Saratoga 1858

a novel of sorts

First Edition

D0107771

By

Hollis A. Palmer Ph.D.

Deep Roots Publications
Saratoga Springs, New York
2016

Published by
Deep Roots Publications
P.O. Box 114
Saratoga Springs, New York

Library of Congress Cataloging-in-Publication Data has been applied for.
LCCN 2016937037
ISBN 978-0-9819528-5-7
ISBN (ebook) 978-0-981528-9-5

To:
All who came before and made Saratoga what it is today;
Those who are here now as stewards of a truly unique place;
And for those who will follow by choice not chance.

Acknowledgements

First and foremost Donna, Sandy and Ralph who helped me
appear coherent and Jim for giving me another great cover.

This book is fiction!

The building imagined by the author as Morrissey's Casino, was at
the time the home of a wealthy family. It was never a casino.
Morrissey's Casino was never robbed.
Judge Baucus's family's story is sad but not the one in the book.

Pictures and illustrations

The map is from the period.
There were two choices when it came to the limited pictures in
this book; use illustrations from the period or pictures that are
current. Fearing that readers, who are not local, may not
understand how much of Saratoga's past can still be enjoyed it was
decided to use current pictures in the hope that the book would
attract people to come to the city and try to envision the story.

Other Books by Hollis Palmer Ph.D.

Victorian Era True Crimes
To Spend Eternity Alone
Crime in Time Journal
Maggie's Revenge
Victorian Rules
Curse of the Veiled Murderess

History
Saratoga's Great Ladies; Broadway and Franklin Square
The Batcheller Mansion
See and be Seen: Saratoga in the Victorian Era
(winner of the Ruth Emery Award)

Business
Everything Matters

Fiction
Mahogany Ridge

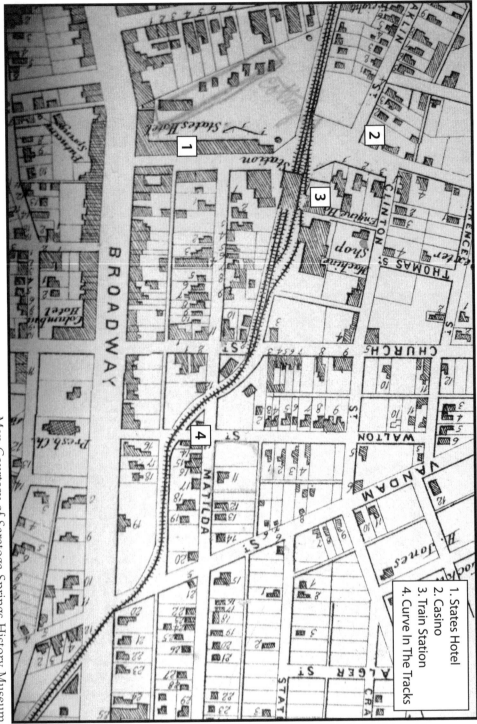

Map Courtesy of Saratoga Springs History Museum

1. States Hotel
2. Casino
3. Train Station
4. Curve In The Tracks

Settling In

JUNE 5th 1858

In the summer of 1858 the fastest and most comfortable way to travel is by rail. With an economy built on tourism, the railroad station in Saratoga Springs is conveniently placed in the middle of the village. Less than a block from the States Hotel and two short blocks from the Union and Congress hotels, the station is surrounded by boarding houses, warehouses, and a multitude of retail ventures.

Those fortunate enough to be able to afford an excursion to the village disembark to the sounds of trunks slamming from the baggage car to the deck, hack drivers screaming for riders, people pushing to find their belongings, and a general turmoil that puts even the busiest of airports today to shame. Into this mayhem each day, four trains arrive from the south and three more from the north. Hundreds of visitors disembark seeking primarily one thing, to **See and be Seen**. As the season evolves, hundreds more will leave daily because they have spent their allotted funds or stayed for as long as their family's business will allow. There is even a group, however small, that have left because they have accomplished one of the most significant objectives of a visit to Saratoga – they have become engaged and have to return home to plan their upcoming nuptials.

Visitors to the village are separated by wealth. The railroads have three levels for paid riders, first through third class, with the most expensive cars in the back away from the smoke of the engine. There are even the occasional guests who can afford their own car, which is at the extreme back of the train. Once in the city, guests continue to segregate themselves economically by the selection of the hotels where they stay.

The most affluent visitors stay at the States. The rising middle class take rooms at the Union or Congress and those who are struggling stay at lesser or older hotels. There is even a group who elect to stay in boarding houses. People who arrive without reservations might find themselves sleeping in private homes or even the livery.

On this day, James Marvin, the owner of the States, goes to the station to meet the first train of the summer. Stately in appearance, Marvin has the air of an executive. As the noon train pulls in, Marvin is approached from behind by his light hearted nephew, nineteen year old Jacob. Both are fashionably dressed in gray frock coats, white shirts, and ties. Jacob begins the conversation, "So another season begins."

Somewhat surprised, Marvin turns to his nephew. "What brings you here?"

"George and his family are supposed to arrive on this train," Jacob answers, referring to his friend and former classmate, George Batcheller.

"From Cambridge? I am surprised they are able to arrive so early."

"Uncle, you know Mr. Batcheller; he inevitably feels that the day is already wasted." They both smile. Sherman Batcheller is the owner of a woodworking factory near the waterfalls north of the village. His company started out manufacturing wooden spoons and bowls. A decade before, the senior Batcheller had established a bourgeoning source of sales, wooden washboards. His company now employs twenty men. Jacob inquires, "So what will the season bring?"

At that moment the whistle of the northbound noon train signals it has come to a complete stop. There is the sound of people's voices as they begin unloading. Marvin speaks over the commotion. "As the summer social capital of the country, I have the feeling that this will be a season loaded with political tension, rumors, romance, the occasional robbery, and, in general, intrigue."

"How will that make it different than last season?"

"I did not say it would be different." Marvin pauses, looking over the crowd. "I believe that in these times, being what they are, there will be a greater intensity this season."

There is no platform, so the passengers are forced to climb down the steps between the cars. The narrow steps of the train are a problem for the women passengers, who are all wearing hoop skirts wider than the steps. The more sophisticated women place one hand on the front of their skirts, holding them in place. No lady would want a stranger to catch a glimpse of her stockings.

The station bustles with people. There are porters moving trunks, hack drivers trying to grab bags and trunks, and arriving guests trying to

2

find their trunks among the pile near the baggage cars.

Marvin looks toward the back, the first class section, where he recognizes the Stiles family. The Stiles' only son, ten year old Todd, jumps from the second step. Thomas, the father, has continued to lose his battle with weight, and is the second member of the family to disembark. At least in his own mind, Thomas, a true southern gentleman, turns and offers his hand to his wife, Cora, a perfectly proportioned lady with a natural presence, and a full decade younger than her husband. The final members of the family are the two daughters, Sarah, eighteen, and Sadie, seventeen. Both the girls are attractive. Fortunately for the Stiles, their daughters are the same height and weight. This permits them to wear each other's dresses at the hops and balls. The fashion of the day requires that Cora, Sarah, and Sadie wear dresses with hoop skirts. Sadie, the last to disembark, does not hold down the front of her skirt as she goes down the steps. Her ankles show. Sarah frowns at her sister's gaffe.

Once on the platform, the Stiles are joined by three well-dressed African Americans who traveled third class near the front of the train, immediately behind the baggage cars. The male servant, forty-five year old Benjamin, is wearing a red livery jacket that shows off his strong build. Seeing Mr. Stiles, Benjamin waves acknowledgement, then moves to collect the family's baggage.

The women servants, forty-five year old Josey and twenty year old Missy, are wearing plain black dresses. Josey is attractive; however, Missy's striking looks cause most of the men in the station to turn. Both women servants carry their simple carpet satchels as they join the Stiles women. Missy and Josey put their bags down at the feet of the Stiles women then go to help Benjamin.

Among those in the first class section is one tall, powerfully built man, John Morrissey, whose rugged face covered by a short beard and immense size make him stand out from the crowd. Although well dressed in a frock coat and tie, he fidgets as if the clothes make him uncomfortable. Morrissey is scrutinizing each building and each person in the horde.

A thin, demur young woman, extremely well dressed in a hoop skirt, Catherine Cook carries a parasol and a small purse. Catharine is accompanied by her stern looking father. Having no luggage, a sure sign they are from the village, father and daughter depart quickly. Automatically Catharine opens her parasol as soon as she gets in the sunlight, and then takes her father's arm as they walk away. Her actions are so smooth they appear to flow.

Near the end of those in the second class cars is the Batcheller family. Jacob's friend George Batcheller recently graduated from Harvard Law School at the ripe old age of twenty. He is thin and intelligent looking. He offers his hand to his older sister, Helen. Helen's fashionable dress and bonnet does little to hide the fact that she is tired from the trip. Sherman Batcheller, who worked hard his entire life, is rough around the edges. George and his father each wear frock coats that are a little worn.

Also in the second class area are the first members of the gaggle of dowagers to arrive. This pack plans to spend their summer criticizing everyone and complaining about everything. Dowager in Europe is a title used to show rank; in countries used to nobility this is considered an honorable title. In the democratic Saratoga it has taken on the derogatory meaning of someone who is aloof and constantly negative and condescending. To each of Saratoga's dowagers, the only persons who act virtuously or look refined are their fellow members. They are immune to the fact that no one outside the group wants to speak to them.

The widow, Mrs. Brewster, is the unofficial leader of the pack. Mrs. Jackson is her pathetic sidekick. Both are dressed in clothes that are a couple of years old. They appear unhappy; they always do, as they mill about the station looking for their trunks. Naturally, it is one of Mrs. Brewster's trunks that is found overturned with the contents spilled onto the ground.

As Marvin turns away from Jacob to greet the Stiles family, he murmurs, "Now the season begins." Capable of writing a book on etiquette, Marvin automatically starts by shaking Thomas' hand. "A pleasure to see you Thomas; I hope your trip was pleasant." He turns to each member in the family as he speaks. "Miss Sarah and Miss Sadie, you are even more beautiful than you were last year, if that is possible." Although vain by nature, the girls blush over the attention of such a sophisticated and handsome man.

Marvin rubs Todd's hair. "Did you get sick on the boat this year?"

Todd tries to duck under Marvin's hand. "No, I am too old to get sick." There is a fresh, disrespectful tone of a child who assumes status is inherited.

Marvin ignores Todd, and takes Cora's hand. "You look as charming as ever." Marvin holds Cora's hand a moment longer than necessary.

Benjamin is busy piling up the family's numerous trunks as the women servants pick up the ladies' suitcases and hat boxes and place them in the pile with the trunks.

A group of eight colorfully dressed women rush from around a corner onto the station floor. Their dresses are shorter and more brightly colored than everyone else's. The women, all between the ages of 18 and 25, collide with the arriving passengers. Occasionally one of the women actually touches one of the men new to the village, a forbidden deed in the Victorian era. It is obvious that the women are desperately trying to board the train before it departs. No one in this group is concerned about anyone seeing their legs as they shamelessly climb the steps to the train. Knowing the women are prostitutes, the arriving women turn away, acting like those in the group do not exist. Many of the men take the opportunity to catch a glimpse of leg.

The last of the prostitutes flirtatiously squeezes Benjamin's strong arms as she passes him. "Where have you been all winter?"

A second prostitute grabs the flirt's arm, pulling her toward the train. "Hurry up. The judge said fifteen minutes."

"We still gots five minutes," the flirt calls out so all can hear. "That's time 'nough to earn a dollar." She yells to Benjamin as her friend desperately pulls on her arm. "You's as big as they say?"

Finally, the two prostitutes board the train. As the train starts to pull out of the station the flirt takes out a hanky and begins a mocking wave to those at the station. Everyone does their best to ignore her.

Jacob approaches the Batchellers, who are near the area where luggage is being unloaded. Out of excitement at seeing his best friend, Jacob breaks tradition and shakes George's hand first. "George, my dearest companion, how was the year at Harvard?" Before George can answer, Jacob realizes his mistake and turns to Sherman Batcheller, offering his hand. "Mr. Batcheller, how was the graduation?"

The stoic Sherman talks as if giving a political speech, "If it were not for George's speech, it would have been singularly unimpressive."

George automatically defends his alma mater, "Harvard is a collection of America's best, both those of proven intellect and those who are our future leaders."

Jacob cannot help but be sarcastic. "I think Yale and Dartmouth would question that claim."

"And they would be wrong!"

"Helen, you deserve credit for tolerating these two on such a long journey."

"Their constant banter was a challenge." She picks up her lone bag. "I am not sure that even the opportunity to shop in Boston made it worthwhile."

"I do not question that they were constantly endeavoring one-upmanship," Jacob concluded.

Sadie watches a poorly dressed white man in working clothes deliberately bump into Benjamin, then stare, defying Benjamin to act. Benjamin continues pulling the family's trunks to the side. The man smiles and jolts Benjamin a second time. Benjamin remains calm and signals for a wagon to be brought to transport the Stiles' numerous trunks. The man is about to elbow Benjamin a third time when he notices Morrissey's glare. Instinctively the man slinks away.

George gives Helen a brotherly hug then shakes his father's hand. Sherman holds Helen's hand as she steps into an older worn carriage that has been sent to pick them up.

Jacob and George begin walking toward George's boarding house. Each has a suitcase in his outside hand and they hold George's trunk suspended between them.

"Have you confirmed where you will board?" Jacob inquires. A true friend, he was helping with the trunk, not knowing how far he would have to carry it.

"I will be staying at Mrs. Webb's boarding house," George clarifies. A look of dread comes over Jacob's face. He realizes it will be two long blocks before he can put down his burden.

The lobby of the States is alive with people who have just arrived on the train, all trying to check in. Upon signing in, one of the numerous porters grabs the guests' bags to carry up the grand staircase. A few guests, mostly women, are sitting in the overstuffed chairs waiting for a nod from their husbands that they are registered. The women, sitting or standing, are all waving their fans. In the case of the younger women, the fans are not for the heat but rather a way to send messages to one another.

The lobby has tall windows to allow as much natural light as possible. Between the windows are twelve foot tall elaborately framed mirrors. Sarah and Sadie are examining themselves in one of the mirrors while Marvin talks to Cora. Dutifully Thomas looks on. Morrissey is waiting anxiously in the background for an opportunity to talk to Marvin. To the careful onlooker, Cora is more familiar with Marvin than is appropriate for a married woman.

"May I prevail upon you to volunteer to be on the entertainment committee again this year?" Marvin asks. It is the practice of the large hotels to ask the long-term guests to serve on committees. One of the most important is the one that organizes the season's entertainment.

"Mr. Marvin, volunteer is hardly the correct word. I will consider the committee; however, you should be mindful there was rarely accord last year." Cora avoids looking directly into his blue eyes.

"I must insist," Marvin pleaded. "I want this year's grand ball to be the most magnificent ever, one so special that the children will be talking of that evening to their grandchildren."

Cora waves her fan over dramatically and smiles at Marvin. "Thank you for your confidence. Do you have a theme in mind?"

"That would be the committee's decision."

"It would be presumptuous of me to believe I could speak on behalf of the committee but I think a masked ball could be interesting."

"And I agree." Marvin smiles at Cora, then hands the cottage key to Thomas who has been leering at the various ladies in the lobby. Marvin closes the conversation, saying to Thomas, "I have arranged for a bottle of bourbon to be sent to your cottage." Led by Todd, the Stiles family starts toward the door to the hotel's private park.

Like many of the guests who are spending the entire season in Saratoga, the Stiles have rented their own cottage. The cottage they will occupy consists of a foyer with two parlors and a small servants' kitchen/workroom on the first floor. There are four bedrooms on the second floor; one for Todd, one for the sisters, and one each for Thomas and Cora – wealthy husbands and wives do not share a bed. The third floor, which is merely a finished attic, has four rooms for servants. The family will take their meals with the guests staying in the hotel.

Back in the lobby, Marvin walks toward the desk when Morrissey cuts off his path. "Mr. Marvin, allow me to introduce myself; I am John Morrissey." There is a slight Irish accent. Morrissey extends his hand. Marvin accepts it with some reluctance.

"The same John Morrissey who was in the village last summer, I presume?"

Despite knowing that his reputation precedes him, Morrissey continues his self-introduction, "Yes sir. Finances required that I stayed at the Congress last year. However, this has been an excellent year and I have engaged rooms in your fine establishment for the season."

"I assume the rooms will not be used for business," Marvin cautions.

"Absolutely not; they are for my family. I was wondering, however, if you might know of a building I could rent for my business."

"I am sorry but I do not." Marvin lingers before asking a question to which he already knows the answer. "Why do you seek a place in Saratoga?"

"Because it is Saratoga; everyone who is anyone will be here during the season." Marvin and Morrissey continue taking the measure of one another. "Surely Mr. Marvin, you will admit the rich deserve the best and Saratoga is the summer habitat of the rich."

Marvin changes the topic, "All of my properties are already leased and I believe most of the others suitable to your needs are also gone."

"I am confident you will find something," Marvin says insincerely before he turns to his post near the front desk.

Morrissey watches Marvin, then turns and walks out the front door.

Before they have officially checked in, four of the dowagers have commandeered rocking chairs on the front piazza. These are the same chairs in the same place as they occupied the previous season. The chairs are arranged in a crescent shape so that each of the coven can see the front steps and sidewalk. As self-appointed queen of the cluster, Mrs. Brewster occupies the center seat. Mrs. Jackson, who is knitting, sits to her right. Mrs. Brown has the seat to Mrs. Brewster's left. Only in her late thirties, Mrs. Brown is sent to Saratoga each summer by her husband, who would rather be alone then share the 'pleasure' of her company. Mrs. Brown busies herself darning a glove. The three old guard are joined by the newest and youngest member of the group, Miss Strong. Only in her mid-twenties, Miss Strong has the misfortune of inheriting her position among the dowagers from an aunt who is ill and stayed home. Although quiet to the point of appearing meek, there is something intriguing about Miss Strong. All four women are wearing simple dresses with little flounce. Probably their most noteworthy characteristic is how unhappy they all look.

Morrissey walks out the door across the piazza and down the front steps.

Mrs. Brewster serves the first of the season's rebukes, "He may be dressed in the best clothes but he does not appear to be a true gentleman."

"I have heard he is a sporting man," adds Miss Strong, trying to fit in.

"I have heard the same," scowls Mrs. Brewster. "If that is the case, why does Mr. Marvin keep his company? The senior Mr. Marvin never would have allowed such a man to stay at the States."

"Mr. Marvin may be an innkeeper, but he is also a man. What man does not want the company of others who enjoy the sporting life?" Mrs. Jackson pauses to be sure that all are listening. "I understand that Mr. Marvin was once quite the rider." The implication is that he raced horses.

The other women nod assurances.

George unloads his trunk, placing the clothes in the lone dresser. Jacob is sitting in the only chair, running his hand up and down the curtain, examining the material. Both men have hung their frock coats on a stand.

Jacob sarcastically swings his free hand. "This room will definitely impress the girls you smuggle in. Of course, getting past Mrs. Webb will be a challenge."

"There will be no sneaking in of anyone. I intend to be accepted at the bar by autumn and will need all my time to prepare." George continues to unpack. "I anticipate being in the office every day by 9:00; I will allow myself an hour for dinner at 1:00, then back to the office until 5:00. I know that will be much more time than anyone else, but I plan to prove my worth."

Jacob's expression shows disbelief. "George, George, George, whatever am I going to do with you? This is the place and this is the season. Mornings at the springs, afternoon strolls on Broadway, evening walks beneath the stars, and a hop or a ball every night. George, this is the time to flirt, the time to live a life that makes poets jealous."

"Jacob, Jacob, Jacob, whatever am I going to do with you? This is the time of America's needs, a time of action, a time for doing. Despite the Dred Scott decision, or maybe because of it, slavery has to end. It is our time to make our marks." He stresses 'our.'

Jacob shakes his head, stands and looks out the window. "What has Harvard done to you?" Before George can answer, he continues, "George, did you ever think that you are too political? There is nothing wrong with a summer's attraction and a winter of action."

Knowing his friend has seen something out the window, George joins Jacob. The two gaze down on Catharine Cook. Dressed as she was at the station, Catharine is on the porch of a grand house across the street. She is sitting on the swing reading. They watch as her father comes out of the house onto the porch. As Jacob is about to speak, Reverend Beecher walks up the steps of the Cook's porch.

Catherine holds a book whose title is in French while she gently pushes herself in the swing. Her father, dressed in a frock coat, comes out carrying a thin stick with a flame from which he lights his pipe. He takes a drag. "Lovely afternoon." Looking directly at his daughter, he adds, "Are you going for an after dinner stroll?"

"Broadway will be there tomorrow. Today is for the pleasure of this gentle breeze."

"Catherine, you constantly confuse verse with life. Life is not what one reads about; it is what one experiences."

"Is that why you are going to the Sheehan's this evening? Because you know that the widow, Mrs. Putnam, will be there?" Catherine does not stop her all wise daughter persona, "Should I consider her one of your experiences?"

"Although its better days may be over, my life is still going. Yours has yet to start."

Catherine doesn't answer. She gazes up at the window where she sees George and Jacob looking at her. Neither moves to get out of her gaze.

The Reverend Beecher, thin and academic looking, walks up the steps. "How good it is to see you both out enjoying this fine afternoon."

"To what do we owe the honor of this visit?" Cook asks.

"I was walking by and merely wanted to say hello and ask one more time if Miss Catharine would be willing to sing in the choir."

"Reverend Beecher, I have told you many times that my voice was meant to be heard when I was reading, not singing."

Reverend Beecher bows slightly, "I think your voice charming under any circumstances."

"George, that is out of your league. Last season she was the hostess at her father's dinner for President Buchannan. Her father would not let her consider a lowly college graduate who only owns three jackets." Jacob points at one of the coats. "One of those has a hole in the elbow." Tricked, George looks at the elbows of the coat - it is worn but there is no hole.

"Don Quixote had his windmills; maybe it is time for me to have mine. You are the one who implied I am too stoic."

"That is as it may be, but do not expect me to be your Sancho Panza."

George does not answer and returns to unpacking his trunk. Eventually he adds, "I must finish unpacking. Tomorrow I begin work at Mr. Beach's office."

"Tomorrow you become a mole; today we have time for a stroll." Jacob tosses George his hat and coat to put on.

Despite the family's wealth, the Stiles daughters' room is simple. There are two single beds, two dressers, two wooden chairs and a washstand. Two trunks are standing on their ends, serving as makeshift dressers. Dresses are hanging from a rope that has been hung across the

10

room to increase storage. There is a rope hanging beside one of the windows to be used in case of a fire. This is all that is needed because the girls, like all the other guests, are expected to spend their time in the parlors, park, piazza, at the springs, and at the balls. People do not spend time in their rooms.

Cora and the older servant, Josey, are busy unpacking the girls' clothes. Josey puts one of the girls' undergarments in a dresser.

"This will be the summer of my girls. Sarah is eighteen already and Sadie barely seventeen. I will be busy chaperoning them every evening, gathering stories to tell their daughters." Cora holds up a series of her daughters' evening dresses as she speaks. Originally from the Baltimore area, Cora has an acquired deep southern accent.

"It will be some kind of summer. Pretty as she is, the gentlemen will be a callin' on Miss Sarah all the time and her dance card will be full for every evening." Josey looks at Cora. "There ain't no need to concern yourself about Miss Sadie though, that's unless there's some young minister sulkin' about. And you don't have to worry about that, no young minister can afford the States, they're all down at the Union."

"Five fancy dresses for each and six dances a week; we will be spending all our afternoons sewing flounce so that they are the best dressed young ladies here." Cora shakes her head, "As a mother of two girls of age, I simply hate the unwritten rule that a lady never wears the same exact outfit twice."

"It will be worth it, Mrs. Stiles. I remember when I stayed in one of these same cottages and sewed and sewed and sewed the flounce for you."

Cora places her hands on her hips. "It wasn't so bad, was it?"

"It wasn't bad then and it surely won't be bad now. The good Lord willin', I will be sewin' for Miss Sarah's daughters someday."

"I am sure you will be. Now I insist you must tell me if you see either of the girls visiting with men in the park. And whatever you do, be sure to get the names of the men. I know these Northerners will be hovering around like vultures."

"I could save myself time and just gets the names of all the men at the hotel now, 'cuz they will all be a hangin' around Miss Sarah."

Todd runs into the room. "Mother, they have added an archery range to the park. I was practicing and I will be the best shot by the match at the end of the summer!"

"I am sure you will be."

Morrissey enters the newspaper's office. A bell attached to the top of the door rings, signaling the door is opening. A young clerk/reporter, Walter Pratt, is leaning on his elbows at a stand up desk reading a proof of the weekly paper. Instinctively he looks up at Morrissey.

Morrissey, showing his confidence, starts talking without introducing himself. "Good afternoon. I was wonderin'; do you have a list of available storefronts or buildings that might be for rent?

"At the beginning of the season, I am sure we do not. Everything worth renting has been hired for weeks. I believe that even most of the undesirable buildings have been leased."

"What about a school buildin' or barn?"

"None, I am sure."

"Are there any large houses for rent?"

"This is going to be a big season. Everything I know of has been rented for weeks." Walter's exasperation is evident. "This is Saratoga Springs." Walter stares at Morrissey. "You may want to try the Lester Brothers; they have opened a new real estate office on Broadway. They are specializing in renting properties for the season."

"Where on Broadway?"

"Above Steinbeck's Dry Goods Store; you enter on the right."

"Thank you, you have been most helpful." Insincerity rings in Morrissey's tone as he turns and walks out the door. The bell chimes.

"Irish, no chance," Walter says under his breath.

Todd is well ahead as Cora, Sarah, and Sadie stroll on the sidewalk. The women all carry parasols, but because they are on the shaded side of the street, their parasols are closed and being used as walking sticks. Morrissey is walking on the other side of the street, looking up at the windows on the second and third floors.

"Mother, why did we have to get here so early? The dances don't start until Friday and that is merely a hop," Sarah pleads.

"And in Savannah, yellow fever break outs the start of the first week of June," answers Cora.

"Looks like all the same stores to me," complains a bored Sarah.

Sadie uses her parasol as a pointer as she corrects her sister. "That fancy goods store is new and so is that sweet shop."

"Are you proud of yourself; you found the only two new stores in the village? Why do you always have to correct me?"

"I don't. I only correct you when you are wrong. It is hardly my fault if that is frequent."

Sarah shakes her head. "Mother do we have to take her every time we stroll? I would rather stay in the cottage with Todd than deal with her."

"We will stroll each day and," Cora pauses and then emphasizes, "we will behave like fine southern ladies."

Sadie uses her parasol to point one more time at a store just being set up. "That jewelry store is new. I am amazed you didn't see that one first!" There is a man painting the name of the store on the window.

Cora does not raise her voice. "Ladies!" Morrissey is walking in the front door of the jewelry store.

The store has only two display counters and the shelves along the walls are only half full of bric-a-brac. The clerk is examining newly arrived jewelry when Morrissey enters. "I'm sorry sir; we are not open for business," the clerk explains to Morrissey. "It will be at least another week before we officially open our doors. I suppose I could show you something if you know exactly what you want."

"I am not a customer at this time." Morrissey continues to look around.

"Then how may I help you?"

"It is I who hope to help you. Since you are not open, how would you like to rent this store space to me for the season? I will pay you more than you would make all season and you may have the building back in September."

"My shelves and goods are due in this week. I will be open in plenty of time for the true season."

"That is as it may be; however, I need a place for my business. I am willin' to pay you $5,000 for the season. That has to be at least twice what you are anticipatin' earning. Think of it, a profit before you open the door and you do not have to work for it."

"That is an attractive offer. However, like every other merchant in the village, I need the season to pay for the year."

"I am offering you what you would make for the year, paid in advance."

"What type of store would you put in that makes you so sure that you can make enough to pay me such a generous amount?"

Morrissey responds, "My business is providing what the public seeks."

The dining room in the States is less than a third full for supper. Guests are clustered in family groups, friends, couples, and the rare single male. The four dowagers are sitting together looking at everyone else. Morrissey is sitting alone at one end of a long table with Marvin standing across from him. "Mr. Morrissey, I hope your search went well."

"It is too soon to be sure. I was able to put in a bid on a storefront this afternoon. It is on Broadway, which would prove ideal."

"So you have a place?"

"The young merchant told me he needed the night to think about it. I am confident he will see the merits of my offer."

"I thought I saw on the reservation that your wife was joining you."

"She will be here within the next few days. I wanted some time to make my business arrangements before she arrived."

"Wives are such a comfort. 'Nieces' can cause such a distraction." Both men are well aware of the practice of men registering their mistresses as 'nieces.'

"I have no need or desire for a 'niece.' When you see my wife you will understand." Pride is evident in Morrissey's voice.

"You are indeed fortunate."

"My life has been about overcoming obstacles." As Marvin walks to another table, Morrissey's mind flashes back twelve years to a darker period in his life.

Morrissey is in the foyer of a bordello in Troy. Two interior doorways from the foyer are covered in burgundy drapes. The sounds of a piano can be heard along with background voices, both male and female, along with occasional laughter. Although only sixteen, Morrissey's size allows him to be the bouncer.

Morrissey sits on a hard wooden chair reading a book at the bottom of the staircase just inside the entrance. A petite prostitute dressed in her bloomers and corset makes no effort to cover up as she comes down the stairs. Suggestively she pulls a hand rolled cigarette from a case in Morrissey's shirt pocket. She watches Morrissey as she lights the cigarette from a gas light. She sits on the arm of Morrissey's chair.

"So how's it goin'?" she asks. Dropping the sound of "g" at the end of words is common in Troy.

"Quiet night; only ten guests so far."

"And two of those were my Tuesday night regulars. Well, at least it's givin' you a chance to work on your readin'."

Morrissey opens the book. "What does con-tem-pla-tion mean?"

"It means to think about. That was a really long word for you to get through - good job, John." She brushes his hair like he was a little kid.

"I been meanin' to ask, why did ya ever leave teachin'? Yus good at it."

The little prostitute waves her arms in a mocking gesture. "Cause this life looked so attractive."

"Ain't yus the one who's always tellin' me not to use sarcasm?"

"The word is 'aren't,' or better yet 'are not'; not ain't, and yes that is my role - yours is learnin' to read." She again rubs Morrissey's hair.

"So why did ya leave?"

"Because I was fool enough to believe the superintendent when he told me his wife was dyin' and he was goin' to marry me as soon as she passed into the next world." Morrissey stares at her, waiting for her to finish. "Seems a ruined woman is not fit to be around children but a defiler can go to church, ask forgiveness, and go ahead with his life. And, just so you know, his wife miraculously got well."

There is the sound of a woman screaming, followed by the scraping of furniture upstairs. In response, Morrissey hurdles the banister and leaps up the stairs two steps at a time. With only one door closed, Morrissey immediately knows the origin of the sound. He opens the door and finds one of the girls naked to the waist, kneeling on the bed, holding her client's wrist as he pulls her hair. The client's free arm is drawn back, getting ready to punch her in the face. Morrissey hooks the man's arm and, as if working with putty, Morrissey puts the client in a half nelson. Effortlessly Morrissey literally lifts the man off his feet and pulls the man through the doorway into the hall. Morrissey speaks for the first time. "That will be enough of that."

"Get your hands off me. That bitch bit me," the client warns.

Morrissey puts the client in a full nelson and wrestles him down the stairs. The little prostitute opens the outside door. "If she bit ya, she had a damn good reason."

"I'll kill her for this!" the client threatens, as Morrissey carries him down the outside steps.

When they reach the street, the client keeps shouting, "I want my money back!" Morrissey finally puts the man down but holds the back of his shirt. "I'm gonna' go to the police to file a complaint." Morrissey turns the client around, and holds him off the ground by his vest. The client continues to call out. "I'm goin' to get my friends and we'll be back." Morrissey and the client's faces are inches apart. The client's pants hang on his thighs.

"Yus goin' home. Yus goin' straight home and if'n ya ever come near this place 'gain, I will personally break every finger on your hand." Morrissey takes a breath and gently puts the client back on his feet. Morrissey mocks the client by straightening out his vest like he is a valet. "Then how will ya take dictation at the courthouse?" Morrissey watches as the client pulls up his pants and starts to walk down the street.

Morrissey climbs the steps to the bordello where he is met by the little prostitute holding his book. She taunts, "Needed a break from your readin'?"

"Sarcasm!" Morrissey criticizes.

"By the way it is 'you' not 'ya,'" she corrects. Morrissey takes the book from her hand.

During the early Victorian era, the hotels of Saratoga were on the American Plan, which meant that meals and entertainment were included in the cost of the room. Under the American Plan guests took their meals at their hotel, were entertained at their hotel, and relaxed at their hotel. They could even charge purchases to their rooms. The downside was that it was not good manners to enter a hotel where you were not a guest unless you were visiting a specific person. Those who came to the village would spend the season socializing primarily with those from their hotel had it not been for one major natural phenomenon, the mineral springs. The springs were the epitome of democratic. Anyone in the village, regardless of hotel, or even boarding house, was able to visit any of the springs. Although a trickle of people went to the springs throughout the day, the springs were the social center before breakfast. Since a visit to Saratoga was all about seeing who else was in town and being seen oneself, daily social rituals started with a visit to the springs.

Even though it is 8:30, the normally high point for the springs, this early in the season there are only forty people present at Congress Spring. As if by requirement, the servants stand further back than the guests with the slaves, and free blacks even further to the perimeter. The springs may be the most democratic place in the village but they are far from politically correct. There is a woman sitting on a wooden folding chair who is playing the violin. She has the case open so people can tip. There is a dipper boy who reaches down into the fountain to collect fresh water to fill the glass of anyone who comes up to the rail. He works for tips.

George and Jacob stand at one of the pillars sizing up the crowd. Jacob has a glass of water in one hand, George does not. James Cook finishes his glass of water and leaves and walks in the direction of his grand Victorian house on Circular Street. The newspaperman, Walter Pratt, stands among the slaves holding his glass of water and mingling. The slaves are weary of his intentions. George and Jacob eye him questioningly. Mrs. Brewster and Miss Strong are near the walkway used to go to the hotels; the two examine everyone with a critical eye. The Stiles sisters, dressed in white dresses, stand at a second pillar. Todd is running around. Jacob looks at the Stiles sisters and raises his glass in a mock salute. He turns to George, "Now that is why people come to Saratoga each season."

"Last year you were in love with one of Vanderbilt's daughters and this year you are ready to fall in love the first week of the season," George reminds his friend.

"And, with any luck, I will fall in love each week of the season," Jacob boasts before he continues, "Oh no, that would mean I could only fall in love 10 times before fall. That simply will not do."

"I am with your uncle on this. We will be delighted if you only fall in love 10 times this summer." George's exasperation shows. "Are you ready for breakfast?"

"Not before I say hello to those lovely southern belles. 'Belles,' I like that term. I think I will go ring them." Jacob pats George on the back, walks toward Sarah and Sadie. George shakes his head and moves toward his boarding house, passing Mrs. Brewster and Miss Strong.

Miss Strong, who has not been to Saratoga in several seasons, remarks, "Strangest custom I have ever experienced, walking to the springs for a tumbler of water before breakfast; yet everyone seems to partake."

"It is not the waters one seeks here, it is the news," explains Mrs. Brewster.

"News?" Miss Strong's naivety shows.

"You know, who danced with whom, who was caught talking to whom, and who is no longer speaking to whom," Mrs. Brewster explains.

"I so loathe gossip," asserts Miss Strong.

"Oh me too; me too." The insincerity is evident in Mrs. Brewster's words.

William August Beach is the leading attorney in Saratoga and arguably the leading attorney in the state of New York. He counts among his clients Cornelius Vanderbilt. For over a decade Beach has been involved in every major court case in Eastern New York, both criminal and civil. Beach is a courtroom attorney, a performer; he dreads what he feels are mundane tasks such as writing wills or contracts. For tedious work he has partners and a series of young men reading for the law. It is into this assemblage that George Sherman Batcheller is throwing himself.

Apprehensively, George climbs the stairs to Beach's offices as the bells on the church ring nine times. Life has come easy for George. A strong memory, excellent elocution, and family connections have given him an advantage over his peers. These will not matter to Beach. George knows that his mentor only cares for victory.

Beach's Saratoga office occupies the entire second floor of one of the larger buildings on Broadway. The first floor is a series of private stores. The outer or public office has dark wainscoting with all the furniture stained dark. In the receptionist's office there are book shelves on two walls filled with law books. The windows to the street below are open; George can hear gentle street noises including the clumping of horse's hooves. George walks to the desk of the overbearing male secretary, Dexter. Dexter's desk is very neat, appearing unused.

"My name is George Batcheller. I am here to begin reading for the law under Mr. Beach."

"Of course you are. Please be seated," says a cold Dexter pointing to a set of chairs along the wall. George takes a seat in a stiff wooden chair and looks at the clock. Within ten minutes three men in their early twenties enter, one at a time. Each of the men examine George as they pick up folders at Dexter's desk. One-by-one each enters the same room off to the left. Not one says a word to George.

Like all the grand hotels, the States has separate men's and women's parlors. As the church bell rings, Marvin and Thomas Stiles are sitting in leather wing-back chairs. Each is smoking his morning cigar. Thomas speaks first but it is an old conversation. "My dear Marvin, there is no question but that it is a difficult issue. What those in the north fail to understand is that to Southerners, our peculiar institution is both a social and economic necessity. Congress will never make it illegal and we will never give it up." He is referring to slavery. Marvin does not answer, choosing to remain silent on such a volatile issue. Thomas continues after he takes a long drag on his cigar. "There is a prevailing belief that the Negro is inferior to those of European descent. Preachers, in all the churches in Savannah, cite verses from the Bible where slavery is practiced." Thomas pauses one more time to take a puff from his cigar. "It is the belief throughout the south that it is the white man's duty to protect and train those of color."

Marvin is finally drawn into the discussion. "As a hotel owner catering to a worldly clientele, I have learned to avoid political discussions; however, I would point out to you that here in the Springs, with fourteen churches, you will find but one minister who will defend what you call a 'peculiar institution.'"

"There is also the issue of what would happen if those in bondage were suddenly freed. In Savannah those of color outnumber the white population and the issue is even graver in Charleston." Thomas supposes his beliefs are held by every logical person.

"Among many of our guests, regardless of where they are from, you will find that they believe that the Dred Scott decision will lead to war. You will forgive my bluntness, but though it is your legal right, I wish you had not brought slaves with you."

"I only brought two, my wife's and my daughters' ladies. My father freed Benjamin years ago. My wife treats her lady as well as any servant is treated in the hotel and my daughters and Missy would be lost without each other."

"I will be spending my entire summer trying to squelch conversations on slavery. As a friend, I would suggest you do the same." Marvin starts to rise adding, "Rare is the person who changes his view to embrace the institution."

George listens to the church bell ring eleven times. From the stairway there is the sound of boots. Beach enters, looking thinner than George remembered. In a well-practiced habit, Beach looks the outer office over, noticing George. Beach speaks in a courtroom voice, "Ah, Mr. Batcheller, I presume. Good to have you join our firm," extending his hand to George. Beach grabs George's hand firmly and gives it a hard, almost painful, shake. "You might as well get started. James Cook has asked that some mortgages be reviewed. Do you know Mr. Cook?"

"Yes, before his wife became ill, he used to stay at our house when he went hunting in the Adirondacks."

Beach walks to Dexter's desk and picks up notes. "So your father was a Whig?"

"Yes, and like Mr. Cook, he is now a Republican."

"And like the rest of the Republicans, he probably doesn't believe in slavery and supports temperance and women's suffrage." Beach does not wait for an answer. "Dexter, give Mr. Batcheller the bank mortgages sent over by Mr. Cook." Beach turns to George, "When you are finished, take them over to the Cook's house. It is on Phila Street."

"Will you want to see my notes before I take them?"

"Mr. Batcheller, James Cook never makes a mistake; your review is perfunctory; that is why I gave it to you." Beach, holding various notes, enters his office.

When George reaches Dexter's desk he is handed a thick manila folder. Dexter points in the direction of the office where the three men had entered previously. Folder in hand, George enters the office assigned to the clerks. He finds the three other law clerks, Lawrence, Frank, and

James, sitting at small wooden desks. Books are piled irregularly in front of each. The clerks are busy either writing or researching. There is no desk for George, so he sits at the long library table. Not one of the other clerks speaks to him.

Josey and Missy are among the most sophisticated of the Stiles' slaves, but they have been deprived of any education, causing them to speak in a colloquial manner. Josey is busy cleaning Mrs. Stiles' room and Missy pretends to help. Josey remarks, "We's gets so much done when they's in the park list'n to the music."

"Wouldn it be nice to jus list'n to the music and not have to work?" Missy dreams.

"There's yus go's agin think'n high thoughts and get'n all righteous."

"I wasn't sayin' we was doin' it, I jus sas it would be nice."

"An' I thin' it would be real nice if you done your share of the work."

"I have more expected of me then yus ever will." Missy thinks she is holding a secret that has been a rumor in the household for months.

Josey stops cleaning and stares at Missy. "But no more'n use'd to be asked of me."

Each of the large hotels in Saratoga has its own private park. The parks are used by the guests for reading, writing letters, painting, and wandering the paths. To entertain the guests, Marvin has engaged a piano player. Sarah, who had been painting, gathers her watercolors and walks across the park. She enters the family's cottage and starts to climb the stairs to the bedrooms.

Hearing her sister approach, Sadie moves quickly from her chair by the window and places a book under her pillow and returns to her chair where she picks up her needlepoint. On the stairs Sarah calls out to her sister. "Sadie!" Hearing no response, Sarah enters as Sadie is sitting down. "What are you hiding?"

"Nothing." Her voice belies her words. Sarah just stares. Sadie breaks the silence. "Just a book."

"You were reading again? We are here among the best possible beaux in the country and you sit alone reading a book."

"Just because they are present does not mean they are interesting." Sadie defends herself.

Sarah paces the room. "Interesting, what is interesting?" Sarah gets more sarcastic with each word. "The sons of planters only want to hunt, ride, and brag about their fine thoroughbred horses. Oh yes, and to complain about the quality of the bourbon. When they get older, they add lounging on the veranda and sleeping to their busy itineraries." Sadie's face shows she is unimpressed by her sister's diatribe. Sarah continues, "That is why I am here. I am going to marry a man from the north, a professional man who goes to his office each day, goes to his clubs in the evening, and dances every dance at the ball on Saturday evenings."

Sadie has heard enough. "A man like Jacob Marvin I assume. What about his friend; what is his name, George Sherman Batcheller?"

"Mr. Batcheller is way too consumed with himself, too serious by a mile. He may be smarter than Jacob but he is not as handsome and I doubt if he can dance a lick."

"And with Mr. Jacob Marvin, what will you talk about over dinner?" There is a sardonic tone to Sadie's comment.

Sarah defends herself. "I said a man like Jacob; I did not say that Jacob was the man. We will talk about his clients or his store. We will discuss where the children will go to school and what we will do with mother and father when they are too old to live alone." She giggles, "I will suggest with you."

"That may be, but I am going to find a man who wants to discuss ideas, who brings me flowers each day," Sadie romanticizes, "a man who reads me poetry in the evening."

Sarah continues walking around the small room. "Then you are also going to marry a man from the north. If you are going to impress a southern man you must always avoid topics of literacy. If not, you will make him run from you as if you had the plague."

Sadie defines her sister's role. "Sarah, you are the sparkling dilettante of the family. Despite what you may think, it is not all about good looks and companionship. My beau will provide bright conversation at the dinner table and in the evening."

"I could have holiday dinners with a brother-in-law who is all you want, as long as he is not a solitary thinker." Sarah has her limits. "Who could possibly be attracted to a writer or painter? They are too conceited and self-centered." Sarah quickly reaches under her sister's pillow and pulls out the book *Twelve Years a Slave*. "Oh Sadie, how could you. Mother and father would kill you if they found this. If you are not sent to Gran-ma-ma's you will be banned from the dances all season, and then who will I sit with?" She catches herself. "Not that I plan to sit at all."

"If you tried to read it, you would see it is a classic example of the author trying to find the extreme example. Father and everyone we know would never treat our slaves like he describes in the book." Sadie tries to show the book as something different than its reputation.

Sarah throws the book on the bed and walks toward the door. In exasperation Sarah says, "If you must read, bring a book out into the park," she pauses, "and make it poetry."

Sarah picks up her writing materials and walks out, leaving Sadie alone in the room. Sadie picks up the book, sits back in her chair, and returns to her reading.

Josey and Benjamin are gathered in the alleyway behind the cottage. Benjamin is smoking a cigarette he rolled for himself while Josey hangs out the family's clothes to air. He starts to preach, "They buy yus the best servants' clothes to show that slaves are treated better'n white servants. It is all a show."

Josey takes issue. "That shows how little yus know, Benjamin Stiles. They buys us the best clothes to show how well off they is."

Benjamin refuses to yield. "Yus can say it any way yus want, but the honest truth is that they brought us up here to show all the Northerners that slavery isn't evil."

"That's easy for yus to say; yus free. But Missy and me, we's got to mind our p's and q's."

"I's agree you do. I's not so sure about Missy." Benjamin implies inside knowledge.

"What's yus mean by that?" Josey demands. Benjamin throws the butt on the ground, steps on it and walks back into the cottage.

George, dressed in his newest frock coat, walks up the steps, and rings the bell at the Cook's house. He fidgets, shifting his weight between feet as he waits. Just before he is about to give up, the butler opens the door. "I have a package for Mr. Cook."

"Mr. Cook is not here; you may leave it in my care." The butler's language and manner is formal even by Saratoga standards.

"Thank you, but I think it will be better if I come back later; when is he expected?"

Catharine appears from the parlor door holding the book she has been reading. Her finger is between the pages, marking her place. "I am Catharine, Mr. Cook's daughter. Would you be allowed to leave the package with me?"

"I am quite certain that would be permissible," George assures her. "I am sure you do not remember me, but I am George Sherman Batcheller.

Our fathers visited each other often before our mothers became ill."

"I remember. You are from Batchellerville; how is your family?"

"Like you, my mother passed a few years ago. The others are well. My sister is engaged and will marry this summer. My father is the same as always." George speaks as if Catherine remembers his father.

"What do you mean when you say 'the same as always'?"

"My father runs his woodworking business with an iron fist, and his family the same way."

"Mr. Batcheller, excuse my familiarity but I have always wondered why you constantly use your middle name."

George's explanation sounds like a recording. "My family is very proud of their connection to Roger Sherman, the only man to sign the Declaration of Independence, Articles of Confederation, and the Constitution."

"That sounds rehearsed," Catherine critiques, "although it does show deep roots."

"Humble lives of late," George says, noticing that the book she is reading is entitled *Notre Dame de Paris* by Victor Hugo. He speaks first in French. (Author's note: as the languages change, the English version follows in italics). "Apprèciez vous le livre?" *Are you enjoying the book?*

"Il a besoin d'un développement de la personnalité, mais l'intrigue est intéressante." *It needs some character development but the story line is interesting.* She switches to Latin. "Have vos legere librum?" *Have you read it?*

"Non, sed nunc quod classes sunt super sum frui relegere of avunculus Tom scriptor Cameram." *No, but now that classes are over I am enjoying a reread of Uncle Tom's cabin.* He switches to Spanish. "Lo ha leído?" *Have you read it?*

"Sí, por supuesto. Me parece que siempre es mejor para leer a los clásicos en su lengua materna. " *Yes of course. I find it is always best to read the classics in their native language.* Catherine switches to German. "Haben Sie das Kommunistische Manifest von Karl Marx?" *Have you read the communist manifesto by Karl Marx?*

"I am sorry but my German is weak. I did read a translation of Marx's work. As we all know, 'Language is the armory of the human mind, and at once contains the trophies of its past and the weapons of its future conquests.'" George quotes Coleridge.

"Ah, and people of humor are always in some degree people of genius." Catherine matches his knowledge of literature stroke for stroke.

"My compliments, you know your Coleridge as well as your languages."

"So you do not give a lady a warning before you give her a test?"

"My apologies if my words appeared as a test; although, if it were an examination, you would have received an 'A.'" George bows slightly as he hands the thick folder to Catharine. After she takes her father's folder, George turns to leave.

As Catherine speaks, he turns back to her. "When shall I tell my father that you will be back to collect the papers?"

"There is no need; they are in final form." George again turns to leave.

"Since you are working with Mr. Beach, perhaps you might call some time to meet my father."

George is taken off guard by the offer, "I would like that very much; perhaps later in the week?"

"Let us say Thursday. Father is usually home by 5:00." Catharine turns and reenters the house. As the door closes she says, "I will tell him to expect you."

George leaves the porch; a proud smile appears.

The Lester Brothers' office is simple with two wooden roll top desks facing the wall with a table that can be used for meetings in the center of the room. Willard Lester's coat is hanging on a rack. Not expecting guests or clients, he is in a tie and vest reading the newspaper. The windows are open to the street and the rhythm of pedestrians and carriages permeate the air. The peace is broken by the sound of the bell ringing as Morrissey enters. As the door shuts, Morrissey asks, "Mr. Lester?"

Lester rises and offers his hand. "Good afternoon. Willard Lester, how may I help you?"

"My name is John Morrissey. I am looking for a suitable site to open a business. They told me at the newspaper office that you were the man to see." Morrissey plays to Lester's ego.

"Perhaps, if you had been here a week ago, or better yet a month ago, that would have been true. At this point everything has been rented. I only wish I had more listings; I could fill any and all in a day," he brags.

"What about a stable or livery?"

"A stable, what kind of business are you opening?" Lester's curiosity is peaked.

"It will be for entertainment."

"In a livery? You must forgive my confusion."

"A livery would be the last option. What I need is a space near the hotels," Morrissey confides.

"Mr. Morrissey, I can assure you there is nothing available in the village, let alone near the hotels." Morrissey's departure is held up by Lester. "Then, Mr. Morrissey, I assume you will not be opening a business this season."

"Oh, I will be opening a business within the week; when I set my mind to a mission, I succeed." Morrissey exits to the sound of the bell.

After Morrissey leaves Lester mutters, "Irish."

The collection of rocking chairs on the piazza continues to grow. Mrs. Brewster, the widow Mrs. Brown, and Miss Strong are joined by two new members: Miss Lee and Miss Place, both in their mid-thirties. Each woman is wearing a hoop dress. The coven is watching those who walk by on the street. Each of the ladies, except Mrs. Brewster, has a book open on her lap, but none are reading. Mrs. Brewster has knitting – at the rate she is going, she should have the scarf done by Christmas.

Marvin, the supreme host, nods to each dowager as he says her name. "Good afternoon Mrs. Brewster, Mrs. Brown, Miss Lee, Miss Strong, Miss Place. It is so good to see you all again this season. I certainly hope that you had a healthy winter season and took in several plays." There is more than a hint of disingenuousness in his words.

The women all speak cordially to Marvin then look to each other for assurance. Mrs. Brewster even attempts to flirt with Marvin. "Mr. Marvin, you know I only attend the opera; theatricals attract such a disreputable element, both on the stage and in the audience."

Mrs. Brown attempts to explain, "There were several Shakespearian plays in Philadelphia. My former husband had a box each season and I have continued to subscribe ever since his untimely death."

Miss Lee makes a critical summary, "The most interesting performance in Hartford was 'Our American Cousin.'" She looks at everyone then focuses on Marvin. "You simply must see it."

"When it plays in Albany or Troy I will make a point of going to a performance. Ladies, have a good day." Marvin tips his hat and walks to greet others on the porch.

"I should be going to my room to lay down for a brief rest. The excursion yesterday was such a strain. Do you believe they misplaced one of my trunks?" complains Miss Strong. "I must remember to pack a sleeping gown in my personal bag in case this ever happens again."

Not to be outdone. Mrs. Brown contributes to the woes, "One, only one; they told me two of mine will not get here until today."

"I will escort you," Miss Lee concurs, "a short nap would be good for me also."

As the Misses Lee and Strong head from their chairs to the door,

Mrs. Brown waves her kerchief as if hailing a hack. "Please hold on my dears, I could use a rest myself."

With those in need of rest gone, the dowagers continue in hushed tones led by Mrs. Brewster. "Untimely death, my, my; the only thing untimely about her husband's death was that he did not have time enough to put his pants on before he passed! You do know that is why she imagines that every un-escorted woman in the hotel is someone's niece. It makes her such a shrew."

"I never noticed. Under the circumstances Mrs. Brown always seems very pleasant to me," responds Miss Lee.

"Pleasant, I am the pleasant one," assures Mrs. Brewster. "She is a disagreement waiting to happen, and that Miss Strong, despite her wealth, if she does not find a man this season, she shall have to accept the role of spinster."

"Twenty-four is not that old." Miss Lee defends her young friend.

"Twenty-four! She's twenty-seven if she is a day," demands Mrs. Brewster. "I suppose with all her money she will be able to buy a husband someday or, more likely, one will find her."

The Masonic Lodge in Saratoga is primarily one large room on the second floor of an older hotel. There are chairs capable of seating at least fifty around the perimeter, all facing in. The grand Marshal's chair and two assistants' chairs are on a raised dais on the east end of the room. When Morrissey enters, there is single member present, Harrison. Harrison is busy putting clean glasses in the only cabinet in the room. Seeing Morrissey enter, Harrison smiles. "Good afternoon, how may I help you?"

Morrissey introduces himself as he walks across the room toward Harrison. "My name is John Morrissey. I am a Mason from the Brooklyn Lodge, although I spend almost as much time in the Troy Lodge."

Harrison's response is one that is well practiced. "Welcome to our fair village."

Morrissey gets straight to business. "I am interested in renting a space for the season."

Harrison gives the standard response. "If you are looking for lodging, the major hotels should still have rooms. Mr. Marvin at the States is a fellow Mason; remind him of that and he should be able to help. There is also Mrs. Webb's boarding house if you are staying for the entire season."

"I have engaged rooms. What I need is a commercial space where I can operate a business."

"I'm sorry, I cannot think of a single space that is available," Harrison remarks. Morrissey is examining the lodge's room.

"What about the lodge hall? I would pay handsomely."

"We have meetings all season. It is a time for our fellow members, from around the country, to come and to share."

"Wouldn't the lodge be better off renting this floor and holding meetings on the next floor?" Morrissey is pointing toward the ceiling.

"What is the nature of your business?"

"I am goin' to establish a gentlemen's clubhouse, a place with an honest reputation and a fair game."

"If you are indeed a fellow Mason, then you would know that we would never allow our lodge to be used in such a manner."

"I am a Mason, and the lodges I attend offer such activities." Morrissey leaves; as he closes the door Harrison's jacket opens and his police badge shows.

Harrison whispers, "Damn Irish, which lodge started letting them in?"

Morrissey climbs the eight steps and walks through the main door of the States. Four of the dowagers, Mrs. Brown, Mrs. Brewster, Miss Lee, and Mrs. Jackson are sitting in rocking chairs. The day has warmed up and most of the women have fancy fans to cool themselves. There are two men sitting in the chairs usually occupied by the dowagers.

"It is not going to be a good season, not good at all. Any season that starts with this much discord is bound to become dreadful. The hack drivers are more obnoxious than ever, and," Mrs. Brown points with her collapsed fan, "those men are sitting in our chairs."

Mrs. Brewster reestablishes her leadership, "Everyone knows that those chairs are ours. Those have been our chairs for many seasons. I swear, when the senior Mr. Marvin was operating this establishment he would have walked right up to those men and told them to move."

"Rude, it is simply rude, for men to assume that they can sit in any old seat. If etiquette keeps declining at this rate, in no time at all men will be drinking hard alcohol on the piazza." Miss Lee's support of the new temperance movement is obvious.

Mrs. Brown joins in, "That is as it may be. I will not see it twice! If I ever see a man having a drink on the piazza I will check out that very morning and go to one of those Methodist institutes."

"Did you see the dress that Miss Sarah Stiles wore to breakfast? I swear, if it was cut any lower it would be illegal; so much for Southern modesty." Mrs. Brewster enjoys adding fuel to any fire.

"In Hartford the minister would banish her from church and no lady of character would call on her mother. I assume none of you will be calling on Mrs. Stiles." Miss Lee refers to her hometown.

At that moment, Sarah, wearing a low cut dress, walks out of the hotel on the arm of the Reverend Mr. Beecher. Knowing that his church's support comes from those who attend in the summer, Beecher tips his hat as he and Sarah pass the four dowagers. Looking at the dowagers, Sarah has a knowing smile. After descending the stairs, Sarah and the Reverend turn and walk in the direction of the Methodist Church.

There is a new organ on one side of the altar in the Methodist Church. Reverend Beecher's voice shows his pride. "Isn't it marvelous? It was a gift from one of our seasonal parishioners."

Sarah is impressed. "It is beautiful. May I play?"

"That is the reason I brought you here. I so look forward to hearing you play on Sunday mornings."

"You flatter me Reverend Beecher; I am not nearly good enough to play at services." Sarah releases the Reverend's arm and walks to the organ's bench.

The Reverend watches the sway of Sarah's skirt as she walks. As she sits on the bench he remarks, "You have been blessed by God with many aspects of natural beauty."

Uncomfortable with the remark, Sarah places her hands on the keyboard and demonstrates she is talented. Reverend Beecher stands just behind her and looks down at the low cut dress.

Even in the middle of the day the lack of adequate windows leaves the tavern across from the railroad station dark. Morrissey, carrying a small satchel, enters. He instantly notes the bartender, rag in hand, talking to two locals. In the back of the bar four men are playing cards at one of the six tables.

Morrissey puts the satchel at his feet and rests his arm on the bar." As the bartender approaches, Morrissey says, "You look like a man who knows his community. Could you tell me of any buildings that are for rent?"

"I can help you get a drink, some crackers, and maybe even a room. This time of year, for a building, you would have to ask at the newspaper office."

Morrissey orders, "I'll have a beer; make that a boilermaker."

"Oh an Irishman - I thought you looked like one," the bartender quips.

"I've already tried the newspaper office."

The bartender pulls the beer and pours whiskey into a shot glass and places both in front of Morrissey. "My father owns the warehouse across the street from the station. Last time I talked to him there was still space available. What do you want the building for?" The bartender holds the shot glass above the beer. Morrissey nods and the bartender drops the shot glass into the beer.

Morrissey looks at the four men playing cards. "I am going to open a clubhouse, a place for gentlemen to wager in an honest game."

"No need to ask my father, he would never allow gambling in one of his buildings."

Morrissey turns his eyes toward the ceiling, "What about your second floor?"

"Not interested."

"Two thousand for the season; paid in advance." Morrissey opens the case so that the bartender can see the cash inside. The bartender continues drying a glass, then silently continues cleaning up.

The door from the third floor hallway to one of the servant's rooms in the Stiles cottage opens slowly. Thomas Stiles peers into the hallway. When he is sure no one is coming, he slips out. Missy is reclining on the bed. Her lower body is covered by a sheet. Her bare back is the last thing Thomas sees as he closes the door, adjusts his belt, and slithers away.

It is a beautiful afternoon, warm without being hot. The fine weather draws the Stiles family and a crowd of over a hundred to the park at the States hotel where a string quartette is playing. Sarah is painting the scene with watercolors and Sadie reads a book of poetry. Todd is at the archery range. Jacob brashly approaches the Stiles sisters.

"Miss Sarah Stiles, I assume?"

"There is no need to be coy, Jacob. A couple of the dowagers saw you speaking to me at the springs this morning and by now an alarm has been spread throughout the hotel."

Jacob ignores her snip. "Miss Sadie Stiles, I presume?"

"Thank you for trying to bring me into your little tryst but I am not interested."

Jacob returns his attention to Sarah. "Apparently we are having a tryst. I thought that it was simply a chance meeting of a southern belle and a true gentleman from the north."

"Excuse my sister, she has an over developed imagination. Sadie sees devils in every bush and those who would assault the flower of a good woman hiding behind every tree," Sarah attempts to explain.

"I see only what is visible," asserts Sadie.

"Since I did not appear from behind a tree or even a bush, what do you see when I talk with your sister?"

"A potential brother-in-law."

Sarah becomes stern, "Sadie, how dare you?" She then turns her attention to Jacob, "I apologize for the impertinence of my younger sister."

"No need to apologize. Perhaps she really does see what is visible."

Cora approaches carrying a wrapped bundle. "Good afternoon Mr. Marvin. Saratoga has certainly provided us with some beautiful weather," she says, treating Jacob very formally. "I was wondering if I may prevail upon you to introduce some of the young men at the hotel to my daughters."

Upset, Sarah and Sadie speak in unison, "Mother how could you!"

Cora ignores their protest. "I believe that Sadie in particular would like to meet young Mr. Walter Pratt. The word around the hotel is that he has quite a future as a writer."

It is Sadie's turn to protest. "Mother!" Sarah smiles at her sister's embarrassment.

Jacob acknowledges his role as host, "Like Miss Sarah and Miss Sadie, he is usually at the springs in the morning. I will be glad to oblige the next time he is there or, for that matter, I will do proper introductions when any of the other fine single men, who are spending the season, are at the spring."

Cora looks up at the cloudless sky. "The weather looks good for tomorrow. They will be at the Congress about 8:00." Having established that she will do what she determines is appropriate, Cora ends the afternoon's visit. "Girls, it is time to get ready for supper."

The two Stiles daughters gather their possessions. Sarah takes a little too long and bends a little too far over to pick up her paints. Her hoop skirt goes up slightly in the back; Jacob has a clear view of her ankles. After Sarah has finally gathered her painting supplies she turns to be sure Jacob noticed before she joins her mother and sister, returning to the family's cottage.

Morrissey is sitting silently at the same long table he occupied the previous evening. There is a couple at the other end of the table; the remainder of the table is empty. The man, Oscar Bennett, is significantly older than the woman. Marvin approaches the table with an envelope in one hand. He greets Bennett with a firm handshake. "Mr. Bennett, how good to see you. I see you brought along another of your nieces this year."

Bennett talks with his mouth full and points with his fork. "Yes, yes, this is Edith. She's, she's..." he appears to be having trouble remembering how he registered his companion, "my sister's daughter. She is also from Pittsburgh."

Ever the gentleman, Marvin smiles at Edith, "I hope you enjoy your stay. Will you be with us for the entire season or will one of your 'cousins' be joining you later?" There is more than just a hint of sarcasm in Marvin's comment.

Edith is undaunted. "I plan to be here for the entire season, although," Edith raises her eyebrows, "it might be interesting if one of my cousins or even my aunt did join us."

Marvin is forced to smile at her candor. "If that should happen I am sure you will be quite happy. Whatever you do, be sure to enjoy our hops and balls, they start Friday evening. Remembering his manners, Marvin asks, "Have you two met Mr. Morrissey?" Marvin turns to introduce Morrissey. "Mr. Oscar Bennett, Miss Edith, let me introduce you to Mr. John Morrissey. Mr. Morrissey, let me introduce you to Mr. Oscar Bennett and his niece Miss Edith. Now when you should meet in the hotel or park, you may speak."

Marvin leaves the Bennetts, intent on speaking with Morrissey. "So has your search been successful?"

"Not at this point. It appears that every convenient facility has been engaged for the summer."

"As I expected, even the hotel's advanced bookings are up from last year. So you have given up?"

"I am not in the practice of givin' up. At this point I am considerin' rentin' a large tent for the season."

"A tent would still require a space to set it and it would get terribly hot under a canvas tent in the summer." Marvin's words are not comforting.

"I could always raise the sides to let in a night breeze, but that would take away some much needed privacy."

"You are facing a dilemma." Marvin hands the envelope to Morrissey. "By the way, this came for you."

Morrissey waits for Marvin go to another table before he opens the envelope. It is a telegram that reads *Equipment packed and ready to ship. Should leave by Friday.* Morrissey crumbles the note.

The crowd at the railroad station is larger and noisier than the previous day. This time the last car is a private Pullman. On the steps of one of the first class cars, a young woman moves in close to a mature couple. Morrissey identifies her as a pickpocket. He witnesses her trying to move next to the older man. She notices Morrissey glaring at her and leaves.

One moderately attractive woman, Mary, stands back from the pack watching for her own trunk. She is traveling alone - a true break from custom.

Morrissey sees his very attractive wife, Susie, coming down the steps from the first class car. He walks swiftly toward her. It is obvious even to the casual observer that they both care very much for each other. Once they hug, Morrissey gives her a gentle kiss on the cheek; she is too much of a lady to return the gesture. Arm in arm they walk to the baggage car to gather her trunks. Effortlessly, Morrissey gathers her two trunks and three suitcases. Everyone gives him space. Susie brings her husband up-to-date. "Lil' John will enjoy being with my mother for a few days. I wanted time to settle in; besides, mother loves doting over him." Morrissey signals a hack to take his wife's luggage to the hotel. The hack driver appears only too happy to be carrying Morrissey's luggage.

"And she will spoil him. You know she lets him eat all the sweets he wants and when he gets here he will be sick for two days."

"A grandmother's right." She changes topics, "How has your search gone?"

Morrissey is exasperated. "Not well."

"You were unable to work out an arrangement with Mr. Marvin? You were so sure he would see the value in your proposal."

"He made it clear he was not interested. I think he wants to let the private games go on but nothin' too public."

"John, you cannot blame him, he does have the reputation of the hotel to maintain."

The door to one of the baggage cars opens and three younger women and one very large middle aged black man rush out. The three women use one hand to hold up the fronts of their well-worn skirts so they can run faster. In their other hands they have what appears to be a pillow case stuffed with clothes. Holes can be seen in their stockings. The man's run is more of a lumber. He is big enough that, with the possible exception of Morrissey, no one will try to stop him.

Pauline, at 22, the oldest of the three tramps calls out, "Run, run yus fools"

Janet, the youngest at 17, replies, "Dun't calls me no fool, I knows when to run." Antoinette, 20, just laughs.

Morrissey taps Susie's shoulder, making sure she is catching the show as the women and the man make a successful getaway.

Looking back down the train, Morrissey sees a couple, John and Ethel, both about fifty, thin and poorly dressed, get off the third class car. The decrepit couple clutches two very worn bags apiece. John takes a sip from his flask then hands it to Ethel, who also takes a sip. Morrissey whispers to Susie. "The old ones are with them."

John watches as Pauline, Antoinette, Janet, and Bob make good their escape. John reassures Ethel, "I know'd they'd make it jus' fine."

"Shut's up and carry the bags. Yus thin' yus know'd everythin'," she answers. The two struggle with the bags.

Morrissey smiles at the show to which he was just treated.

A team of four beautiful white horses pulls up to the station. The carriage driver holds the team while two footmen jump off the back of the carriage; one crosses the station's wooden platform and opens the door to the Pullman car. The second opens the door to the carriage. Madam Jumel, a tall, thin, regal woman, gracefully exits the Pullman and walks to the carriage. She looks about forty, but if the stories about her are true, she is much older and clearly she is of undeterminable age. Those in the crowd watch Madam Jumel climb into the carriage and be carried away.

The crowd at the springs has grown to well over a hundred. This morning a woman is seated on a folding wooden chair playing a flute. Among those in the crowd are Sarah, Sadie, and Cora. Sarah and Cora all have on simple yet stylish cotton dresses. This early in the day they are excused from wearing hoop skirts. It looks as if Sadie has simply pulled her dressing gown over her night dress. All three women are holding tumblers of water. Todd is admiring the fine horse tied to the hitching post.

Walter Pratt, holding a glass of water, is among the servants. He is wearing the same suit jacket that he has worn all week.

The entire dowager coven, Mrs. Brewster, Mrs. Brown, Mrs. Jackson, Miss Lee, and Miss Strong, stand off in a corner near the path to the hotels. From their vantage point they can see everyone who comes or leaves – at least those who matter.

Madam Jumel looks better than women half her age. Everyone, male and female, looks on with envy. She is well dressed with leather gloves and a scarf. Her glass is crystal.

George and Jacob are standing next to each other near one of the pillars. Jacob has a glass of water, George does not. George and Jacob stare at Madam Jumel. "She's back for another season," George remarks.

"I doubt she would ever miss and the springs would not be the same without her," observes Jacob.

George says admiringly, "No matter what has happened to her, she holds her head high and looks askance at her detractors. To me, she epitomizes elegance."

"Sometimes I wish I had gone to Harvard. If I could talk like that I would be Le beaux extraordinary." Jacob fakes a French accent.

"You do well enough now filling your dance card. Furthermore, Harvard would disavow any connection."

Jacob changes topics, "As the hotel owner's nephew, I have a duty to perform." George looks questionably. "Whenever one of the guests wants an introduction, it is my responsibility." Jacob reflects briefly, "Do you think this antiquated rule of never speaking to anyone without a formal introduction will ever end?"

The Victorian gentleman George answers, "I would certainly hope not. Can you imagine life if a man could approach a woman, to whom he had not been introduced, in a grocery or a library? With such behavior polite society would collapse in a single generation."

Jacob walks over to Walter; George remains by his original pillar. "Walter, I think we have guests who you would like to meet."

Walter is instantly sarcastic. "Jacob, how good to see you." Jacob ignores the comment, taking Walter's arm as he leads him to the three Stiles women.

"Walter, I would like to introduce you to Mrs. Cora Stiles and her daughters, Sarah and Sadie." Jacob points to each woman as she is introduced. "Ladies, this is Walter Pratt. Walter is one of our village's aspiring authors. He writes for the Press. Walter, I am sure that you must agree that we are to be grateful to the unpleasant climate in Southern cities each summer, as it causes them to send their finest lilies north to enjoy our resplendent atmosphere."

Walter politely takes each woman's hand as they are introduced. "Mrs. Stiles, Miss Sarah, Miss Sadie, it is indeed a pleasure to meet you. How long will you be with us?" Walter attempts to hold Sadie's hand for a second longer than normal. Sadie pulls it away.

"It is nice to meet you; we have engaged a cottage at the States for the season. Who is that lady in the green dress?" She is referring to Madam Jumel.

"That is Madam Jumel," Jacob informally does his duty one more time, "the widow of Steven Jumel and the former wife of Vice President Aaron Burr."

"She has climbed a very long way." Walter adds his anecdote.

Jacob cautions, "That is not proven. What we do know is that she is one of the classic beauties of our times and that she honors our springs each year with her presence. I would like to think that our mineral waters have helped contribute to her lasting beauty."

"She is as beautiful as they say. I have heard of her but never expected her to look so stately." Cora's admiration shows.

"Just wait until you see her promenade in her four horse carriage this afternoon."

Jacob cannot resist the opportunity to give a compliment, "Her beauty pales beside yours and your daughters."

"Jacob you are becoming too bold." Cora gathers her litter. "Girls, shall we go to breakfast?"

Disappointed that the meeting is being cut off, Walter presses, "It was a pleasure meeting you. I hope to see you another morning." The girls wave but don't answer. As she walks away, Sadie drops a handkerchief. Walter hesitates for a minute then picks up the handkerchief, noticing the embroidery. He starts to call after her but puts it in his pocket. Jacob returns to George.

Madam Jumel is talking quietly to a bald man who is much shorter than she. George and Jacob can be seen trying to listen in to what Madam Jumel is saying.

The coven is gathered at the pot stirring gossip. Mrs. Brewster throws the first mud. "Look at that woman, so overdressed for this hour. I would wager she never went home last evening."

"That is the infamous Madam Jumel," Mrs. Jackson reminds the others.

Mrs. Brewster attempts to add fodder to the stew. "Now there is a woman with a checkered past. I would never be seen in public if I had lived a life such as hers." The other four dowagers gather closer. "You know they say her mother was a fallen woman and, some say, that she fell into the same fate when she was young."

"I have heard the same, but, I have also heard that the story was created by people who were jealous." Mrs. Jackson stresses the word jealous.

Mrs. Brewster defends her conclusions. "Well, you can be sure I am not jealous of her."

"I would not imply that you are, only that that was what some say was the source of the story." Mrs. Jackson always leaves people wondering if she really means what she says. "We do know that she was married to Mr. Jumel and that he was a fabulously wealthy man and, after he passed, she married a Vice President."

"The first was much older and," Mrs. Brewster pauses for

emphasis, "'French.' The second was tried for treason. That is hardly a marriage record anyone should endeavor to replicate."

Mrs. Jackson changes the topic. "Perhaps not, but you do know who that little man is who is talking to her?"

"Probably some pretender after her supposed wealth," Mrs. Brewster suggests.

"No, that is our former President, the honorable Martin Van Buren," Mrs. Jackson says proudly.

The day is warm. Five of the dowagers, Mrs. Brewster, Brown, Jackson, and Misses Lee and Strong, have assumed their regular rocking chairs on the piazza of the States Hotel. Marvin and Thomas are sitting in rocking chairs at the far end of the piazza. Bennett and Edith are sitting near the main entrance. It would be considered a compliment to say that Bennett looked thrown together. His rough, wrinkled appearance is in sharp contrast with Edith, who is well dressed.

A slight middle aged man is standing near the bottom of the steps of the hotel. There is nothing noteworthy about him except for the silver toothpick in his mouth. There are seats available; however, a second man is walking up and down the piazza as if in search of a seat.

All knowing Mrs. Brewster fires the first volley, "You do know why that man is standing at the bottom of the steps?"

Mrs. Brown makes the mistake of answering. "Of course; he may think he is fooling people but everyone knows that he is trying to catch a glimpse of a lady's ankle as she ascends the stairs."

The wind taken out of her sails, Mrs. Brewster becomes aggressive. "I shall have to call over one of the waiters and have him removed. Back in the day, when the senior Mr. Marvin was operating the hotel, a man like that would have already been sent on his way."

Miss Lee fans herself. "It is just disgusting the behavior and boldness of the men this season. The poor innocent young ladies who climb those steps would never suspect that there was an old man leering. A thing like that would never happen in Hartford."

Flustered by what she has just heard, Miss Place blushes. "Oh my, I was just thinking he was standing there when I came back from the springs. I certainly hope he did not see my stockings."

The true shrew, Mrs. Brewster becomes disparaging. "Miss Place, I do not think you have to worry. I am sure it was the younger ladies who were capturing his attention."

"I think he would look at any well-turned ankle," Miss Place rationalizes.

Mrs. Brewster signals a waiter. "Then we shall have to have him removed." When the waiter comes to Mrs. Brewster she points her parasol at the man at the bottom of the stairs. The waiter nods understandingly and heads toward the man with the silver toothpick. In a very quiet voice the waiter talks to the man at the bottom of the stairs. The man glares at the dowagers then reluctantly walks away.

Mrs. Brown changes the topic. "When I was downtown, I could not help noticing those young Stiles girls shopping in the fancy goods store. The way they spend money, they better marry for it."

Mrs. Brewster passes judgment. "There is no question but that that is exactly their intention. That is why they stay at the States; is this not where all the money and the politicians stay?"

Miss Strong defends her generation. "If they are not to have a good season when they are young, when will it be their season? Each piece of fruit is ripe for such a short period."

Mrs. Jackson becomes motherly. "You talk as if your time is over. Miss Strong, you will have your day and I would guess it will be this very season."

Two couples get up and leave the piazza, leaving their seats open. The man who has been walking up and down the piazza remains on patrol. Thomas and Marvin watch him from their chairs at the end of the piazza. Thomas puffs on his cigar, "Do you think he will ever land?"

"Not for a while, he is too busy showing off his new silver handled cane," Marvin observes.

"To whom?"

Marvin demonstrates his ability to read people. "He is an example of not knowing the difference between seeking and deserving attention; seeking is from everyone, deserving is from someone."

Bennett and Edith watch with great care the incident with the man at the bottom of the stairs. Bennett is reminded of being asked to move the first time he and Edith went to the dining room. "Damnest place I ever stayed. Even if a man's here first he can be ask'd to move fer someon' else," Bennett grumbles.

"Now Oscar my darling, you promised not to make a scene." Edith pats his hand.

"I ain't make'n no scene, I jus' make'n a point." His voice has become louder.

"Well, now we know that that table is reserved for Mr. Vanderbilt; we won't be taking it again."

"I don't care. If'n I's there first."

Edith and Oscar go silent as Morrissey and Susie walk up the steps and enter the hotel. "She is one fine lookin' littl' filly," Oscar says too loud.

As the Morrisseys enter the lobby, a young messenger is calling out, "Telegram for Mr. Morrissey, telegram for Mr. John Morrissey." With all the activity in the lobby, people barely notice the porter. Morrissey signals the messenger by raising his hand. Seeing the gesture, but unsure if he has it correct, the porter asks, "Mr. Morrissey?" Morrissey reaches in his pocket and pulls out a silver coin, which he gives to the messenger. The messenger looks at the coin, and then smiles, acknowledging it is a much larger tip than normal. The messenger walks back to the telegraph office, hoping that the tip is an omen.

"John, you should not show off. Humility, remember humility," Susie admonishes her husband.

"He needs it much more than I do," Morrissey responds, opening the envelope. Susie studies her husband's face, looking for clues about the telegram.

"Good news?"

"Under different circumstances."

Catharine Cook is sitting in a tall wicker chair on the front porch of her father's house, reading a book. Her chair is arranged so that her back is in the direction George is walking. As George passes on the opposite side of the street, he does not see Catherine. After he passes, she watches him over the top of her book. To her dismay she sees the Reverend approaching on her side of the street. Climbing the steps, Beecher removes his hat. "Good afternoon, Catherine. May I join you?"

"Reverend Beecher, what an unexpected surprise," she says as he climbs the final step.

"It was such a beautiful afternoon, I felt compelled to take a break from preparing this week's sermon and take the opportunity to stroll among God's creations." He stands awkwardly.

"The weather is most pleasant," she concurs.

"May I have a seat?"

"My father is not at home and I fear that some may get the wrong idea."

"Even on the front porch, in the afternoon? I am a man of God."

"I would not want anyone to make insinuations."

"Then I will have to ask your father for permission to join you in his absence." Undeterred, the Reverend turns and walks away.

Morrissey and Susie are sitting in the parlor of their suite looking over the gardens of the hotel. To be cool, Susie is in a silk dressing gown sipping a glass of water. Morrissey, dressed in his coat, is smoking a cigar. The windows are open and a light breeze is blowing the curtains. "What was in the telegram?" Susie asks.

"It was from Richards. He told me the equipment is already on the way. He assumed I would need it by Friday."

"So they rushed to ship it?"

"Yes, it should be here in two days. Without an address, he sent everything to my attention. Now I will have to meet each train." He takes a puff on his cigar. "The croupiers are also on their way."

"Do you think that all the space is suddenly rented because you are Irish?"

"That probably closed some of the doors, but not all."

"So you have tried the newspaper office, the real estate office, major land owners; have you tried the priest?"

"Susie, my business is not one that God is known for supportin'."

"Not God, the local priest. Promise him jobs for his parishioners and see where it goes." Morrissey looks appreciatively at Susie while he takes a puff on his cigar.

"Mr. Marvin seems like a very nice gentleman."

Morrissey rises and goes to the window. "He is a very successful businessman and has the rare quality that everyone seems to respect him."

"You always say that every man has either a vice or an anvil. What is Mr. Marvin's?"

"I don't know." There is a long pause. "Yet." Morrissey stares out the window.

Susie stands and pulls up her dressing gown. "Now what do you say we appreciate the fact that Lil' John is not here."

The crowd has grown to well over a hundred. The violinist is back. Cora is dressed for the day; Sarah and Sadie are wearing elegant night-coats tied at the waist. Todd is chasing a duck into the pond. The younger women are all wearing night-coats instead of dresses; apparently what happens in Saratoga stays in Saratoga. The dowagers, Mrs. Brewster, Brown, Jackson, and the Misses Lee and Strong are gathered by one post. They face in different directions so that nothing escapes their combined gaze. Walter appears nervous as he leaves the servants area and moves to the spring. Madam Jumel and Van Buren are near the rail.

George and Jacob are at their usual post. Jacob is looking appreciatively at the Stiles sisters. George looks at Madam Jumel and Van Buren.

"They are back. Can you just imagine what they are talking about?" George is impressed by how naturally the two handle their stature.

Jacob shakes his head very slightly. "It does not matter; however, what does matter is what the Stiles girls are talking about." Jacob gives George a gentle nudge. "Oh, watch this." Walter has Sadie's handkerchief in his hand as he nervously approaches her.

Walter builds up his courage. "Miss Sadie, I believe you must have dropped this yesterday."

"Why, thank you." She pretends that she is not sure of his name. "You are Mr. Pratt, I believe. How did you know it was mine?"

"Please call me Walter. I thought I saw it fall from your hand; by the time I recovered it you were gone." Sadie unfolds the handkerchief, noting that it has been washed and ironed. "I could not help but notice the initials. The embroidery is excellent, my compliments." He is fidgeting and having trouble making eye contact.

"Thank you Mr. Pratt, and thank your mother for washing and ironing it for me."

Having witnessed enough, Cora suggests, "Sadie, I think it is time we should be leaving." Sadie gives Walter a smile as she joins her mother and sister.

Jacob speaks quietly to George, "My call is he will try his best and fail miserably." Jacob raises his voice as he talks to the Stiles women. "Mrs. Stiles, Miss Sadie, and Miss Sarah, may I have the honor of your company on the way back to the hotel?"

Cora responds, "Jacob, you have mastered the ability to make one wonder whether you are being polite or sarcastic. We will accept your offer as if it were meant as a courteous gesture." Walter watches for any special recognition from Sadie as the group gathers; none happens. Jacob holds out his arm for Cora.

"Todd, come along now," Cora calls out for her roving son. Todd joins them and the five exit the park in the direction of the hotel.

Josey and Missy stand with other servants and slaves on the perimeter. There are many more servants than slaves. Even among this group there is an informal ranking; the servants stand closer to the spring than the slaves. One of the hotel servants says to Josey, "You may dress better than we do but you are still a slave and we's free."

"I may be a slave but I's eat better'n, dress better'n, and live better'n than yus ever will," Josey responds.

"Can you go to the church on yur own? Does you have any money of yus own? Can you decide not to work a day if'n you don't wants to?"

Missy intercedes, "We can go tos any church we want; we jus wans to go to the same one as the masters."

"Call it what yus like, you can be beaten and sold without no justice."

"And you can be fired and go hungry jus fur bein lazy." Missy is fired up. "Howz duz you keep a job anyhow?" There is a general snicker among the servants and slaves until Walter approaches, and then they all go silent.

George has moved as close to Madam Jumel and Van Buren as he can get without being too obvious. "Will you be going to his reception?" she asks Van Buren.

"To watch such a simple man try to show pomp, I could not and would not miss the opportunity, after all, to dine with the President."

The priest's office is decorated as a business office with dark woods. A picture of Jesus, a second of the Virgin Mary, and a crucifix provide the religious overtones. The walls on two sides of the room are bookshelves. The middle aged priest is in black robes, which serve to accentuate the whiteness of his hair and the redness of his nose. Morrissey and the priest are seated on hard wooden chairs that are at a conference table. "And what can I do for you my son?" The priest has a heavy Irish accent.

"Father, this is my second season in Saratoga. Perhaps you have heard of me?"

"I don't recognize you from your attendance at services, but I do recognize the name."

"My wife attends services regularly and gives generously to the causes of the church." The banter is over; who will run the meeting is not yet determined, but instead put on hold. "Father, I have come to Saratoga to establish a business. It is a business I have been engaged in for some time and have done very well."

The priest flashes back to Susie. "I remember her. She has a lovely voice."

"Father, I run an honest business, even if the business itself is not within the frameworks of the law. Unfortunately, here in Saratoga I have met with nothing but closed doors."

"Because you are Irish, Catholic, or because of the nature of your business?" asks the priest, now focusing on Morrissey.

"Probably some of each; it could be worse." Morrissey pauses. "I could be black." The priest nods assurance. "Everyone knows that there are many private games in town. Last year there were at least two public clubhouses; one in a livery stable and one over a local tavern. All the sporting men know that my clubhouses in New York and Troy are

41

successful and that I run an honest game."

"I may be able to help." The priest leans back in his chair. "Recently, all of the young ladies, who were boarding at Mrs. Quinn's house, were given the fifteen minute rule. There is no way she will be able to replace so much talent before the season. I suspect her house may be available."

Morrissey is reminded of the incident at the train station the day he arrived in Saratoga. "You know father, I think I saw them at the station."

The priest smiles, "Judge Baucus is a tough man. I have been told that they ran when he ordered that they had fifteen minutes to be out of town or fifteen days in jail. I am glad to hear they made it."

"Where is Mrs. Quinn's house?"

"It is the big white one across the tracks and kind of in back of the States Hotel. It is the one with four round pillars."

"I know the place. Do you think she would rent to me?"

"Rent, no; but I do think you could buy the house. I am sure Mrs. Quinn would like the money to open another establishment in another community and to be rid of Saratoga."

"You know my business. Do you think I will have trouble with the neighbors?"

"I think that for one season they will be glad to have a business such as yours rather than one similar to Mrs. Quinn's. After all, sins of the pocketbook are forgiven far quicker than sins of the body."

"Thank you father, you have been a big help." Morrissey rises.

"There are two more things," the priest mandates. Morrissey sits back down. "You need to come up with a way to assure everyone that locals will not be allowed in your establishment. That restriction alone will cut the condemnation of the community in half. It is okay for the guests of our village to lose their money; it is not okay for the fathers of our working families to lose their hard earned wages."

"That can be arranged." Thinking the meeting is over, Morrissey again begins to stand.

"I said two things," the priest reminds Morrissey. Morrissey sits. "I expect to see you at services."

"My wife will be there. As you said, she has a beautiful voice and, I might add, a generous purse." Morrissey rises and walks toward the door without looking back.

"Mr. Morrissey." Morrissey stops but does not turn around. "I assume that none of my congregates will be involved in your endeavor." Morrissey opens the door and leaves.

On Broadway, an excited Morrissey catches up to Susie, who holds a bag with purchases. The street is busy with people shopping. Seeing his expression of joy, Susie says mockingly, "How was your meeting with the priest?"

"Fantastic! I think there may be an answer."

"Is it all resolved or can I help?"

"The priest gave me a lead on a location. He says that I need to be able to assure that no one from Saratoga enters the clubhouse."

Susie looks in the window of the jewelry store as she thinks. She turns to Morrissey, "There are two ways to solve that problem; require a hotel room key to enter or hire a local who knows everyone in the village."

"Better yet - both! You are the woman behind the man," he says, walking away.

"And Mr. John Morrissey, don't you ever forget it." Morrissey smiles as he hustles off in the direction of the hotel. Susie continues shopping.

Marvin and Thomas are sitting in leather chairs in the gentlemen's parlor. Marvin has chosen a seat that allows him to watch the front desk. He notices Morrissey at the desk. The clerk is handing Morrissey the valise he had with him at the tavern earlier. During the conversation between Thomas and Marvin, Morrissey takes the bag and exits. "If it keeps up like this, it will be a very hot summer," Thomas comments.

"I feel you are correct. A hot summer increases the number of guests and the numbers at the balls. What have you decided regarding your slaves?"

"I did not realize that I was expected to decide anything." Thomas pauses, "As I said, the ladies of my family would so miss their servants. I could never send them home."

Morrissey climbs the few steps to a Greek revival house and rings the bell. A huge black bouncer answers the door. "Is Mrs. Quinn in?" Morrissey asks.

"Who may I say is calling?"

"Mr. John Morrissey." He says handing the bouncer his card.

The bouncer steps back, allowing Morrissey to enter the foyer. There is heavy stuffed furniture in the room and paintings of naked women on the walls and a grand piano. "Wait here. I will see if she will receive you."

The bouncer walks to a door near the back of the foyer. Morrissey paces anxiously, looking at the paintings that adorn the walls. A door near the front of the foyer opens, revealing Mrs. Quinn.

She holds out her hand, "Mr. Morrissey, I presume."

Morrissey extends his hand graciously. "Mrs. Quinn. You must excuse me. I heard about your troubles and want to be of some assistance."

"I have a sudden commodity shortage; do you have a supply?"

"No. I am not in that line of work, but I am in a position to offer you cash for this fine house."

"Mr. Morrissey, I doubt that you have the amount that I would expect."

"And what would that amount be?"

"You know what they say about location. I am three buildings from the States, a long block from both the Union and the Congress and yet this house cannot be seen from any of them, a useful option for those with suspicious wives or jealous nieces."

"That is true, but it is not a price."

"I am afraid I would have to have at least eight thousand dollars and that would have to be in cash."

"Is there a lien or mortgage on the property?"

"I am not in a business where people would lend to me. I may help the occasional banker out but he would never dream of helping me. The house is paid in full."

"I only have four thousand with me today; getting the rest will take some doing. You can rest assured I can raise the funds. I will meet you at 10:00 tomorrow morning at your lawyer's office to draw up the necessary documents."

Mrs. Quinn offers her hand for a second time. "The office of Mr. Beach; it is across the square."

"I will see you there."

The States lobby is busy. Morrissey descends the stairs with a small black book and walks up to the desk clerk asking, "Where is the telegraph office?" Before the clerk can answer, Marvin approaches.

"I understand you had a successful afternoon Mr. Morrissey, my congratulations." Marvin takes Morrissey by the arm and leads him to a corner of the lobby.

"Thank you. News travels fast." Morrissey is surprised that Marvin knows already. "I would like you to know that we have made arrangements that should make our presence suitable to those who live in the village."

"How so?"

"We will only be open to guests of the village; no locals will be allowed inside. We will have our own men handle any situations, so that we will not be a burden on the local constabulary."

"Those are excellent ideas. How will you live up to those promises?"

"Those who enter will have to show a room key. And I will have one local man stand watch on the porch."

"Excellent, might I impose on you to tell me if any of my guests seem to be losing more than they can afford?"

"That would not be an imposition. You will excuse me; I need to make some financial arrangements."

"I thought you had the matter resolved."

"It is close; I need additional funds, which I am sure I can raise with one or two telegrams."

"How much do you need?"

"Do you know someone who might have access to several thousand dollars? I would pay 50% interest payable at the end of the season."

"Those are very generous terms. The person I know thinks long term. He would want joint interest in the business, not just one season's revenue."

"If I could operate the business under my terms, that might prove acceptable."

"The person I know would not want his name associated with the enterprise. As long as the business was run honestly, he would not interfere. How much do you need and by when?"

"Five thousand by 9:00 tomorrow morning." Morrissey asks for more than he really needs.

Marvin offers his hand, "Consider it done."

Morrissey watches as eleven men get off the first train of the morning. One, Ringer, is small with large wire rim glasses. He looks like he has successfully avoided the sun for years. The others are all large, not the type one wants to make angry. Even among this oversized group one man, Richards, stands out. The freight car door opens and the men begin moving crates onto a waiting wagon. Morrissey moves next to Richards. "Is it all here?"

Richards looks at the collection of crates. "By the looks, I think that someone added a few extra." There is general laughter among those struggling to unload the crates.

"Are the important ones here?"

"There should be five marked with red circles and three with blue squares." Richards looks at the crates. "They're here."

In a tenement apartment near the coal yard are the three worn sisters from the train, the man who calls himself their father, and the woman he lives with. The room has a wooden table with two unmatched wooden chairs, a full size bed, and an extra mattress on the floor. None of the pieces match. The two older girls, Antoinette and Pauline, are sifting through a small pile of stockings on the old table trying to find any without holes. When they find the best of the lot, they put them on. No one demonstrates any modesty. Their speech is inner city poverty.

The father wants an income. "Where's yuse goin' to be workin' t'night?

The youngest of the girls, Janet, begs off. "I can't work t'night, I's got my curse."

"Yuse always got da curse ans yuse probly gots a sore throat too. I know'd we shu'da left yo in Albany - let yuse starve," John threatens.

"Wish yo'ad."

"I here'd on da porch that dey's open'n a gen'lemen's club ove' on da square. We sh'uld be able to make rent money dere." Pauline has already found the rumor mill.

The toothless woman they call mother tries to advise the daughters. "Da Square? Dey will bust yo sur's shoot'n dere. It's too close to da States. We ain't got bail money so don't go gett'n yuse sel'se in trouble bys gett'n' greedy."

Pauline is the business woman of the group. "D'at may be, but we's always better off'n we's follow da money."

Antoinette has always looked out for her younger sister. "I dink's we ough' take a night off to scope da village - see where it's safe and were s'not."

It has been too long since John has had a drink and his mood shows. "There ain't no nights off'n Saratoga. We's needs to make money while we can."

"It don't make no difference tonight - the club aint open anywho." In town only days and Pauline knows the schedule.

Jacob sits in the wooden chair leaning back so the front legs are off the floor. His feet, with his boots on, are up on the bed. He watches as George puts on his best jacket and checks himself in the mirror. "So today you meet the father. How does someone from Harvard tell the refined lady's father that he is scheming to embrace his daughter before the season is over?"

"One does not. What a Harvard man does is show respect for the daughter and interest in the father's ideas. Handled with diplomacy, the father hopes that the Harvard man will be embracing his daughter. Furthermore, I don't scheme." George attempts to correct his friend.

"You may not think of it as scheming but I can assure you that the father of your victim will see it that way."

George slaps Jacob's legs off the bed, making him sit upright. "That is because in your case the term fits. In mine, it is inappropriate."

"Really?" There is a long pause before Jacob continues, "Will you be taking her to the dance on Saturday?"

George walks out the door leaving Jacob in the room.

Mary, the single lady who got off the second train, is staying at the Marvin House, a small hotel with a room overlooking the front porch of the States. She leaves the window open but closes the curtains. She walks over to the wash stand and pours a bowl of water to wash with. She takes off the top of her dress, chemise and corset. Naked to the waist she uses a cloth to wash her face, under her arms and the front of her body. She looks into the mirror, "Well, Miss Mary, you made it to Saratoga, now the question is, do you have what it takes to do it?" She lifts the front of her skirt and continues to wash off.

The lobby of one of the best hotels in Troy is decorated with dark heavy woods. There is an open staircase leading to the second floor. Only the desk clerk Nelson and the porter are on duty. Suddenly there is what sounds like a gun shot. "What the hell was that?" Two more gun shots sound in quick secession. Nelson and the porter look at each other, and then look upstairs. "Sounded like gun shots to me," Nelson continues.

"Me too," the porter agrees. There is the sound of a door slamming. Nelson and the porter waste precious moments looking at each other.

Finally, Nelson rushes around the main desk as he yells to the porter. "Go get help!" There is the sound of another gun shot.

Frank Baucus causally appears at the top of the stairs. His hand takes the railing as he walks down. Nelson, hustling up the stairs, passes Frank. The two do not acknowledge each other. Frank walks out the front door. Nelson walks down the hall until he comes to a door that is slightly ajar. Cautiously, Nelson opens the door. On the floor, in a puddle of blood, is Mansfield Baucus. Mansfield did not rent the room but Nelson recognizes him as he had been a guest on several occasions in the past. Nelson rushes to his side and attempts to intervene.

Frank Baucus walks along the street until he finds a police officer. Boldly, Frank walks up to the officer and hands him a pistol.

As George reaches the steps of the Cook's home, a messenger catches him, "You're Mr. George Batcheller?"

"Yes."

"Mr. Beach sent me to get you. He said it is imperative you come to his office immediately."

"Tell him I will be there presently. I need to stop here for a minute."

The messenger is used to a person jumping at Beach's name. "He said immediately."

"And I said, after I deliver a message." As the messenger starts fearfully running down the street, George walks up the steps and rings the bell.

The door is answered by the butler. "Mr. Batcheller, Mr. Cook is expecting you, do come in."

"I must speak to Mr. Cook. It is important."

"I will see if he is ready to receive you." George waits patiently until Cook enters the foyer from the library.

"I thought this was to be a social call. What is so important?" Cook inquires.

"I wish I knew. A messenger from the office just told me that Mr. Beach needs to see me immediately. I must apologize for having to leave so abruptly."

"Mr. Beach would not send a messenger unless he felt it was essential. Be on your way." George does not realize that Catharine is standing just out of sight on the second floor where she has been listening to the conversation. She has on one of her best dresses. As George closes the front door she turns and goes back to her room.

The Reverend Beecher stops walking and watches as George walks down the street. He then climbs the steps to the Cook's house and rings the bell. The butler answers the door.

"Is Mr. Cook accepting callers?"

"I will see. Please wait here for a moment." The butler turns and walks away without offering to let the Reverend enter the house.

Cook, walking from the library door, opens the front door, gesturing for the Reverend to enter the foyer. "Reverend, to what do I owe the honor of this unanticipated visit?"

The reverend removes his hat upon entering and fidgets with it during the remainder of his visit. "How nice it is to see you. I was wondering...I was wondering...I was wondering...if I might ask your permission to call on Catharine and to sit with her on the porch."

"Reverend Beecher, I am sure that if you truly know my daughter, then you know she is very strong willed. She and she alone will determine who will be welcomed to call."

"When I called earlier, she implied that I would need your permission before I could sit with her."

"Then you have your answer. Good evening Reverend." Cook turns and returns to his study, leaving Reverend Beecher looking totally confused.

The guests are gathering for supper. When Morrissey and Susie reach the door the maître d steps aside and Marvin takes his place. Marvin escorts them to a small table near the musicians.

Morrissey understands the importance of being seated by the host. "Mr. Marvin, why don't you drop down tomorrow to see my new building? I would like you to feel comfortable suggesting my establishment to men of quality."

"That is a very generous offer. Shall we say noon? That way I can be back for dinner at 2:00."

"Noon it shall be. May I provide somethin' to eat or drink in your honor?"

"You will be busy enough getting established. Please, I would prefer that you do not go out of your way on my account." The two men shake hands. The wine steward appears with a bottle of wine. "Until tomorrow, I assume the wine will suit your taste. It is with my compliments." Marvin moves on to the Stiles family.

Marvin speaks to the entire family, "I hope you are all enjoying your stay. Cora, I have just been notified that President Buchannan will be arriving next week. He will be staying for two weeks. I think it only fitting that the hotel hosts a reception in his honor. I have taken the liberty of reserving the ladies' parlor tomorrow at 3:00 for the Entertainment Committee to meet."

"Who else is going to be on the committee?"

"I have contacted the Commodore and he has agreed to send Miss Mary; Mrs. Astor is here and Mrs. Osgood (another Vanderbilt) will be arriving in the morning. I have not heard from Mrs. Corning or Mrs. Davidson, but I believe they will make every effort to attend."

"No other southern ladies?"

Marvin looks dubious, "Is that a problem?"

"There did seem to be an under representation from the south last year."

"I will see what I can do to correct the imbalance."

A messenger enters and talks to one of the waiters. The waiter points to Mrs. Brewster. The messenger walks over to her table. "Mrs. Brewster?" She fails to tip the messenger. She opens the telegram. It says, "One family went missing."

Two weeks before, Mrs. Brewster is boarding her carriage. The back of the carriage has three trunks and two bags strapped down. There are two dozen slaves gathered to see her off, including the field hand, Nate, his wife, Mattie, and their children, Adam and Eve. Mattie's mother, Nanny, leans on a chair near the family's humble cabin. The overseer helps Mrs. Brewster get comfortable. He says, "Now you have a nice time in Saratoga."

"You take care of the plantation and let me worry about myself," admonishes Mrs. Brewster.

"It looks like a good crop this year, so don't go worrying about how much you spend."

"And you mind yourself. I don't expect to hear any issues with the slave women when I get back."

The overseer steals a looks at Mattie. "Oh, you won't hear of no problems." The carriage starts down the dirt road.

Beach's personal office is meant to impress. There are two large leather chairs facing the desk. There is also a conference table with six wooden chairs. There are law books along one wall. Beach is seated as George enters. "I said I needed to see you immediately."

"I assumed you would not want one of your best clients to be stood up when an explanation was simple to provide."

"Have you heard the news about Judge Baucus' son?"

"Mansfield or Charles?"

"Then you have not heard. Mansfield was shot dead in Troy less than an hour ago." George is too stunned to respond. "I always expected he would be shot by a jealous husband, not by his own son. Do you know Frank?"

"We have met. He was a year behind me at the Fort Edward Academy."

"I need you to go to Troy on the next train. Be sure that Frank Baucus does not talk to anyone. It is your job to keep him quiet until I get there." Beach collects his thoughts before continuing, "I will go to the manor and meet with his grandfather and his mother. Send me a telegram after you have met with young Frank." Beach pauses for a second time. "Pay any bail required; tell the judge that you are from my office and I guarantee the money. Do everything you can to get him out of jail and away from jailhouse witnesses."

Marvin and Morrissey walk out onto the porch, exiting the casino. Marvin remarks, "Mr. Morrissey, my compliments. You have done an excellent job. Before I leave, I need to ask one more favor." Marvin seems hesitant, "In the event one of my guests should over indulge, would you please send a man so one of my porters can escort him safely to the hotel?"

"No need, if one of your guests needs an escort, I will provide it. Neither of us wants to see a dissatisfied customer."

"Thank you and good luck." Marvin walks back in the direction of his hotel while Morrissey leans against one of the pillars and lights a cigar, watching Marvin leave.

Morrissey speaks to himself "Successful is the man who provides what men need. Wealthy is the man who provides what men want."

Congress Spring

The President's Visit

The simple cell Frank Baucus occupies has two cots. Frank, dressed in wool pants, suspenders, and a band collar shirt buttoned to the top, is sitting on one of the cots. His back is against the wall, his head is held down, his legs are drawn up, and his hands are hanging over his knees, making him appear almost in a ball.

George enters wearing the same clothes he wore to the Cook's house and carrying a valise. The jailer closes and locks the door behind him. As George stares, the jailer reluctantly walks away. After placing his valise on the empty cot, George offers Frank his hand, which is taken without emotion. "Frank, it is good to see you again; I believe it has been at least two years." Frank does not respond.

George sits formally on the edge of the second cot. "How are you holding up?" Frank remains silent. As George continues to speak, Frank slowly sits up. "I am here on behalf of Mr. Beach. He told me to tell you that it is imperative that you do not speak to anyone until you meet with your mother or him."

The reference to his mother makes Frank come out of his shell. "Have you spoken to mother?"

"No, but by now I am certain that Mr. Beach has met with her. I would not be surprised if they are on the next train down."

Frank remains absent of emotion. "You know I did it." He pauses to look at George. "My mother had suffered enough. I was not going to allow him to hurt her ever again."

George looks around to be sure Frank has not been heard. "Frank, you should not talk about it; not even to me. You have to understand the other prisoners or one of the guards can be listening and they can be called to testify."

"What difference does it make? As soon as I saw him fall, I walked to the precinct house and turned myself in. I confessed!"

"Frank, for your mother's sake," George lowers his voice, "if not for your own, stop talking about what happened."

"You have no idea how hard it was to live with an insane man hanging around, the constant threats."

George appears concerned as he again looks around. "Frank, I have to insist you stop talking." The two go silent as they hear the guard walk by banging his club on the bars of the cells. When the guard is well away George continues, "On the way in, the guard told me you have been arraigned already. How much is bail?"

"The judge said something about no bail; something to do with an imminent danger to society."

"I am sure Mr. Beach can get that straightened out as soon as he gets here. Do you need anything - food, water?"

"No, they have treated me fine."

"You look tired; you should try to get some rest."

"I suppose I can lie down but I doubt that I will sleep. What hotel will you be at? Just in case I need you."

"No hotel. I will be spending the night right here. I need to be sure you do not talk to anyone." George fiddles with the latch to his valise while looking despairingly at his surroundings. "How about a game of chess?"

"I suppose."

George rises and takes off his suit jacket. He looks at the makeshift cot with distain. He sits back on the cot and takes out a chess board and pieces.

The crowd at Congress Spring is the largest in years. One has the feeling that everyone in the village is present. There is constant buzzing and movement as people change groups. With George in Troy, Jacob is alone near the post where he and George usually stand. Walter is near the servants on the perimeter. The dowagers are near the main sidewalk to the hotels, buzzing and pointing about all who pass. Catharine stands off by herself.

Sarah, Cora, and Sadie walk into the area of the spring. After successfully getting a glass of mineral water, they stop by one of the posts. Todd runs ahead to be near the Deerpark. Cora reminds her daughters, "Remember, we are ladies of the south. We do not engage in the idle gossip that will be flying around. We just listen."

"Do we know either of them?" Sarah asked.

"I honestly do not remember them," Sadie adds, showing unusual support for her sister.

Cora thinks about how to describe Mansfield and Frank. "The son is very quiet; he appears painfully shy. I would doubt either of you would remember him. His father attended a couple of the dances last year and was at the grand ball." The girls show no signs of remembering either of the men. "The father had a thick mustache and was loud, boisterous, and I understand, a bit of a philanderer."

"Sounds like most of the older men who were at the grand ball. I am sorry, but I cannot place him," Sarah remarks.

"That is only because he is not in the top ten best looking or wealthiest men in the village." Sadie returns to their normal rivalry.

"Ladies!" Cora's voice is stern.

Walter walks by the Stiles women on his way to Jacob. As he passes Sadie, Walter smiles in her direction but does not get a response.

Walter is unusually affable with Jacob. "I never would have thought Frank capable of using a gun. He hated his father; everyone knew that, but to shoot him?"

"All people have a side they try to conceal from others," Jacob observes.

"I heard that Mr. Beach sent George to Troy. He must have earned his trust very quickly." Walter fishes for a quote.

"George makes an impression," is all Jacob offers.

Walter looks at Sadie as he speaks. "That he does; I admit I am jealous."

Jacob looks at Walter then follows his gaze to Sadie, "No need to be, George has his sights set on another target. You must excuse me, duty calls."

Jacob walks over to Catharine. "He obviously impressed Mr. Beach if he was sent on such an important mission."

Catharine maintains her formal facade. "And good morning to you, Jacob Marvin. I am not familiar with whom or what you are talking about."

"I am sorry. I understood that Mr. George Sherman Batcheller was to be at your house last evening when he was snatched away by the demands of Mr. Beach and the errors of one of the finest sons of

Saratoga, Mr. Frank Baucus."

"I believe you are correct; Mr. Batcheller was to have met with my father last evening. I do not believe I was included in their plans." She thinks back to how she felt as she was preparing for George's visit.

"You did hear what happened?"

"All one has to do is listen for a few minutes to know that Frank Baucus shot his father. What does that have to do with Mr. Batcheller?" Catherine emphasizes her point by looking around. "Rumors love a good tragedy."

Jacob boasts about his friend, "In the heat of the moment, with all options open, Mr. Beach chose young Mr. Batcheller to go down to Troy to handle the situation until he could get there."

Miss Strong passes Catharine and Jacob on her way to join the coven.

"Patricide; deliberately taking of one's own father's life must never be tolerated. Remember the good book says 'Honor thy mother and thy father." Mrs. Brewster has placed herself in the center of the crescent of dowagers. As if to wash some unpleasant taste out of their mouths, each of the dowagers takes a sip of water when she finishes speaking.

"I believe it is 'Honor thy father and thy mother," corrects Mrs. Jackson.

"Trivial!" Mrs. Brewster plays down the gaffe.

"He will be hung for sure." Mrs. Brown gets political. "If only women could be on juries, crimes like this would end forever!"

"I disagree. I do not think that fine ladies should be exposed to the language that is common in trials. Just imagine for a moment hearing the dreadful details of a murder or the tales of what happens in a disorderly house." Mrs. Jackson has mastered the art of correcting a person without it becoming a conflict; that is, with the exception of Mrs. Brewster.

"I heard he was defending his mother and that his father fired two shots before young Frank fired the first one." There is an air of anxiousness in Mrs. Brown's voice.

Mrs. Brewster cannot stand to be corrected. "I know my source well and she is much more connected than any other. She told me that all the father did was attempt to pull a handkerchief out of this pocket. There was no gun."

"No, I heard on the piazza that Mr. Mansfield had a gun. It just misfired." Miss Place shows the range of the rumors.

"I disagree. The woman who cleans my room told me that the poor father never pulled the revolver from his pocket." Miss Strong at least has the courtesy to tell her source.

Miss Lee remains nervous. "All this violence and only thirty miles away; I fear father will order me home this very day."

"Fiddle faddle, there is no reason for anyone to go home. Just because something like this would never have happened in Hartford is no reason for your father to call you home." Mrs. Brewster stresses the word Hartford.

"And I am sure it would not have happened," Miss Lee challenges, "if the senior Mr. Marvin was still with us." Miss Lee and Mrs. Brewster glare at one another.

George and Beach stand across from each other in the dimly lit hall outside a meeting room in the Troy jail. Beach's valise is on the floor. George is holding his. The lower part of the walls are wainscoted. The upper portion of each office door is glass to allow in as much sunlight as possible.

Beach breaks the silence. "We will give Frank and his mother a few more minutes before we talk strategies with them." He smiles, "You spent the night in the cell?"

"He was brooding. I felt it was in his best interest that he not be left alone to create witnesses."

"You have worked for me for less than a week and already you have spent a night in jail. I would say you are off to a rather auspicious start."

"I also had to miss a meeting with one of your most important clients."

"Oh yes, let us not forget that you stood up Mr. Cook." Beach chuckles.

The park is full but it is not a normal morning in the park at the States Hotel. The morning concert is being performed by a string quartette. Guests are set up to paint or write; however, they are ignoring the music to gather in small clusters and engage in gossip about the Baucus affair. Morrissey walks from the back piazza up to Marvin. The two look at the crowd rather than to each other as they speak. "Would you be so kind as to thank your associate for becoming my silent partner?"

"You just did."

"I assumed as much."

"I would have expected nothing less. The ability to read people is an essential element in our field." Marvin acknowledges the similarities in their businesses. "Are you ready to open tonight?"

"The faro and roulette tables are set up and I have arranged for tables for card games. Next week we will begin accepting bets on special events." He looks for some evidence in Marvin's expression that he is pleased; there is none. "We will open the doors at 5:00."

"That early?"

"I would expect that it will be closer to 9:00 before the real action gets underway."

"When will you be closing?"

"This being the first night, we will remain open all night."

"I am not sure anyone told you, but the Sabbath is always respected in Saratoga." Marvin advises, "Saturday nights you should close by 4 in the morning and not open at all on Sunday evenings."

"However, if I were the only place where entertainment was available; I should be very busy."

"For one week. By the time you opened on Monday the sheriff would be closing you down. This is Saratoga, not Brooklyn. Here the Sabbath is sacred. Although we have an afternoon concert to 'sooth the soul,' even the States does not have the band play in the evening."

"Thank you for the advice. In one way that is better, all my workers can have the same night off."

"All things happen for a reason."

"There is one problem that I have not resolved. I have not been able to find a person from the community who is willing to stand on the porch to assure that locals do not enter."

"What happened when you asked the priest for recommendations?"

"He felt there was enough animosity toward Catholics without one being considered a snitch."

"Interesting." Marvin reflects, "Have you asked the police?"

"For help?" Morrissey is flabbergasted at the idea.

"The rule in Saratoga is simple. If the police do not see a problem or no one files a complaint, there is no problem. You could hire a policeman to stand on the porch. As long as he did not see what was transpiring inside he would take no action."

"Convenient. But what about a complaint?"

"Anyone who files a complaint against a gambling or a disorderly house to have witnessed the illegal activity, which means they were inside. The local newspapers always publish the name of the complainant." Marvin takes a drag on his cigar, "Tends to make their lives rather uncomfortable."

"That would serve as a deterrent."

"Indeed, it has in the past."

"So now I am off to hire two off duty police officers." Morrissey walks off toward the back entrance to the hotel, passing the dowagers who are sitting on benches.

"A little bird told me that that Mr. Morrissey is opening a clubhouse just a few doors from the hotel," Mrs. Brewster apprises her troupe.

"The same little bird chirped in my ear," Mrs. Brown pipes in.

"I am sure that gambling is not the only sin that Saratoga will host this season," notes Mrs. Jackson.

"This is why my father dislikes me going to Saratoga alone, he knows the type of happenings that transpire. This is becoming more and more a center for sin," squeaks Miss Lee.

Morrissey approaches a police officer, Smiley, who in the age before uniforms, is only identifiable by the badge on his vest. "Excuse me sir, my name is John Morrissey." Morrissey waits for a response; when none is forthcoming, he continues. "And you are?"

"Deputy Smiley." He introduces himself but does not offer his hand.

"Of course you are." Morrissey cannot restrain his smile. "Mr. Smiley, I am opening a business on the Square. It is in the building formerly occupied by Mrs. Quinn."

"Are yuh goin' inta the same business?" Smiley is obviously hopeful.

"No, but I would like my business to be assured a quiet presence. Would you be interested in working nights after you finish your shift?"

"What would yuh be payin'?"

"How much are you making as a deputy?"

"A dollar fifty a day," Smiley brags.

"Then I think you should make two dollars fifty a night."

"I's can be there. What kin' of business you runnin'?"

"That is irrelevant. I would like a second officer; can you make a suggestion?"

"If'n it's okay with you, I can brin' one with me tonight."

"That would be fine." Morrissey takes his leave and walks toward the States. Smiley thinks he has put one over on Morrissey, he only makes ninety cents a day.

Frank's mother, Amanda Baucus, is sitting at the far end of the conference table. Frank sits to her left as Beach and George enter. Before he sits down Beach takes notepaper out of his valise, then takes a seat at the opposite end of the table. George sits across from Frank.

Beach looks at his notes, "Amanda, Frank, you both need to understand that this will be an uphill battle. We are not in Saratoga where everyone knew Mansfield and what he was like." He pauses to let them take in his inference. "To a jury in Troy made up of Democrats, we are outspoken Republicans from Snooty Saratoga. That will not make us popular. And the fact that two aldermen from Troy were convicted of embezzlement in Saratoga County last year will only add to the desire for revenge." Beach pauses for a second time, allowing them to digest the side issues. "The district attorney will consider it a feather in his cap if he were able to bring down the grandson of one of the most prominent families in Saratoga."

Amanda interrupts, "But Frank only acted out of fear for his own safety."

Beach ignores Amanda and turns to Frank. "Is that what you told the officers when you were arrested?"

"Not exactly."

"What exactly did you say?"

"The truth."

The memory is still fresh in Frank's mind as he tells the story of how he was on a street in Troy carrying a small valise. He fails to mention that he was nervous as he looked for the sign for the Mansion house. Finding it, he enters. "I told them that I arrived in Troy the afternoon before and checked into the Mansion House. After I placed my suitcase in the room, I walked to my father's boarding house. Like I expected, his landlady told me he was not in. So I left the note requesting that he visit me."

Frank remembers sitting in a chair fidgeting with a pistol. He put it in his pocket then took it out and then returned it to the pocket. "He never came that evening. It was not unusual for father to be out all night. I told them that I barely slept. I just sat in a chair with my pistol in my hand waiting for him. For fear I would miss him, I never even took meals the whole day."

"I had finally fallen asleep sitting up when I heard a knock on the door. It was about 6:00, and before I could answer, my father opened the door on his own. When he came into the room, I asked him if he had written to mother again. He just smiled and said 'and what are you going to do about it, tell my father?'" Frank paused. For the first time he begins to show emotion. "That is when he reached in his coat pocket and I shot him."

"Is that all you told the police?" Beach asks. He has not taken any notes.

"They wrote it all down; you can read it for yourself."

"I will." Beach turns his attention to Amanda. "I need to start working on bail so Frank does not have to spend the weekend here. Assuming arrangements can be made, I doubt they will allow Frank to leave the county. Do you know of a respectable family he can stay with?"

"You get him out of this God awful place. I will get the two of us rooms." Amanda commands, "Assure the judge that he will be under my care and supervision."

Beach returns his attention to Frank, "Who was the judge who arraigned you?"

"Judge Tremain."

Beach looks directly at Amanda, "I will defend Frank, but knowing the politics of this city, I suggest we have a second attorney. And yes, I think it should be a Democrat. How do you feel about Levi Smith or Martin Townsend?"

"They are both good men. Either would be fine."

Beach begins to pack his case, "Very well for now; we need to get started. Mr. Batcheller and I are going to leave you at this time. I will go see Judge Tremain about setting bail, then engage either Smith or Townsend. Mr. Batcheller is going back to Saratoga to start researching possible defenses. Amanda, do you need him to do anything for you when he gets back?"

"Mr. Batcheller, first let me say thank you for staying the night with Frank, I wonder who else would have done that." For the first time her eyes appear warm. "When you get to Saratoga, if you would be so kind as to stop by the manor and tell Frank's sisters and grandfather how he is doing. Tell them that I am staying on. I have clothes enough for now but tell Clara that I want her to pack a trunk in case I need it."

"It would be my privilege." George and Beach stand to leave.

Beach holds papers in his hand. "Frank, just in case I have a problem getting the judge to set bail, remember do not talk to anyone about your father, what happened, or your plans." George and Beach exit, leaving Amanda to talk to her son alone.

In the hallway outside the conference room George and Beach stand across from each other. "Thank you again for staying with Frank. If you had not, he would have been accused of saying things that he might, or might not, have said. With you there, those from the jail cannot be enticed to provide manufactured evidence."

"I thought it was the best course of action."

Beach hands George paper to write notes. George scribbles as Beach dictates. "When you get to Saratoga stop by the manor and tell the Judge what is going on. Then I want you to go to the office; tell Lawrence that I want him to research all cases on momentary insanity; tell William that he is to research all cases on the use of a gun for self-defense - tell him to focus on cases where the victim did not have, or show, a weapon. Tell James to research cases where the judge refused to set bail; tell him to focus on cases where the person who, until that time, had been a responsible citizen."

"What do you want me to research?"

"We are going to need character witnesses on both Frank and his father. Start interviewing people in Saratoga who knew them; now on your way." George, holding the paper, walks out in the direction of the train station. Beach starts down the hall in the opposite direction when Amanda comes out of the conference room. "Mr. Beach, a moment."

Instinctively George also turns. He realizes Amanda wants to talk to Beach alone and continues on his way. Beach turns and walks in her direction. "I do not condone what my son has done, but you must understand his father made the entire family's life hell on earth."

One of the incidents Amanda was referring to occurred eight years before. The foyer of the manor is lit by a single candle. There is a loud bang as Mansfield enters the house and knocks over a metal vase containing cut flowers. He begins to pick up without trying to hide the effects of the alcohol. Amanda enters the foyer from the parlor. She is dressed in her night clothes. She is pregnant.

"Oh Mansfield, not again."

Mansfield struggles to stand straight and waves his hand in an attempt to point. His words are slurred. "Damn right again. Anyone married to you has every right to drink. Hell, I believe it may even be considered a requirement."

"Mansfield, remember the children," Amanda says, trying to quiet her husband.

"How can I forget the little bastards? Are any of them mine?"

"Keep your voice down; you will awaken the entire household."

"Nag, nag, all you ever do is nag. Nag is a good name for you. You are nothing but a worn out horse." Amanda approaches Mansfield, her arms open to console him. He pushes her away. Amanda begins to cry, but fearing the children will hear, she approaches him once more. Mansfield's eyes fixate on her. He draws back and punches her squarely in the cheek. There is a muffled scream as she falls; her stomach hits the floor. Trying to regain her footing, she tips over the cane rack.

Judge Baucus entered from his office. "That will be enough of that." He demands, "Get out of this house."

Mansfield opens the door to leave. "Take her side. Take anyone's side except your own son's." Mansfield slams the door.

The Judge approaches Amanda and sees blood on her skirt. He calls out, "Mrs. Smith come immediately." An African American servant, Mrs. Smith, enters from the kitchen and begins to help.

At the top of the stairs a younger Frank is crouched in a ball cowering against the railing.

The sound of the train pulling out of the station is simultaneous with George reaching the porch of Baucus Manor. Knowing he is the bearer of bad tidings, he is hesitant to knock. As he reaches for the doorbell, Judge Baucus opens the door from the inside. The Judge is slightly stooped and appears to have aged overnight.

"Good afternoon, Judge. Apparently you heard the train."

"Yes, yes, all of them since last night. We knew Amanda would be sending word as soon as she could. Please come in."

The Judge holds the door as George enters the foyer. George looks up at the top of the stairs where the four children have gathered. Cognizant that the children are listening, George asks, "Do you want to speak here or would you prefer we go into the parlor?"

The Judge looks over his shoulder at the children. "Excuse me; I am so anxious that I forgot about the little ears. Please join me in my office." The two men move to the Judge's office adjacent to the foyer.

The Judge's office is still set up like a small courtroom, which was its former use. The Judge has a large desk at which he can sit on a stool or stand behind. It is in this room that, a decade before, the Judge heard appeals. George finds himself looking around. His words sound rehearsed, "Mr. Beach is working on getting Frank released on bail. He is sure that the judge will not allow Frank to leave Rensselaer County so Mrs. Amanda is taking rooms. She and Frank will be staying in Troy until this is over."

"Mr. Beach is one of the best trial lawyers in the state. I am sure that is why he represents Mr. Vanderbilt. He will do what he can." The Judge's age is apparent in his voice.

"Mr. Beach anticipates that there will be as many political aspects to the trial as factual and that is why he is engaging a lawyer from Troy to assist."

"Mr. Beach is correct." Details over, the Judge asks about his favorite grandchild, "How is Frank?"

"Given the situation, he is all right. The entire affair has made him very quiet." George hesitates before adding, "So that you know, he made a full confession before I arrived."

The Judge is staring at the spot on the floor where George is standing. It is like he is in a different time. "Daniel Webster stood in that exact spot when he argued a case before me." For reasons that will plague George for years, the Judge adds, "May you go on to have such an impact on this country."

Six of the dowagers, Mmes. Brewster, Brown, Dillon and Jackson and Misses Strong and Place, are clustered together on two benches in the park at the States. Each dowager is putting away her knitting, writing implements, book, or writing paper, whatever it was she brought to pretend she was engaged in something besides gossip. The band is packing up from their afternoon performance. Jacob and Sarah are seen strolling arm in arm in the background.

A man, nearing forty, walks by the dowagers and stares as he tips his hat at Miss Strong. It is all the action it takes to stoke the fire in Mrs. Brewster. "Well, I never. Miss Strong have you been properly introduced to that man?"

"No."

"Such boldness." Mrs. Brewster continues her lecture to Miss Strong, "Looking directly at a lady to whom he has not been properly introduced. I certainly hope you did not acknowledge his advances."

Mrs. Brown defends her younger companion, "Millicent would never encourage such behavior."

"Well I certainly hope not," lectures Mrs. Brewster. "Has he been introduced to any of you?" The dowagers all shake their heads. "Then he must be an upstart or Mr. Marvin would have introduced him to at least one of us. Such a season; it would not have been like that when the senior Mr. Marvin was running the hotel."

Mrs. Brown touches Miss Strong's hand then whispers in support, "I will endeavor to ascertain who he is."

"Thank you." Miss Strong has a smile for the first time since she arrived in Saratoga.

The dowagers turn their attention to Jacob and Sarah, who are sitting alone on a bench. "It does appear that they are becoming a set," acknowledges Miss Place.

"It would seem perfectly natural. She wants money and he will inherit this hotel and neither has a lick of sense," Mrs. Brewster criticizes.

The crowd in the dining room at the States has grown. The room is at least two-thirds full with people dressed for dinner. Among those in attendance are Bennett and Edith. They are at their assigned seats at the opposite end of a long table where Morrissey has been seated. Marvin and Jacob are both circulating among the guests.

Marvin stops near Bennett and Edith. "Mr. Bennett, how have your excursions to the springs been each morning?"

Bennett speaks with a mouth full of food, "No, never go. I certainly woul'n't wanna get a reputation fer wakin' up with no damn roosters."

Marvin turns to Edith, "Miss Edith?" He knows she understands that it is her turn to answer the same question.

"I have not yet been, but I understand it is quite the daily social event." She flirts with Marvin.

"Like all of Saratoga, it is the place to see and be seen; however, in the case of the springs, it is more of a morning ritual. Of late, in the afternoon, more and more of our young people are engaging carriages to visit the springs and the geysers south of town.

"What of your lake?" Edith asks.

"It is an excellent way to pass an afternoon. If you go, be sure to do two things: take a ride on the paddle wheeler and be sure to have some Saratoga Chips out at Moon's Lake House."

"I have heard they are excellent."

"They are quite the new fashion, a plateful for only 22 cents. The only problem is that you will not be hungry for supper."

Bennett interrupts, "I 'ear there's a new club'ouse."

"So I have been led to believe."

"Yuh don't 'ave to wear no damn jacket on a ho' night like tonight, do yuh?"

"I am not aware of the dress code." Marvin takes his leave. Edith and Bennett both note that the Morrisseys have been moved from the end of the table to a table by the band.

Marvin smiles as he greets, "Mr. Morrissey, Mrs. Morrissey."

"Mr. Marvin, I would prefer to be called Susie. Mrs. Morrissey makes me sound old."

"Calling a lady by her first name is somewhat foreign to my tongue but I shall endeavor to comply with your wish." Marvin directs his attention to Morrissey, "If I might see you for a minute before you leave?"

"Susie, will you excuse me for just a moment?" Morrissey is

already rising. His asking was merely a formality.

"It can wait until you are finished with your dinner."

"Mr. Marvin, you are too busy a man to have to await me."

Ever the gentleman, Marvin makes his apologies. "Excuse us Mrs. Morrissey…Susie." Marvin and Morrissey move to a more private area.

Marvin whispers, "It has just come to my attention that requiring your patrons to wear coats and ties to enter would add a rare sense of respectability to your establishment."

"An excellent idea; I shall post one of the men at the door to ensure the code is followed. Do not be surprised if some of your guests come back to the hotel in search of a coat."

"I assure you that word of the dress code will be out by the time the third man returns to the hotel."

Jacob is talking quietly to Miss Strong, the youngest member of the dowagers. "It would be my pleasure. I will do it tomorrow either at the spring or in the park."

The ladies' parlor is filled with overstuffed furniture. Mirrors for primping are between the windows. Present for the meeting to plan the Presidential Ball are Mary Vanderbilt, the youngest of the Commodore's daughters; Mrs. Astor, the wife of the New York real estate fortune; Mrs. Osgood, a second of the Commodore's daughters; Mrs. Corning, wife of the Albany railroad baron; and Cora Stiles. Each woman is dressed in the dress she wore to dinner.

Cora attempts to chair, "Ladies, it has been suggested that the hotel host a reception in honor of the President's upcoming visit."

The head of New York City society, Mrs. Astor, agrees, "I would think that there could be no question but that a reception would be given. However, before we proceed, I believe the first question should be who is going to chair the Committee for the summer. I suggest Mrs. Osgood."

Mrs. Osgood declines, "Thank you for your support. My daughter will be coming out in the fall and I will be much too busy planning her ball to serve as chairperson. I suggest Mrs. Corning do the honors."

"That is simply impossible." Mrs. Corning also declines. "My heart is too weak and it will be all I can do to attend the functions. There is no way I could preside. I guess the chair will fall to Miss Mary."

Cora sits with her hands clutched in her lap as she tries to hide her look of disappointment at not being considered.

Mary Vanderbilt assumes the lead, "I will have to adjust my plans.

I was not planning on spending the entire summer in Saratoga, but given this responsibility, I shall make whatever changes are required. How do we hold a reception for a single man? I mean, has anyone ever done so?" The women all look at each other, unsure of the protocols.

Mrs. Corning offers a suggestion, "I know that when Russell Sage was a widower, there was at least one dinner held in his honor. It was just like any other dinner. I believe his niece served as the stand in."

Mrs. Davidson enters; she is somewhat younger than the rest, with the exception of Miss Mary Vanderbilt. "It was Sage's sister-in-law who stood in," Mrs. Davidson points out. "Who serves as hostess at the Executive Mansion?"

"It is Buchannan's orphaned niece, a Miss Harriet Lane. Will she be coming with him?" Mrs. Osgood shows she is knowledgeable of Washington's protocol.

"A niece in Saratoga, who really is a relative, how novel; that being the case, I suggest we make it a dress ball." Mrs. Corning is amused even if the others are not.

"Since it is the President, I suggest we decorate the room in red, white, and blue and encourage all the ladies who attend to wear one or all of those colors; after all, at this point we are still a union." Mrs. Astor glares at Cora. The rest of the women follow her gaze.

"Then we are in agreement." The young Miss Mary was raised to plan this type of event and takes the lead. "I would ask Mrs. Corning to make arrangements for the flowers and to ask Mr. Marvin if he could arrange for the Fourth of July flags and bunting to adorn the ballroom. Mrs. Astor, would you please arrange the musical selections with the band. Mrs. Davidson, would you please see to the food table; and Mrs. Stiles, if you could arrange for the sale of tickets? If any of you need additional support, feel free to ask non-members to contribute." The meeting over, Mrs. Osgood, Miss Mary Vanderbilt, and Mrs. Astor remain seated while the other three women get up to leave.

About of mile south of the States hotel there is a spring that shoots the water at least ten to twelve feet into the air. The spring is located in the center of a rock in the middle of a creek. Over the years, the minerals from the spring water have formed a crown that looks like a mushroom. Known locally as Spouter Spring, it differs from a geyser because the water is not hot.

Jacob, Sadie, and Sarah are standing at the railing overlooking Spouter Spring. Jacob arranged for them to use one of the hotel's carriages. The girls are dressed for an afternoon carriage ride. Jacob is dressed in his usual frock coat and tie.

"Oh, isn't this romantic?" Sarah gushes, "I am so glad you invited me along."

"This place is romantic in the evening, definitely by moonlight. In the afternoon, it is merely a tourist attraction." Jacob shows his cynical side.

"So you say." Sadie is not accepting Jacob's comment about the spring only being romantic by moonlight. "I doubt you asked my sister here because you wanted to make her feel like a tourist."

"Sadie, you truly are the evil sister, constantly trying to weave falsehoods into innocent gestures. With your tongue, it is a wonder I have any friends left; but it explains why you do not have any." Sarah attempts to put her sister down.

Ever the diplomat, Jacob asks, "Sadie, do you deny that this is a unique site?"

"No."

"Then as a proud Saratogian, why should I not want to show it to you and your sister?"

"Are you going to show this spring to that dreadful group of ladies who gather on the piazza every day?"

"Probably not, but as the future owner of the hotel, if asked, I would take them."

"But you admit that you would not ask them as you did Sarah."

"I asked you and Sarah, after I asked your father if it would be acceptable."

"You may remember this excursion any way you want; I know the truth." Sadie has an all knowing glare.

The first two to approach the casino on opening night are Smiley and Harrison, the man from the Mason Lodge. They climb the few steps and knock on the door. The door is opened by Richards, whose sheer size is intimidating.

"We are looking for Mr. Morrissey," Smiley says timidly.

"Wait here." Words like these from Richards hold anyone in the exact place he or she is standing. Richards closes the door, leaving the men on the porch.

It is a little over a minute before Morrissey opens the door. Richards stands behind Morrissey as they join the two other men on the porch. "Mr. Smiley, and who do we have here?"

Smiley speaks first to Morrissey, "Dis here is Chief Harrison, I told you I was gunnatuh bring along anodder man." Smiley then turns to Harrison. "Dis here is Mr. Morrissey." Morrissey and Harrison stare at each other realizing they met at the Masonic Hall. Eventually the two shake hands.

Unsure why the Chief of Police is present after Marvin had assured him that there would not be a problem, Morrissey asks, "So we meet again. What can I do for you, Chief?"

"I understand you're looking for off duty police officers."

"I desire to run a quiet business and to keep the locals from entering. Since the police officers would know all those from the community, it seems that hiring an off duty officer is a good idea."

"Oh the idea is most excellent; it's just that I would rather select the officers myself. That way the right men get the additional money."

"Chief Harrison, I apologize for not coming to you first. In my rush to open, I forgot to follow protocol. You making the selection is suitable to me." Morrissey wants to be sure that the rules are clear. "Your men do not come inside and they insist that those who wish to enter have a hotel room key. Anything that happens inside, my men will handle."

"That sounds fine to me."

Smiley becomes concerned, "Does dat mean I don't got's no's extra work?"

Morrissey immediately recognizes the new protocol. "That depends on the Chief. However, for tonight, I would like you to stay on."

"Mr. Morrissey, it appears we have reached a suitable arrangement." Harrison is satisfied. "I just want to be sure our job here is just to ensure no locals go inside, correct?"

"Correct."

"In the event I allow all of my men to have a night off, and I will be filling in, what will my salary be?" Harrison inquires.

"Since your men will be making $2.50, I think it only appropriate that you make $3.50."

"I was thinking five dollars," Harrison ups the bid.

"But of course." Richards opens the door for Morrissey.

Marvin, intent on speaking to Cora, greets the Stiles women as they walk across the park at the States. As Cora and Marvin begin to talk, the sisters sit on a bench out of hearing range.

"Mrs. Stiles, I understand that the committee is planning a ball in honor of the President."

"That was the decision of the group."

"I also understand that they failed to select you as chair. I am disappointed; I was looking forward to our working closely."

"Since being the unofficial hostess of the States is so important in social circles throughout the country, it became apparent that one has to be from the North to chair the committee."

"That is too bad; but also probably true. I will add some members from the South."

"That would be most kind of you." Cora touches Marvin's arm in appreciation.

With the smile every young boy has upon stealing his first kiss in elementary school, Marvin turns and walks back to the hotel. The sisters rise from the bench and walk ahead of their mother in the direction of the family's cottage. With her children not looking, Cora glances over her shoulder one last time at Marvin.

Cora's gaze is interrupted by Sarah, "Mother, is it true what they say about Mrs. Marvin?"

"That depends on what it is that you have heard."

"They say that she is never seen. Some say that she is locked away in a room of his house; others say she had to be put in an institution."

"I have heard similar stories, but remember, we are southern ladies and we do not take part in idle gossip."

Sadie's insight shows, "Mother, if there were no gossip in Savannah, no one would have a thing to say." At the cottage door Cora turns to look back at Marvin but he is already inside the main hotel.

Mary's room seems even more humble when compared to the accommodations of the Stiles family. Mary has a washstand, single bed, dresser, a trunk which is being used as the closet, and a single wooden chair. With the hour of the evening hop approaching, Mary struggles to tighten her own corset. When it is tight she ties it and pulls on her large hooped dress. One has the impression she is trying to look plain. She looks into the mirror. "Saratoga, I am here." Mary brushes down the front of her skirt with her hands and goes out the door.

It is opening night at the casino. With hops at the States and Union, it is the long married men and men who are single in Saratoga who are in attendance. There are groups of men at the roulette tables, crap tables, and playing faro. Morrissey's dress code is enforced so the men are all dressed for an evening out.

Morrissey is standing prominently in the middle of the main

room, a place he will occupy most of the summer. Richards approaches, "My congratulations! Opening night and we are full; even the rooms upstairs are all engaged with private games."

"I knew Saratoga needed a quality clubhouse." Morrissey looks around, "We may have tonight but before the season is over, I fear, we will have competition."

"With all the trouble you had finding this place, where will anyone else open?"

"In one of the cheaper hotels or in the back-room of a tavern; there are always people who can smell money and will chase that odor."

"If you are right, what can we do?" Richards loves a good fight.

"We need to be the best there is. I have decided to model myself after Mr. Marvin and model the casino after the States." Noticing Richards questioning look, Morrissey continues, "Marvin is an artist. He plays people like they are musical instruments. He remembers the name of everyone he has ever met and makes each person feel special."

"That is a very high compliment."

"He deserves it. I will spend every evening circulating; and, like Mr. Marvin, I will know every guest - what he drinks, and how much he can afford to lose. Richards, we are going to set a new standard in gaming, even higher than our clubs in New York, Brooklyn, and Troy."

"If anyone can do it, it is you."

"Let us hope for a big winner this week. Nothing draws a crowd like the idea the house can lose." Morrissey moves to the roulette table and starts talking to a recent winner.

It appears that everyone in the village is present at the Congress Spring. Although it has been several days since the shooting, there remains a constant buzz of misinformed rumors.

The usual characters are all present, with George and Jacob at their usual post. Sarah, Cora, and Sadie are near the dipper boy. Walter is again talking with the African American crowd. The dowagers line the walkway in. One who did not know their personalities would compare them to an honor guard. The dowagers go silent as Catharine walks up to the spring with Clara Baucus, Frank's sixteen year-old sister. Clara has a black band around her arm and a black bonnet. After getting water the two young women walk to the perimeter.

Catharine whispers, "Thank you for coming Clara, it took a lot of courage."

"They are all staring," Clara observes, "Don't they understand it was my brother, not me? Why should a family be judged for the actions of one member?"

"They are looking, not staring," Catharine corrects her. "They will judge you by your decorum this morning." Catharine takes Clara's elbow. "Show the world how strong you are."

"Right now I do not feel very strong," Clara admits.

"Just being here took courage, more than anyone else here could have mustered." Catharine compliments her.

"Except you," Clara says humbly.

George and Jacob tip their hats as Catharine and Clara approach. "Good morning ladies."

Jacob is more familiar, "Good morning."

Catharine and Clara answer in unison, "Good morning."

"Mr. Batcheller, my grandfather told me you spent the night in the cell with my brother. I would like to express my gratitude. He would have been very much frightened alone."

"He did not appear so. Your family must feel better now that Mr. Beach was able to arrange bail. Will your mother stay with Frank or will your Uncle Charles go to Troy?"

"I can assure you my mother will never allow Uncle Charles to be alone with Frank." Clara discloses a family secret, "Mother does not appreciate his evangelical ideas."

"I have not seen your uncle in several years. I assume his views on God and right have not changed." George makes a statement more than asks a question.

"Oh they have changed; they have gotten sorrier."

"Miss Cook, it is nice to see you. Avez-vous fini le livre?" *Did you finish the book?*

"Oui, il ya quelque temps. Quid legis?" *Yes some time ago. What are you reading?*

"Hic lectio omnium librorum iuris," George answers. *At this point all my reading is of law books.*

Jacob ruins the moment, "Clara, did you realize there were so many foreigners in the village?"

Clara has the first hint of a smile since the news of her brother broke. "No Jacob, I had no idea that I would be exposed to so many languages before breakfast."

"Although it has been a couple of years, I think I heard some Latin, which means that some of the village's guests have even transcended time."

Those gathered at the spring, who did not know Clara before, have learned her identity and are taking turns looking at her. It is natural that Mrs. Brewster would have some criticism to make. "In my day a family living through such a scandal would never be seen in public. Not a single member. They would not have even attended church; they would have had the minister come to the house."

Mrs. Brown flips her fan ever faster. "Times are changing too fast. We are losing all decorum. A confessed murderer's sister at the springs in the morning; it is all too much."

"She should be in mourning," Mrs. Brewster points out. "I mean her father died just days ago."

"I thought that one of the curative powers of the spring was for people in mourning." Miss Strong defends the young lady.

"I heard that the son, who committed the murder, will be one of the pallbearers." Mrs. Brewster shakes her head judgmentally.

"I doubt he will be a pallbearer. That is probably the conjecture of some evil mind. From whom did you hear it?" Miss Strong commits the ultimate sin, challenging Mrs. Brewster's sources.

"I do not recall. I am sure it was someone in the park." The wise dowagers know this means there is no source.

"I do not know if I will be back at the spring tomorrow," frets Miss Lee, furiously waving her fan, "To witness such behavior is just so offensive."

"Oh, you will be back. You could not stand to miss seeing the show," Mrs. Brewster reminds her protégé.

Boldly, Jacob approaches the coven with Ellis, the same man who tipped his hat at Miss Strong in the park days before. "Ladies, I would like to introduce you to Mr. Peter Ellis. Mr. Ellis is spending the next three weeks with us." Ellis nods to each lady as they are introduced by Jacob. "Mr. Ellis, this is Mrs. Brewster, Mrs. Brown, Mrs. Jackson, Miss Lee, Miss Strong, and Miss Place.

"It is indeed a pleasure to meet you all." Ellis is smiling. "I am from Philadelphia. Are any of you fair ladies from the city of brotherly love?"

Mrs. Brown chimes in, "I am also from the city where the country was founded."

Mrs. Jackson jumps in before Ellis says any more. "I am from Lancaster. The home of the President, who I understand, will be joining us forthwith."

"Then we are near neighbors," Ellis confirms. "Do you know Mr. Nicholas Biddle? He is one of my neighbors."

"The banker?" Mrs. Jackson answers, "I have not had the pleasure. Perhaps when we are back in Pennsylvania in the fall you could call, if you venture to Lancaster."

"Perhaps," Ellis says politely, knowing he will never 'venture' to her house.

Jacob and Ellis say in unison, "Good day ladies." Ellis smiles at Miss Strong as he and Jacob leave.

Mrs. Brown takes Miss Strong's arm and the two walk to the dipper boy for a fresh glass of spring water.

"A neighbor of one of the wealthiest men in the country; he must be substantial. Who knows anyone from Philadelphia? We must check up on this Mr. Ellis," demands Mrs. Brewster.

Mrs. Brown adds, "I have a cousin who lives in Philadelphia. She knows everyone."

"I do believe I have an aunt and uncle residing there." Miss Place bolsters the ability to check references.

"Then we will be sending inquiries this very morning. We will write letters while we are in the park for the concert." With everyone willing to do her bidding, Mrs. Brewster feels validated.

Even with the morning concert underway, having all of the dowagers writing to friends and family for references on Mr. Ellis, the park is quieter than usual. The dowagers are gathered on two benches; each woman is busy writing a letter. Other hotel guests are painting, reading, or just listening to the music. One of the hotel's messengers approaches Sadie and Sarah. The messenger does not know the names of the girls so he asks, "Miss Sadie Stiles?"

Having never received a message from a messenger before, Sadie is surprised. "Yes?"

The messenger hands Sadie an envelope with only her name on it. It did not come through the mail. She immediately opens the envelope. Sadie is so excited that she forgets to tip the messenger. Realizing her sister's oversight, Sarah takes out a coin and gives it to the messenger. "Excuse my young sister, she rarely carries money." The messenger walks back to the hotel. "Who is it from?"

Sadie opens the envelope and silently reads the short poem inside. She turns the paper over and checks the envelope, looking for a name. "I don't know, it is not signed."

"Well what does it say?"

"I won't tell."

"Why ever not?"

"Because you will tease me unmercifully," Sadie answers, as she reads the note a second time. "And then you will tell mother and father."

"No matter what, I will tease you unmercifully; however, Miss Sadie Stiles, if you do not let me read it, then I will tell mother and father," Sarah insists.

Reluctantly, Sadie hands the note to her sister. "You must promise to give it back." Sarah smiles as she reads the note.

Lovely Sadie, Maiden Fair
Shall I Confess? Oh, Do I Dare?
You're more than just a lovely face,
I so admire your style and grace.

"My little sister has an admirer. Congratulations, you are becoming a woman."

"Having a young man interested does not make me a woman; if it did, I would have been a woman at nine when Wesley Coates pulled my hair in church."

"That is as it may be, but no one ever sent you an original poem. Who do you think it is from?"

"Just for this one afternoon, I do not want to guess. I want to look at every young man and imagine it is him." Sadie stands slightly straighter and has developed a glow.

Ben has taken Todd fishing and Josey is doing laundry; the Stiles women are in the park listening to the afternoon concert, leaving Missy and Thomas alone in the parlor of the Stiles cottage. "Mr. Stiles dis just ain't right. Da family's right out dere in the park. They coulds walk in anytime," Missy protests.

Thomas ignores her comment, saying in a determined voice, "They will stay until the music ends."

Missy understands that her appeal will be for nothing and goes over to one of the stuffed chairs. "But dat don't make it right."

"Remember, I could have brought one of the other girls; everyone wants to be out of Savannah in the summer," Thomas threatens. Missy knows the discussion is over. She leans over the arm of the chair pulling up the back of her skirt. Thomas unbuttons his pants as he walks up behind her.

"At least let me keep an eye out da window, I don't want us'n to get caugh'." She knows that if they are caught that she will be sold as soon as they return to Savannah. Southern wives may believe their husbands are sleeping with one of the slaves but they do not want to know it.

The music in the park suddenly stops. The leader of the quartet stands up. "We have just received word the President's train is due at the station in fifteen minutes; the concert is ending at this time so that the band may remove to the piazza to play in his honor." Everyone in the park starts packing up. As they begin to walk toward the hotel, Mrs. Brewster moves next to Miss Place. Mrs. Brewster asks, "Did you write to your Aunt?"

"Yes I did. I will post the letter this very afternoon," Miss Place responds bashfully.

"Good, we need to find out about this Mr. Ellis."

News of the President's arrival has spread throughout the village and a large crowd has gathered at the station and lines the street between the station and the States Hotel. The piazza at the States is also full of guests who want to be sure they catch a glimpse of the President.

Like the lord of a mansion, Marvin is standing in front of the door. Van Buren, Cook, three governors, four senators, a Supreme Court Justice, and numerous congressmen have joined him. The group has one thing in common, each member looks like a politician. The group watches as the President's entourage enters the street near the station. Cook, who is standing next to Marvin, speaks, "So he is back."

"With all the pomp and grandeur of an office he may not deserve." Marvin takes the rare opportunity to become political.

"So how will you handle his visit?" Cook inquires.

"With all the pomp and grandeur he may not deserve; this is the States Hotel, there can be nothing less."

"So it is," Cook acknowledges.

President Buchannan, his young niece Harriet, carrying a parasol, and two men in the uniforms of generals walk down the center of the street. The crowd applauds and cheers. When Buchannan and company near the hotel, the band starts playing a patriotic song. Reaching the top of the stairs, Buchannan turns and waves humbly to the throng that has gathered in his honor.

After a respectable time he turns to enter the hotel. "Mr. President, a pleasure to see you again." Marvin shakes the President's hand. The President moves along the line of elected officials and each introduces the man next to him.

Sadie, alone in her room, is sitting by the window in the lone chair. She is reading a book of poems when Sarah enters, clearly upset with her sister. "You missed it." Sarah raises her voice, "You missed the President's arrival."

Sadie remains blasé. "I will see him at dinner and again at supper, and tomorrow at breakfast and dinner and again at supper and..."

Her attitude is too much for Sarah, "We are staying in the same hotel as the President of the United States; all Savannah will be envious! And you sit in our room reading."

"I sincerely doubt that those in Savannah would care." Sadie brings up what is really on her mind, "Who do your really think wrote the poem?"

"Mr. George Batcheller, it would take a Harvard man to make up a limerick as clever as that one."

"I suppose you may be right but I have never seen him looking at me. There are several young men in the hotel who stare, but not Mr. Batcheller." An intrigued Sadie continues, "Why do they call him Mr. Batcheller and Jacob and Walter are called by their first names?"

Sarah counts the reasons on her fingers as she says them. "It is out of respect. He is not a George, he is a mister. He has yet to reach 21 and already he is a lawyer and assisting one of the most famous lawyers in the state, if not the country. He is involved in the most notorious case that is going on this season." She takes a breath, "Whenever I am around him, he makes me want to call him Mr. Batcheller."

"Yes, I suppose that explains it. But can you just imagine what it would be like to be on a picnic and to always feel you have to call your beau Mister?" Sadie's comment makes them both laugh.

Mary Vanderbilt, Mrs. Astor, Mrs. Osgood, Mrs. Corning, Mrs. Davidson, and Cora are seated in stuffed chairs in the ladies' parlor checking last minute plans for the upcoming ball. Marvin clears his throat to indicate there is a man present as he enters with Mrs. Cardozo and Mrs. Devereux; both are very well dressed. "Ladies, I know how much work there is being on the Entertainment Committee. Mrs. Cardozo, from Havana, and Mrs. Devereux, from Mobile, have agreed to help by serving on the Committee." Marvin points to each lady as he introduces her. The Committee members look on politely but one can sense that they are suspicious as Marvin sets up two more chairs, then leaves.

"I was late for the first meeting; did anyone bring up raising money for the Relief Fund? I know that by the end of last season, the fund was nearly depleted," Mrs. Corning reminds her fellow committee members.

"Are you suggesting using the reception for the President as a fund raiser?" Mrs. Astor is offended by the mere suggestion.

"That would be inappropriate." Mrs. Davidson agrees with her idol.

"I am not suggesting anything. I am simply raising the question.

We are all going to want to help when there is an emergency; we should take all appropriate opportunities to raise funds." Mrs. Corning remembers when they ran out of money and could not help the people of a fire in Maine.

"Does anyone have any suggestions?" Miss Mary asks.

"We had a dance at our church where the men paid for the privilege of dancing with the ladies. They raised several hundred dollars." Mrs. Astor makes her suggestion in a tone that implies it is to be accepted.

Reverend Beecher is standing at the head of a casket at the top of one of the small hills in Greenfield Cemetery. There is total of twenty people present for Mansfield's funeral, including: Judge Baucus; Mansfield's brother, Reverend Clarence; Clara; her brother Mansfield, who was named for his father; their two sisters. Marvin, George, Beach, and Jacob are also in attendance. The men are all holding their hats.

Reverend Beecher remembers Mansfield. "His life was a struggle. It is our belief that through his death, Mansfield Baucus has finally gained the peace that so alluded him in life. Amen." Each family member picks up a handful of dirt and throws it on the casket, then walks toward the two waiting carriages.

Clarence, dressed as a priest, approaches his father. "You could not even let me preside at my brother's funeral?"

"It was not my decision; however, had it been, I still would have asked Reverend Beecher to preside."

"Cold father, cold."

Judge Baucus stares down his son. "We needed someone forgiving to help us say goodbye." The Judge gathers the children then walks to his carriage.

The coven is convened on the piazza; Mmes. Brewster, Brown, Jackson along with Misses Lee and Place are present. Mrs. Brewster has the latest in 'news.' "Did you hear that at the reception for the President, in order to dance, the men have to contribute to the Emergency Fund? To me it is like they have decided to sell off our innocent young flowers, petal by petal." She looks directly at Miss Lee and Miss Place.

"Do the women have any choice or are they simply up for sale like a slave in Charleston?" Miss Lee waves her fan.

"I am sure; I am sure." Miss Place feels competitive. "Are there different prices for different women like fine linen or is the price the same for all women?"

"If a lady cannot say no, how will they deal with men who take liberties, or who have failed to bathe?" Mrs. Brown still smiles at the idea.

"Well, I am not for sale. I may be a widow but no strange man is going to touch my hand, even with his gloves on. By the by, has anyone seen Miss Strong?" Mrs. Brewster dreams someone might contribute to a charity for the privilege of dancing with her.

Miss Lee answers, "She told me she was feeling rather faint and was either going for some mineral water or lying down."

In Congress Park, Mr. Ellis and Miss Strong are strolling side-by-side along the path by the pond. It is the afternoon, so the park is far less crowded than in the morning. "My father always loved summers in Saratoga. It is too bad he is not well enough to make the journey. He always said it was the coal mines he owns that gave him such an awful cough."

Ellis does his best to keep the conversation going, "I thought people came to Saratoga for cures for illnesses such as coughs."

"He said he is too weak to make the trip, but with me being his only child, I truly think he stays home because he does not have anyone he can trust to load his trains."

"Owning one's own business can be a burden. My father is always busy maintaining the house where he lives; it has twenty eight rooms."

"And do you dress for dinner every day?"

"Yes, we are into all the trappings; we dress for dinner and even wear jackets to supper."

It is cloudy, making the night very dark. The porch of the casino is brightly lit with a gas chandelier. The attention of two patrons exiting Morrissey's is attracted to the sound of women walking in heels and giggling. The men squint to see down the dark street. Realizing that the women are walking in their direction, one man nudges the other. As the men clear the bottom step they turn to go down the street in the direction of the women. For the first time, they see the women's' bodyguard, Bob, in the background.

Harrison, his silver badge showing, steps out from behind a cedar tree in front of the men. The two men immediately turn around and head in the direction of the major hotels. Harrison turns around and walks toward the two women, stumbling slightly as if he is trying to hide the fact that he drank too much; he did not, it is an act.

Pauline calls out, "I believe yus goin' da wron' way." Harrison smiles to himself and just keeps stumbling toward the two women. "If'n you want, we can help ya back to yo'rn 'otel." Harrison opens his coat, showing his badge.

"If I ever see you in this neighborhood again, it will be me helping you to where you will be spending the night. Now back to Congress Street where you belong." Pauline and Antoinette turn and walk away. Bob waits for them to pass, then follows.

Antoinette raises her voice at her sister, "Dat was too close. I told yus we was a need'n a few nigh's to scope out the city."

Harrison turns and starts walking the half block in the direction of the casino. At the far end of the square he sees what looks to be an un-escorted woman, Mary. She looks around as if she is lost then heads back in the direction of the hotels.

When Mary gets out of Harrison's sight, she appears to step incorrectly and twists her ankle. She continues walking in the direction of the hotels, struggling with each step. A man out for an evening stroll offers to help. "Excuse me miss, are you all right?" Mary ignores him and continues to limp down the street. "Excuse me miss, are you all right? It looks like you sprained your ankle or something." The man calls out.

"Are you addressing me?" Mary asks.

"Excuse me, but you appear to be in pain. I was just about to offer to help."

"I never speak to a man to whom I have not been properly introduced."

"If that be the case, then let me introduce myself. I am Willard Anderson and I am out this fine evening to aid a fair damsel in distress."

"Well, Mr. Willard Anderson, I am just trying to reach the States."

"May I escort you?"

"No, but you can walk near me in case I should fall." Willard walks ten feet behind her, watching the sway of her skirt until they reach the States. "Are you a guest here?" Mary inquires.

"Yes."

"I think before I try to negotiate the stairs to my room I should like to sit in the park for a few minutes."

"May I sit with you?"

"No, but you may sit across from me if you like."

A porter in uniform and the night clerk watch as Mary and Willard walk across the lobby of the hotel and exit to the park. The young porter observes, "I think I am getting this - they are a couple."

"How can you tell?" The clerk is serving as the porter's mentor. "She is not colorfully dressed. She is a wife, not a niece."

It is Saturday morning, the day of the President's Ball. The crowd at the springs is finally back to normal. At the rail, Van Buren and Madam Jumel are visiting with Buchannan and his niece. George has gotten as close to the dignitaries as he can by standing in line for a glass of water. Catharine is standing with Jacob. The dowagers are there. Sadie and Sarah are standing near the pathway speaking in a loud whisper. "I am wearing the red dress," Sarah insists.

"No, I am. You wore it to the cotillion; it is my turn."

"This is the President's reception and, as the eldest, I get to wear the fanciest dress."

"Very well, I am wearing the white silk dress."

"You better tell Missy so she can find the lace insert." Sarah feels she has won the argument. Sadie smiles to herself, "Oh I will."

George, glass in hand, walks up to Catharine, who has a crystal glass in her gloved hand. He asks, "How many glasses of water do you have each day?"

"Only one."

George looks over his shoulder to see if anyone is watching, pours the water from his glass onto the grass. "That is one more than I. I do not know why anyone would drink water a thirsty horse would stick his nose up at."

"Mr. George Batcheller, talk like that is considered treasonous in Saratoga."

"Then go ahead and hang me, but do not bathe my body in this water. I want to meet my maker smelling acceptably. If you look around, everyone has a glass but almost no one is actually drinking this abysmal mixture."

"Mr. George Batcheller, keep it up and you will surely be hung this very day."

"Watch for yourself," he instructs. Catharine looks at the crowd. He continues, "No one is drinking."

"You are right, they are all holding glasses but no one is drinking. So why do they come to the springs each morning?"

George looks at the crowd as he speaks. "Democracy, people are not supposed to enter a hotel where they are not registered. Each hotel has its own park and band so guests don't see anyone all day accept the people from their hotel. From the most humble boarding house to the States, everyone is welcome at the springs. The springs of Saratoga are the great equalizer."

"Interesting; I shall take your observation under advisement."

Sadie and Sarah walk across the lobby when a messenger cuts them off. Knowing who he is looking for, he stops Sadie. "A message for you, Miss Sadie Stiles." Sadie takes the envelope and tips the messenger.

"Well, open it!"

"I will, in the privacy of our room." Sadie clutches the envelope as the sisters continue through the lobby and into the park, which is filled with guests who are writing, painting, and visiting. On the way to their cottage the Stiles sisters pass Mary, who is painting a watercolor of Ellis talking respectfully to Miss Strong. Miss Strong is seated on one of the benches.

Marvin walks up to Mary. "Lovely painting, I am the innkeeper; I thought I knew every one of our guests by name, but somehow I have missed the opportunity to meet you."

"I am not a guest. I am staying at the Marvin House. They told me it was permissible to use this park."

"They told you correctly; we allow those at my cousin's hotel to use our park. I am James Marvin." He extends his hand.

"I am Miss Mary Barden, of Boston." She extends her hand.

Marvin eyes her suspiciously, "Very nice to meet you, Miss Barden; perhaps you would like to have dinner at the hotel today."

"I would like that very much."

"It will be at 2:00; you can hear the bell from your hotel; just tell the maître d you are my guest." Mary watches as Marvin walks away.

Ellis is standing in front of Miss Strong. "I was raised to believe it was the man's role to provide for his family and the woman's to keep a suitable house."

"I was raised in a similar fashion, until I attended Mrs. Willard's Female Seminary in Troy. She taught her students the arts and literature. We were trained to engage in a lively conversation and to be hostesses at great galas." She continues, "Wives are to be their husband's partners."

"I do not see the two as necessarily separate. I believe a woman can be a successful mother, keeper of the house, and contributor to a conversation."

"You are the enlightened man, Mr. Ellis. What have you been reading this summer?"

"I read the financial pages each morning and try to read a book a week."

"What book are you reading this week?"

"Open it, open it!" Sarah persists. Sadie slowly opens the envelope, then takes out the folded piece of paper. No sooner has the paper cleared the envelope then Sarah grabs the note from her sister's hand and turns away to prevent Sadie from taking it back. Sarah reads the note aloud.

> I will gaze tonight from afar,
> Upon your beauty like a star,
> Unseen now, unnoticed then
> Unknown for now, I wonder when.

"How could you?" Sadie is furious. Sarah hands the note back, knowing she has pushed too hard.

"Not Mr. George Batcheller, he would never consider himself unseen."

"So again I can imagine it is every young man who asks me to dance tonight." The poem has made her forgive her sister.

The President walks in the dining room, accompanied by Senator Toombs of Georgia and former President Van Buren. They move to a table in the center of the room that has become the head table by being turned sideways. Among those at the table are General Winfield Scott, Governor John King of New York, Governor William Packer of Pennsylvania - a personal friend of Buchannan, Governor Joseph Brown of Georgia, and Governor Isham Harris of Tennessee. Marvin moves to a seat at the far end.

Buchannan speaks softly, "There is only one requirement to being allowed to sit at this table; there will be no discussion of politics."

Governor Packer fires the opening volley, "My good friend, I would not think of troubling you with politics while we are in Saratoga; by the way, do you think the country could spare a little money to widen the canals?" There is general laughter among those at the table.

"Any and all extra money is needed by the military to squelch rebellions by those feisty Indians," General Scott suggests. There is a little less laughter.

"Any additional moneys should be given back to the states. It is the states that matter most to the people." Governor Brown is a strong states rights supporter.

"Gentlemen, as host, I am forced to insist that any further political comments will be met with a dollar fine, imposed by me and not subject to nullification, secession or appeal." There is general laughter among the group. "I suggest we talk about something far more important to each of us, such as how much we are going to be paying for the dresses our daughters and wives will be wearing to the ball tomorrow evening." To that there is laughter followed by private conversations.

The wives and daughters of those at the head table have set up a second head table of their own. Mrs. Brown brags, "It will be a special pleasure to wear the most delightful dress to the ball. It was made by my eldest daughter. She is so talented."

"After all my years, I still look forward to the balls in Saratoga." Mrs. King glows. "I mean I would, if it was not for those dreadful corsets." The women all laugh in agreement.

"It is making sure my daughters sit properly in a hoop skirt that causes me the greatest concern," says Cora, "especially my youngest."

"Mrs. Stiles will tell you that recently a daughter of one of Savannah's best families was wearing a hoop skirt. Well any way, she fell getting out of a carriage and everyone on the street saw way too much white," relates Mrs. Brown. General laughter and assurances of other such happenings follows. "With two daughters, I will be sewing flounce from now until the dance."

Cora asks Mrs. King, "Who does Mr. Marvin usually bring?"

"That is a question that is never asked."

In the Stiles cottage, Missy, Josey, Cora, Sarah, and Sadie are all working on making alterations to the dresses that will be worn to the ball. Josey reminisces, "Dis takes me back twenty years to when I was working on your momma's dress."

"Josey, do not remind me how old I have gotten," Cora jokingly reprimands.

"Miss Cora, yus ain't got older, yus gotten wiser. An listen up you two girls, yus mother knows what yus wants to happen this evening."

"Missy, make sure that the collar of the dress buttons securely on to Sadie's dress," Cora demands.

Josey looks at the sisters, "I told you she knows wha's best."

While the quartet is playing, Miss Strong and Ellis are walking arm-in-arm around the perimeter of the park. Marvin walks up to Cora, who is sitting near the band. Sarah and Sadie are sitting on a blanket off to the side. "Will the new members of the committee provide the appropriate effect?" Marvin asks.

Cora looks back over her shoulder at Marvin. "Mr. Marvin, you surprised me. Yes I believe they will."

"Those from the North can be so colloquial."

"As can those from the South." Cora pauses. "I am quite over any silly feelings I may have had about the committee. The way my daughters are behaving, I will be quite busy watching over them for the summer."

"I understand your concerns. I have a nephew to watch." Their smile to each other is longer than usual.

In the lobby of the hotel a tall thin man steps up to the clerk who asks, "How may I help you?"

"I have a reservation; my name is Peter Ellis."

The clerk begins looking through the list of reservations, "Of Philadelphia?"

"The same."

"I have your reservation right here. We were not expecting you until the middle of next week."

"The heat was oppressive in Philadelphia; I simply had to get away."

"Luckily your usual room is open, we will not have to move you mid-week." The clerk continues, "So you know we have another Mr. Peter Ellis with us at this time. How unusual."

"How unusual indeed."

Two weeks before at a plantation in North Carolina, Nate, dressed in the well-worn clothes of a field hand, is using a cut log as a chair to sit on in front of one of the four slave cabins. Mattie, dressed as a house slave, approaches from the main house. Nate inquires, "Yus late?" Mattie, without speaking, walks by him and enters the one room cabin. She goes over to the bed where her son Adam and daughter Eve are both asleep, laying end to end on a shared bed. She kneels down and gently rubs both of their heads, taking care not to wake them. After having gained some courage, Mattie stands and exits the cabin.

"Happened again, didn't it?" Nate's voice is an interesting combination of hurt, anger, and compassion.

Mattie sits on the other log for several seconds. "It won't end till the season's over uppin Saratoga and the misses gets back."

Nate looks at the ground defeated. Eventually he speaks. "We's gots to leave 'fore I do sompen the Lord don't like."

"We can't leave Nanny."

"Den we won't," Nate assures her. Mattie is silent.

In the lobby of the States, the program for the President's Reception is on a music stand. The band is warming up in the background.

In his hotel room in Troy, Frank is sitting in a chair reading a book. He stands up from the chair and walks to the wash stand to get himself a glass of water. As he passes the door that connects his room to his mother's, he sees her at her writing desk. There is a pile of sealed envelopes on the side of her desk.

Mrs. Brewster adjusts her hat one more time, then turns to the door where the rest of the dowagers are waiting. They all have their dance cards hanging from their wrists.

Walter has a humble room in his family's home. He puts on his only jacket and takes out his pad and looks over the notes of what he is to be sure to cover for the newspaper.

George puts on his second cuff link. He pulls on his best frock coat and checks himself in the mirror. He opens the door and leaves his humble room.

A door opens in the Cook house and Catharine walks into the hall where she takes her father's arm. Her dance card is hanging from her wrist.

Benjamin adjusts Thomas' cuff links, then helps him into his coat. Benjamin brushes the coat off one more time before handing Mr. Stiles his beaver top hat. Missy and Josey help Sadie and Sarah with their dresses. Cora buttons the black lace collar that fits as an insert covering Sadie's bodice in her white silk dress. Cora says to Sadie, "You are becoming a woman so fast."

Sadie adjusts her dance card, "I already am a lady."

Minutes later, in the hallway leading into the ballroom, there is the line of dignitaries set to walk through the doorway and into the ballroom. The line consists of the members of the Entertainment Committee, their families, and, of course, the President and his attractive blond niece. The Stiles are near the front of the line. Sadie turns to her mother, "Excuse me for just a second." Sadie disappears into the ladies' parlor.

Cora whispers to Sarah, "Where is your sister going?"

Sarah responds honestly, "I have no idea."

There is the voice of the band director heard from the ballroom. "Ladies and Gentlemen, on behalf of the States Hotel, I present the members of the Entertainment Committee." The line begins to move forward. "And the President of the United States, Mr. James Buchannan, is accompanied by his niece, Miss Harriet Lane." As the music for the grand entrance begins to play, Sadie reemerges and slips in line next to her sister; the lace collar has been removed and the top of her cleavage is showing. The line continues to move toward the doorway.

"You will be banished to your room for a week over this, young lady," Cora threatens. As the line moves forward, Harriet Lane, the President's niece, turns, and removes her scarf; her dress is cut even lower than Sadie's.

Sadie whispers, "Modesty holds affection, sensuous draws attention."

Spouter Spring

Accused

The morning after the first ball of the season, the numbers at Congress Spring are greatly reduced. The violinist plays for the few who are gathered. Madam Jumel, who arrived in her grand carriage, stands by herself. Mary, also alone, watches everything. Todd Stiles is off to the side admiring Madam Jumel's horses and carriage. Walter is mingling with the servants, especially the southern slaves. Clara Baucus stands by herself, her head tipped down. The four dowagers, Mmes. Brewster, Brown, and Jackson, and Miss Lee are standing in their usual place near the walkway. Reverend Beecher enters through the gate and passes by the dowagers.

An event like the ball the previous evening is fodder for Mrs. Brewster. "It was one of the vilest scenes I have ever witnessed. The hostess of the Executive Mansion in a dress where her shoulders were visible and cut so low one could see the top of her bosoms. Can you just imagine what Martha Washington or Abigail Adams would have thought?"

"It was the behavior of those Stiles girls that I found offensive. The younger one with a dress cut as low as Miss Lane's and her older sister danced every dance. I counted and she danced three times with Jacob Marvin. Three dances and they are not engaged!" Mrs. Brown criticizes.

"Just look around, they were up so late that they are not even able to take the mineral water their bodies so badly need. I predict they will not even be in church," Miss Lee observes.

"If I were twenty years younger, I would have danced every dance and slept until noon myself." As usual, Mrs. Jackson attempts to stay above the fray.

"Well, if no one else is going to bring it up, I am. Our Miss Strong danced twice with Mr. Ellis and I am ever so certain that I saw them having punch together." Miss Lee brings out the weak link in the coven.

"Why should they not; they are both single?" Mrs. Jackson appears to be rooting for Miss Strong.

"What of Mr. Marvin? As innkeeper he may be expected to dance every dance, but who would have imagined he would dance more than once with Mrs. Stiles, a married woman?" Mrs. Brewster gets to her real issue.

"It was only twice and, if my memory serves, he danced with you and me." Mrs. Jackson is getting weary of the banter.

"That does not excuse two dances with a married woman." Mrs. Brewster always uses the rules of protocol when they serve her.

"If I remember correctly, Mrs. Stiles also danced with President Van Buren, Governor Brown, Senator Toombs, and that Mr. Cook." Mrs. Jackson smiles. "I do believe I even saw her dance once with Mr. Stiles."

"I sincerely doubt that!" Mrs. Brewster relishes casting aspersions on the entire Stiles family.

Walter walks up to Clara Baucus, who has been standing alone. Knowing him her entire life, she asks, "After all this is over, how many years will it be before I am welcome at a ball?"

"Clara, by next year your family's issues will be resolved and you will again be received in all the best homes in Saratoga, New York, and Washington."

"I wish that it were true, but I am cursed. How can anyone survive an insane father, an impatient brother, an evangelical uncle, and a dominant mother?"

"Through the love of a grandfather who is one of the most respected men in the State." Walter thinks before asking, "Is Miss Catharine Cook not calling on you?"

"Catharine did call on Tuesday and I will call on her on Friday, but to the rest of Saratoga, my family is shunned."

"Surely not the Judge?"

"No, he walks on a different plane, but even he is feeling the effects of Frank's actions and my father's history." Clara looks at Walter as if wishing that her grandfather was enough to resolve her plight. "Walter, what will appear in your newspaper tomorrow?"

"It will be a description of the dresses worn, the quality of the music, and how traditions are carried on in Saratoga." Walter gets bolder, "If my editor permits, I may even get away with a tale or two of the loves discovered and the hearts broken."

Reverend Beecher walks past Walter and Clara up to Madam Jumel.

"It is very beneficial that you have chosen to grace our springs this season."

"Have we been introduced?" Madam Jumel stands on protocol.

"I am the minister at the Methodist Church. Those in the ministry are allowed to speak without formal introductions."

"Not to me."

Beecher ignores her comment. "I was hoping to see you later this morning."

Madam Jumel sizes him up before answering, "Why would you expect that?"

"As a leader of the community, your attendance at services would encourage many questioning souls to join us.""

"I think not." Madam Jumel walks to her carriage. Todd, who has been admiring her horses, steps aside. The footman opens the carriage door and she gets in.

For at least two generations, each day after dinner there is an unofficial procession of the best horses and carriages on Broadway. The sidewalks are packed with people watching and waving as the wealthy, flashy, and flamboyant parade for no official reason. For serious shoppers, the procession is the best time to shop, as the stores are vacant. Whenever she is in town, Madam Jumel's grand carriage leads the pageant.

Madam Jumel's driver brags to the footman, "It is so easy to drive on Broadway on Sunday, that I could almost let you take the reins."

"May I please?" begs the footman. There is a loud tap from inside the carriage. The two go instantly silent.

There is an eerie silence as Thomas and Todd walk across the virtually empty hotel park. They are on their way to dinner. "Father, is it always like this?" the boy asks.

"Always on the Sabbath. Don't you enjoy the quiet?"

"It is not what I expect in Saratoga."

"Nor I."

When the Stiles men arrive they find the dining room at the States is nearly full. They join the women who have been seated. Being this late, they will only get dessert. "Are you feeling better?" Cora asks Todd.

"Some."

The Morrisseys, including their four year old son John Jr., are at the table near the music, having dessert. Susie smiles at her husband. "I am glad you have to be closed on Sundays. It gives us a day together."

Susie helps John Jr. with his ice cream. Susie speaks in a baby voice, "Little John misses his father."

"I miss him too." Morrissey defends his schedule.

"You two are never awake at the same time. He gets up shortly after you get home and you wake up just in time for supper."

"It is the plight of all fathers." Morrissey gets defensive, "Farmers and millworkers only see their sons for meals."

"John, you are hardly a millworker, are you?"

The Stiles family stands in unison and prepares to leave. Sarah whispers to her sister, "Mother still not speaking to you?"

"No, but it was worth it. I danced nearly every dance. And I am sure Mr. Walter Pratt will mention me tomorrow in the newspaper."

"Is that how you measure success, your name in the newspaper?"

"In the social column, absolutely." She pauses to reflect. "At least for now."

As the Stiles family walks across the lobby, Todd is well out ahead of the rest. A messenger meets Thomas with a telegram. Thomas tips the messenger and opens the envelope; his face gets serious. Cora waits with Thomas as the girls follow their brother into the park. She asks in a low voice, "Is it bad news?"

"It is from father. He is concerned about the economy and protecting his investments. He suggests I consider going to Europe," whispers Thomas.

"Last year was bad, but why now?"

"Father reads newspapers from all over the country. He is concerned about all the coverage the Republicans are receiving. He fears the rabble rousers from Charleston may really want to secede and he understands what that will do to the cotton market." They again walk toward the door to the park.

Thomas holds the telegram as he and Cora walk out the door into the park. Their children are so far ahead they are entering the family's cottage. Cora does not take Thomas' arm. "Why would what happens in Charleston mean that you have to go abroad?"

"Father has been talking to me for some time. He wants to protect the family and move some of our investments to what he feels are safer places."

"When would you have to leave?" Distress is evident in Cora's words.

"He did not say, but I would guess before the end of the season. He would not want me traveling during hurricane season."

"Despite Sadie's behavior, I would feel better having the family here. Summers in Savannah are so oppressive and unhealthy."

"I see no reason why father's fears should spoil your's or the children's excursion. You should stay on and return to Savannah in September as planned."

Standing at the desk in the lobby is the well-dressed, attractive Ruth Stein. There is a dapper middle aged man standing near her. At a distance, it is not possible to tell if they are a couple or if he is invading her space. Upon reaching the desk, the clerk asks Ruth, "Checking in?"

"You have a reservation in the name of Asa Stein."

The desk clerk searches through papers. "Yes. It is for a two bedroom suite overlooking the park."

"That is correct."

"Are you Mrs. Stein or his niece?" Ruth smiles and looks over her shoulder at the middle aged man before answering in a devilish tone, "This is one Mr. Stein."

A week before in the slave cabin, the children are both asleep in the same bed when their mother enters. She is poorly dressed in a dress with rips on the back and upper part of the front. She tries it hide it, but her walk shows she has been raped. Nate is angry. "Happened again, didn't it? He used you and hurt you." Mattie ignores her husband and sits on the children's bed. She gently rubs each child's head. "We has to leave," Nate insists.

"It will just keep happening until Mrs. Brewster gets back from Saratoga." Mattie is resigned to her fate.

"And it will happen even then; just like last fall." Nate hates the family's plight.

"But not as often. They's all afraid of Mrs. Brewster."

"We's leaving! We get as far as the big bay and there will be preachers and fishermen that will help us get north."

Mattie continues to rub the children's hair as they talk. "They ain't going to help us for nothing and that is all we have, nothing."

"Then we gots to get something worth trading, light things, small things."

"Like the silver and the china?'

"They're too heavy. We need light, like the boy's violin. Hell, he don't like that instrument no how."

"So we get beaten for stealing."

"No worse than we would for 'scaping. But we ain't getting cought."

Mattie realizes that he has a plan. "So we have a useless violin that should get us about a mile."

"Don't go getting down. We can take her thimble collection and her new fur coat."

"So when do we go, Mr. Planner?"

"Tell your momma we leave the next rainy night."

Congress Spring is as busy as it was the day the village learned of the Baucus scandal. The dowagers, Mmes. Brewster, Jackson, Brown, and Miss Lee have assumed their usual position by the pathway. Catharine, Jacob, Walter, the President and Miss Lane, Van Buren, and Madam Jumel are all present. Todd and Walter are on the perimeter with the Stiles' servants.

A group of servants walks toward the spring, passing Mrs. Brewster. "I told you they would not make church. Barely a person from the ball was at yesterday's service."

"How do you propose they make church services more exciting, because they will never make the balls less so?" There is sarcasm in Mrs. Jackson's tone.

"And the children in the park yesterday, they acted totally bored. Are today's children raised without respect for the Sabbath? I tell you by the time they are grown, stores and taverns will be open on Sundays." Mrs. Brewster did make church the day before and feels she has the right to preach.

"That will never happen in America," pledges Mrs. Jackson.

Miss Lee is forced to comment, "Oh my goodness; look over by the gate. It cannot be!" Over Miss Lee's shoulder, Miss Strong and Ellis can be seen entering the area of the spring together.

The extremely attractive Ruth Stein, un-escorted, walks toward the spring. "Now isn't that an interesting addition?" Mrs. Brewster notes, referring to Mrs. Stein.

"Yes indeed, I saw her checking in yesterday - she was not alone. Her companion was old enough to be with one of us," claims Miss Lee.

Sarah and Sadie are standing near the rail, their glasses full. Sadie notices Walter and she nudges Sarah, newspaper in hand; the two walk over to confront Walter. "Walter, are you implying that I am this Miss Coquette, the southern belle, who danced with all the men at the ball… wait, let me read it exactly." Sadie opens the newspaper and reads the quote, "making each feel special, when none are?"

"Miss Sadie Stiles, you are hardly the only girl from the south who danced every dance. If memory serves, your sister also danced every dance. I would like to think that the characters mentioned in the article are composites of those who were there, not specific individuals."

Sadie appears dejected. "Well, that explanation makes me feel even worse. That means you did not mention me at all."

"As you like." Walter knows he cannot win.

"Were the others all wearing a," Sadie again looks at the newspaper, "white dress that was envied by Miss Lane?"

"No, but some were. Did you think your dress was suitable with the President in attendance?"

Sadie gets coy, "Why Walter, whatever did you imagine was wrong with my dress?"

"It was rather audacious."

"Then you did notice. I thought as much." Sadie turns and waves the handkerchief that she had previously dropped at Walter. Sadie and Sarah walk toward the hotel.

Walter watches as they walk away, shrugs, and walks over to Catharine. "Have you seen George this morning?"

"It is hardly my responsibility to know Mr. Batcheller's schedule." Catharine doesn't notice as Jacob walks up behind her.

"That may be, but you did make a handsome couple on the dance floor. Three dances if memory serves."

"Why Jacob, thank you for counting."

Jacob answers Walter's question. "I saw George headed for the 7 o'clock train to Troy; off to visit our local murderer, I should imagine."

"I doubt he would use that description," corrects Catharine.

"What word would he use to describe young, spoiled, compliant Mr. Frank Baucus?"

"I doubt if he would use an adjective," declares Catharine.

"Oh, here he comes," Jacob warns.

"Who?" Before Jacob can answer, Reverend Beecher is standing beside Catharine.

"Miss Catharine, how nice to see you this lovely morning. I find the springs after morning prayers such a refreshing way to start the day." Jacob moves behind the Reverend so he can be seen by Catharine and not by Beecher; he starts to make faces and mimics the minister.

"With so many parishioners to visit, I would have guessed a visit to the springs to be a strain."

"It is never a strain to see you Miss Catharine. Oh, perhaps a strain on the eyes."

"Sir, you take liberties," Catharine reprimands, then walks away without saying goodbye.

The Baucus defense team is gathered around a long table in the conference room at the courthouse. Beach, George, Amanda, and Frank are all seated, along with Levi Smith. Beach makes the mistake of trying to change Amanda's mind. "Amanda, are you sure you want to push to have the trial that soon? It means less than two weeks to prepare."

"You must understand; I do not want my family to be the center of the conversations on the piazzas this season. My son acted in self-defense and I want those at the springs to understand that." She takes a breath, "Besides, if you give them more time, they will use it to manufacture more witnesses."

"But it also shortens our time to uncover people who fully grasped your relationship with Mansfield."

"I will provide you a list of all the names you need. Mr. Smith, do you agree with me?" She tries to divide and conquer.

Smith knows how to be non-committal. "If we proceed with an early trial it looks like we have nothing to hide. But we run the risk of missing a key witness."

Amanda only hears what she wishes to hear. "And there will be no insanity defense. My son is sane; if anyone was insane, it was his father."

"Then I will just allude to the issue, just raising it enough so that a juror or two might think that was the question."

"You will not."

"Amanda, you are tying my hands and endangering your son."

"I am doing neither."

Beach tries the divide and conquer. "Frank, how do you feel?"

"At this point I just want this over."

Beach is exasperated. "Okay, I will ask the judge to set the date for July 5th."

Fancy goods stores are the places where women can gather, chat, and select things to alter the looks of their dresses and gowns. Fancy goods stores are where Saratoga's guests can also purchase unmentionables. At home a woman will only buy a white or cream colored corset; in Saratoga such items are available in red and black. The Stiles women are selecting a new flounce in one of the fancy goods store. Mary appears to be looking at ribbon but is really watching the others. There is a bright red corset on the counter. "Mother, what woman would wear such a thing?" Sarah asks.

"Certainly not one we would associate with," answers Cora. Sadie just smiles.

Mmes. Brewster, Jackson, Brown and Miss Place are examining

ribbon and lace. The dowagers are approached by Miss Strong, who enters alone and walks up to the group. She looks directly at Mrs. Brewster, "You went shopping without inviting me?"

"You seem to be too occupied by your Mr. Ellis," Mrs. Brewster stresses his name, "to want to spend time with us."

"I have found someone whose company I enjoy; why should I not spend time with him?"

Mrs. Jackson tries to smother the fire that is about to erupt. "That is not the question my dear; the question is why would you want to spend time with us?"

As always, Mrs. Brewster ignores Mrs. Jackson. "So we are simply to be fair weather friends?"

"That would be your choice, not mine. I have excluded you from nothing," corrects Miss Strong.

"I do not remember you inviting us on your afternoon stroll in the Deerpark," Mrs. Brewster points out.

Miss Strong holds her ground. "The Deerpark is hardly the place I would have expected you to want to visit. I never suspected that you desired animals nudging up against you, soliciting a handout."

Mrs. Jackson again tries to intercede. "I enjoy the Deerpark but I think it is much more suited for young couples who want a public place to talk in private."

"This white lace is beautiful," remarks Sadie.

"That it may be, but you will get no more until you apologize for your behavior at the ball," Cora demands.

"Mother, if I were to ask grand-ma-ma how you dressed and behaved at every dance and cotillion you went to when you were seventeen, what would she say?" Sadie treads on dangerous ground.

"She would tell you that I may have disagreed with her rules but I never defied them."

"You did not tell me to wear the collar, you just assumed I would. Besides, did grand-ma-ma approve of all your afternoon carriage rides with father, or, what was his name, Mr. Paul Chatfield?"

Sarah has the final word, "Ladies! Remember we are ladies of the south!"

Morrissey is standing in the center of the casino when Richards approaches, asking, "The young man in the light brown suit," Morrissey looks in the direction Richards indicates, "he wants to raise the stakes at the roulette wheel."

"How much?"

"He wants to be able to bet $1,000 a spin."

"Who is he?"

"David Toombs, he's the son of a Senator from Georgia."

Morrissey looks the man over closely for a second time. "How has his play been going?"

"He is about even; maybe ahead a hundred or so."

"For him only, keep me posted on how the play goes."

Pauline and Antoinette are huddled together out of the glow of the gas streetlight a block south of Morrissey's. Pauline looks longingly at the entrance to the casino. Pauline remarks "All dat money, so close and dere's no way to get to it. I bet yah dose men woo' enjoy a goo' evenin'.

"It's when we reach too high dat we's get in'a trouble. We's stayin' righ' 'ere.

Pauline pulls her skirt up to her knee to show her sister a hole in her stocking. "Pa takes so much of da money dat I cain'g afford d'cent stockin's. Man takes one look at dese stockin's and he's knows dat I'm desperate an' he can 'ave me for next to not'in'.

There is the sound of two loud voices coming from the casino. Young Toombs and his friend Hugh are on the porch. "Four thousand... four thousand in a single night; we are going to have a season to remember," Toombs brags.

Pauline and Antoinette look in the direction of the voices. "Our luck may be chan'in," Antoinette comments.

"We be needin' a chan'e of luck."

Antoinette laughs loudly to draw attention. "I thin' it's work'n, dey's lookin' dis way," Pauline observes, then bends over as if to re-tie her shoe exposing considerable ankle. "Das lookin'?" Pauline asks.

Hearing the noise, Hugh and Toombs look at Pauline and Antoinette. Hugh nudges Toombs, "Looks like your lucky streak has not ended. This evening is developing into an excellent foray."

"It would not take much luck or much money to spend some time with those two," Toombs comments.

"How much luck would it take for us to go back to the hotel alone?"

"We would never get them by the porters in the lobby." Toombs becomes sarcastic, "Marvin keeps a reputable house."

"A dollar tip and the porters go blind."

Toombs shrugs his head in the direction of Pauline and Antoinette. "They are not my style. Let's agree to go to a hop tomorrow night where we will meet some suitable company."

"Sometimes you have high standards when none are needed, but a hop on the morrow is better than nothing." From a less wealthly family, Hugh has lower standards than his compatriot.

Getting frustrated, Antoinette remarks to her sister, "Da're lookin' but I don't thin' dey's comin."

"Dey's probabl' saw da 'oles in my 'ose. We make's money t'night, we don't tell Pa and we buy's some decen' clothes." Pauline's voice becomes sad, "Damn and das was good lookin' ones."

Hugh and Toombs leave the porch, walking in the direction of the hotels.

It is a warm morning so the usual contingent is at the springs. A violinist is playing as the Stiles women, Mary, Madam Jumel, George, and most of the dowagers without Miss Strong are present. Walter is near the Stiles' servants. Todd is off looking over the fence into the Deerpark.

Pauline and Antoinette suffer the curse of having been born into the wrong family. Because of their occupation, they are forced by the rules of society to stand further back than even the slaves.

Catharine and Jacob are talking near Catharine's usual post.

Out of breath from rushing, Miss Lee enters the park waiving a sheet of paper. "I received a post from Philadelphia this very morning. It is from my blessed aunt. It must have come on the 7:00 a.m. train."

"Did she speak about Mr. Ellis?" Mrs. Brewster rubs her palms together as if starting a fire.

"Indeed she did. She said that she knows a Mr. Ellis, who is the same age as our Mr. Ellis, and that he is one of the most successful young bankers in Philadelphia." Miss Lee struggles to catch her breath. "He is active in his church, sings in the choir, and is very much single." She points to a passage in the letter. "It says right here his heart was broken a little over a year ago." Miss Lee suddenly realizes how loud she has been and starts to whisper, "When the woman, to whom he was engaged, eloped and got married to an adventurer going to Kansas."

Mrs. Brewster is disappointed; she was hoping for a negative reference. "Before we make any assurances we need to hear from at least one more source."

"In matters of the heart, I always think it better not to interfere," Mrs. Jackson advises. "Mrs. Brewster, whatever is your motive in making these inquiries?"

"I only wish to secure the happiness of Miss Strong; nothing more." Mrs. Jackson's expression shows she disagrees with the explanation.

George arrives and is walking across the pavilion to talk to Jacob and Catharine. When he nears Madam Jumel, she puts her hand on his arm to get his attention. "Mr. Batcheller, I presume?" George is totally taken back. "I am known as Madam Jumel."

George is so shocked that she is speaking to him that he almost stutters. "Yes." He recovers and politely removes his hat before taking her hand. "Everyone in the village knows who you are. It is my pleasure to actually make your acquaintance."

"May I inquire how Judge Baucus is doing during these trying times?"

"The Judge is holding up as well as could be expected. He does not speak of the situation but I can tell he is concerned for Frank."

"When you see him next will you please give him my regards and ask if I might call on him?"

"It would be my pleasure. I am sure he will be pleased with your interest." Everyone watches as Madam Jumel strolls to her carriage.

George joins Jacob and Catharine. Jacob cannot wait to rib his friend. "Are you still talking to me after becoming the celebrity of the springs? I cannot wait to get to breakfast and hear the rumors about how Madam Jumel stopped you."

"Jacob, she merely inquired as to how the Judge is doing." George turns to Catharine, "It is good to see you Catharine."

"It is good to see you also Mr. Batcheller. Might I ask how the preparations are proceeding? I so worry about the Judge and Clara." She pauses, "and Frank, for that matter."

"We have a planning a meeting today. I should have a better answer when next we meet."

"So you are off to Troy?"

"No, we are meeting in Mr. Beach's office."

Mary's gaze is fixated on Walter, who is on the perimeter speaking to the African American servants. She is distracted when Miss Strong and Mr. Ellis enter the park. Miss Strong and Mr. Ellis give Pauline and Antoinette a wide berth.

"Wouldn't it be great to come to da sprin's ev'r mornin'?" Pauline bemoans her fate.

"Yes, I so enjoy haven' people staren' an' lookn' down dere noses at me." Antoinette has no trouble accepting her reality.

"I din't mean as we're now, I meant's we cou'd be."

"An' dat my dear siser's as we'll neve'be."

Ellis and Miss Strong finally reach the rail where he offers, "The springs are the hub of the ritual of see and be seen."

"Then you did not suggest we come for their medicinal properties?" She smiles.

"No I did not. I suggested we come so that everyone would know of my interest in you."

"So now I am a show piece, or is it a prize?"

"Excuse my boldness but to me, you are both." He blushes.

"Why do you think I accepted your invitation to the springs?"

He smiles, "Because of the medicinal properties of the waters." Miss Strong smiles broadly and touches his forearm.

"Why should I want to be considered a prize?"

Ellis smiles even wider, "Because of the medicinal properties of the waters."

Beach is sitting at a large wooden desk but one can feel his persona throughout his entire office. Sitting across from him in order are, fellow lawyer Levy Smith, George, and Judge Baucus. "Levy, how do you feel the jurors will see the letters?" Beach holds a pile of letters that Mansfield wrote to Amanda.

"As you said the other day, they are every bit as much a motive as a threat," Levy gauges.

"George, what is the pertinent quote?" Beach asks.

George looks through the pages until he finds the quote. "I will kill both the boys and the bastard's name will die forever."

Judge Baucus speaks with reserve. "It was obviously a threat, but by omitting words such as 'shoot' or 'poison' or giving a date, there is not a real danger. The question is, what other defense do you have?"

Beach makes an assessment, "Judge, we agreed that on cross the district attorney will make Frank look weak and imply that his one false moment of strength was when he fired first and Amanda will be crucified on cross."

They are interrupted when Dexter, Beach's secretary, knocks and boldly walks in. He stutters, "Excuse me but Mr. ..." Before Dexter can finish saying Beach's name, the Judge's other son, Charles, walks in and boldly joins the meeting.

Charles looks at Beach and then his father, as if daring them to tell him to leave. "I think it is time that we respond as a family and not jump to the whims of that outsider, that upstart, my brother's widow."

Beach is clearly annoyed as he stands unfolding his entire six-foot two-inch frame. "Charles, you are an old friend; I will excuse your intrusion into my office this one time." The act of unfolding allows Beach to regain his composure, "Never take the liberty of entering this office without an invitation again!" Beach sits back down.

"Excuse me, but this involves the family and I am part of the family. Now I am the head of the next generation."

The Judge never loses his equanimity. "This involves Frank, and you are his uncle, not his father. Of late you have not even been much of an uncle."

"We have the family name to protect."

Beach asks a rhetorical question, "And how exactly would you do that?"

"By only calling witnesses to Mansfield's intolerable behavior; leave the rest of the family out of the public eye."

"To protect the family name is to give up on Frank," Beach argues.

"Charles, you have no reason to be at this meeting. I respect your concern for the family but right now my concern is for Frank. I can deal with the family name when the trial is over," the Judge pledges.

"Fear not, the Lord will provide, he always has; he always will." Lacking faith in the courts, Charles falls back on religion.

"Well, unless you can get the Lord to testify," the Judge asserts, "we are going to follow Mr. Beach's advice." There is silence; the Judge, Beach, and Charles stare at each other. George and Levy Smith look like they wish they could melt and flow out of the room.

The Judge asks his son, "Where will you be staying while you are in town?"

"I was planning on staying at the manor."

In a calm voice, the Judge says, "I suggest you make arrangements to stay at the parsonage. I don't want you talking to the children when I am not present." Charles stares at his father, rises, and leaves the room.

"Mr. Beach, you have your challenges and, as you can see, I have mine." The Judge reflects, "I leave Frank's defense to your capable judgment." The Judge turns to George, "When you were at Harvard did you have the opportunity to take any classes in the divinity school?"

"Yes, three."

"Did any of them explain why a man, like my son, who has spent his entire adult life in the study, a man who was humble and preached acceptance, peace, and forgiveness, could be so arrogant?"

"I can say for certain, no, because that question has always plagued me," George declares.

"Mr. Batcheller, you have understandings beyond your years," the Judge says as he rises. Instinctively, Beach, Levy, and George also rise.

Beach walks with the Judge and the two shake hands at the door. The Judge turns to George, "Mr. Batcheller, let us hope you have found some compelling witnesses." He then turns his attention to Beach, "I had two sons and combined, not one good man."

Gathered in their usual chairs on the piazza, the dowagers appear to be enjoying the afternoon. Mrs. Brewster points her parasol in the direction of Ruth and Mr. Stein, who are walking on the street. She drones, "He does look too old for her. Are you sure she didn't call herself his niece?"

"I could not help but overhear them when she checked in. She said she was Mrs. Stein and I have heard him referred to as Mr. Stein."

"Interesting, very interesting," Mrs. Brewster crackles. "Miss Strong, you will be glad to learn that we have taken the opportunity to acquire references on your Mr. Ellis."

"And why would I be glad for that?"

"Because we can now assure you that he is independent and not after your fortune."

"Why was that your concern?"

"With a fortune such as yours, one must be sure that those with whom you associate have your best interest at heart."

Miss Strong stands and picks up her writing papers. "I doubt that that was your objective in seeking references, but it does explain why I will no longer take part in your company." Miss Strong walks across the piazza and enters the hotel.

Sarah whispers as she and Sadie climb the stairs to the piazza, "Do you really believe grandfather will send father to Europe?"

"I do hope so; I would love to see London and Paris." Sadie's eyes glass over.

"What makes you think he would take any of us? I have the feeling that he plans on going alone."

"Mother would never allow that. She will insist that we join him. Imagine a month on the Continent."

"That may be your dream, but I think we will be staying here for the season."

"You only want to stay to be with Jacob! Father will not deny us such a great experience."

"Which of us danced with the most men at the ball?" Sarah lampoons her younger sister.

"Which of us danced three dances with one man and took a

punch break with the same man?" The sisters enter the hotel.

Morrissey and Marvin are taking a break from business, enjoying a cigar on the piazza. Morrissey brags, "I am learning the rules of Saratoga."

"How so?"

"Last evening I had two men try to place a wager on the trial in Troy."

"Which way were they betting?"

"The conversation never got that far; I told them sports betting only. Although, I must admit taking wagers on election returns would be an interesting way to win, since so many are fixed."

The largest landau in the village pulls up in front of Baucus Manor. A footman jumps off the back of the carriage and comes around the side to open the door. Madam Jumel descends and walks up the slate walkway to the door. She rings the bell and the door is opened immediately by the butler, who bows slightly. "Madam Jumel." She enters the foyer where four grandchildren are all peeking around the staircase trying to catch a glimpse of the infamous lady. The Judge enters the foyer from his office.

"Madam Jumel, how good of you to call."

"Judge, it is always an honor to be received by you." The Judge takes her hand and leads her into the parlor. Madam Jumel sits on the couch and the Judge sits in his favorite leather chair. Before the door is closed a footman enters with a tray of tea and cookies. Madam Jumel asks, "Why is it, my old and dear friend, that so many of our conversations take place when one of our lives is in turmoil?"

"Because we both are responsible for so many that it is hard to find a time when there is not disorder in one of our lives."

"Then let us take this opportunity to talk of better times. What have you been reading?" The two seem to sit taller and be growing younger as if the company of old friends brings back more than just good memories.

Thomas and Missy are in her tiny room on the third floor of the family cottage. Both are naked but covered to the waist by a sheet; her head is on his chest. He rarely speaks to her but today is an exception. "I so love Saratoga in the season, it will be a shame to have to leave for Europe."

"Is there any way that yus could bring me along?"

"No Missy, a married man cannot travel alone with a woman even on the Continent."

Missy's hand moves between his legs. "I would make ever so worth your'n time. It would be like havin' your very own sugar with yus coffee every morn." Thomas looks out the window.

Josey is sitting on an overturned wooden case in the alley behind the cottage. Benjamin is standing smoking a hand-rolled cigarette when he says, "I do believe I's going to enjoy Europe."

"You really think Mr. Thomas is going to be takin' you?"

"Well, we both knows he can't takes care of hisself. He needs me to lays out his clothes and to get him places on time."

"There is another servant that can provide all of that and some special services."

"Watch your mouth woman, I seen slaves get the whip for less than that."

"Talkin' the truth is a painful sin; besides, we's in the north here and no whippin' allowed no-how."

Couples are sitting at several of the benches in the park. Mmes. Brewster and Brown are sitting on one side of the park looking very judgmental.

"It is such a beautiful evening," Jacob remarks to Sarah as they stroll in the park. He becomes reflexive, "With the trial starting next week I wonder what Frank is thinking? You do know our families are friends, but not close; perhaps a better word would probably be associates?"

"I would guess that he is nervous and probably full of remorse."

"He had not seen his father in at least two years. Last summer his father stayed at our hotel rather than see his own children who were but a couple of blocks away."

Sarah squeezes his hand for a moment, "There are so many sad stories in Saratoga."

"Most sad stories happen outside of Saratoga and are brought here. The sad stories that occur here are usually those of broken hearts."

"Mr. Jacob Marvin, why do you think I agreed to walk with you this evening?"

"You knew it would be safe. Your sister and brother are in the window of your cottage watching our every move."

Sarah takes Jacob's arm. "If that is the case. Let's give them something to talk about." They continue walking.

A messenger is walking around the park calling, "Message for Mr. Ellis, paging Mr. Peter Ellis." Ellis, who is strolling with Miss Strong, raises his hand. The porter approaches him.

"That would be for me."

"You must be quite the popular man. There are two." Ellis tips the porter and opens one of the notes. It reads, "I know who you are not. It is time to leave the village." Ellis looks around, shaking his head no.

The Mr. Peter Ellis (Peter), who recently checked in, is in the background. He whispers to himself, "So if that is Mr. Peter Ellis of Philadelphia, who am I?"

Thomas holds the door for Sarah as they get ready to walk to the dining room. When they leave their private porch, Thomas says, "Your mother is becoming concerned about the amount of time you are spending with Jacob Marvin."

"But, Father, how do you feel?"

"Sarah, your mother thinks you younger than you are. In point of fact, you are a determined young woman. You know what you want and, I fear, you know how to get it."

"Thank you Father; what does that have to do with Jacob?"

"I would guess everything. Don't remind your mother, but she was your age when she had to leave Saratoga to prepare for our wedding."

Among the crowd at the spring are the dowagers, the Stiles women, and Todd, who is admiring a black saddle horse.

"I saw Mr. Strong checking in last evening. He must have been on the last train from Albany," Mrs. Brown observes.

"So the wealthy father is here to check on his beloved daughter's beau," Mrs. Brewster screeches. One can imagine her concocting a spell.

"Can there be any other conclusion? One has to wonder how he learned of Mr. Ellis." Mrs. Jackson looks directly at Mrs. Brewster, who looks guilty.

"One would have to guess," Mrs. Brewster smirks.

George approaches Catharine, asking, "Good morning Catharine, could I inquire as to your father's plans for this evening?"

"He usually goes to his club on Tuesdays, but I believe he will be at home early in the evening. Why do you want to know?"

"With your consent, I would like to ask his permission to call on you."

"How should I answer?" She is coy.

"With the words your heart feels."

"I shall tell father to expect you at 5:00."

Reverend Beecher walks up to Sarah, Sadie, and Cora, who are visiting by the railing. He attempts to flirt, "Miss Sarah, I will be working on this week's sermon this afternoon; if you were practicing the organ, it would inspire me. Will you be my muse?"

"What an honor, Reverend. She has no plans for today and she does need to practice." Cora takes control.

The Reverend looks at Sarah. "Then shall we say 4:00? I will leave the church doors open." Reverend Beecher walks to greet others who are present.

When he is out of hearing distance, Sarah confronts her mother, "Mother, how could you?"

"Whatever do you mean? For a minister to call you his muse is the ultimate compliment."

"An old hag would be a muse to him. Mother, I never want to be alone with that man. Since you got me into this, you will have to give up your shopping, sewing, or whatever you were planning and go with me to the church."

"Sarah, you are usually such a good judge of character; however, this time I feel you have missed the mark."

Sadie makes a rare attempt to support her sister. "Mother, I must agree with Sarah. There is something in the way he stares."

"Thank you," Sarah says to her sister, and then turns to her mother, "You did hear that Mr. Cook told the good Reverend not to call on Miss Catharine."

The States band is playing in the background when Miss Strong storms off the steps and moves directly to Mrs. Brewster, who is sitting in the park among the coven. "Did you write to my father?"

"But of course my dear child, I wanted him to know how much I appreciated your good fortune at meeting such a fine gentleman as Mr. Ellis." There is not a word of truth spoken.

"You were prying into things that are none of your concern."

"The happiness of all my protégés is of upmost concern to me, as it is of your father. I am sure his heart was warmed by my information."

"Oh his heart was warmed. Let me read exactly what he said." She tries to find the quote in the letter. "He says, 'your mother always distrusted Mrs. Brewster and the hens she roosted with. She said that they are, by their very nature, unhappy and they wish nothing more than to ensure misery on everyone else. That is why I told you to avoid them while at the springs.'" Mrs. Brewster's face is red.

Miss Strong turns to talk to the other women. "Do as you wish, but as for me, I will have nothing further to do with Mrs. Brewster or any who associate with her." Miss Strong turns to leave, then turns back. "Mrs. Brewster, he said to tell you he was saddened by your husband's heroic death at Monterrey, but says that he always understood the reason he volunteered to lead the charge." Miss Strong walks toward the steps to the hotel, head held high.

"Well, I never." Mrs. Brewster is gasping for air. "She will get quite the surprise when she learns her father beat the letter to Saratoga."

Miss Place rises. "That you 'never,' may be the very reason you act as you do. I would rather spend the rest of the summer alone than in your company. I only associated with you because Miss Strong did." She turns to those who remain, "I will hope that my dear friend will accept my apology." Miss Place gathers her few belongings and before she leaves, Mrs. Brown and Miss Lee join her. The three walk toward the hotel. Mrs. Jackson remains.

"Thank you for your support; today's young people have no respect for values and tradition." Mrs. Brewster is offended.

"Oh you misunderstand," smiles Mrs. Jackson, "I am not here to support you; I am here to watch how you connive to get out of this predicament that you created. My guess is that you will pack up and leave on the next train."

In the main lobby Jacob walks up to his uncle. "Two big stories to follow at the same time; it is too much for the guests, a trial in Troy and the execution of Mrs. Brewster in our park. We would have less to talk about if the hotel were on fire."

"The problem is that dowagers can never be made extinct; cut off the head and they grow another body and the original body grows another head. Suddenly you have two coteries."

"But their chief rivals will be the other group."

"They always seem to have enough vile left to attack other guests. By the way, what is going on between you and Miss Sarah Stiles?"

"I enjoy her company."

"She is not the type to toy with; be careful."

"For once, Uncle, I do not believe I am toying."

"Then I repeat, be careful."

In the Cook's parlor, Mr. Cook is holding a glass of bourbon. George, looking nervous, holds a similar glass.

"What would you be offering my daughter?"

"Although my current worth is limited, my income is secure and my prospects are excellent."

"You know there will be problems meeting her expectations. Catharine has already hosted dinners for two presidents, three Supreme Court Justices, two governors, and the occasional senator and congressman."

"I would hope that if she were to fall in love with me that she will share a dinner nightly with the President."

"Rather high goals wouldn't you say?"

"That may be, but they are realistic."

Cook raises his glass as if to salute. "Mr. Batcheller, if I should see you sitting on the porch, or walking to the park with Catharine, I would be most pleased."

Morrissey, standing in his usual spot, is approached by Richards, who stands so that Morrissey can look over his shoulder at Toombs. "You were right, he is the kind who wins one night and thinks he can win all the time. I have him down about a thousand as of now."

"Did you check the sources of his money?"

"Slave labor."

"How big is his plantation?"

"It isn't a plantation that they talk about. His father has over a hundred slaves that he hires out, the men to unload boats at the docks or to do construction work. As for the women, he hires them out to work as house servants and laundresses."

"So he earns his money from another man's sweat. Let us see how he loses his money. Keep me posted."

Ellis walks across the park to where Misses Strong and Lee are sitting, listening to the concert. He has a warm smile. "Good morning ladies." He turns his attention to Miss Strong. "If I am able to engage a carriage for an after dinner drive, would you grant me the pleasure of your company down to what they call the Spouter Spring or we could go to the lake if you would prefer?" He turns his attention to Miss Lee, "Naturally I hope that you will join us as a chaperone."

Miss Strong asks her friend, "Would you like to see the Spouter? I am told it is a delightful setting and a pleasant way to spend a hot afternoon."

"I have heard nothing of this spring; is it a great distance?"

Ellis answers, "I am led to believe it is only a couple of miles.

Some of the guests have walked there. There is an omnibus that goes near but I think they are often too smelly and uncomfortable for fine ladies like yourselves."

"It sounds like an adventure. How long would we be gone?" Miss Strong wonders.

"I will engage the carriage for three hours, that way you will have time to pick wild flowers for your rooms."

Miss Strong turns to her friend pleading, "Miss Lee, would you accompany us?"

"It would be my pleasure." Ellis rises and walks to the hotel to hire a carriage. When he is gone, Miss Lee adds, "He is the proper gentleman and unmarried."

"That he is. His manners are impeccable; one has to wonder why he never married." Miss Strong appears to have doubts.

"Where did he go to school?" Miss Lee inquires.

"I do not think he ever said, but it must have been one of the best in New England."

In the men's parlor, Thomas Stiles and Marvin are sitting in leather chairs, both holding glasses of the best bourbon. Thomas asserts, "I would have to admit, it will be enjoyable to visit England and France again. I am less sure about Germany."

"When would you be leaving?"

"I received a telegram this very afternoon in which father asked me to leave before the first week in August. Please do not mention it to my family as I have not shared the information with Cora and the girls."

"I must admit I will miss your family, they are always smiling. It would appear that Jacob will be host to a broken heart."

"Oh, my family will not be accompanying me. They will stay the season and return to Savannah when the weather changes."

Marvin is surprised by the news. "Will not your daughters want to join you?"

"I am sure Sadie will but she has already been to Europe. If anyone was to go with me it would be young Todd."

"How would you manage with him alone?"

"Oh I do not plan on taking him. My man Benjamin will be staying on. He will mind Todd in my absence."

"He will have the easy part. Mrs. Stiles will have the more difficult task watching the Misses Sarah and Sadie." The two men smile and raise their glasses.

The Stiles sisters walk into the lobby holding packages. They are met by the messenger who smiles, saying, "Miss Sadie, you have a message."

Sadie takes the envelope, tips the messenger and speaks as she is opening it. "Please wait just a moment." She reads the telegram:

> *Our paths crossed to-day,*
> *Your beauty kept me at bay.*
> *I often wonder if all is lost*
> *And if you cared who it cost.*

Sadie speaks to the messenger who waits impatiently. "This will only take a moment; I have been working all day on what to say." She walks to a small table and quickly scribbles her response.

Sadie hands the note to the messenger. "I understand you may not be able to tell me who sent this message, but nothing stops you from being sure that the sender gets this." She gives him a generous tip.

In the second floor hallway, Ellis knocks on the door. It takes a few seconds, but it is opened from the inside. He looks very nervous as he walks in.

Richards and Morrissey are in their usual spots in the center of the gaming room. "You were right about young Mr. Toombs." When Morrissey does not answer Richards continues, "He is down over two thousand this evening. He can't leave the roulette wheel."

"Has he asked for credit?"

"Not yet, but I checked with the window and they told me he only bought twenty-five hundred in chips, so he will be running out soon."

"Does his father know he is coming here?"

"They are in the same cottage at the States, so my guess is that he knows."

"To lend him anything over a thousand, his father will have to sign the note. " Morrissey's eyes are focused on a medium sized, nondescript man of about forty. He does not appear to be playing any of the games but he looks like he is mentally measuring the room. Morrissey asks, "Who is that man?"

"Never saw him before. Want me to find out more?"

"If you can, there is something about him."

With the trial about to start, the entire village is at the springs. The dowagers are divided into two camps: Mmes. Brewster and Jackson, who are joined by two pledges, Mmes. White and Dillon; Misses Strong, Lee, Place, and Mrs. Brown form a second group. Pauline and

Antoinette are on the perimeter.

Walter, Jacob, Sadie, and Sarah have finally made it to the rail to get some water. Jacob asks Walter, "Why are you smiling?"

"I did an unnamed article about the incident that caused the dowagers to split. The editor is running it today. No one is named but we all know who I am talking about."

"Walter, do you think it is fair not to identify the person you are writing about? Innocent people could be mistaken for those who are guilty," Sadie asks.

"That is less likely than those who are guilty not realizing it was about them."

"Do you think it is right for someone to write something and leave it unsigned?" Sadie looks into his eyes.

"It depends on what they write. There are people who desire anonymity or fear being known."

"So you believe that there are people who wish to forever remain unknown?" Sadie challenges.

"I suppose, but I would guess that most people want to be identified at some point. Remember yourself and the white dress."

"So it was me you wrote about in that article!" Sadie is elated.

"That is not what I said." Walter attempts to clarify.

"But it was what you meant. I was the envy of Miss Lane!" Sadie smiles, grabs her sister and walks off toward the hotel. Walter shrugs and walks over to where the servants gather. Mary walks in front of the group and over to the edge where she stands near Walter, trying to hear what he is saying. Walter is talking to the African Americans who are present and pointing to a small man; among the group is Missy.

Walter points to an African American. "That is him, Solomon Northup, over by the little spring. He is the one whose story became a best seller." The African Americans around him look at him as if they have no idea what he is talking about. Walter continues, "He was born near here a free man. He was tricked into going to the Capital City for a job; when he got there he was sold into slavery. He was a slave for twelve years before he was able to get a message out and be freed." Realizing that no one seems to care, Walter walks away.

One of the male servants looks to the women around him, "Don' go believin' those fairy-tales. I heard that one mys'self and my mas'er told me it was nutin' but a lie made up to make's slaves wan's to run away." Missy watches Northup closely.

With the park still crowded, George boldly walks over and begins a conversation with Pauline and Antoinette. "Miss Pauline St. Claire, I believe?" He pauses. "I am George Sherman Batcheller. I am working with Mr. Beach on the Baucus trial."

Pauline is almost too surprised to respond; when she does, it is in her best behavior. "Why's yes sirs." She cannot remember the last time a man treated her as a person.

"I have met with several people from Troy who told me that you have been acquainted with Mr. Mansfield Baucus, the writer."

"I knowd him. I knowd him preddy wells. An' he surely know'd me." She giggles.

"If you were a witness how would you describe your relationship?"

"A lady neve' tells." Antoinette breaks out laughing at her sister's comment. Even George smiles.

"Would you be able to say whether he generally carried a gun or not?"

"When he's with me his pockets are empty." She smiles. "He alway' puts a gun on the dresser."

"We may be calling you as a witness."

"Won't do you no good. I can't afford a train trip to Troy jus' to testify in some damn trial."

"At least not one that is not her own," Antoinette jokes.

George turns his attention to Pauline. "If we were to call you, we would pay for your ticket."

"Maybe yah should talk to my sister - she know'd him almost as well as me."

"Thank you, but I do not believe having sisters testify as to his character would be helpful."

"That means you won't be talking to my ma either. She talked to him more'n once when she was younger." Antoinette breaks out laughing.

The day is cool for late June but that does not distract the dowagers from their daily ritual of observing those who wished to be ignored. Sitting on benches in the park are Mmes. White, Brewster, and Jackson. They have been joined by two new dowagers, Miss Clark and Mrs. Jefferson. A sixth dowager, Mrs. Dillon, rushes to join them.

"Well, it is obvious we had the wrong impression about Mrs. Stein. She may have appeared as a lady but I saw something last evening that has forever changed that conception," Mrs. Dillon reports.

"Do not waste time trying to be coy, you saw something, tell us," Mrs. Brewster commands.

"I am not sure what I saw. I will leave the conclusions to each of you." Mrs. Dillon pauses to be sure she has everyone's attention. "Last evening, just as I was about to put my shoes out to be polished, there was a knock on a door down the hall. When I opened the door I saw this devilishly looking handsome man standing three doors down. The door was opened by Mrs. Stein. She gave the man a quick kiss and pulled him into the room." She nods her head to ensure that they all know, "The kiss was on the lips."

"There are not a lot of ways to interpret that kind of action, are there?" Mrs. Jackson flinches.

"Did I mention she was in a white satin sleeping gown and without a robe?" If Mrs. Dillon had not witnessed it herself she would not have believed such a story.

"So you are saying she is having an affair?" Mrs. Brewster declares.

"I am not saying anything except what I saw with my own eyes." Mrs. Dillon recoils.

Mrs. Brewster says something that even she knows is insincere. "Well, I am not going to tell Mr. Stein. Are we all agreed he will just have to learn about his wife for himself?"

One of the States' carriages is parked on the grass across from the Spouter Spring. Miss Lee has taken the opportunity to pick wild flowers. Miss Strong holds Ellis' arm as they look at the spring. He explains, "It is everything people talk about. I am no scientist but it is obvious that the minerals in the water are forming a yellow white mushroom rock."

"Makes one believe in the power of nature. Look how the leaves are being eaten by the minerals." Miss Strong has always looked for fossils in her father's coal.

"This must be an incredible sight with a full moon." Ellis shows his romantic side.

Miss Strong picks up on his tender feeling. "Mr. Ellis, surely those are the thoughts of an aspiring poet."

"I am hardly a poet, a dreamer, yes, but not one skilled enough to commit his thoughts to paper."

"Where did you go to school?" she asks.

"I went to Deerfield Academy for a time."

Miss Lee approaches with a bouquet of wild flowers in hand. "Did you know my cousin John Lee? He is about your age."

"The name sounds familiar but I cannot place it to a face. I was not able to finish my studies; my sponsor died and I had to return to help my family," Ellis explains.

"When we were introduced, Jacob mentioned that you were not staying the season. When will you be leaving?" Miss Strong fears she will miss an opportunity she truly wants to explore.

"I will be leaving a week from Sunday."

"So soon?" is all she can say. Taking his elbow tighter, they walk back to the carriage.

"It is all the time I can afford."

Mrs. Stein is reading a book on the lawn while the band plays in the background. Colonel Parker, carrying his cane and wearing a bowler, walks up to Mrs. Stein. The Colonel bows politely before he speaks. "Mrs. Stein, I presume. Please excuse me for speaking without having been properly introduced; I am Colonel Parker of Richmond."

"I accept your apology but I hardly think anyone will be too concerned since we are in a busy park."

"Ah, but you are quite mistaken," he asserts.

"How so?"

"Everyone in the park is talking about you. If I were 20 years younger, I would be added to their list of victims of what I hope is idle scandal mongering."

"Whatever are you talking about?"

The Colonel blushes. "Please excuse my bluntness but it seems that a young man was seen entering your chambers last night."

"Really." Mrs. Stein rises, and turns to Colonel Parker. It is an automatic action as she takes his arm saying, "Colonel, one should not automatically believe everything one hears." She smiles in the direction of the dowagers. "Or sees for that matter. Allow me to explain." They walk toward the back entrance to the hotel.

George is walking on Broadway on his way to Beach's office when he notices Catharine and walks up to her. "Catharine, how fortunate to see you." Catharine looks him in the eye and silently walks away. George looks stunned by her behavior.

Mrs. Brewster's group is seated in their usual chairs. Nearby Walter is uneasily rocking in one of the chairs. He has a bouquet of flowers nestled beside him as he keeps a watch down Broadway. Sadie and Sarah come into sight, walking back toward the hotel. At the same time a group of ten young college age men come around the corner. The college men are boisterous and have several bouquets of flowers. They are handing out individual flowers to each of the seemingly attractive women. Both Sadie and Sarah get a flower from one of the bouquets as the men rush off. Laughing at their good fortune, Sadie and Sarah climb the steps to the hotel.

Sarah remarks, "Only in Saratoga do we see such behavior without anyone being offended."

"But now I have to wonder, was one of them my poet?" Sadie looks at the departing group.

The church bell rings twice as Sadie notices the abandoned flowers in the rocking chair. She picks up the bouquet and looks to the dowagers. "Did any of you see who left these flowers?"

"Oh, it was nobody. I am sure you may take them," says a snide Mrs. Brewster.

The dining room is crowded with those seeking supper. The dowagers are seated together. Ellis and Miss Strong are seated together, awaiting dinner. Miss Strong's back is to the door. A waiter accompanies Mr. Strong as he walks up to the table to join his daughter. Miss Strong does not see her father until he is at the table. Mr. Strong coughs, signaling his presence. "Father, how wonderful to see you." Her instant smile becomes an instant look of concern. "Is everything okay? I thought you were too weak to make the trip." Against all rules of protocol, she stands, throws her arms around her father's neck and hugs him as if she were a little girl, "I am so glad to see you."

As father and daughter hug, the second Peter Ellis walks up to the table. "Mr. Strong, I believe; I am Peter Ellis, the banker of Philadelphia." Miss Strong looks at all three men, trying to determine what to do.

Mr. Strong points to the original Ellis, "I believe that this is Mr. Ellis of Philadelphia."

"I am," says his daughter's beau.

The father recommends, "Interesting. Perhaps we should all sit down."

The new Peter Ellis stares at the first Ellis and begs off. "Please excuse me, but I do not feel comfortable with that suggestion. I will take my meal with the gentlemen I came with." The new Ellis walks away.

Mrs. Stein walks in on Mr. Stein's arm. Colonel Parker is walking a step behind. The three walk up to the dowager's table, where she says, "My dears, I have been told that you felt you were the witness to an unusual occurrence last evening." Her eyes lock on Mrs. Dillon. "you were not."

All the dowagers fidget; Mrs. Dillon more than the rest. At that moment the young man from the previous evening joins Mrs. Stein, Mr. Stein, and Colonel Parker. Mrs. Stein points to the young man and says, "I would like you to meet my husband, Daniel Stein, my father-in-law, Judge Stein, and of course my new and very dear friend, Colonel Parker." She now locks eyes with each dowager in turn. "Let me see. With your loose tongues, you are sitting together, while my honest and quiet nature allows me to have dinner with three of the handsomest men in Saratoga. I guess there really is a just God." The three Steins and the Colonel move toward a smiling Marvin who has saved them a choice table near the band.

Miss Strong and her father are both seated in chairs by the windows in his room. Trying to suppress his cough, Mr. Strong gets out, "I suppose you would like an explanation."

"You know very well I deserve one." She is both happy to see her father and upset he did not tell her he was coming.

He coughs lightly. "It all started five days ago when I received a letter from your Mr. Ellis. He asked me if I were well enough to join you in Saratoga or if I would prefer to receive him in Strongsville. He had something of a serious nature to discuss with me." The daughter listens intently. "I wired him inquiring as to the nature of what he wanted to discuss." The father is running out of breath. He coughs softly. "He wired back saying it had to do with you but it was something he wanted to speak about in person." He coughs again. "I told him I would be over directly."

"With your health, why did you not have him come to you?"

"If it concerned you, I should be near to you when it was discussed." Another cough. "I arrived last night, where upon I went to Mr. Morrissey's." he smiles. "I might add, I won." He takes a drink of water before continuing." A man of my age should have known better; I slept most of the day away."

"Are you all right?"

"Better than that, far better." He pats her hand. "I met with your Mr. Ellis this afternoon. It seems that he came to Saratoga to celebrate the first anniversary as a mortgage officer at a bank in Philadelphia." The cough returns. "He related that when he first saw you, you were simply dressed, as were your associates. He did not realize for several days that you came from an established family." He coughs yet again. "By the time he learned of your worth, he already had developed strong feelings for you. He told me today that he would cease all contact if that is what I wanted."

"But he attended Deerfield and his father lives in a house with 28 rooms. Did he lie to me?"

The father has a knowing smile. "He told me his father is the butler in a house of 28 rooms. His father's former employer took a liking to your Mr. Ellis and sent him to Deerfield. Unfortunately, the man died and your Mr. Ellis had to come home."

"But he led me to believe he was wealthy."

"Did he, or did you make the assumptions?"

She takes a moment to think. "Father what should I do?"

"Follow your heart; it knows what is best for you." He coughs, and then continues, "Did your Mr. Ellis try to get you to elope and get married?

"No."

"He is not a pretender; he is an honest working man, just like I was when I met your mother."

"But what will people say when we get back to Strongsville?"

"Unless I am seriously mistaken, they will say you chose a man who loves you and that the mineral waters of Saratoga actually do work once in a while." He smiles as he coughs.

Mr. Cook is sitting on the porch of his mansion, having an evening cigar. George walks by, builds his courage, then walks back to the porch. George speaks from below the steps. "Mr. Cook, I fear I have in some way offended your daughter." George is in wonder. "I would apologize if I knew in what way I offended her."

"It is my understanding that you are not taking proper care of whom you are seen associating with at the springs."

George has to think. "I fear there has been a dreadful misunderstanding." Cook just stares at George waiting for an explanation. "Mr. Beach has assigned me the task of finding witnesses that would be willing to testify as to Mansfield Baucus' character. Many of those from Troy mentioned a woman who is of late in Saratoga - a Miss Pauline St. Clare."

"I have been led to believe that she is not one that a gentleman would be seen talking to, let alone at the springs."

"I never would have talked to her there, or anyplace else, had Mr. Beach not needed her for the defense of Frank. I could think of no better place to talk to her than one that was public."

Catharine has been silently listening at an open window in the parlor. She exits the front door, and walks up to George. "If you should ever need talk to her again or any other of her vocation, you will tell me in advance. I did not appreciate being told when I could not defend your actions."

"I humbly apologize. It was not my intention to hurt you or your feelings in any way," George gasps.

"Then say no more of it. I think you should take me for a walk so that others will have nothing to gossip about." She steps down from the porch, takes George's arm and they walk toward the hotels. "Never forget," she says sternly, "We are blessed and cursed by our families and judged by our friends."

Judge's Office
Saratoga Springs History Museum

Trials

The defense team is using one of the conference rooms in the Troy Court House for the last planning session before Frank's trial. George, Beach, and Smith are sitting along one side of the long table; Amanda and Frank are sitting across from them. Beach tries to explain the problems.

"Amanda, without considering a momentary insanity defense, we are relying totally on self-defense. Even if I were trying to be optimistic that will be difficult. The police and hotel workers will testify that when they arrived, Mansfield's hand was still in his pocket and no gun was visible."

"But they will also testify that he had a gun. They could have put it back in his pocket," Amanda reasons.

"What possible motive would they have for moving his hand and the gun back into his pocket?"

Amanda has a cold stare, "To get a charge of murder and prevent an argument of self-defense." She turns to George, "You only have to be able to prove that everyone knew Mansfield carried a gun."

George looks to Beach before he speaks, "We have five witnesses who will testify that they often witnessed Mansfield with a pistol."

"There is your threat," Amanda proclaims.

"A history of carrying a gun is not the same as seeing the gun or using a gun. To claim being threatened we would have to put Frank on the stand. That is unwise because it leaves him open to cross-examination."

"We have the letters in which Mansfield threatened to kill both the boys," Amanda points out.

"How would we get the letters into evidence? Besides, if we try to use the letters, it establishes motive more than a threat. Mrs. Baucus, you have to allow me to plea momentary insanity." For the first time Beach called her by her formal name.

"Absolutely not! Besides, how often does a plea of momentary insanity work?"

"Not often, but I assure you claiming self-defense when the person had not shown a weapon works even less often."

"Mr. Beach, you have won millions for Mr. Vanderbilt, you will win my son's freedom for me." She glares at Beach. "You will be ready in two days." Amanda rises, signaling the meeting is over.

Five nights before, the rain was not heavy, but it was constant. Nate drags a set of old clothes on a rope through the woods down to the creek, then returns and enters the humble cabin. "Trails been lain. Dem dogs will follow it down to the river." Nate picks up Eve. Little Adam is carrying a violin case. Mattie and Nanny carry heavy sacks of things they will trade along the way.

"Now's everyone steps exactly where I's do." Nate leaves the house, taking small steps so everyone can follow without stretching. After they pass the trail, Nate puts Eve down. The family watches as Nate picks up a rope. On the other end is the carcass of a dead woodchuck. Nate pulls the dead woodchuck back over the exact trail they had just walked. He returns, dragging the dead woodchuck a second time. He then throws the carcass down a hole. "That'll confuse the dogs and everyone'll thin' we wents toward the creek."

They gather their meager belongings and move silently off. Mattie is in the lead, with everyone else stepping exactly where she does. Nate is last so only his large footprints will show.

At the springs one can feel that the entire village is anxiously waiting for the trial to begin. It will add more scandal, disgrace, and dishonor to the village than all the couples who eloped the previous summer. People are trying to stake out where they will stand at the springs each morning, not for the minerals, but rather for the trinkets of gossip that are the true nourishment of the spring.

Mmes. Brewster and Jackson are the only dowagers along the path. Van Buren is talking to a group of men near the spring. Sarah and Sadie are trying to nudge their way through the crowd to get near the dipper boy. Todd is on the perimeter. Walter is talking to the servants. The group of young men who handed Sadie the flowers is gathered over to the side.

Jacob and George are standing along their usual post. A tall bookish man in his mid-20s comes up to the spring. Jacob smiles, "You know who that is?"

"He does not look familiar. Should I know him?" George is perplexed.

"You should; he is a fellow lawyer from Vermont. A year ago he was the defense attorney in one of the most famous capital crime trials in the history of the Green Mountain State." George looks at his friend, then the lawyer. Jacob is holding back a laugh, "Do you have time enough to hear the story of a great trial?"

"If it will take less than a half an hour; I am due at the office by 9:00."

Jacob puts his hand on his friend's shoulder. "Come join me for breakfast at the hotel. That will give us plenty of time." Jacob and George leave the spring, walking toward the hotel.

Even after the Stein fiasco, Mrs. Brewster is full of venom. "That little Miss Perfect, Catharine Cook, never should have accepted his excuse. He may have claimed he talked to a woman of the night in a public setting to avoid accusations, but that Mr. George Sherman Batcheller is just like every other man. You can rest assured he wanted more than just her testimony and she would sell anything any man wanted, even an excuse."

"What makes you so sure?" Mrs. Jackson awaits this answer.

"Men are all alike."

"And your former husband?" Mrs. Jackson askes sarcastically.

"He was no better than any other man cursed as he was with his yearnings." It was a rare confession from Mrs. Brewster. "However, as a lawyer, he would not have allowed himself to deal with someone of her caste."

Mrs. Jackson smiles to herself.

Looking at the raucous group that handed out the flowers, Sadie speaks to her sister, "They were moving so fast, it is all a blur. I do know that there were at least two, and I think three, who gave me flowers." She looks whimsical. "How will I ever learn which one he is?"

"Your mysterious admirer is smitten with you. He will write you another poem."

"If only I could be sure of that. I did hear they were from Madison College - wherever that is."

"If you are going to marry a professional man, you will need to learn about all the good schools. It is in a little village called Hamilton,

New York," instructs Sarah.

"They were all very handsome."

"Not all," corrects Sarah, "I must ask, how do you account for the flowers that were left on the chair?"

"You cannot believe they were for me. My poet would never have left without handing me the flowers."

"Unless he was unsettled by that bunch of rowdy fraternity boys."

"My poet would never be intimidated. He is bold and called by adventure."

Sarah has a suggestion. "I have it, you could walk away and I will watch to see which one's eyes follow you." Sadie does not answer but starts walking toward Walter.

She smiles at him, "Walter, how was yesterday?"

"Disappointing."

"How so?" She looks over his shoulder at the college boys.

"I thought I had a date, but I was wrong."

Sadie continues to glance at the fraternity men. "You must be heartsick, how could any girl treat a noble person, such as yourself, with such a cold heart."

He has caught that her eyes are not on him. "It seems with the greatest of ease."

Sarah joins her sister and Walter. "Either they are all interested in you or none are. They all just kept looking back and forth between us." Sarah turns her attention to Walter. "Good morning."

"What?" He is honestly confused.

"Those fraternity boys gave us flowers yesterday and Sadie is trying to establish which one is her poet."

"Poet?" Walter sounds as if has no idea what Sarah is talking about.

"Sadie has a secret admirer who keeps sending her poems."

Walter looks at Sadie to see her reaction; she continues to try to steel glances at the fraternity men. He looks only casually. "Do you really think any of them capable of writing poetry?"

"Walter, be kind," Sarah reminds him of his etiquette. She turns to Sadie. "We should be going." Sarah and Sadie start walking toward the hotel.

Madam Jumel and Van Buren have been standing near the dipper boy. She asks, "How do you deem the trial will go?"

"I sincerely believe that it will be unencumbered by facts and doubt that justice will be served."

"Then you believe that politics will prevail."

"No, no, I believe it will be a battle for the emotions of the jury. Everyone knows he did it; the question is, was there a good enough reason?"

"As a man, a lawyer, and a father, how do you feel it should go?"

"I only thank God women cannot serve on juries or young Frank Baucus would be free for sure."

"Your honor, I am surprised by your aspersions on the character of women."

Van Buren speaks with sincerity, "No, my dear Madam, you miss my point. I cast no aspersions but rather praise the delicate gender for having compassion, understanding, and thoughtfulness."

On their way back to the hotel Sarah comments to her sister, "That was interesting. I do not remember telling Walter that the poetry was original." Sadie is lost in thought.

Jacob and George are sitting along the wall at one of the smallest tables in the dining room. Jacob takes a sip of his coffee,

"It was a year ago; just before the season. Our friend, let's call him Mr. Justice, had recently set up an office in a former one room school a little north of Bennington."

"It was just before sunset when Mr. Justice looked out the window and saw an old beat-up farm wagon pull up outside with two huge, bearded, middle aged woodsmen. When they got off, one tied up the team while the other lumbered toward the office. Neither spoke as they walked up the steps to Justice's office. They walked directly in the door without knocking.

"Yus a lawyer, ain't you?" the first lumberman stated more than he asked. The second lumberman never spoke; he just looked intimidating.

"Accepted to the bar last month," Justice assured him.

"Well, we be needing your services."

"What is the nature of your business?"

"We's caught us a killer and some of the boys jus' wan's to hang him. Cooler heads has prevailed so far and insist that he get him a fair trial - then's we hang's him."

"I have never handled a capital case," Justice implored.

"I don't remember asking yus history. I think yus should get's some of your books together and come with us'n."

Justice felt compelled to ask, "When is the trial scheduled?"

"As soon as yus gets dere."

"Who will pay my bill?"

"You will get the standard fee for our town. Now get packing." The

second lumberman held open Justice's leather briefcase as Justice selected a couple of law books at random and put them in the case. The three men exited the office. Lumberman 2 put the briefcase in the wagon before he boarded. With only one seat on the buckboard, Justice was squeezed between the two huge men.

"How will I get back?" Justice wondered out loud.

"Don't yus go worrin' about dat. One of us will get yus home safe-n-soun'."

"Who was murdered?"

"A mother and three of her younguns. The farmer could hear her screamin' but couldn't get dere in time to helps." The second lumberman spoke for the first time. The wagon began jerking its way toward the mountain. Jacob continues telling the story. "So it took about 45 minutes to get there. They were on truly back roads and since they were in the middle of nowhere, and in Vermont, that is saying something."

They looked over and Justice appeared to be getting motion sick as the wagon bounced along.

"How much further?" Justice moaned.

"The barn is jus' 'round the next corner." The gate was open, the wagon turned in. In the background the outline of an old house and barn could be seen. The wagon pulled up in front of the barn. Several other carriages were on the lawn and light could be seen though the gaps between the boards that made up the barn walls.

The second lumberman picked up the valise and took it inside. Justice walked toward the barn like both his legs had fallen asleep. Inside Justice could see that the barn had been made to look like a makeshift courtroom.

The judge was a man in his late fifties with a long white beard. The judge was sitting at a makeshift table meant to signify the front of the room. The prosecutor, a man in his forties, looked like a lumberjack. There was a crowd of 35 - 40 men mingling about the room. They all looked like they were brothers of the two men who brought Justice to the barn.

"Bout times yus got here," the judge demanded.

"Now can we start?" The prosecutor seemed upset that there was even a need for a trial.

"Your honor, I need some time to talk to my client," beseeched Justice.

"No needs for dat," the judge replied.

"Your honor, as a judge appointed by the courts of Vermont, you know that I have to have time to prepare the defense and the opportunity to visit with my client is essential to that defense." Justice was white from both the trip and fear for his own safety.

"First off, smarty-pants, I's not a judge, jus' a justice of the peace." The judge waved his arms while he corrected Justice. "And dese boys here is just about all the voters in the town so I know's any of my rulin's gunna stand."

The crowd started rooting, "Yeah, get's on with it. We waited long enough."

The prosecutor leaned over toward Justice. "Do yus self a favor and don go rilin' the Judge. Just plead da case innocent."

"Your honor I must object," Justice declared.

"Now dun't yus go objecting an' dragging dis here trial on. Iff'n you do start actin' like an uppity city lawyer, I's gunna hold you in contempt," the judge threatened.

Justice tried to remain the professional, "On behalf of my client I plead not gulity."

"Das more like it," the judge affirmed, "Mr. Prosecutor, let's get dis case a movin'."

The prosecutor began his opening statement, "Your honor, da people will show that da defendant killed a mother and her three offspring. And for dat crime the defendant should be hung by the neck until dead."

"Objection, where is the jury?" Justice was beginning to get it through his thick head that this was just a Kangaroo Court.

"I dun told yus no objections. Dat will be a dollar fine for contempt of court, an fur yus information dis entire town will serve as the jury."

The prosecutor said, "I's calls Bob Barnes." A man in a straw hat stood up and walked to the front of the room. He casually sat down.

"Bob, yus ain't gunna lie is you?" asked the judge.

"Never have - never will." Justice was stunned by the oath accepted by the judge.

The prosecutor asked, "Bob, what happened?"

Bob explained, "It was about 3:00. I was makin' a deposit in the outhouse when I hears this horrible screamin'. I know'd right away it were my Rosey." He turns and looks at the judge, "Well I's grabbed leaves and cleaned me self up as fast as I could. By the time I got's outside, Rosey an all three of her young'uns was dead." Bob waved his hands to demonstrate the extent of the blood. "There was blood everywhere. I looked toward the woods and seen the defendant ducking between two bushes."

The judge asked the prosecutor, "Any more questions?"

"Nope."

The judge turned to Justice, "Well, have at it."

Justice sharply asked, "So you did not actually see the defendant kill your Rosey or her children."

"Is dat a question? It sounded more like a statement tos me," Bob replied.

"Did you actually witness my client kill your Rosey?" Justice corrected himself.

"Yus got me - but I did see him run off."

"Bob, yus can goes back to yus seat. Mr. Prosecutor do yus have any more witnesses?" Bob rose, and took his seat as the prosecutor called his next witness.

"I would like to calls Taylor Barnes." Taylor stood and went forward to be sworn in.

"Taylor, yus ain't gunna lie is you?" The judge asked the second witness.

"Judge, yus knowd I only lie when I's drinkin' and to my wife. She ain't here and I's only had a little so far today."

Justice rose to his feet, "I must object, we cannot allow a witness in a capital case who publicly admits to having been drinking."

The judge responded immediately, "Now dat's gunna cost yus another dollar - I told yus no objections!"

"But your honor."

"Nuther dollar."

Justice appealed, "But I did not object."

"Sounded like one to me. Nuther dollar." The judge called out. Justice sat down, perplexed.

"Taylor, did you see what happened at your brother's place?" the prosecutor asked.

"I cums by my brother's place a little after it happened. It was a mess." Taylor looked to the judge for support, "Jus' so's yus know's, I seen the defendant hangin's around my place a couple a days before."

Satisfied that justice was being done, the judge asked, "Mr. Prosecutor, any further question?"

His response, "The prosecution rests."

"Mr. Justice, any questions?" The judge asked.

"Taylor, let me be sure I have this correct. You did not see the crime; the only thing you saw was the mess after and my client hanging around a couple of days before," Justice summarized.

"Yus know, for a lawyer, yus ain't too smart. You didn't ask me brother a question and now you ain't askin' me one."

Justice glared, "Did you see the crime?"

"Nope," Taylor responded and those gathered laughed.

"No further questions your honor."

In the State's dining room George comments. "Jacob, I am sure this is going someplace, but at this hour I haven't the time, nor the inclination, to figure it out. I have to be in Troy in an hour.'

"Not a problem, we will finish the story tomorrow over breakfast." Jacob smiles.

"If I am back. I may need to stay in Troy for the trial."

The courtroom in Troy is far more formal than the one in Bennington. Filled to capacity, there is a general commotion while those gathered await the judge. In the 1850s all jurors, regardless of the crime, were male. Frank's jury is seated. Knowing they are going to be seen by many in the city, the men on the jury are wearing their best suits – actually, in most cases, their only suits.

George, Smith, and Frank sit at the defense table with Beach. Amanda, Clara, and Judge Baucus sit on the bench behind. District Attorney Bingham is joined by two young attorneys. Bingham has always been a rival of Beach and is looking forward to this trial as a way to vindicate several previous courtroom losses.

The room goes quiet as the judge enters and takes his seat. With no ceremony, he calls on the prosecutor. "Mr. Bingham, call your first witness."

The first witness introduces himself. "My name is Dennis Nelson and I am the desk clerk at the Mansion House." His booming voice indicates he is proud of his position.

District Attorney Bingham asks, "On the evening of June 7th, 1858, you had cause to send for the police. What made you call for them?"

"I was working the front desk. Mr. Mansfield Baucus came in and asked for his son's room number. I offered to send up a messenger but he insisted on going up himself."

"Did he give a reason for his visit?"

"None that he gave me."

"What happened when he went upstairs?"

"Well, a few minutes later I heard what sounded like three gun shots, then I heard a door slam and then what sounded like another gun shot."

"Did anyone else enter the hotel after Mansfield?"

"Not that I remember."

Beach, standing very tall, moves very close as he cross examines Nelson. Beach has learned to dominate the room by pulling his shoulders out. "You said you heard three shots, then a door slam?"

129

"Then another gun shot," Nelson injects.

"How long was it between the first gun shot and the last?"

"Not more than a minute or two."

"Which was it, a minute or two minutes?"

"I am not sure."

"Were the shots in rapid succession or were they about evenly spaced, or were there gaps between the shots?"

"The first three were pretty close together; there was a gap before the fourth."

"How long was the gap?"

"I'm not sure."

"But you are sure there was a gap?" Beach stresses the point.

"Not a long gap but there was some time in between."

"How long would you say it was between the first shot and when you went to investigate?"

"Not long at all. I mean, I passed Frank Baucus on the stairs."

"At the top of the stairs, the bottom of the stairs, where on the stairs?"

"It was at the bottom of the stairs."

"When you got to the room, was the door open or closed?"

"Open."

"You referred to the victim as Mansfield Baucus. Did you know him before the shooting?"

Nelson smiles for the first time. "Mr. Baucus had spent several afternoons in our hotel."

"Under what name did he register?"

"Oh, he never registered. He came to visit with one of our other guests."

"Who was that?"

Nelson looks at the judge, trying to avoid answering. The judge nods, indicating that he has to answer. "Mrs. Anna Lanagan."

"The wife of James Lanagan?"

"The same."

"The same James Lanagan who operates the resort on River Street?"

"The same."

"The same James Lanagan who was recently released from jail?"

"The same."

"No further questions." Beach closes and sits down.

Bingham has a question on re-direct. "Mr. Nelson, I believe you may have misspoken in your testimony; you said you heard three shots, a door slam, then another shot. Are you sure that is the order of the events?"

"You heard correctly."

"There is no way that you heard the door slam first or last?"

"Nope, you heard correctly." Nelson is getting nervous.

Beach rises to begin his re-cross as Bingham returns to his seat. "Was there anyone in the room when you got there?"

"No, I was the first to arrive."

"And you testified the door was open, is that not correct?"

"That is correct."

"No further questions." Beach returns to his seat and sits very tall.

Bingham calls his next witness, Deputy Sheriff Charles Burns. Known for being a joker on the stand, the courtroom is packed to hear Burns' testimony. The deputy takes his seat in the front of the court after the oath has been sworn. Bingham asks, "What did you see when you entered the room in the Mansion House?"

"There were three people in the room. I recognized dem all as employees of the hotel. And of course, Mansfield Baucus was lyin' on the rug; his knees was pulled up toward his chest like he was in pain."

"Was he in pain?"

"I felt for a pulse and there was none, so I figured his pain was pretty much over."

"Did you see a gun?"

"Not at first. But when I checked his coat pocket, I found a pistol."

"Was the pistol in his hand or in his coat?"

"Both." There is a snicker in the courtroom and Bingham stares at Burns. "He had the pistol in his hand but his hand was in his coat pocket."

Beach, on cross examination, pushes the point of the location of the gun. "So can you say for certain that he had not pulled out the gun and put it back in his pocket after he was shot?"

"That's a damn stupid idea. You mean he put the gun away as he was dying?" There is a chuckle in the room.

Beach acts out the actions as he asks the question, "Can you say for certain that he did not put the gun away, or even that it had been half drawn and, as he fell, he pushed his hand deeper into his pocket?"

"I never heard of no one who ever done that."

"But then you have never interviewed a dead man?" It is Beach's turn to get general laughter; when it calms down, Beach resumes, "or have you?" There is more general laughter. Burns has been outdone.

Beach is cross examining Dr. Bontecou, the county medical examiner. The doctor is answering a question regarding his experience.

"I have performed over one hundred post mortem examinations."

"What did you learn when you performed the one on Mansfield Baucus?"

"He was shot three times, although only one of the wounds would have probably proven fatal."

"And what made that shot critical?"

"It was the shot to the heart. Mansfield Baucus' death was almost instant."

"Was Mansfield shot in the front or in the back as was reported by several newspapers?"

Dr. Bontecou points to the locations on his own body as he indicates the location of the wounds. "Mr. Baucus had to be facing his assailant. One bullet entered his left leg, a second wedged against his right collar bone, then there was the shot through his chest that hit the heart. We also found what was left of a bullet in the wall of the room."

"What was the maximum distance between the wounds?"

"From the thigh to the collarbone is about 26 inches."

Beach treats the doctor as a professional. "Is it your expert opinion that only the shot to the chest would have proven fatal?"

"Yes."

"From your examination was there a difference in the distance between where the assailant stood and the victim?"

"There may have been. There was powder residue near the wounds to the collarbone and the thigh. There was no such stain in the area of the chest."

"What conclusions would you draw from that information?" Beach is on to some point he feels will help Frank.

"I would not draw any conclusions but it would suggest that the assailant was closer to Mansfield when two of the shots were fired than at the time of the fatal shot to the chest."

"Were the bullets from the same gun?"

"That is impossible to say. The bullets were of soft lead and had broken apart. I could not even testify with certainty the caliber of the gun."

Bingham examines Price, a second deputy. "As deputy sheriff, part of my beat is Federal Street in Troy. I was walkin' the beat when the defendant walked up to me, bold as could be, and handed me a pistol. He told me he had just shot his father."

"So you considered that a confession?" Bingham asks rhetorically.

"I sure enough did. He confessed mor'n once. Like I said, he did on the street and then when I got him back to the jail."

"What reason did Frank give for killing his father?

"He really didn't give none. He just said he shot his father."

On cross-examination Beach goes after Price. "He wasn't upset at all. He talked to me just like he had just done a public service and shot a rabid dog."

"Do many men, who recently shot someone, appear to 'not be upset?'"

"Nope. The three men I arrested before for murder had plenty to say."

"What about the others' emotions; were they angry?"

"Dey was all either mad as hell or scared near to death."

"So you would characterize Frank Baucus' behavior as unusual?"

"Unusual! Hell, it was nuts." There is universal laughter from the balcony.

"What type of gun was it that Frank handed to you?" Beach asks.

"It was a Colt Pocket Pistol."

"Excuse my lack of knowledge of handguns, but is that not what they call a six shooter?"

"Nope, a Pocket Pistol only holds five cartridges."

"Did you have a chance to examine the weapon?"

"Of course." He looks at Beach like he has a second head.

"How many unspent bullets were left in the chambers?"

"There was two."

"Mr. Price, just one more question; actually, it is more of a clarification." Beach has moved so that Price is looking directly at the jury. "The defendant said he shot his father, not that he killed his father; is that not correct?"

"Same thin'," Price looks at the jury.

"No Mr. Price, it is not; someone can be shot and not be killed," Beach says as he faces the jury, making sure they have heard his point. Bingham is becoming concerned about details.

On re-direct, Bingham asks Price, "Mr. Price, was the gun still warm when Frank Baucus handed it to you?"

"Oh yes, it was recently fired." Price feels relieved to be back on easy questions.

Price leaves the stand. Beach sits upright in the chair and has the expression that he has just trapped Bingham.

Mmes. Brewster, Jackson, and White are gathered in their usual chairs on the piazza. One chair is empty. Mrs. Stein exits the hotel on the arm of Reverend Beecher. Seeing the dowagers, she releases the Reverend's arm and goes over to the coven. "Good afternoon ladies, who are we crucifying today?" No one responds. "I see you are unable to speak when you owe someone a public apology." No one responds. "An empty chair, a great many of us in the hotel truly wish there were more." No one responds.

Reverend Beecher attempts to relieve the pressure. "Mrs. Stein, let us proceed."

"Well ladies, I am on my way for a private viewing of the new organ." She twists the screw tighter. "I am sure that each of you has already had your private viewing." Mrs. Stein returns to Mr. Beecher and they walk in the direction of the church.

"Ladies, we must address the problem caused by Mrs. Dillon's mistake. She placed us in a very bad light." Mrs. Brewster shows no blame for the situation.

"Indeed, indeed, I have never been so embarrassed." Mrs. White is clearly embarrassed.

"Now that surprises me." Mrs. Jackson is not letting anyone off the hook.

"Ladies! If we take Mrs. Dillon back into our confidence, who knows what other mistakes she may make." Mrs. Brewster is convinced she has deflected all fault.

"If we do not accept her, then we must remember that each of us is but one mistake away from absolute banishment." Mrs. Jackson smiles.

Mrs. White fans herself out of nervousness. "Banishment or embarrassment, oh my-my, I cannot decide."

Mrs. Brewster pushes Mrs. White, "You need not trouble your thoughts. It shall be banishment."

"Without a trial or appeal?" Mrs. Jackson fakes being appalled.

"This is not a court of law, this is an assembly based on trust - those we cannot trust cannot be part of the assembly," Mrs. Brewster declares.

"Will we have others join us now that we have been shown to cast unfounded disparagements on others?" The stress shows in Mrs. White's tense facial muscles.

Mrs. Jackson shows her cynical side. "That is exactly why others will want to join us."

The defense team, Beach, George, Smith, Frank, Amanda, and Judge Baucus, is planning during the court's dinner break. "I suggest we do not put on a defense. It is my belief that they failed to prove that Frank killed his father."

"Whatever do you mean?" Amanda is one decibel below a scream.

"Frank's gun had been fired three times. There were four shots fired in the room. Are they going to expect the jury to believe that Frank reloaded one bullet on his way to the police station?" Beach shows the principle point in his closing argument.

"You are willing to risk my son's life on the idea that the jury will believe that some unknown person came into the room and shot Mansfield after Frank left?"

"Any defense will mean that we will have to attack Mansfield's character." Beach argues.

"Mansfield must be shown for being what he was."

Beach turns to the last logical family member. "Judge, it is your son and your grandson, what do you feel?"

"My son was not a good man, my grandson is. If we do not put up a defense, people will always wonder. I agree we cannot put Frank on the stand but we can admit to the foibles of Mansfield."

Beach speaks to Frank, "It is your life. What do you want?

"I wanted him to leave my mother alone; I shot him. If I must pay for my actions, it is what the Lord wants."

In desperation Beach looks to George, "Let us hope that your witnesses stand up."

Bennett is sitting at a table with five other men playing blackjack. Scooping up his chips, having won, Bennett almost shouts out, "Hells bells dis is one hell of 'n evenin.' I's gunna take my winnin's and treat my niece to a bottle of the best champagne Mr. Marvin has."

The dealer looks to Richards to be sure he is not in trouble for losing the casino's money. "Congratulations, Sir; that is quite a haul you have there. Please come back another evening." Bennett stands and pulls the chips into his hat.

"I'll be back; yus can count on dat." Bennett leaves the table to cash in his chips.

Richards warns Morrissey, "It is the Toombs kid; he has lost all his winnings and the thousand that we allowed him in credit. He wants the house to lend him another thousand."

"I'll talk to him." Morrissey talks to two other patrons on his way to young Mr. Toombs who is with Hugh. "Mr. Toombs, I believe."

"Yes, yes," Toombs talks to Morrissey like he were a servant.

Morrissey asks, "How can I help you?"

"I would like to have my credit extended by a thousand dollars."

"I understand you already are indebted to the house more than the usual limit."

"That may be, however, I am a gentleman and my debts are always honored."

"Who honors your debts?" Morrissey asks.

"If I cannot do it myself, my father will cover the rest."

"Good, than have your father come in and I will extend him the credit."

"Mr. Morrissey, you insult me by not taking my word as a gentleman."

"You would be well advised to be very careful what words you use in my presence." Morrissey's look scares Hugh, who begins to pull gently on Toombs' arm.

Hugh whispers to his friend, "Let's just leave."

Hugh and Toombs walk a couple of steps away from Morrissey and then Toombs says, "Not until I win my money back."

Hugh tries to reason with him. "How? You don't have any money to bet with."

Toombs watches as Bennett counts his money. "We will," Toombs smiles, "in a few minutes."

Bennett puts the money in his jacket pockets and walks out the door. When Toombs and Hugh start to walk to the door their path is cut off by Richards. "Going someplace?"

Toombs responds, "Yes, to our hotel. Get out of our way." Richards just stares at Toombs. Exasperated, Toombs raises his voice, "I said get out of our way."

Morrissey comes up behind Toombs and Hugh. "I thought you were a gentleman. A gentleman would never raise his voice without a good reason."

"We are leaving but this lummox is blocking our way," Toombs shouts.

"Yes, you are leaving. Richards, would you be so kind as to see that these," Morrissey stresses the next word, "gentlemen make it safely to Division Street."

Toombs and Hugh are standing near the desk when Bennett enters the lobby. A big winner, Bennett brags to the night clerk. "Would you have the porter bring up a bottle of yus best chilled champagne?"

"That would be my pleasure," the clerk gives his assurances. "Your room number again?"

"I's in 384. Yus are gunna bring glasses?"

"Of course."

"Make it two glasses," Bennett insists as he heads for the stairs.

Toombs grabs Hugh. "Let's go for a stroll, it will be an hour before the old fool is asleep."

"Going to be just like when we were back in school?"

"Just like."

"They made it back to the hotel," Richards reports back to Morrissey.

"The man watching the faro table…" Richards looks to be sure he knows who Morrissey is watching. "I think that is the same suit that the watcher had on the other night."

Richards focuses on the non-descript man. "I think you may be right."

Morrissey shakes his head. "I don't like it."

"It may not be stylish but it is colorful," Richards jokes. Morrissey's expression indicates he is not kidding.

Jacob continues to tell George the story of the murder trial. *"So the trial in Vermont had been going on for an hour when the prosecution rested."*

Justice appealed to the judge's sense of fairness. "Your Honor, it is impossible for me to put on a legitimate defense. I have not been allowed to interview my client or compile a list of witnesses."

"That's true enough. But it don't make no never-mind cause the trial is gunna end tonight. Do you wants to put on a defense or not?"

"Not being familiar with the community, I cannot even draw upon character witnesses."

A huge man sitting in the crowd stands up saying, "Judge, if all he needs is a character witness, I's as familiar with the defendant as anyone I know'd."

Justice looked at the judge for direction. "Okays John, gets yus self up to the chair." The man who came forward was the biggest man in the room. "John, yus ain't gunna lie, is you?"

"No sir, I give dis court all the respect it deserves." There was a moment of laughter.

"Goes ahead, Mr. Justice."

Justice approached his witness with trepidation. "John, it is John, right?"

John shook his head, "That's what my momma told me."

"What is your last name John?"

"Why do yu need to knowd that? Everyone in the courtroom know'd who I am and I don't like you and don't want you to know my last name."

Justice looked at the judge for guidance - he got none. "Very well, John, what can you tell us about the defendant?"

"He came from a family of killers. Killin' was as natural to him as goin' to the bathroom in a chamberpot is to you or off the porch is to me and da boys in dis here room." The audience snickered.

Jacob leans back with his coffee. "The reports were that Justice's closing argument was a work of art. He allegedly quoted Shakespeare, Chaucer, Ben Franklin, and the Bible. When it was over, those in the audience gave Justice a standing ovation."

At the moment that the applause started to wane, a young boy came running in with a note he handed to the judge. "It seems that Taylor and Bob took it upon they's selves and hung the vermit; so's there' no need to make a ruling in the case." The crowd murmured its agreement with what happened.

Justice was in some ways relieved but worried, "What about my fee?"

"Oh yeah, the town pays a dollar a day for the attorney iff'n a resident can't pays dem selves. Now take away from that the four dollars yus owe for contempt of court and yus owe the town three dollars."

"You're saying that I have to pay the town for having come here against my will to represent a defendant I did not even meet?" Justice was truly perplexed.

The judge came up with a solution, "Tell's you what. You go up to Gallow Hills with John and bury the body and we call it even."

"It was all more than Justice could take. He only wanted to get out of that barn and out of that town for that matter, so he agreed to go with that huge witness, John, to give the body a decent burial. They took the buckboard up onto the mountain. When they came around the corner in the wagon they found a fox hanging from a tree branch. It had a sign hanging around its neck. The sign said 'God forgive me; I only did what came natural when I killed those four chickens.'"

Jacob laughs at himself. George smiles.

The dining room at the States is buzzing with whispered conversations, most about what is happening in the Baucus trial. It has kept the community so engaged, that the fact that two married women ran away with single men this week, normally the focus of summer breakfast, was virtually overlooked.

Mr. Strong and his daughter are sitting at the end of a long table. "Father, I never tire of hearing how you and mother met."

"That is because we never told you the truth. What you heard was a glorified version of a majestic couple." He coughs. "We were more normal. When your mother and I met, I was a teacher who had struggled for three years and was finally able to buy a farm. I thought that my future would lie in what I could raise on the land; as it turned out, it was on what I could raise from under the land."

"When you bought the first farm, you knew there was coal underneath?"

"No, but I suspected as much. 'Bout that time your mother had a small inheritance from her grandparents. I mean small." He coughs. "We could have used the money to build a better house or barn." He coughs. "It was about that time that I found a pocket of coal while digging the well. We talked it over and we agreed I would go to the tax auction and try to buy another farm just down the road."

The daughter is concerned and wants her father to stop talking. "You always did love her, did you not, father?"

It is a story he wants to tell. "Indeed I did. So many young people marry in the heat of passion or for some imagined fortunes, or out of desperation. Ours was a love born out of respect and hard work." Miss Strong listens to the real story, told for the first time. "That same year I did not plant crops, but used the growing season to open up a vein of coal. Your mom helped, she used to push the wheelbarrow out of the mine with you strapped to her back like an Indian baby." He coughs. "By the time you were three, we had twenty families working for us. By the time you went to Miss Willard's School, we were up to a hundred families and now there are close to a thousand."

"So mother helped?"

"From the beginning. She was always there for me. Never forget we started out poor and worked our way up." He coughs. "For you, it will be very different; you will start out rich and will probably end up very rich."

"Father, are you worried about Mr. Ellis being after my money?"

"Not as much as you."

"Father, what do you think of Mr. Ellis?"

"It really doesn't matter."

"I want to know."

"He is an honest man who dearly cares for you. You could do much worse, but not much better."

"So if he asks for your permission, you will say yes?"

Strong coughs. "I already did. It has been too long since I have seen you smile so much."

Marvin is talking to Morrissey while almost everyone in the park is reading the account of the trial in the newspaper. Bennett, pulling

Edith dressed in her night clothes, is looking for Marvin. "I was robbed. Last night someones gots into my room and stole over two thousand dollars."

Marvin simultaneously gets defensive and starts an investigation. "When did this happen?"

"Middle of da night; I'ad my winnings from Morrissey's place. I cums home an' orders a bottle of champagne fur Edith and me to celebrate. I falls asleep around about 2:00 and whens I's wakes up, duh money's gone."

"I will check with the porters and hall boys and see if anyone saw anything suspicious," Marvin assures his guest.

"I t'ought dis was suppose' to be a safe 'otel."

"It is a safe hotel and we have a safe in which to place your valuables. Give me a couple of hours to investigate."

"I's goin' to the police," Bennett grabs Edith's hand and charges back to the hotel.

Morrissey asks Marvin, "Do me a favor, ask the desk clerk when young Mr. Toombs came into the hotel."

"Do you know something?"

"If I knew, I would share it with you. I don't know, but I do have reason to suspect. You must understand that a robbery in your hotel makes you look bad; the robbery of one of my winners makes me look even worse."

The defense has started with Beach calling Jarred Porter. Jarred is a very large man. Those in attendance watch intently as he rises and takes his seat. "Mr. Porter, how did you know Mr. Mansfield Baucus?"

"I run the South End Tavern. For the last six months or so, Mansfield Baucus cames into my pub almost every Wednesday and Saturday night."

"How would you describe his behavior when he was in your establishment?"

"He'd come in, order a cup of the soup of the day and a draft; course, when's he were finished with 'em, he switch to bourbon for the rest of the evenin'."

"And how long did the rest of the evening last?"

"Depended. If'n he found the company of some of the boys to his likin,' he would be right pleasant, if'n he didn't, then he would get into some kind of argument and I would 'ave to ask him to leave."

"How often did you have to ask him to leave?"

"Every Wednesday and Saturday night." Porter leans back to

general laughter.

Bingham cross examines Porter. "Was Mansfield ever in a fight in your establishment?"

Porter gets serious. "No one's ever in a fight in my place. Now what happens when's they get outside; dat's another matter."

"Did you ever see Mansfield Baucus in a fight outside your establishment?"

"No, but I heard of two or three."

"I did not ask you if you heard of fights; that would be hearsay, I asked if you saw any fights."

Porter gets sarcastic. "Good sir, I am so sorry I missed your technical nuance." He leans back in the chair. "Nope, I never saw a fight, course there were those three different black eyes and the occasional fat lip that I did see. I guess they was caused by the soup of the day." The courtroom erupts in laughter.

Pauline, wearing a new dress and new shoes, keeps running her hands over the material of the skirt, which is the best she has ever worn. She is enjoying her time in the witness box. "Misser Mansfield done lik'e spendin' time with me. He treated me ever' sos kindlee."

"How did you and Mansfield Baucus spend your time?"

"Well, we're kin' of lik' onna date."

"So he took you to dinner and the theater?" Beach asks.

"No, whats we're doin' was mor lik' lat'r on in da date."

"So you had tea with crackers or cake?"

"No, lik's whens yus get 'ome, n' I never heerd it call'd cake. Yus a fancy un." There is a combination of laughter from the men and gasps from the ladies in attendance.

"Have you ever been arrested?"

Pauline is proud of herself. "Why Misser Beach, I've ne'er be'n arrested. Whatever woul' I have been arrest'd fer?"

"When you were with Mansfield, did he ever have a gun?" Beach inquired.

"He us'a gentleman and alwa's put 'isn gun on the dresser a'fore he tooks off 'is pants."

Bingham has his hands full on cross examination. "Miss St. Claire, were you paid for your testimony?"

"W'y no'ir."

"Are those not new clothes you are wearing?"

"Yesir, dey is."

"And who paid for those clothes?"

"Misser Beach."

Bingham makes the mistake of getting arrogant. "So you were not paid for your testimony. You just received a new dress and shoes."

"'nd new stock'ngs." Pauline pulls up her skirt past the ankle to show the stockings. The women in the room gasp so she pulls it up a couple of more inches.

"Misser Beach said I'd 'ave new clodes cause all my odder clodes 'ad holes and if'n I 'as sittin' in dis box yo might sees my legs through one of da holes. He said he did't want yus to get distracted. Dus yus want to get distracted, Misser Bing'm?

The courtroom erupts in laughter, even the judge smiles and a group of men in the balcony applaud. The judge turns and glares a warning to the group but they continue to clap.

That evening Richards walks out onto the porch of the casino, pulls a cigar from his pocket, and lights it from the flame of the gas light. He goes over to talk to Smiley. Smiley smiles as he sees Pauline in her new dress walking on the sidewalk across the street. She smiles and curtsies in his direction. At that moment Toombs and Hugh round the corner on their way to the casino.

"Hello little lady; my friend and I are going to the casino to win some serious money. Where you going to be about midnight?"

"Well sirs, it is a Thursday night so I can be any ol' place yus wans me to be."

"I do have a second requirement. If I do come around to see you later, do you promise to keep your mouth shut? You sound like a cow." Toombs takes Hugh's arm and leads him across the street to the porch.

Richards enquires, "Did you get some more money?"

"Not that it is of your concern big man, but I have over two thousand."

Toombs thunders past Richards into the casino. He stops at the cashier's window.

Richards follows Toombs and Hugh through the door and heads for Morrissey. "You were right; he just bought two thousand in chips."

"Before he sits down, bring him to my office. Bring along his little friend as well." Morrissey walks in the direction of his office.

Richards signals a man almost as big as himself and walks over to Toombs. He whispers to his charge, "Mr. Toombs, come with me."

"I will do no such thing!"

Richards grabs Toombs' arm so tight that he winces in pain. "I apologize; that was not a request." The second big man looks at Hugh, who instantly agrees to go along without being touched. The group enters Morrissey's office.

Morrissey is leaning against his roll-top desk smoking a cigar. With his hand, he gestures for Toombs and Hugh to sit down. They take seats in two hard juror chairs. "I will ask you exactly one time. Where did you get the money?"

"My father gave it to me so that I could win back the money that I lost the other night." Morrissey looks at Richards, who grabs Toombs' left arm and holds it to the arm of the chair. Morrissey hands the cigar to Richards, who places the flame end of the cigar against the back of Toombs' hand. Toombs starts to scream, but the sound is instantly cut off by Morrissey's hand covering his mouth.

Morrissey turns his attention to Hugh. "Your name is Hugh, I believe." Hugh nods, unable to speak. "Where did you get the money?"

"We borrowed it from an old man who won last evening."

"Now we are getting somewhere." Morrissey releases his grip from Toombs' mouth. "Mr. Toombs, I will take it upon myself to return the money on your behalf. I believe two hundred is missing but I will make that up. You, however, will be on the midnight train to Montreal. An associate of mine will wire me when you arrive." Morrissey watches Toombs' face to be sure he is listening, "and you will not ever be back in Saratoga."

Morrissey looks to Hugh. "You will leave tomorrow for wherever you would like to go. Tonight your friend wants to travel alone." Morrissey walks out of the office and into the casino. Richards offers Toombs a handkerchief to cover his wound. The front of Hugh's pants is soaked.

Morrissey walks up to Marvin and hands him an envelope. "You can call off your investigation. I located Mr. Bennett's money." Marvin just looks at the envelope. "There is no need to notify the police, the matter has been resolved."

"You know who took it?"

"As do you." At that moment Toombs enters the lobby from the park carrying a carpet bag. His hand is wrapped in a handkerchief. He walks across the lobby and out the door to the street. "I forgot to mention, there will be one less for breakfast."

"Do you want credit?"

"No need." Morrissey leaves for his casino.

Beach, George, Smith, Frank, Amanda, and Judge Baucus are gathered in the conference room discussing last minute strategy. "I think

143

we made our point yesterday; to go further means that members of the family will have to testify."

"I am willing to testify," Amanda persists.

"To what?" Beach does not see any merit to her taking the stand.

"To the way Mansfield treated me and the threats he made."

"That might explain why you shot him; what does that have to do with Frank?"

"There are the letters where he threatened Frank and little Tracy." Mansfield Jr. goes by his middle name, Tracy.

"Those are reasons to call the police, not to shoot someone."

Judge Baucus speaks in a calm controlled voice. "I could testify to Mansfield's nature." Everyone in the room is suddenly uncomfortable.

"Judge, are you sure you want to do that?" Beach asks.

"I do not wish to do it; however, for the sake of justice I will."

"Frank, how do you feel?"

"I love and trust my grandfather. No one could do better."

Judge Baucus is on the stand. The courtroom is silent. "From the time he was a boy, Mansfield was difficult. He resented his brother and most of his sisters." The Judge reflects, "I think he resented me the most."

"Was he ever violent?" It is the most caring voice Beach ever used in the courtroom.

"Yes. He had to go to three different boarding schools because he was constantly in fights."

"And as a man?"

"He was never a man. He always wanted to be a man, but he never made it." The courtroom remains silent; the Judge bends over, talking to the rail in front of his chair. "To be a man means to take responsibility. Mansfield did not show restraint; perhaps he could not. He was searching for something, but not knowing what it was, he was never able to find it."

"You have heard other witnesses describe Mansfield using some unpleasant terms. As his father, is there anything you would disagree with?"

"No. He was a man of bad habits."

"One more question." Beach hesitates for impact, "Did Mansfield ever carry a gun?"

"Always."

"No further questions."

It is obvious that Bingham is uncomfortable with Judge Baucus as a witness. The presiding judge asks if Bingham has any questions.

Bingham shakes his head no, whispering, "No questions."

Judge Baucus does not move. His hands are clasped on the rail in front of his chest as if he is in prayer. The presiding judge orders, "Then we will adjourn for the day; closing arguments will be tomorrow. I have an engagement in the morning; court begins at 1:00."

The overseer is looking off in the general direction of the river. His son comes up on a horse and leads a second horse. The owner of hounds has the pack of four on leashes. "With the kids and the ol' lady, they can't have gotten far," the overseer says. The hounds' owner releases them. They take off following the fake trail.

The dogs follow the trail to the bank of the river and then run back and forth, howling. The overseer and the dogs' owner put a leash back on the hounds. Talking to his son, the overseer looks at two skid marks in the mud. "They had a raft all made. You get back to the house and grab my shotgun. I'll ride to Murfreesboro to get a posse. Dem ol' boys will cost me a roast pig and a keg of beer." He shakes his head in anger. "Dat Nate gunna pay dearly for dis." The boy rides off in the direction of the plantation, while the owner and the dogs go in another direction. In the water there is a log stuck against a downed tree. If they had turned it over, they would have seen it was used to make the marks in the mud.

Mmes. Brewster, White, Jefferson, and Jackson are along the perimeter. Across Congress Pavilion from them are Miss Place, Miss Strong (standing very tall), Mrs. Brown, and Miss Lee. Jacob is standing with Catharine and the two Stiles girls. As usual, Walter is over in the area where the servants gather. Pauline and Antoinette are standing behind the servants. Everyone is buzzing about the trial.

Mr. Cook, Van Buren, Judge Baucus, Beach, and George walk in as a group. They approach Madam Jumel, who is standing by the rail to the spring. They smile and shake her hand.

"Well, do't dat jus' beat all. Dey walk in jus' like dey own da place," Pauline remarks.

"Dey probably do. Aldough I 'ave been told dat a Mr. White owns da springs," Antoinette informs her sister.

"I thin' I'll goes over tu say hello to dat Mr. Beach and his handsum young par'ner, Mr. Batchelle," Pauline threatens.

"Yus be was'n yus time. I heared dat Mr. Batcheller 'as his eyes set on dat Miss Cathar'ine Cook. Yus know'd da one who's comes dun here ever' day by herself," Antoinette tells her sister.

"Well den, I'ss jus' go an say hello to dat Mr. Beach," Pauline says as she walks over toward the group of men.

Seeing her coming, Beach excuses himself and walks over to her. "Miss Pauline, I would like to thank you for your testimony. You did very well."

"I's on mys way to say tank yus for the fine dres yus bought for me. Ifn yus ever needs anoder favor, yus jus comes on by, I'll give's yus a fine even'n," Pauline promises.

Madam Jumel separates from her group, intent on saving Beach from Pauline. With the practiced skill that only someone who has walked on both sides of the street can muster, she gives Pauline a polite smile with a look that says never come near this man again. Madam Jumel addresses Beach, "William, please escort me back to my carriage, I need to discuss a matter with you." Madam Jumel and Beach walk politely away. A dejected Pauline returns to Antoinette.

Marvin enters, making a rare appearance at the spring. "However the jury finds, it will be an interesting day in the history of the village."

Cook concurs, "Regrettably, I would agree with you. It is too bad that we find our momentous days are somehow linked to a tragedy, rather than a celebration."

"The biggest incident of my career was one of the smallest events in my life," Van Buren assures the group. "None of you were here when Mrs. Clinton turned her back on me at the States Hotel." The former President remembers one of the more embarrassing moments in the village's history when the wife of the Governor turned her back on the President.

"My uncle owned the hotel at the time and I was a messenger. I remember it well." Marvin politely changes the topic. "I hope I am correct when I say my biggest day has yet to arrive."

Although an older widower, Cook agrees, "We all hold that aspiration for you and even for ourselves." Cook walks away from the others to join George. "Mr. Batcheller, when do you expect a verdict?"

"Closing arguments are this afternoon; Mr. Beach believes that the verdict will be in late in the evening, maybe even early in the morning."

"That being the case, might I invite you to dinner on Saturday so that I can get your perspective on the trial?"

"It would be my honor."

"Shall we say 8:00?"

"I look forward to it."

"My daughter will be joining us." Cook rejoins Marvin, Van Buren, and Beach.

Mary has spent the morning walking around the spring area. She notes that once again Jacob is with Sarah.

Like most of those gathered, the discussion is focused on the trial. Jacob asks Sarah, "So from what you have heard, how will the jury find?"

"I do not know. In Savannah he would be found guilty, but here I am not so sure."

"Why would he be found guilty in Savannah?"

"Because his father never drew the gun. His actions would be considered cowardly, unmanly, as if he broke some code of chivalry."

"Why do you think the answer might be different here?"

"Because your men are not attached to some antiquated code of honor; you do not have duels, you are not even taught to fence."

"Nor do you have slavery." Sadie joins in.

"You oppose slavery?" Walter overheard Sadie's comment.

"If I were to inherit my father's estate, the first thing I would do is free all the slaves." She takes a breath, "Then I would hire a boat to give them passage back to Africa."

"Sadie, watch what you say," her sister corrects her. "There are always ears about."

"Let them listen. It is not like I want to date or think blacks are equal to us, I just think they should be free to come and go. They need to return to Africa because those in the south, especially the poor whites, hate free blacks.

"What made you come to these beliefs?" Walter is intrigued.

"It was not our slaves; no, father and mother treat them well. Our slaves dress better than the free whites who work in the docks. It is the dreadful stories I hear about how they are treated in Charleston or on the plantations that I find wicked."

"Do your parents know how you feel?"

"They would never believe it, even though Benjamin is a free man and works alongside the household slaves. The strange part is that because he is free, he is not allowed to sleep in the house and has to provide his own home. I have seen where he lives; he would have a much nicer home and actually live better if he were still our slave," Sadie explains.

"But he would not stand as tall," Walter noted, walking off.

Mrs. Brewster acts like the incident with Mrs. Stein never happened. "They will convict him for sure. Just you wait to see the Baucus family hide after everyone knows the eldest son will hang."

"The Baltimore papers did not cover the trial that closely, but from what I understand, they have no choice except to convict," Mrs. White adds. "I mean did he not confess?"

"There will be a conviction for sure." Mrs. Smith tries to fit in.

"So Mrs. Dillon has chosen to leave the hotel?" Mrs. Jackson stares at Mrs. Brewster.

"So I have been told." Mrs. Brewster is standing erect.

Mrs. White worries, "Where will she be staying?"

"Some place in Sharon Springs, or so I have been told," Mrs. Brewster gloats.

Mrs. Jackson speaks quietly to Mrs. White. "That is what banishment looks like."

Across the springs, the former dowagers have gathered. Miss Lee wants to take the high road. "We should make it a practice to not speak evil of others. I suggest we start by not talking any further about this terrible trial."

"That will make us unique; I truly believe that that is exactly what everyone else is talking about." Miss Strong worries less about what they talk about than how they act toward others.

Miss Place demonstrates her sensual side. "Then we must agree to talk about the absolutely delicious men. Who is that man in the gray hat?"

Another new member, Miss Houghton, answers, "I believe he is Mr. Meyers of Biloxi. If I am correct, his father is one of the largest slave traders in all of Mississippi."

Walter and Jacob have been watching all the mini drama at the springs. Jacob asks, "Walter, how much space is the newspaper saving for the story?"

"The entire front page; innocent or guilty, we have the story written both ways."

"Have you heard of Miss Sadie's mysterious poet?" Jacob appears wise as to the identity of the poet.

Walter blushes, "I have heard mentioned that someone is sending her notes, then he gave her flowers in the street. I was going to write it up as a story."

"So you subscribe to the belief that one of the college boys wrote the poems?"

"Who else could it be?"

"Yes, who else," Jacob smiles.

The grounds of the park are crowded with people listening to a pianist as Marvin walks up to Bennett. "I have something for you." Marvin hands Bennett the envelope; Bennett looks inquiringly. "Mr. Morrissey took it upon himself to investigate who robbed you," Marvin explains.

"Who was it?"

"He did not tell me the reprobate's name, but he was able to return your money. He also made arrangements for the person to leave the village."

"Whats 'bout the police?"

"That is up to you."

"I'll go tuh Morrissey's t'night to express my t'anks in person."

"I am sure you will."

During closing arguments, Beach is animated as he walks back and forth before the jury. "The prosecution should never have brought this case forward. They totally ignored major points. First, the gun held five shots. Four shots were fired in the room. When Officer Price received the gun from Frank there were still two un-fired cartridges. Are they going to expect you to sit in the jury room and believe the defendant reloaded it on the way to the jail?"

Beach takes a long pause before changing points. "Second, Mr. Nelson, the clerk in the hotel said, and I quote from the record," Beach picks up a copy of the transcript, "'I heard three shots, a door close, and another shot.' If Frank had fired the four shots, he would have shut the door either before he fired or after he left, not halfway through the shooting."

Fully aware how to use drama, Beach takes a long pause before changing points. "Third, keep in mind that Mr. Nelson explained that Mansfield was a regular guest of Mrs. Lanagan, the same Mrs. Lanagan who is married to James Lanagan, who you will remember just returned home from on holiday paid for by the good people of Troy." There is general laughter in the audience.

"Fourth, I would point out to you that Frank never said he killed his father. He said 'I shot my father.' Could that explain the bullets to the collarbone and the one to the leg? And even the one in the wall?"

Again Beach takes a long pause before changing points. "I could spend a lot of time talking the particulars of Mansfield's behavior, but you all heard it already and with the delicate ears of the ladies present, I do not wish to return to specifics. It is painful enough that his poor father, Judge Baucus, one of the most respected men in the State, had to come and testify in open court to the nature of his son's character."

Beach makes a critical point of the defense's role, "Now the prosecution will tell you that the defense did not prove that Mr. Lanagan or anyone else was in the hotel and pulled the trigger or even tried to explain the missing shot. That is not the role of the defense. It is only the role to raise reasonable doubt, to show that the prosecution took the easy route in their investigation. In the case before you today, the doubt is far beyond reasonable."

While Beach paced during his closing argument, Bingham is professorial delivering his closing at a podium. "My learned adversary, Mr. Beach, has raised some interesting questions in his closing argument but he did not put anyone on the stand to prove his conjectures and that is exactly what he offered, conjectures. He wants you to ignore Frank Baucus' own words that he shot his father. That when he handed over the gun to the arresting officer, it was still hot."

Bingham mimics Beach and takes a long pause. "There are few things in the world more unfortunate than a husband who shoots his wife, or a son who shoots his father, but it does happen and when it happens, the law calls for the offender, in the case of murder, to be hung."

Judge Harris is very practiced in charging a jury. His style is almost ministerial. "You have heard a well presented case. Both the people and the defendant were well represented. The case is now in your hands. You are to go to the jury room and, based on the evidence you heard in this courtroom, find the defendant innocent or guilty."

At eight that evening the court house bell begins to ring. The streets are instantly filled with people who want to be present when the verdict is read.

The audience is noisy as the last juror settles in and the bailiff calls the court to session, "All rise." Judge Harris enters and takes his seat behind the bench.

Judge Harris bangs his gavel, trying to bring silence. "There will be order or I will instruct the bailiffs to clear the courtroom." It takes time for the crowd to go silent. When there is order the judge asks the foreman, "Has the jury reached a verdict?"

The foreman is not used to speaking in public. He tries to speak in a voice loud enough for all to hear, "We have."

Judge Harris asks the jurors, "Do all of you agree on the verdict?" There is general nodding of heads by the jurors.

The foreman is unsure if he is supposed to answer. Finally he adds, "Yes."

"How do you find the accused?"

One reporter in the stands asks a second reporter, "Will justice be served or will politics prevail?"

SCENE AT SARATOGA.

Harper's Weekly 20 August 1859
Courtesy Saratoga Springs Public Library

Decisions

The slave family finds itself spending the night in a damp musty cellar with walls and floor made of cold stones. The children are sharing a rope bed with Nanny. Nate and Mattie are on a mattress spread on the floor. The lone candle is almost burnt out. Nate attempts to calm Mattie. "We needs to get some sleep. We's gotta wake up 'bout an hour before sunrise. Minister says that he knows of a boat owner that will take us all the way up to the Susquehanna River."

"I can't swim an' I don't like boats." Mattie refuses to be calmed.

"It'll be all right." Nate gives Mattie a gentle hug. "It'll be all right."

The courtroom is filled beyond capacity. Beach, Frank, Smith, and George are seated. Amanda, Uncle Charles, and Judge Baucus are seated directly behind when the judge asks, "On the charge of murder in the first degree, how do you find the accused?"

The foreman answers in a loud clear voice, "Guilty."

The room erupts in a combination of cheers, tears, and threats. Amanda hugs Frank whispering, "This is not over." She scowls as she shakes hands with Smith and George. She deliberately ignores Beach's hand. Judge Baucus sits quietly.

"Justice has not been served," declares Amanda several times as she turns and storms out of the courtroom.

The bailiffs shackle Frank, then lead him shuffling out of the room.

Beach packs up his leather case. Looking at George he asks, "Or has it?"

Before leaving the room, Judge Baucus looks at Beach, "Amanda is Amanda, let her go her way. You must begin the appeal process." He

153

continues almost to himself, "I will use whatever influence I have to see that Frank is safe." The Judge shakes George's hand, "You did a fine job finding witnesses. Now you and my grandson are leaving the harbor called home on very separate voyages."

With the ruling in the Baucus case less than twelve hours old, there is a crowd at the springs. Those who are the most prominent are closest to the spring, with the servants around the perimeter. Mmes. Brewster, Jackson, White, and the newest member, Mrs. Dallas, are near the path to the hotels.

Always willing to preach, Mrs. Brewster lets her feelings be known. "Through his one foolish act, he has destroyed his entire family's reputation. A thing like that would never happen in North Carolina."

"Nor Baltimore," assures Mrs. White.

"Mrs. Dallas?" Mrs. Brewster is testing the initiate.

"There must have been something more than in the newspapers. I was not expecting this outcome." Mrs. Dallas hedges on her opinion.

"What were you expecting - a son admits killing his father - what more is there to know?" Mrs. Brewster appears to be questioning her decision to allow Mrs. Dallas to join the coven.

George walks up to the horde. To everyone's surprise, he is smiling, "Good morning ladies, I must correct you ever so slightly; he never admitted killing his father, he only admitted shooting his father. There was a shot unaccounted for." Having publicly challenged the coven, George leaves to join Catharine.

She has walked to the springs with her father but stands alone. George is in a better mood than she expected. "Catharine, your father invited me to your house for dinner this evening. I look forward to a lively discussion of the trial."

"Father was much impressed with the reports of Mr. Beach's performance. I am sure he will be filled with questions."

"Hopefully, I will be able to answer most."

"It is too bad father chose a Saturday night as it will interfere with your ability to go to the ball."

"That is why I came over. Would you mind if I asked your father for his permission for you to accompany me to the ball after our dinner this evening?"

"Father will say the choice is mine. Because you have been occupied, I will accept your invitation on such short notice this one time. In the future you will provide me with suitable time to prepare."

"It would have been proper this time, were I assured that I would be back in the village for the evening. Excuse me while I talk to your father." George takes the short walk to Mr. Cook.

At the entrance to Congress Park, Amanda, wearing black, Clara, and the Baucus children are at the top of the stairs entering together. Amanda is walking with her head held arrogantly high, the rest seem humble.

Mrs. White fires the first verbal volley, "If one did not know better, one would think it to be the procession of the winners instead of the parade of the defeated."

"She hardly appears vanquished or even sorry. My goodness, the Judge is not with them. A man of stature in North Carolina would never be seen out for a year after the murder of his son." Mrs. Brewster smiles to herself. "Perhaps there is some culture in Saratoga after all." She is referring to Judge Baucus excusing himself.

"In Boston, they may have been out, but they would have stayed on the sidelines," Mrs. Dallas comments.

Mrs. White makes it personal, "Did you hear? Miss Strong has been asked to the ball by Mr. Ellis."

"Why ever should I care?" snarls Mrs. Brewster.

Jacob asks Sarah, "What color dress will you be wearing this evening?"

"I think I will be wearing light blue. Why do you ask?"

"With your permission, I will have a wrist corsage sent to your cottage."

"Tell the florist blue and white flowers with a white ribbon."

Sadie has been concerned about Todd. She finally finds him eating an apple near a horse and buggy. She scolds her brother, "Todd, you must stay closer to the springs or I will tell mother that you are wandering again."

"I don't want to waste my time at the smelly old spring; there are so many beautiful horses to see."

Sadie places her hand protectively on her brother. "It is the culture of the springs that matters, not the water."

"To you and Sarah, not to me," Todd gives the grateful horse the core of the apple.

In the lobby, Marvin is talking to one of the clerks when Thomas approaches. "It's official; I leave Thursday for New York City. I will depart for Europe on Sunday."

"We will miss you. What members of the family are joining you?"

"None. The family will be staying on. For this excursion it will just be me; I am not even taking Benjamin."

"How long will you be in Europe?"

"I am uncertain. Father is interested in investing in a textile factory in Manchester."

"Not Massachusetts?"

"Father feels the United States ends at the Mason-Dixon Line, but somehow extends via the Gulf Stream to England." He smiles, repeating a well-used expression.

"We all have interesting perceptions."

"Father would not want me to return until the hurricane season is over, so I would guess I will be in Savannah in November."

Frank is sitting on his cot in the jail trying his best to ignore the constant jabber of the other inmates. "So all your fancy connections didn't do you one drop of good," one inmate yells.

"Of course they did, all he got was life in prison, if'n it had been one of us it would've been a hangin' from a short rope," corrects a second inmate.

"You know after five, six years in prison yus gonna wish they hung yus," the first inmate counters.

"Old Frank hanging from the end of a rope, his legs dancing to a rhythm that his mind made up. Now that would be some sight," the second says through his coarse laugh.

"You ever see a man hang?" the first inmate yells.

"Go easy on him boys, I don't thin' we heard the end of his fate jus' yet," says a calmer more resourceful prisoner.

Frank sits with his back against the wall as the inmate in the adjacent cell's hand comes around the wall and places a Bible on the floor of Frank's cell.

Benjamin has carried Thomas' trunks down from the upper floor with the anticipation of getting them packed today. "Will you want both trunks in your cabin or will one be placed in storage?"

"The cabins are so small. Pack ten days' worth of clothes in one trunk and the rest of my clothes in the second trunk. Do not bother with formal evening wear for the cabin."

"I would enjoy going wid yuh sir."

"I would appreciate your services also Benjamin; however, this is one trip I have to make alone." Benjamin begins packing some of the clothes in a trunk that has built in shelves and drawers. "You may take the time I am gone to work for someone else. Any money you make you can keep for yourself."

"How can I work for someone else and still keep an eye on Mr. Todd?"

"Todd is very independent, as long as he is in one of the parks, he really does not need anyone to watch him."

"Then I will ask Mr. Vanderbilt if I can help with his fine horses."

Thomas smiles knowingly, "That is an excellent idea. Just avoid the Vanderbilt women, their men are exceedingly jealous." Benjamin continues packing as if he missed the comment.

In the parlor of the Baucus manor, Madam Jumel and the Judge are having tea together. The Judge confesses, "To have to speak in public about things you do not want to admit to yourself is more painful than I would have imagined."

"Mansfield's behavior was no reflection on you and in no way tarnished your reputation."

"But it was. Even as adults, our children reflect the values they were taught."

Having no children of her own, Madam Jumel remains quiet, relieving the tension by patting the Judge's hand.

"No dear Judge, children reflect what they have learned, not what they were taught - teaching and learning are two very different phenomena."

"Then how do I explain why Mansfield turned out as he did?"

"Judge, you cast a huge shadow, one too big for Mansfield to ever fill. He knew that and decided to live in darkness and not to cast a shadow."

"Then in some way I drove my son away?"

"No, he ran away of his own volition."

Amanda enters the parlor without knocking. "Judge, I have just received a telegram from the Governor's secretary; he has agreed to meet with me this evening. I plan to begin a discussion for a pardon for Frank. I will be leaving for Albany on the 3:00 train. You and Mrs. Smith can tend to the children." She turns and shuts the door before the Judge can answer.

"I live from crisis to crisis. What happened to a genteel retirement?"

"You are too dynamic to ever consider retirement. Do you need company when you go to visit Frank?"

"Thank you, but I can manage on my own. I suspect that prison is not a place where Frank will do well."

Madam Jumel stops patting the Judge's hand and gives it a gentle squeeze.

Cora and Thomas are sitting across from each other in the parlor of their cottage. The tension is so heavy it fills the room. "So when were you planning to tell me that the trip was official."

"I only just learned that father had the trip planned this morning."

"Yet you are to be in the city by Thursday?"

"Father is an impatient man. When he makes up his mind, nothing slows him down."

"So I am supposed to be responsible for the children for the rest of the summer?"

"Sadie and Sarah are among friends; Todd plays well alone. Besides, Benjamin can help with Todd."

"So you are not taking Benjamin?"

"No. I will be fending for myself."

Cora asks frigidly, "Are you taking anyone else I should know about?" Thomas adjust his cuffs but does not look at her.

Cook and George are having coffee at the table in the Cook's dining room. Having cleared the table, the butler stands near the sideboard. The pile of dishes shows that a third setting has been used. "So you feel there will be an appeal?" Cook wants reassurance that his assumption is correct.

"I am to begin drawing up the paperwork on Monday."

"Your personal feelings?"

"Clearly there was reasonable doubt. Frank fired three shots, but there were four bullet holes. Mansfield was shot three times and there was the hole in the wall. There was also the sequence of events: three shots, door slams, and then a shot." He pauses, gaining the confidence to add, "I am quite certain that if the trial had been in Saratoga County, the verdict would not have been the same."

"Interesting perspective. According to the newspapers, when the clerk got to the room, the door was open. Perhaps the door that he heard slammed was to another room?" George and Cook stand as Catharine walks in carrying a boutonniere. She is dressed for the ball.

"Interesting indeed." George is not referring to the case.

Both men remain standing. Catharine begins pinning the boutonniere on George's lapel. "Mr. Batcheller, that will be enough talk of Saratoga's biggest scandal. Tonight you give me your undivided attention."

"It would be my pleasure."

In Saratoga during the season there were hops almost every night with several balls each season and a Grand Ball that brought the season to a close. Guests dressed better for the balls than the hops, making them the most important places to be seen. Women and men had dance cards with the type of dance listed next to the number. A gentleman would ask a lady to dance, she would agree and both would list the other's name next to the number of the dance. This practice is where terms such as 'her dance card was full,' meaning the lady was very popular, 'save me a dance,' and 'wall flower' originated.

If one did not have a partner in advance, it did not necessarily mean he or she would not dance, as uncommitted people could be asked at the beginning of a dance.

Throughout the evening, elegantly dressed men and women walk back and forth between the ballroom and parlors. If one did not want it known that he or she did not have a partner, the gender specific parlors offered a place to gather out of sight.

Period dance music can be heard in the background at the second ball of the season at the States. Jacob, dressed elegantly, and Walter, in a suit that is too big, are standing at the punch table awaiting Sadie and Sarah. "So as the society reporter, you get to attend all the dances for free." Jacob takes a shot.

"And as nephew of the proprietor, you pay the same price." Walter returns volley for volley.

"Shall we call a truce, at least for the evening?" Jacob offers.

"That seems mutually unfair."

"Who do you believe is Sadie's poet?" Jacob ponders.

"You know I was thinking of putting that to the readers in Monday's column."

"I suggest you do not use her name."

"I never use the person's name. My columns refer to the people by a pseudonym."

"You do know Sadie will see through any mask you give it," Jacob advises.

"It is not her that I am concerned about."

"Then whom?" Jacob wonders.

"The poet, he remains anonymous for a reason."

"Then he is foolish; he has captivated her by his intrigue. It is time to announce his intention and reap the benefit of his skills."

At that moment Sadie, Sarah, and one of the college boys, Ralph Vincent, comes through the doorway from the ballroom and walk up to Jacob and Walter. Sadie is excited, "Walter, Sarah and I want you to meet

Mr. Ralph Vincent, of Buffalo. He just confessed to being my poet."

Sarah has a flirtatious snicker, "Come little sister, let us freshen up." Sarah hooks Sadie's arm and they go through the door to the ladies' parlor.

Walter asks, "So when did you become her poet?"

"About 10 minutes ago. Before that I was an engineer for a young lady from Cincinnati and before that a member to the rowing team for a young lady from Buffalo," Ralph brags.

Jacob responds, "Looking to add to your dance card?"

"No, trading up, the last one's father had grain elevators. This one's father has a plantation."

The ladies' parlor is crowded with elegantly dressed women of all ages. The only women who have seats have been in the parlor for some time. Sadie and Sarah are checking their appearance in one of the mirrors. While checking her hair, Sarah asks, "So little sister, how do you feel now that you have discovered your poet?"

"Ralph is not my poet. He is a pretender in the first right." Sadie continues to freshen her makeup. "However, I do believe I am on to my poet."

"What are you up to?"

"Discovery. My dear sister, discovery." Sadie stands up and waits for her sister.

The Stiles sisters finally get back to the cottage at 3:30 in the morning. Not wanting to have Josey or Missy pry into their evening, they help each other out of the dresses and corsets. They turn away from each other as they take off their chemise and bloomers and put on their sleeping gowns. It is only then that Sadie notices that Sarah forgot to pull the shade down in her window.

Jacob enjoys the prearranged view from a bench in the park.

The morning after the second ball, the crowd at the springs is very light, a point Mrs. Brewster cannot help but note. "It will be this quiet all morning. It has been after each of the balls this season. The young people today sleep their lives away."

"The ball did go until after 3:00 am," notes Mrs. Dallas. "Had I stayed to the end, I would probably still be asleep."

"Missing mornings at the spring are one thing, but I assure you they will miss church again," Mrs. Brewster preaches.

"Things will get very interesting starting soon; there is a rumor about that Mr. Stiles is leaving for Europe this very week. That means

160

that the Stiles daughters will be without a father's protection," reports Mrs. White.

Although relatively new to the coven, Mrs. Dallas has learned who is fair game. "It should be quite the summer watching Mrs. Stiles manage those two girls all by herself."

The ever judgmental Mrs. Brewster has more porridge to add to the pot. "It also means that Mrs. Cora Stiles will be on her own. Now I think that will be even more interesting than what happens to her daughters." She purses her lips. "I saw her dance three dances again last evening with Mr. Marvin."

"I certainly hope that before disparagements are bantered about that everyone checks their sources and their own history. As for Mrs. Stiles, she will do fine. Attractive children are easier to manage than those who are plain. They have more options," Mrs. Jackson advocates.

"I disagree, I think she will have a handful with Jacob and that so called reporter Walter," Mrs. Brewster holds.

"Sometimes I wish I still had a husband to send off on a journey. Then I remember how mine behaved around other women and am glad to be alone," reminisces a sad Mrs. Dallas. At that moment Mrs. White and a new member, Mrs. Davis, enter from the street; they are both out of breath.

Mrs. White is out of breath from hustling to the springs. "You are not going to believe what we just learned. Oh excuse me, this is Mrs. Davis, a friend of mine from Pittsburgh." She tries to correct her oversight. Unable to catch her breath, she gives up. "Oh you tell them."

"Two couples from the Constitution Hotel eloped last night. Two in one night!" Mrs. Davis reports. At the time, eloping meant only to run away together. Couples could elope without getting married.

"The Constitution has always had a dubious reputation. When those at the front desk cannot see the stairs, anyone can slip into any room," Mrs. Brewster explains.

"Oh when did you stay at the Constitution?" slams Mrs. Jackson.

"Well I never," Mrs. Brewster defends herself.

"Then how did you know that the stairs are not visible from the desk?" Mrs. Jackson presses the point. A pall hangs over the two.

Mrs. Davis tells of her source, "Two of the ladies staying at the Constitution went to Lake George for the day. When they came in on the southbound train they saw one Miss Violette Woods, or at least that is what she called herself. She and a Mr. Dunkin were taking off on the 7:00 train." Mrs. Davis has no trouble gloating, "Apparently when she and Mr. Albert Woods took a two bedroom suite everyone believed they really were uncle and niece, she being only about sixteen and Mr. Woods, the poor gentleman, being nearly sixty. The two were seen in the parks and even at the springs. She held his arm like a niece."

Mrs. Davis relishes the attention she is receiving. "Well, at the hop last weekend Miss Woods danced three dances with young Mr. Dunkin. He was doing everything for her, fetching punch, saving her seat. Now everyone was concerned about the breaking of the three dance rule but you must understand, Mr. Dunkin is hardly pleasant on the eye, and she being so beautiful, no one suspected much." Mrs. Davis takes a breath. "Apparently during the day, they snuck her trunks out of her room and down the hall to Mr. Dunkin's room. Well, this morning the porter at the hotel told me that Mr. Wood realized that his diamond shirt studs, gold cuff-links, and all his cash were missing."

Having learned from Mrs. Dillon's mistake, Mrs. Davis hedges her conclusion, "Now I'm not saying Miss Woods, or whatever her name is by now, took them. I'm just saying it was an interesting coincidence."

The dowagers all look totally concerned and offended by such going ons. Mrs. White raises the question they all wanted to know, "You said there were two, do tell us about the other one."

Mrs. Davis looks at Mrs. Brewster, "Are you sure your heart can take more news?"

"Pay her no mind, she needs bad news to survive," Mrs. Jackson says snidely.

"Well if you are sure." Mrs. Davis is anxious to begin. The dowagers all nod assurances. "The second lady was Mrs. Lewis. She engaged rooms for the season. You may have seen her down at the springs. She had a little boy about five and a girl about three. The children always wore light colors which matched their flaxen hair. She appeared to be a good mother, from a good family. Mr. Lewis is an attorney in the City and has spent three weekends and one week here so far this summer. Last weekend, a man, who we were led to believe was Mr. Lewis' brother, showed up."

Mrs. Davis pauses to let the news settle in. "At the hop, he danced twice with Mrs. Lewis and neither danced a single dance with anyone else. If it were not for the fact that he shared such a strong resemblance to Mr. Lewis, every tongue in the hotel would have been wagging."

"Well yesterday afternoon, Mrs. Lewis' mother arrived unexpectedly. At supper I noticed that neither Mrs. Lewis nor Mr. Lewis' brother were present. Today, I heard - let me stress I heard - that they were seen leaving the lobby of the hotel together yesterday late in the afternoon."

"We have at most one elopement a summer at the States; apparently the Constitution is where the profane action takes place," Mrs. Brewster comments.

"That may be, as that may be, but I doubt any hotel in the world has more uncles taking their young nieces on excursions than at the States." Mrs. Jackson smiles.

The women take sips from their cups in unison.

Josey is trying without much luck to get Sarah and Sadie out of bed. Sarah makes her feeling known. "Josey, leave me alone, there is no reason to get up on a Sunday morning in Saratoga."

"You need to goes to the spring and to eat. You danced all your energy away last night." Josey is getting frustrated.

"I will wake for dinner, leave me alone." Sarah is getting angry.

Knowing it is a losing battle, Josey prepares to leave. "We's gunna sees what yus momma says."

"Fine." Sarah opens her eyes just long enough to be sure Josey is gone.

"What a dance." Sadie is waking up. "I danced with seven gentlemen."

"And you discovered the identity of your poet."

"Not yet but he is about to unveil himself."

"What makes you so sure?" Sarah says without turning over.

"Weaknesses to the male personality. Men cannot keep a secret."

Sarah wants to get more sleep. "Get your rest now, mother will make us get up for church in a couple of hours." The sisters roll away from each other; Sadie's eyes remain open.

Frank is sitting silently on his cot, his back against the cell wall. The voice of one of the inmates calls to him. "We's gunna be sayin' good bye soon. I was talking to the guard las' night. Yus goin' to either Albany or Auburn."

A second inmate joins the dialog. "Yus better hope for Albany, Auburn is a place dat is so bad, even I'd be scared."

"They's gonna have fun wid da pretty rich boy in Auburn. Da guards are so mean dere dat dey beats a prisoner an hour jus' to keep track of the time," the first inmate adds.

The man in the next cell whispers, "You there."

Frank gets down on his knees and whispers back, "Yes, thank you for the Bible."

"Don't go listening to those fools," cautions the man in the next cell. "If they knew anything they would not be in here."

"They do seem to know what is going on," Frank points out.

"They should, they have been in here more than they have been on the streets. You keep your spirits up. I followed the newspaper and it seems that you have a family that will get you out. It is just a matter of when."

"The congregation is leaving the church. Members stop to shake Reverend Beecher's hand. Cora speaks as she greets the minister. "An excellent service, Mr. Beecher."

"The spirit of the Lord was with me today. I understand that some changes are in store for your living arrangements. Let me say that with Mr. Stiles gone it would be even more important to have your daughters be industrious and practice the organ. That way they will at least be close to their spiritual father."

Cora looks at the line behind her. "We will speak when you are less busy." Cora and her daughters start walking away.

Todd is last of his family in line; he speaks as he shakes Rev. Beecher's hand. "I will try to get my sisters involved. They can be difficult." Reverend Beecher smiles as he watches Todd catch up with the rest of his family.

The dining room at the States is full. Susie Morrissey is enjoying Saratoga and the time she has on Sundays with her husband. "Overall, how would you say the summer is going?"

"I am doing as well as I should have expected. This heat spell is bad for business."

"Heat spells do not last long in Saratoga."

"That is why so many Southerners come here."

"That may be one reason." Susie acts better informed.

Thomas tries to reassure his family. "I have assured your mother that you will be very well behaved in my absence. Your mother has been instructed not to buy you new dresses for the Grand Ball unless you have followed her every wish."

"With you away, who will a young man talk to if he should want to call?" To Sarah, social protocols are important.

"Your mother and I always consult on issues involving you children. She can speak on my behalf."

"May I invite Jacob to visit Savannah in the fall?"

164

Thomas looks at Cora for guidance. Cora answers, "A proper lady never invites the man. You will have to wait until he asks permission."

"He will ask permission and then can he come?"

"We will have to wait until we see his intentions before we can answer."

Thomas wonders about his younger daughter. "Sadie, you have been unusually quiet."

"I was sure you would take me. I was a little girl the last time we were in Europe. It was so long ago I barely remember it. Besides, it would give me a chance to practice my French." Sadie has not given up on the excursion.

"Your grandfather and I will be too busy to watch over you. This trip is business, not pleasure."

"You could bring Missy along to watch me."

"That would not be a good idea," Thomas answers.

Cora glares at Thomas, then Sadie.

On the piazza Mmes. Brewster, Jackson, White, and Dallas are rapidly and vigorously fanning themselves. Mrs. Brewster points to Bennett who, to escape the heat, has removed his jacket and tie and unbuttoned the top two buttons on his shirt.

Edith attempts to avoid an incident. "Mr. Bennett, I fear that those dreadful women are looking at you."

"It's so bloomin' hot, I's 'bout to go rents a room in 'n ice house."

"I seriously doubt that those dreadful women will accept any attempt to get cool," Edith reasons.

"A man sitting on the piazza without a jacket. It never would have happened when the senior Mr. Marvin was operating the hotel," Mrs. Brewster remembers.

"It is the unbuttoned shirt that I find offensive. That type of behavior is just rude." Even Mrs. Jackson is offended.

"My, my, the perfect one actually complains." Mrs. Brewster enjoys the slip by her rival.

"I never maintained I was perfect, only that one should try to forgive and be sure before they criticize. That was the behavior my parents and minster taught me to emulate," elucidates Mrs. Jackson. Mrs. Brewster, knowing she has been put down, stares at Mrs. Jackson.

"I believe that they are serving ice cream with dessert this evening to cool us off," Mrs. White offers.

Marvin approaches Bennett, "Mr. Bennett, as hot as it is, we still require that all gentlemen wear a jacket and tie while in the public areas."

The perpetual diplomate, Marvin offers an alternative, "Although he is closed on Sundays, I have heard that Mr. Morrissey has opened the garden behind his establishment for men who feel the need to be refreshed."

"Damn, strangest place I'ver 'eard of when a man's gots to roast just to catch a little breeze."

"Why don't you go down to Mr. Morrissey's garden while I take a sponge bath," Edith encourages.

"You know's a sponge bath does soun' like a good idear." Bennett leers at Edith.

In the tenement apartment Pauline, Antoinette, Janet, and John are sitting on the available chairs. Ethel sits on the table while Bob sits on the floor ogling the women. In an effort to cool off, Pauline, Antoinette, and Janet have removed their dresses and corsets, and chemises. They are sitting in just their bloomers. All three young women are dipping old pieces of cloth in a bucket of water and running the damp cloth over their bodies. The window is open but the curtain does not move.

"I hered downtown dat's close to a hundred degrees." Pauline breaks the silence.

"Well, dat means we gets a nigh' off, dare won't be no business when it is dis hot," Antoinette assures her sister.

"It's okay, I's got my monthly anyway," Janet submits.

Their father intercedes, "Yus always 'ave yur monthly. Yus don't gets o'er it soon I take yus to a doctor I hered about in A'bany and have it turn'd off'n ferever."

John's eyes are fixated on the young women as they try to cool off. Noticing where his gaze is fixed, Ethel hits John with a towel.

"John you stop lookin' at yus daughters dat way," Ethel orders.

"Me, it's Bob who's starin'."

Pauline picks up the bucket and walks brazenly over to Bob. He looks aside. She offers a compromise, "Bob yus goes down da hall an' get's 'nother bucket of water an' yus can see anytin' yus wants to see." Bob just continues to look away.

"Well I guess I'll jus' 'ave to go gets it meself," Pauline announces. Without covering up, Pauline takes the bucket and walks out the door.

Sarah and Sadie are laying on their beds in their underwear; a large reed fan is rigged above their beds. Missy is working the foot peddle that moves the fan. They have a pan of water and are using a washcloth to dampen their arms and faces. They occasionally pull up their bloomers and dampen their legs. "I truly believed father was going to take me with him to Europe," Sadie pouts.

"Just be thankful he brought us to Saratoga. There may be five or six days this warm all season, but in Savannah it is this hot for a month."

"If I were in Europe, I could go to museums and visit the old castles. Those are both cool."

"Father and grandfather will be busy the entire time. They would not take you to museums."

"I do not need them to take me, I could go on my own."

Sarah changes the subject. "So who is your poet?"

"He will reveal himself at Saturday's hop."

"What makes you so sure?"

"I will get Walter to run a story challenging him to come forward."

Sarah looks all knowing. "Interesting."

Mary is sitting in just her bloomers next to the open window. While talking to herself, Mary bathes with a washcloth and sips a glass of wine. "Well Miss Mary, are you going to take action or not?" She pauses as she dampens her body. "If you are successful, the rewards are beyond your wildest dreams." She pauses as she dips the cloth and washes again. "If you are wrong," shaking her head, "don't even think about that option." She puts the cloth in the washbasin.

Two guards have a hose that they extend down the hallway. The first guard yells, "Hot in here, boys?" The guard starts laughing as the water is turned on. He walks down the row of cells hosing down the prisoners. He gets their clothes, beds, floors, and walls wet.

Just before they get to his cell, Frank grabs the Bible and places it where a brick is missing over the top of the cell door.

The guard turns the water off. "Now that will cool you off." He laughs as he leaves the cellblock, pulling the hose behind him.

"So rich boy, feel better after a swim?" the first inmate yells.

The second inmate laughs, "Don't know about you rich boy, but that was the first shower I ever had dat I enjoyed."

Frank whispers to the man in the next cell, "It did feel good."

"But in a wet bed, the lice breed faster. There will be hell to pay in about a week."

"I had time enough to protect the Bible." Frank takes the Bible from its hiding space.

"Or maybe it is just showin' you that it is protectin' you."

Frank shakes his head.

After a refreshing storm, the crowd is back to normal size at the springs. Walter, as usual, is talking with the slaves. Mmes. Brewster, White, Jackson, and Dallas are near the rail by the dipper boy. Pauline and Antoinette are near the perimeter.

"Dat was some storm last night weren't it?" Pauline tells her sister.

"Coll'd it of'n nuff dat I slept," Antoinette agrees.

"Why's it dat dese women feel dey are better den us anyway. If'n dey was better, dare men folks would be spendin' dare evenin's with dem, not us," Pauline wonders.

Antoinette answers, "Oh dey's bedder. Dey gets to select who dey spen'dd time with while we's da ones selected."

"If'n dat's true, dat's we're da ones selected, why are we not lookin' down our noses at dem?" Pauline gets philosophical.

"Cause we do it fer cash an' dese fine ladies do it for houses, maids, an' fancy dresses," explains Antoinette.

"It dun't seem fair." Pauline is perplexed.

"Sis'er, yus can be sured it'sn't fair. Da problem is dat in dis game of couples, womens never win an' dey rarely gets to choose how dey lose." Antoinette has it figured out.

"It is confirmed, I was there when the porter was moving Miss Strong's trunks from her room this very morning - six in all. She must be going home," Mrs. White informs the cluster. "To plan the wedding I am sure. I am sure they are to marry under the Harvest Moon."

"Never too soon. What is she thirty? Thirty-five?" Mrs. Brewster speculates.

"Twenty-six," Mrs. Jackson says in a firm voice. "I would guess we will see them back next season with a baby."

"Probably why she left so soon - necessity," Mrs. Brewster conjectures.

"Do not cast aspersions without evidence," corrects Mrs. Jackson.

"Or she might just want to be sure her father sees her happy. His cough gets worse with each passing day." Mrs. White looks for the silver lining.

"I suppose. Baby or daddy, either way, time is running out," Mrs. Brewster snarls.

Thomas is working on paperwork at the desk in the parlor of the family cottage. Missy enters without knocking. "Mr. Stiles, I needs to talk to you."

Thomas is distracted. "What is it, Missy?"

"Mr. Stiles, I done missed my monthly."

"How late are you?"

"Over two weeks. I's never late."

"It's probably just from the stress of coming up here combined with knowing I will be leaving."

"No sir. I know there is life growin' insides me."

"There is no way you could know that. Do you know whose baby it is?"

"There ain't never been no one but you."

"We will talk about this when I get back. Don't you go saying anything to Mrs. Stiles or Josey."

"Josey's already guessing on account of my not needing any old rags." Thomas just looks out the window.

Frank lays on his cot reading the Bible. Intermittently, he scratches because of the bug bites.

"Auburn was the color of my girlfriend's hair and will be the place to find ol' rich boy." Inmate One laughs at his own joke.

"You know ol' rich boy, there is a surefire way to handle Auburn. When dey finish checkin' you in, you turn and punch the guard in the nose. That way dey put you in solitary and you'll be safe," Inmate Two offers.

"Solitary will not be a problem for rich boy, he don't talk to no-one no how," reasons Inmate One.

"Psst," The inmate in the next cell tries to get Frank's attention. "Don't go paying dem no mind. Just keep reading the Bible. Somewhere in there are the words that are the answer to your problems."

"I have already read the Bible cover to cover twice."

"But those times, you were not looking for answers to the current questions." Frank opens the Bible to the New Testament.

Beach is sitting at his desk, George across from him. Beach looks proud. "I am going to do something I have never done so soon before. George, I am going to recommend you for the bar after just a month in my office."

"I am surprised sir; thank you very much."

"You are going to be a great lawyer, why not let you get started? I expect you to stay on in this office as an associate. We can talk partnership in a few years." George is speechless as Beach explains the rest of his plan. "We do not have enough space in the main office so your

169

office will be down the hall. You can use the law books; just tell Dexter when you take one out."

"Thank you again, I will not let you down."

"You do realize, it will be some time before the men at the Albany Club let me forget having your Miss Pauline testify in a murder trail." Beach blushes. "She did have fun with old stodgy Bingham." Beach smiles at the memory. "You do know she is smarter than most people would guess."

"And wiser," George offers.

"Your office is the third door down the hall."

The room is so small there is barely room enough for George's desk and chair. George enters and looks around. He places his brief case on the desk, sits in the wooden chair, and rubs his hand over the wood of the desk before he leans back. Leaning back causes him to bump his head on the bookcase behind. He smiles.

Lynwood Harbor, on the Chesapeake Bay, is a sheltered shallow water port only used by local fisherman. There is a twenty foot fishing skiff with an area under the seats originally for the storage of fish. The fish boxes have been removed to have a place to hide escaping slaves. The entire family is squeezed into the area under the seats. The crew consists of a fifty year old captain and his crew of one.

The captain explains the rules. "Now, as soon as we get out a mile or so, I let you out. But you will have to stay below the rail so no one sees you. Remember exactly where you are now 'cause if another boat starts getting close that is where you will have to hide."

Fear is obvious on Mattie's face. Nate understands the dangerous situation the captain has put himself in. "Thanks you sir."

"I hates the water," Mattie says under her breath.

The captain and the sailor lift the seat top into position to hide the family. The sailor unties the boat, pushes it along the dock, then jumps on at the last possible moment.

Thomas is coaching Todd at archery in the park. "While I am gone, you will be the man of the family. It is up to you to watch out for your sisters and your mother."

"Father, I am the youngest; they will not want me to be watching out for them."

"Then you will have to become more like an Indian. Move silently but always keep the women in your sight. Make like you are on a scouting mission and have to report what you see to the chief." Thomas points to himself on the word chief.

"They will know I am watching."

"Not if you are very skillful. You are excellent with a bow and arrow, now become excellent as a scout." Todd ponders the idea.

Jacob walks over to Sarah, who is writing a letter. "I see you made it home after the ball."

"Is that all you saw?" She is coy.

Thomas is sorting the few belongings to be placed in the carpet bag as Josey walks in the doorway. "Mr. Thomas?"

"Come in, Josey."

"Yus knows me, Mr. Thomas, I always says my peace. I dun't mean no harm. Jus needs to say what is." Thomas stands watching his wife's servant. "It ain't right you goin' off'n leavin' Mrs. Stiles with all these responsibilities."

"My father has sent for me. Europe is not my idea."

"That may be as that may be, but Mrs. Stiles gots one daughter 'bout ready to fall in love, iff'n she hasn't already, one daughter 'bouts to get into some kind of trouble, and a son that is 'bout to wander off. Not to mention that I think one of the women in this household dun got herself in a mess of trouble."

"Cora is a strong woman, she can handle the girls and whatever issues they create," Thomas reassures his wife's lady.

"No sir, the issue is not Mrs. Stiles, it is you. You dun runnin' off rather than face yus responsibilities."

"That will be enough of that. You are way beyond your bounds." He raises his voice. "Be silent now."

Josey talks quietly as she closes the door. "Whether I talk or not don't change the situation, it jus' makes it clear." Thomas continues to sort his personal items.

Judge Baucus is seated at a table in the conference room of the jail. He has a package in front of him when they bring in Frank. "How are you doing?" Before Frank can answer, the Judge pushes the package across the table. "Mrs. Smith sent you some supplies. There is a loaf of bread, some apples, pears, and a few peaches. They have all been checked over by the guards."

"Thank Mrs. Smith. I am not so well. The cells get devilishly hot. Of course, the guards are experimenting with a new system to cool them off."

"How is that?"

"Not important." Frank has already learned not to complain if

171

nothing can be done.

"I am sure you know that Mr. Beach has already started the appeal process."

"Mother told me she was going to ask the Governor for a pardon."

"You can hope for that, but do not think that a pardon is an easy route. A pardon is a political nightmare. Not out of justice, but out of fear for how the opposition will use it. The Governor will not even entertain the idea until after the election in November. And then only if he loses."

"November is not long."

"If he wins, he will still not consider a pardon until he is going out of office, which could be two more years. Your best option is an appeal." Frank is despondent as his grandfather continues. "There is one thing I can probably do for you. I will endeavor to get you assigned to the prison hospital. It will be safer and those around you will be less dangerous."

"I know nothing about medicine."

"You will learn to be a nurse. In the meantime, are you still writing?"

"Every night."

Judge Baucus hands over two notebooks. "Keep track of what you see and feel. It may prove useful later."

All the sails on the boat have been set. The slave family is all lying out on the deck. Each is sitting or lying below the rail. Mattie is obviously seasick. Nate asks the captain, "Why are you doing this for nothing?"

"Penance."

"What's penance?"

"I made my fortune bringing people like you to this country to be sold. Then I found God. So now I spend my life helping them get free. It is the ultimate irony."

"People like me?"

"Darkies. Made thirteen trips; five to Africa and eight to Haiti, bringing in over a hundred each trip. Lost a couple hundred along the way." Nate just looks as the captain continues. "If'n the wind keeps up, we should be in the river by tomorrow night."

The casino is extremely crowded with every game table full. Richards is standing next to Morrissey. They look in opposite directions. "You know that suit that keeps reappearing? The blonde guy by the roulette wheel is wearing it tonight," Richards points out.

"Are you sure it is the same suit?"

"The last time we saw someone in it, I took the liberty of burning a small hole near the slit in the back with my cigar. That is the same suit."

172

Morrissey examines the man. "Want me to bring him over?"

"Not yet, but keep an eye on him. Do you know why Ringer wants to see me?"

"I'll let him tell you himself." Bennett joins Morrissey and Richardson.

"Mr. Morrissey, Mr. Marvin said dat you were instrumen'al in da return of my's lost funds." Morrissey just stares. "Well sir, I mus' tell ya that I plans on doublin' da money tonigh'."

"I wish you the very best. How is your niece enjoying her stay in Saratoga?" Morrissey smiles.

"She's gettin a bit expensive, what's with all da balls and hops. But she does make herself worthwhile some of the da time." Bennett gives a bawdy snicker.

Morrissey is gentlemanly. "Please give her my best."

Morrissey walks through the door to the cashier cage. There are three men who work the two cashier windows. Ringer, known for his wire glasses and very pale skin, is in charge. "You wanted to see me?"

Ringer is nervous. "Mr. Morrissey, it was terribly hot in the city last week. My daughters got sick. I was wondering if I could bring my family up to Saratoga until it starts to cool off."

"Even if a room were available, I do not pay you well enough for you to afford a place in the village." Morrissey thinks of options. "You could probably rent a place in Ballston or in the country."

"That's just it. I was looking at the four rooms over the woodshed. I could clean those up well enough to make my wife and the girls comfortable."

Morrissey ponders his options. "That sounds like a reasonable arrangement if it is good enough for them. I'll ask Mr. Marvin if he can spare some old beds and linen."

"That would be most generous of you, Mr. Morrissey."

"When will they get here?"

"I will need a day to get the space cleaned. I will tell my wife to purchase tickets for Thursday or Friday." Morrissey smiles proudly and walks out the door into the casino.

George is sitting in a chair and Catharine is on the couch in her father's parlor. Her skirt covers the entire couch. "I am very proud of you. A member of the bar so soon after graduation. Surely you are the first in your class."

"Probably not, one of the Adams was in my class. His father probably got him approved upon graduation. I cannot complain, I have

173

had a very good summer. Although I am sure Frank Baucus would not agree."

"What will happen to Frank?"

"He will be off to prison by the first of August. I know Mrs. Baucus would like him to be in Albany Prison but I suspect he will be in Auburn or Attica."

"I have been told that those are very rough places; I fear Frank will not hold up." She changes her attention to George. "Enough woeful conversation, what is next for you?"

"With luck, a couple of years of private practice, then politics."

"With what goal in mind?"

"I will probably start as a village trustee, move to president of the village, then assemblyman, and if all goes well, governor."

"You do reach high."

"With the right support, anything is possible."

"What do you envision as your biggest obstacle?"

"There are two: the war that cannot be avoided and finding the right woman to share my adventure." The door to the parlor is opened by the butler; Cook enters carrying a tray of champagne and three glasses. He places the tray on a sideboard. "I understand that congratulations are in order." Cook begins to pour the drinks. When the glasses have been filled, he raises his, "To the village's newest attorney, may he win many cases and at least one heart."

Catharine looks him in the eye as if to say, 'How could you?'

Josey is sitting on the back steps of the family cottage. Missy is taking down the laundry. Josey decides it is time to speak. "I know you have missed your monthly. Did you tell Mr. Thomas?"

"I haven't missed nothing."

"Don't you go lying to me," Josey warns.

"Besides, if it were true, why would I tell Mr. Thomas?"

"Cus it is his. Just like Ruby's little girl and Betty's boy; they're all his children."

"Now you are the one who is lying. Mr. Thomas would never have anything to do with the likes of Ruby or Betty. Besides, Mrs. Stiles would never let him mess around with farm hands. Those are both Benjamin's children."

"Girl, you are a dreamer. Years ago Mr. Thomas took a poke at me more'n once. He's just like any other man, when it comes to keeping warm, he ain't got no pride. Besides, Mrs. Stiles don'n care, she figures we's taken a burden off'n her."

"Well, if it were true he would let my baby be free."

"Girl, yus got to grow up."

Benjamin comes out the back door. "So ladies, what are you buzzing about tonight?"

"Benjamin, it seems yus about to be a father again." Josey grins. Benjamin looks at Missy's stomach.

An anxious Amanda is seated across the desk from the male secretary to Governor King, who says, "Mrs. Baucus, with the convention less than a month away, you must understand that this is not an appropriate time for the Governor to be even considering pardoning anyone."

"This is not anyone, this is the grandson of the last Chancellor of the State. A Whig turned Republican, just like Mr. King, and one of the most respected men in the state."

"Mrs. Baucus, I assure you that the Governor has followed the case with great interest and has sympathy for your son's plight, but he will not be able to intercede at this time."

"When will be the right time?"

"A pardon would be difficult to arrange in the foreseeable future."

"Would you arrange an appointment for me with the Governor tomorrow? I wish to speak to him directly."

"I am sorry, but the Governor is at his home in Queens."

"So how was your evening, Mr. Bennett?" Morrissey is polite.

"Not as good as I 'oped. I guess I len' yus a couple of hun'red dollars. I'll be back tomorrow to get my money back."

Morrissey places his hand on Bennett's back and sees him to the door. "Tomorrow night it is, although I would advise you to spend more time with Miss Edith."

"I spent plenty of time wid her dis afternoon." Bennett smirks and nudges Morrissey.

Richards comes in from the side. "John?"

"The little snake in the suit slipped out. I was watching him, then all the sudden he disappeared."

"He must have cashed out and left."

"Not possible. I was only distracted for a second. He did not have enough time to cash in his chips and leave."

"Have the croupiers check to make sure he was not able to do anything to any of the games. While you are at it, check to make sure the cards are all unopened."

Richards brings the night's cash in to Morrissey's office. "The cashiers have balanced out. Jones was off five dollars again. Do you want me to do something about it?"

Morrissey bends down and opens the huge safe as Richards hands him four large bags full of cash. "He's a good man. Tell him that if he is off again it will come out of his salary."

"You already gave him that warning," Richards reminds Morrissey.

"Then tell him I wanted to take the money out this time but that you talked me out of it. That way he owes you a favor." Morrissey closes the safe and he and Richards exit into the main room of the casino. The two look around one last time, then exit through the front door.

After they leave Swanson, the little man in the 'suit,' crawls out from under one of the tables, smiles, and slips to the door to the basement. Swanson descends the stairs, opens a basement window and crawls out.

The boat is moored in shallow water. The family is lying on the deck ready to move back into the cutouts under the seats if necessary. The captain is standing up looking at the nearby shore. The captain sees a lantern swinging, "There's the signal." The family starts climbing over the side and into the waist deep water. Nate holds Eve in his arms and Adam is riding on his shoulders. He has the violin tucked under his chin. Mattie and Nanny both hold the sacks with their meager belongings as they climb over the side. As the family reaches the shore they are led by the crewman to another man, William.

The crewman urges them on. "Come on, come on! We need to cover about three miles before the sun comes up."

William takes the lead and the family follows in close order with the crewman at the back.

Four guards enter the cell block. Two are holding chains with cuffs. The first guard calls out, "Jefferson, Moran, Baucus, get up. Yus go'n for a little train ride." The guard opens the three cells and pulls the prisoners to their feet. When they are in the hallway, the guards chain them together by putting on a string of cuffs on their right hands and on their right ankles.

Frank looks into the cell next to him before he leaves. "Thank you. You are a good man."

"That is one thing I am not. Jus' ask my wife's lover - oh yeah, you can't, he's dead." He laughs, "Remember, don't smile, don't look anyone in the eyes, and the less you say the better off you'll be.'

"And what advice do I give you?"

The man in the adjacent cell leans back and examines the bounty that Frank was given by Judge Baucus. "Thank you for this."

Mrs. King, wife of the Governor, is hosting Amanda for a private tea. "Tell me Amanda, how is the dear Chancellor holding up?"

"His health is good but, like me, he is concerned for Frank. The two are very close."

"So I would assume."

"I would like just a few moments of the Governor's time," Amanda pleads.

"I am sure you would, but the Governor has sworn to me that he will not do any political business until after the convention next month. He needs this time to rest."

"I only wish a moment of his time."

"No Amanda, let us both accept that you want something that is much more than a moment of his time." The two women stare at each other.

John, Ethel, Pauline, Antoinette, Janet, and Bob are all on the stoop of the tenement building.

Pauline whispers to Antoinette, "I do believes dat da man who stands down un duh porch of duh casino most nigh's likes me."

"Which one?"

"Da one dat never goes inside, spends every nigh' walkin' ups and downs da porch." Pauline instinctively flutters her eyes.

"Dat's Smilee, he's a policeman durn duh day. He dun't like yus, me or anyone else who dun't follow da law," Antoinette explains.

"Yus wron' 'bout dat. I seed da way he looked at me." Pauling continues to dream.

"He's may looks but he's lookin' to either bust yus or gets a littl' for free," Antoinette advises.

"If'n he tooks a liken' to me he coul' gets all he wants for free," Pauline promises.

John is appalled by the idea of free. "Damn it girl. You ain't given nuttin' away for free."

"Pa, I's get's da chance to gets out of dis business, I' gunna dus it." Pauline makes her feeling known.

John has his own priority of jobs. "What wou'd you do? Work in a factory, clean up other people's chamber pots fer next to nuttin'?"

Pauline is defensive, "Dats what happen to my's money nows."

"Hey girl, yus shut up, your mom and I need money. We savin' up to open our own house," John dreams.

"Yus have a'ready if yus stop spen'in' all yus time down at da Congress Bar." Antoinette enters the foray on her sister's side.

"Hey girl you stay out of dis. 'side, I have one awful case of rumatism. I suffer every day," John claims.

"Yus dunt feels nutin after noon," Pauline argues.

John brings his fist back. Ethel catches his arm before it starts forward. Ethel is stronger than John. "You hit her an' you lose five maybe six days money. Not even you are that stupid." John stares at each woman in turn.

The slave family is enjoying a simple breakfast of biscuits and oatmeal in a Methodist Church. William explains what is next. "For the next few hundred miles you will be the guest of Quaker families. Get some rest; we leave at sundown.

Nate attempts to calm his wife's fears. "Well, our boating days are over, from here on we will be walking."

"Why all these people help'n us?"

"I don't really know. I guess they just have a feeling of right."

"It ain't bout being right."

Amanda walks out on the pier to a lone fisherman. "Governor." She makes a formal greeting.

"Amanda, I suspected you would come; just not so early." The Governor has misjudged Amanda, not a wise move for any man and even more of an issue for a politician.

"Then you know why I am here."

"Of course, and the answer is 'No' for now. Perhaps after the election, but not before."

"If they have not already, they will be sending Frank to Auburn within the week. He is too frail to survive in that horrible environment."

"Thurlow Weed and his gang of war lords would use any pardon against me and the Democrats would win in November. You will have to wait."

"For justice?"

"Given your son had a trial, most would say that justice has been served and any actions by me would be unjust. However, do not be surprised if Frank finds himself in the prison kitchen or hospital. Things will be safer there." Amanda holds her ground. "That is all. You will leave now before anyone recognizes you." Amanda walks in the direction of a waiting carriage.

Ringer is at the train station watching the passengers disembark the train. Included among the passengers is Mrs. Ruth Ringer, her eighteen year old twin daughters Jennie and Jesse, and their younger sister Dolly. Ringer helps the women down from the train, giving his wife a kiss on the cheek. The women are all weary from the excursion; however, they move to the baggage car in search of their trunks.

The entire Stiles family is present, along with Benjamin and Josey to see Thomas off. Benjamin is supervising the loading of two trunks. Thomas will carry his carpet bag on the train.

"It is so good to see you all." Ringer is trying unsuccessfully to hug each of the women.

The mother can never be pleased. "It is good to be out of the city, but the weather here is not a lot better."

"It cools down at night," Ringer assures his wife.

"So you say," Ruth says without conviction.

Ringer gives his three daughters a common hug. "Girls, it is great to see you. You will have such a good time in Saratoga."

"Where are these wonderful springs?" Jesse has read up about the village.

"What she really wishes to know is, where are all the young men?" Jennie counters. It is obvious that the twins see life differently.

"I can speak for myself! Father, where are all the handsome young men?" Jesse laughs at her own joke. Her sisters join in but not Ruth. With the trunks located, the Ringer family walks off in the direction of the casino.

Todd gives his father a long hug. "Father I will miss you."

"Remember, while I am gone you are the man of the house. Keep an eye on your mother and sisters."

Todd talks in a conspirator voice. "Just like an Indian."

Sarah gives her father a hug and kiss on the cheek. "I will miss you. Tell grandfather I miss him."

"I will."

Sadie gives her father a hug, then steps back without speaking or kissing him. Cora gives Thomas a brief hug, then whispers in his ear, "Did you leave me another mess to clear up?"

Thomas boards the train and waves to his family as if Cora had not spoken. "I should be home by the first of November."

The Stiles family is walking back to their cottage. Josey and

Benjamin walk behind. Sadie mumbles, "It was unfair, father should have taken me."

Todd does not agree. "No, he should have taken me. Instead, I am stuck here with three women to watch over."

Sarah puts a reassuring hand on Todd's shoulder. "I shall do my best to keep you very busy." Cora does not speak.

Upon reaching the park, Sadie looks around for Walter. She sees him talking to Missy and walks directly toward him. As Cora and Todd walk to the cottage, Sarah stays back waiting for Sadie. As Sadie approaches, Missy silently leaves Walter and moves toward the cottage.

"Walter, what mischief are you up to with my servant?" Walter blushes but does not respond. She continues, "I need you to do me a favor."

"What do you have in mind?"

"You write the gossip column that appears on Friday, do you not?"

"That is written by Penelope Perfect."

Sadie corrects him, "Do not be coy with me. I need you to write something in the article that makes my poet begin writing again."

"Why? You already know it is Mr. Vincent."

"I warned you about trying to be coy with me. You know he is nowhere near clever enough to be my poet. But he was a handsome dance partner."

"You want me, someone less clever than even Mr. Vincent, to challenge your poet to come forward?"

Sadie stares defiantly. "You will have it in tomorrow's column."

"I will see if Penelope can include something," Walter says as Sadie walks toward her cottage without saying goodbye.

On the east side of the road, three men who had worn the 'suit' to Morrissey's, Swanson, Elmendorf, and Nolan, are standing in the grass. There are four horses tied to a downed tree.

"I am positive that there will be more money than any place I have ever robbed," Elmendorf assures his compatriots.

Swanson shakes his head. "I am not sure we can get in. I'm pretty sure we can get out, but that is a Troy Safe and unless we learn the combination, we will never crack it in time. If we try to blow it with dynamite, we will wake up the entire village."

Nolan is pessimistic. "It cannot be done. It would take at least eight men to lift the safe onto a wagon, a heavy duty wagon to hold the weight. We would need two Clydesdales to pull the wagon. When we reach the dirt roads out of the village the weight would make ruts a blind man could follow." They all look at the face of the unidentified person who is leaning against the tree.

"You have another idea don't yus?" Nolan begins to smile.

Sarah is reading the newspaper in the park. "I have no idea how, but you did it."

"Did what?"

Sarah reads from the newspaper aloud. "To you, sir, the hidden one, whose poems made her days brighter; without them now, she's lost her sun, I implore you sir, to write her."

The sisters smile with delight. Sarah continues, "and it is signed 'The Southern Coquette.'" Both girls beam.

"Now I must make Walter pay for calling me a coquette," Sadie vows.

"Why must he pay; he wrote your article?"

"Because he must. Bright men must be taught the benefit of an even brighter woman."

Author's Collection

Leave it to the Ladies

The season, being half over, means a daily routine has set in among those who are here for the entire summer. As in past years, the sequence is: the springs in the early morning; breakfast; mid-morning spent listening to music, reading, writing or painting in the parks of each of the hotels; dinner; shopping on Broadway and watching the daily carriage procession; supper; then the most important part of every day, the ball, or hop.

This year Morrissey's Casino has changed the ritual, since, for the first time, there is a venue that is strictly for men. The unforeseen consequence is that the casino is drawing eligible bachelors away from the balls and dances.

One thing that has not changed in generations is that a collection of dowagers meet each morning at the springs. The individuals in the dowagers' group have changed but the scowling faces and tedious personalities remain the same. They have come not to rehydrate their bodies with the spring water's minerals, but to refill their cup of scandal with fresh gossip.

It is July 22 and the dowagers are all in attendance at the spring. Reverend Beecher stands to the side admiring the young women. Walter is talking to Missy; everyone has come to assume it is to gather information about the Stiles women for his articles. George walks into the springs with Catharine on his arm. To be together this early in the morning at the most public place in the village is to show commitment.

"Well, I guess there can be no doubt about it now, the two are making it clear they are the Saratoga young couple of the season." Mrs. Brewster speaks the obvious.

Mrs. Jackson notices two young boys taunting two girls. She nods to Mrs. White to look in the direction of the children. "The cycle of life continues." Her reminiscence turns to despondence, "It has been too long since a man pulled my hair."

Mrs. White smirks, "It is so interesting to observe as each generation discovers love. They always believe they are the first."

Mrs. Jackson speaks to Mrs. Brewster. "Have you always been such a skeptic or was it an acquired affliction?" Mrs. Brewster glares at Mrs. Jackson but does not yield.

Sadie leaves her sister to join Walter and Missy. "What are you two talking about?" Missy fears she has become too familiar and leaves for the hotel.

"The fresh air," Walter remarks.

"Walter, you are a terrible liar."

"What do you mean? Air and spring water are elements we all share, regardless of our social standing."

"Walter, you sound like an abolitionist." Sadie watches as Walter walks alone down to the spring without commenting.

Guests and residents alike line Broadway as the daily procession of over twenty carriages is in full swing. It is the custom that Madam Jumel's open carriage pulled by four matching horses is in the lead. Like all ladies at the time, she is in the seat that faces forward. If there had been any men, they would have faced backward. As she passes the States Hotel, a small cart pulls out behind her, cutting off the next carriage. The cart is pulled by a single ungroomed mule pulling what looks like a service vehicle. The driver of the cart is dressed in worn-out livery that had been discarded. There is a single male, Thompson, in the back of the cart sitting on a wooden crate. Thompson is the man who gave Benjamin a hard time at the railroad station the first day of the season. Thompson is wearing an old dress.

Madam Jumel, unaware of the cart, waves gaily to the people on the street. Thompson watches Madam Jumel and mimics each of her actions. The crowd starts to laugh and cheer. As the carriages get to the Union, the children start to point at Thompson. A young boy in the crowd calls out, "Madam Jumel and Miss Jumel." Madam Jumel turns around, and for the first time, sees the cart behind her.

Madam Jumel's driver asks, "What would you like me to do, Madam?"

With the courage that has carried her through many challenges, Madam Jumel responds, "Proceed as usual." The driver continues down Broadway.

At the entrance to Congress Spring, the procession passes Morrissey and Richards standing on the walk. "That was not funny," Morrissey criticizes.

"Should they be told as much?" Richards is also offended by the crowd's treatment of one of the village's noblest guests.

"The fool driving should leave the village. As for the little man, bring him to me," Morrissey commands.

The cart and mule pull up in front of the doors of a livery in the less affluent portion of the village. Richards comes out the door. "That was quite the little show you put on."

"Do you believe he paid me five dollars for one hour of fun?" The cart driver boasts, unhitching the mule.

"Where did he get that much money?"

"Don't know'd and don't care." The driver has a hard quality.

Richards moves directly in front of the driver, who tries to ignore him and continues unfastening the mule. "I wouldn't do that."

"Why not? Damn mule needs to be cooled off."

Richards puts his massive hand on the cart driver's dress livery and pulls him close. "You and that damn mule are leaving the village right now." Richards releases the cart driver and mockingly straightens out the wrinkles he put in the coat. "And you won't be back." Richards start to walk away.

The driver calls out, "Never?"

Richards just turns and stares at the man, who has his answer.

Judge Baucus pulls his simple two wheeled carriage up in front of Madam Jumel's home. He descends from the seat and ties the horse to the hitching post in front of the house. Older and slightly lame, Judge Baucus opens the gate and walks to the front door where he pulls the bell. The door is opened by a servant to whom he hands his card. The servant signals for the Judge to enter the foyer. A door off the main hallway is opened by Madam Jumel; her face is still flushed. Without a word being spoken, she points in the direction of the parlor. She enters, followed by the Judge. Judge Baucus closes the pocket doors then sits on an uncomfortable padded chair that was pointed to by Madam Jumel. "My dear, I fear you may have been offended by the actions of a couple of fools. Surely you will accept my apology on behalf of the village."

"Judge, you may well be the backbone of the village but you do not speak for it." To keep from facing her guest, she fusses over cut flowers that are in the front window.

"It was only two men and they were not even residents," he pleads.

"Two acted, others laughed."

"It was a shameful act but not meant to offend. Perhaps embarrass, but not offend."

"So you say. I will be leaving tonight for urgent business in the city."

"If you leave, the fools will have won."

"And if I do not leave, I should be the fool," she rationalizes.

"Perhaps not." The Judge looks at her. "You are a resourceful woman, you can think of a way to end this on your terms."

Morrissey works at his desk, his back to the door. Richards pulls Thompson in and forces him into a wooden chair. Morrissey continues to work. Thompson fidgets in the chair. "What was that little show about?"

"Did you like it?" Morrissey stares silently at Thompson. "I got twenty dollars for it. Twenty dollars!"

"Who paid you?"

"Some lady."

"What lady?" Morrissey demands.

"I don't know her name. She saw me at the springs, came up and offered me twenty dollars to have a little fun."

"Do you think Madam Jumel thought it was fun?""

"Probably not. Snooty ladies like her never see's the fun." Morrissey just stares. Thompson tries to buy his way out. "I'll give you ten dollars to give to her."

"That won't be necessary. You know that big maple branch that hangs over Broadway?" Morrissey asks. Everyone knows the branch as full size stage coaches can barely get under it. Thompson nods his head. "Tomorrow, after Madam Jumel's carriage passes, you are going to climb that tree with a saw and cut off that branch."

"Sure." He is relieved that he is going to escape with such a minor punishment.

"And you will be sitting on the branch while you cut."

Thompson suddenly realizes the nature of his punishment. "That's fifteen feet up. I'll be killed sure as hell."

"Let's see if everyone sees the fun tomorrow." Morrissey takes out a twenty dollar coin and hands it to Thompson.

"You are right; you may be hurt in the fall. If you don't do it, I guarantee you that you will be hurt in 'A' fall."

After looking around the park for a few seconds, Reverend Beecher sees Cora sitting on a bench reading a book. He sits on her bench without asking permission. "Good afternoon, Mrs. Stiles. The storms last evening helped break the heat." He looks at the cloudless sky. "Events such as those remind me to appreciate God's unlimited power."

"The weather is much more pleasant."

"With your husband gone, I would like to offer male guidance for your three children."

"You are persistent, Reverend."

"I prefer to call it responding to the needs that the Lord identifies."

"The children will be fine. Benjamin is always there if we need him and I am certain Mr. Marvin would assist if necessary. But thank you for your kind offer."

"It was more than an offer, it was more a challenge."

"How so?" Cora inquires, becoming worried about his motive.

"Your daughters have very strong wills. Taming them must be quite the task."

"I have no desire to tame their wills. It is their strength that assures me they will make the correct decisions." Cora holds up her book. "If you will excuse me Reverend, I need to finish this chapter before the reading club meets this evening."

Reverend Beecher stands and walks over to Mary, who is painting a watercolor. "I do not believe we have been introduced; I am Reverend Beecher."

"The fact that we have not be introduced is even more reason to wonder why you are standing here."

"The formalities of introductions are less relevant for ministers who are always looking to enhance their flocks."

"I am not a sheep and suggest you arrange an introduction before you attempt to speak to me again."

Reverend Beecher walks toward the door to the hotel, passing Marvin in the doorway. Marvin comes into the park. Seeing Marvin, Mary immediately starts packing up her watercolors.

Cora sees Marvin, stands and walks up to him first. "Mr. Marvin, do you have a minute? I must talk to you about a delicate matter."

"I always have time for a member of the Stiles family."

"It has to do with the Reverend Mr. Beecher. My daughters first brought it to my attention but now I agree; he is troubling to women."

"How so?"

"He is always trying to get a woman alone. He has tried with each of my daughters and now he has even tried with me."

Marvin smiles. "One would have to give him credit for good taste." He can see by her expression that Cora is not amused. "What does he do?"

"So far it is not what he does, but how he does it. It almost feels like he is looking at me without my dress."

"Do your daughters feel the same way?"

"They would never describe his behavior in those terms. But yes. Sadie will not even play the organ because she will not be alone with him."

"Let me see what I can do."

"Thank you, I am sure you will do something." Cora turns and begins walking toward her cottage.

Mary sees Marvin alone and walks up to him carrying her painting supplies. "Mr. Marvin, I am not sure you remember me, my name is Mary."

"Barden from Boston. You are staying at the Marvin House."

"Very good. May I suggest you keep a careful eye on Reverend Beecher? I fear he may not be all he professes to be." Mary and Marvin continue their conversation with Marvin looking over Mary's shoulder, watching the sway of Cora's skirt as she walks away.

The eleven-thirty train is unloading in Ballston. Swanson, the man who disappeared in the casino, is looking for one of his cohorts. Several passengers look around, spot the people they are meeting and leave. Others look for their luggage. One fairly well dressed man, Michael, stands at the car door looking. From his vantage point he spots Swanson on the far side of the depot. When he finally greets Swanson, the two shake hands. Michael inquires, "Am I the last?"

"No, but most everyone has been here. You will visit the casino tonight, and then take the midnight train back to Ballston Spa where a house has been rented."

"How many will be involved?"

"The plans are not final but at this time it looks like we will need eight men." They pick up Michael's single carpet bag and walk toward a small simple house.

"So how have you been since last we met for the Waterford Bank?"

Morrissey and Richards meet at Morrissey's normal spot in the middle of the room. Morrissey looks in the direction of Michael. "I already saw the suit," Morrissey says.

"What do you think is up?"

"I am not sure, but it has to be some kind of scam. My guess is they will all show up one night and try to rig one of the games."

"How can they, they only have one suit between them." Morrissey and Richards chuckle.

"Keep your eyes on him. I want to know anyone he speaks to." Morrissey goes back to being the host. Richards walks over to the side of the room where he resumes watching the crowd.

Pauline is walking slowly from their safe corner on Franklin Street in the direction of the casino. Antoinette is talking to a potential customer. "Well dat sir would cost yus a dollar. Course for another dollar yus can have da whole night."

"Let's go for the dollar and if I feel it is worth it, I will give you the other dollar for the rest of the night," the gentleman suggests.

Antoinette takes the man's arm as they walk in the direction of one of the lower class hotels. "Oh it'll be worth it sur' nuff. Yus be thin' of spen'in the week wid me for we's dun."

When Pauline is directly across from the casino she stares flirta-tiously at Smiley. "Hey, what you doin'? Yus know Harrison don't want yus near here." Smiley uses the comment as an opening, not a threat.

"Harrison ain't 'ere, is he? Yus the man in charge 'night."

Smiley's chest puffs up slightly, "I guess I am, but this is a good position and I dun't want to do nuttin' to lose it."

"What time yus gets dun?"

"'Bout 4:00."

"I'll sees yus den down the next corner - lessen yus too tired."

"I'll be there and you will be the one who is left too tired," he boasts.

"We will jus see 'bout dat won't we." She finally has someone she cares about.

Richards and Morrissey are busy in the office closing up. "He never spoke to anyone the entire evening. All he did was play a couple of hands of Faro and a few spins of roulette."

"It is easier for a group to scam a card game than one of the wheels." Morrissey thinks for a moment. "Although they might be planning to modify one of the wheels. Have the croupiers check the wheels every shift just to be sure. If you ever see two of them here the same night let me know immediately."

"I have never seen any of them twice."

"Who's behind it?"

"None of them, they are not smart enough. Oh, they are smart enough to know not to mess with you, but dumb enough to try something."

"Just in case they are just visiting us and they are really after one of the hotels, talk to Putnam and Hathorn. I will talk to Marvin."

Smiley's bedroom is humbly furnished with a pair of twin beds, a dresser, and one chair. The room is on the second floor of a boarding house overlooking nothing of interest.

"Yus do liv's simply," Pauline examines the room.

"Up 'til I gots the job with Mr. Morrissey, I had to share a room with two other guys. Now things are lookin' up."

Pauline begins unbuttoning her dress. "Ben a while for yus?"

"A couple of months, maybe more." He is sitting in the chair watching her undress.

Pauline pulls the dress over her head. Her corset is loose but she unhooks it rather than having to retie it later. She has a flask attached to the garter at her thigh. Pauline takes a sip, and then hands the flask to Smiley. "Bet yus wish yud been where the flask has been." Smiley looks at Pauline in her bloomers and chemise. "Yus can look all yus want. In a few minutes yus'll be able to touch."

Smiley is engrossed as Pauline removes her chemise. Her boldness fascinates him. Naked from the waist up, Pauline walks over to Smiley, straddles his legs and starts unbuttoning his shirt. "I'm glad yus was savin' yus self for me." She kisses his neck.

"Who says I was savin' myself for you?"

Pauline continues kissing his shoulders and neck. "You did iff'n yus wants a freebie."

"Savin' it all for you."

Pauline pushes the shirt off Smiley's shoulders and resumes kissing his neck. She realizes that it is the first time in a long time that she has kissed a man because she wanted to.

The small two bedroom house in Ballston Spa is sparsely furnished. In the main room there is a table with mismatched wooden chairs. Dirty dishes and glasses litter the room, along with a pair of empty whiskey bottles. The table top is clear. What was supposed to be the dining room has three mattresses on the floor. Eight men: Swanson, Michael, Elmendorf, Nolan, David, Peter, Phillips, and Shorty are scattered throughout the house. The church clock strikes two.

The house was selected for two primary reasons. It is close to the Ballston Spa train station and it is in a neighborhood where, if you pay in cash, no one asks any questions and forgets anything they may have witnessed.

Shorty is gazing out the window. "It's time."

The men start moving to the table; the door opens and Edith and Bennett walk in. Edith immediately moves to the end of the table. "Let's get started." She sits, waiting for the last of the men to sit down.

"This is going to go like the North Adams job. Peter, you need to get a pair of pants and cut the legs into masks."

The park is full. Sarah, Sadie, and Cora are sitting on two benches across from each other, reading, while Todd is at the archery range. Morrissey is talking with Marvin on the back porch. "I'm not saying that they are planning to hit one of the hotels, but they are up to something."

"The three large hotels all have safes with clerks and porters on all night. Hitting one of them would be difficult, if not impossible."

"The vaults at the banks would be just as difficult." Morrissey is stumped, "Nothing else makes sense."

"Except your place."

"Impossible. We open at dusk and are open until almost dawn so there is no time to break into the safe," Morrissey reminds Marvin. "It took ten men to move the safe in, so no group is going to take it out."

"They could blow it," Marvin suggests.

"If they were to use dynamite, it would wake the whole village. There would not be time to get away. "My guess is that they will hit one of the hotels in the early hours of the morning. They will have to meet someplace. Since my place is logical, if I see more than one of the men, I will send a courier to warn you."

"I have never said this before, but I think you are wrong," Marvin criticizes.

"One of us is," Morrissey admits.

Across the park, Jacob approaches Sarah. "Miss Sarah Stiles, what a surprise to see you here."

"Oh yes, it must be, I have only been in this park at this time every day for five weeks."

"I never noticed."

"Your banter lacks humor." She becomes bolder, "Is there anything else you may have missed?" Jacob blushes.

"Sadie, has the newspaper article helped expose the poet?" Jacob inquires.

"Not yet, but it has only been two days."

"Obviously he is shy. Do you feel it is wise to push him too hard?" Jacob cautions.

"If he cares, he will consider me encouraging, not pushing."

"There is no question but that he cares. Perhaps you have insulted him in some way."

"How can you insult someone if you do not know who they are?"

"By ignoring the obvious." Jacob's comment causes Sadie to think.

Cora talks to her daughters. "I need to speak to Mr. Marvin. I will meet you back at the cottage."

Morrissey has left when Cora gets to Marvin on the back porch. "Mr. Marvin, a moment of your time."

"Yes, Mrs. Stiles."

"It has come to my attention that some of the male guests maintain more than one room in the hotel or, on occasion, rent a room at a second hotel," Cora asserts. Marvin does not respond so she continues. "I know that there is some kind of gentlemen's code, but I wish to know if my husband had such an arrangement."

"I can assure you Thomas had no such accommodations."

"Do the women guests ever have second rooms?"

"I am sure it has happened."

"With my husband gone, I may need a private place to get away from the children." She looks at Marvin.

"If you should ever need a private place, see me personally, and I will make the arrangements."

At four a.m., there is not much taking place in Saratoga. Shorty is walking on Franklin Street carrying two bolts of dark cloth. When he reaches the casino grounds, he ducks into the shrubs. He looks around several times. Certain that no one is watching, he opens the basement window that Swanson came out of several days before. He hides the bolts of cloth in the basement, and then climbs back out the window. When he is certain no one is watching, he continues his walk toward Broadway.

The crowd along Broadway is double what it was the day before.

There were twin rumors permeating the village; one is that Madam Jumel would again lead the procession; the second is that she has secretly snuck out of the village the previous night. Everyone wants to witness which one is true. As the carriages turn onto Broadway, Madam Jumel's carriage is again leading the procession. As the carriage passes a group, the people erupt in cheers and laughter. The great lady is sitting on the seat facing backward. Her arms are crossed and as the carriage passes, she is seen holding a dueling pistol in each hand.

As Madam Jumel passes the maple tree she sees her annoyance, Thompson, standing with Richards. Thompson begins climbing the tree. He goes out on the infamous limb and starts to cut the branch with the saw between himself and the trunk. People see what he is doing and start to point and laugh.

Just as Madam Jumel's carriage turns off Broadway onto Circular Street, the branch cracks and Thompson falls fifteen feet to the ground. Richards walks away.

Madam Jumel's House

Robbed

Dark, dank with stone walls, a dirt floor and no lights, the basement of the Union Hotel varies dramatically from the grand rooms enjoyed by the guests. Using a candle to find their way, Shorty and Swanson enter a dark storage room carrying several old newspapers and a canvas bag of tools. Swanson stands against the wall and starts walking toe to heal. He carefully counts his steps. "Right here." Shorty takes out a saw, attaches the handle and starts cutting one of the joists.

Across the street at the Constitution, Elmendorf and Nolan are in the basement under the front desk. Under their shirts they have stuffed old towels and they each have a can of kerosene and matches. The space under the front desk is not much more pleasant than that at the Union; however, there is a small window that provides some light. The room is cluttered with old tools and discarded furniture.

At Congress Spring it is a beautiful sunny morning. The violinist is playing to a receptive audience. The topic of the day is the hop that will be hosted by the Union. Among the large crowd that is present are the dowagers, the Stiles family with Todd over admiring the team that brought Madam Jumel, Judge Baucus, Cook, Marvin, and Police Chief Harrison. The single women are all eyeing each other as combatants about to enter the ring of availability. The men, young and old, are focused on the women, young and not too old.

Mrs. Brewster distinguishes more than was actually the difference. "Another Saturday, another hop. At least there is not a ball to keep the young people up all night."

"Hops are ever so much more fun than a ball. Everything is so much more relaxed." Mrs. White flutters her fan.

"With less jewelry and glitter, those at the hop have to impress with their personalities," comments Mrs. Brewster. "How novel."

Mrs. Jackson shoots the opening volley of the day, "Mrs. Brewster, when was the last time you danced?"

She answers to the group, not Mrs. Jackson. "I danced with Mr. Marvin at the first hop. I did something to my ankle and it has hurt ever since."

"As we age our weight increases and our bones weaken." Not having had breakfast, Mrs. Jackson is devouring Mrs. Brewster.

"Are you implying I am fat?" glares Mrs. Brewster.

"If the shoe fits - Oh yes, your shoes are too tight," Mrs. Jackson smirks at her victory. Mrs. Brewster glares at Mrs. Jackson, who offers a sweet smile.

Madam Jumel is standing among the most successful men in the village: Judge Baucus, Cook, Marvin, and Chief Harrison. Marvin directs his words to Harrison. "Morrissey is concerned that a gang is about town who are in the process of planning something."

"In your opinion is he correct?" Harrison wonders.

"It has been five years since there was a serious crime in the city. One could argue that we are about due."

The Judge speaks for the first time in public since the trial. "We have attracted quite the list of guests this summer. It would only be natural to expect some interest by those too lazy to earn their own fortune, but ambitious enough to take one from others."

"With bonds and stock certificates now being numbered, disposing of them is very difficult," Cook rationalizes.

"But not impossible," the Judge points out.

"Thus the issue is jewelry." Madam Jumel, who has had some of her jewelry robbed, comments. "There are so many fences in New York City who will pay pennies on the dollar, then sell to jewelers who will reset the stones for dimes on the dollar. It is an endless cycle."

Swanson has cut halfway through three of the joists. He and Shorty take the newspapers they brought with them and start stuffing them under the floor boards above their heads. Shorty notices a kerosene lamp, which he picks up and shakes to learn if there is any liquid in it. Hearing the splashing of the kerosene, Shorty says, "We're all set."

"Pour this on that pillow over by the bed-frame," Swanson instructs. Shorty pours the liquid on the pillow and hands it to Swanson. Swanson stuffs it up under the floor joist then tells Shorty, "You leave now. I will see you back at the house." Shorty peeks out the door, then leaves.

Swanson looks over his work, lights a piece of wood and starts the pillow and newspaper on fire. He slips out the door and up the back stairs. When he reaches the street, he hears the sound of the fire alarm. The bell of the hotel begins sounding and people begin first walking, then running, from the hotel. The horse drawn fire truck pulls up to the front of the hotel. After stopping for seconds at a cistern, six firemen rush in, carrying buckets of water. A second group of firemen puts a hose in the cistern, while a third starts unraveling a hose to run into the hotel. The men who put a hose in the cistern return to the pumper and start pushing down the pump bar.

People from other hotels rush into the street to help with the fire at the Union. Elmendorf turns to Nolan. "It's time." They pour the kerosene on the towels they have and stick them in the rafters. Nolan lights the towels and they slip out the door onto the crowded street.

It takes several minutes for those fighting the fire in the Union to realize that there is a second fire in the Constitution. By the time the Constitution fire is noticed, there is black smoke pouring out of the cellar window. Walter happens to be walking by and notices the smoke. Someone inside the Constitution starts ringing the fire bell.

While others rush out the front door, Walter rushes in the delivery door to the basement. Although the smoke is heavy, Walter is able to locate one of the burning towels and put it in a pail that is discarded on the floor. Instinctively Walter turns the pail over and the fire is extinguished from lack of oxygen. In the dark he finds a broken ax handle which he uses to pound on the fire, then turns his attention to the second towel. He gets the second towel drooping over one end of the handle and walks out the basement door.

The fire chief is talking to Putnam, the owner of the Union House, and Hathorn, the owner of the Constitution. "They were deliberate." He turns to Putnam. "We got here fast enough that there was little real damage from the fire." The chief wipes the sweat from his brow. "It looks like they were trying to cut their way into your safe, got tired and decided to burn the rest of the way through. You probably need to reinforce three maybe four joists but you should be fine in a day or two."

Putnam shakes the chief's hand. "Chief, thank you and your men. Get a keg and charge it to me." The chief turns over his hand, finding a five dollar gold piece.

"I am not a contractor so I don't know how much damage you have," the chief says to Hathorn. "Probably not much, but since the fire was right under the safe, I would get an engineer to look it over to be sure it is safe." Like his neighbor, Hathorn shakes the chief's hand. When the chief looks in his palm, he finds a ten dollar gold piece.

Marvin, Hathorn, and Putnam are sitting in Marvin's office having a glass of white wine. Putnam, the oldest man there, speaks first. "Damnest thing. In both cases they were right under the safe. What I don't understand is what could they possibly have believed they were doing? Even if the safe had fallen through, they never would have been able to get anything out." Marvin just listens.

Hathorn takes a sip. "Excellent vintage," he compliments Marvin. "You know how it is, always make your guests feel safe. I have ordered three metal shipping boxes from the Troy Safe Company. They should be here on the afternoon train. After dinner I will allow guests to place their valuables in the boxes. What I need to ask of you is if I can place the strongboxes in your safe for the weekend."

Putnam adds, "I must ask the same."

"It would be my pleasure to help you out; however, it is the peak of the season and I doubt I could get more than one box in my vault."

"Any other hotels have a vault or space in their safes?" Putnam asks.

"I doubt it, you could try the jewelry stores," Marvin suggests.

Putnam is skeptical, "They are all too small."

"I suppose we could hire armed guards," Hathorn advocates.

"That is an option. Keep in mind, Morrissey has the biggest portable safe they make. It has to be over ten square feet inside. You probably could get space from him," Marvin points out.

"Would you be so kind as to ask him? You have a far better relationship with him than I do." Putnam has never been to Morrissey's.

"It would be my pleasure to help."

The volume is extreme in the dining room of the Union Hotel. It is not the acoustics of the room, it is the anxiousness of the guests at the idea of almost being robbed and fire in the hotel. There is the tinkling of glasses. When the crowd finally quiets down, Putnam speaks. He is speaking to over a thousand people without a speaker system so his aged voice keeps getting weaker.

"Please let me finish my announcement before you ask any questions. To set the record straight, the fire this morning is considered to be the act of an arsonist. To ensure that our guests are safe, there will be a boy posted in the basement at all times." Putnam takes a drink of water to try to save his voice. "The fire was directly under the safe and there is a minor concern about the strength of the joist. A contractor has been here and assures me that the repairs will be completed by Monday.

For those who wish, we have arranged for three of the largest safe boxes which can be used for your valuables. Mr. Marvin, of the States, has offered us room in his vault." He takes another sip of water. "You should assume that anything you place in the boxes will be tied up until Tuesday. There will be agents present for those who wish to insure their valuables."

Carlos Delmonico speaks with a Cuban accent. "Mr. Putnam, we thank you for your statement. Are you moving your personal items to the safe deposit boxes?"

Putnam had no plans to use the boxes himself, but understands people wanting security. "Yes, I don't have as much as many of the guests, but if there is room I will be using a small part of one of the boxes for my wife's jewelry."

The scene at the Union is replicated at the Constitution.

Three tables have been set up in the lobby of Union House with a clerk at each. Four tables have been set up at the Constitution. In both cases there are clerks providing envelopes for people to place jewelry, bonds, and other valuables. There are couples waiting at each table. There are also insurance agents offering to provide coverage for the contents of the envelopes at an exorbitant price of one percent of the value for one night. As the hotel owner, Putnam is supervising the operation. Hathorn has his son helping at the Constitution.

At the first table at the Union, Clerk One states, "Mrs. Firestone, two pearl necklaces, three rings, two sets of diamond studs, two pair of gold cufflinks, two gold chains, and a pearl studded belt."

The insurance agent next to him says, "Insured for three thousand four hundred and twenty dollars. That will be thirty four dollars, twenty cents." The items disappear into a large envelope. Mr. Firestone pays the insurance agent and then Firestones walk away.

The second couple takes the place of the Firestones. The clerk announces what is going into the envelope, "Mrs. Wrigley, nine bonds, four stock certificates, three necklaces, six bracelets, and a gold pocket watch with chain and fob."

The insurance agent clarifies, "We only insure the jewelry; the bonds are numbered coupons so they do not need to be insured."

Mr. Wrigley claims, "Then insure the jewelry for twelve hundred dollars."

"That will be twelve dollars," The insurance agent claims. The items disappear into a large envelope and the Wrigleys walk away.

The insurance agent says to Putnam, "The way I see it, there will be close to two hundred and fifty thousand in jewelry insured today. That is a neat little two thousand and a half in fees." He grins, "There will be some serious celebrations tonight."

William B. Astor and D. C. Blair approach Putnam. "Mr. Putnam, could we have a moment of your time?" asks Astor.

"But of course," Putnam automatically responds. The three men step to the side of the lobby.

"As you know, we both have private boxes in your safe. We would feel better if we were able to keep our valuables in the boxes rather than expose them in the lobby and have the items placed in envelopes. We were wondering if you knew of a jewelry store or bank that would have room in their vaults."

"I do not; however, I am sure that, if he has the space, Mr. Marvin would not mind having the boxes placed in his care." Putnam does not like having to recommend a competitor.

"That would be most accommodating of him," Astor comments. Satisfied that there is no reason for further concern, Astor and Blair join their wives.

Sadie, Sarah, and Cora are among the numerous guests in the park when a messenger walks directly over to Sadie. The messenger hands an envelope to Sadie, "Miss Sadie Stiles, I believe." Sadie opens her clutch and takes out a coin, which she hands to the messenger. Content at having just touched the hand of one of the most attractive young ladies in the hotel, the messenger walks away, blushing.

"So your poet is back," Sarah prods.

"I do not know, I have yet to open the envelope."

"Are you going to?" Sarah means is she going to open the envelope while they are in the park.

"What if it is something I do not wish to read? I would be sad at the hop tonight." Sadie is concerned.

"Or it could be something grand that will make the dance even better." Sarah sounds encouraging but is really just nosey. Reluctantly, Sadie opens the envelope. "Well?" Sadie reads the brief message silently a second time. "Well?" Sarah insists.

"I do not know how to take it," Sadie says reluctantly. She reads the note aloud.

> *"You ask why I stopped writing*
> *And why it seems we're fighting*
> *Although the results could be frightening,*
> *I'll try to be enlightening.*
> *Let me explain my reasons plain*

For why I currently abstain.
You want boys to be your toys
And thus your actions are filled with ploys;
You crave affection, seek attention,
Yet real emotions ache from suspension;
While doing this, you always miss
He who truly wants your kiss."

Sadie puts her hand with the poem in her lap.

"He misses you," Sarah reassures her little sister.

"It sounds like he is scolding me."

"He is," advises Cora, who has remained silent. "If you feel you deserve his criticism, write back; if you feel he is wrong, then let it end." Sadie looks to Sarah for guidance.

Morrissey, Marvin, Hathorn, and Putnam are supervising the placement of the two private safe deposit boxes in Morrissey's safe. In addition, four men are needed to carry in each of the three even larger boxes from Wells Fargo. "We will barely be able to get one of the large ones to fit in my safe," Marvin acknowledges. "We are lucky you agreed to let us use your safe."

"You are welcome to the space; however, I am sure that the larger boxes will not fit." Morrissey looks closely. "I am sure we have room enough for the contents, just not the boxes."

Putnam is looking older than he did at dinner. "I am concerned about the contents being taken out of the boxes."

Morrissey offers a solution. "Since we are closed on Sundays, we only have tonight to be concerned about. Why don't you send over one of your security men to sit in my office tonight while the safe is open? We will close the door at 4:00 in the morning and the doors of the safe will not open again until Monday afternoon."

Putnam looks relieved. "I will send my son."

"A good choice," Morrissey says, patting Putnam on the back. Marvin, Morrissey, Hathorn, and Putnam look on as the men open the safe deposit boxes and start putting the envelopes wherever they will fit on the various shelves of Morrissey's safe.

A frustrated Sadie finds the messenger who brought her the earlier message. "I would like you to take this envelope to whoever sent me the message earlier today." She tries to hand an envelope to the messenger, who is clearly reluctant to accept it.

"Is he expecting it?" the messenger inquires.

"I certainly hope so." Sadie tips the messenger a dime. "Can you tell me when it is delivered?"

"Consider it done." The messenger walks to the door to the lobby, happy with his windfall. Sadie follows at a distance. Sadie reaches the back door just as the messenger is leaving through the front door. She rushes after him, sure she will lose him on Broadway.

The street is crowded; however, Sadie is able to follow the messenger for over a block before she loses him in the crowd. Disappointed, Sadie turns and walks back to the hotel.

The bell over the door of the newspaper office rings as the messenger enters. Recognizing his associate, Walter stands. The messenger holds out the envelope Sadie gave him. "I have something from her." Walter takes the envelope and immediately opens it.

> *Poet dear I have some fear,*
> *Not of pain but of what to gain,*
> *By finding caring in one who is daring,*
> *To express himself in verse. What a curse!*

The message continues with a plea,

> *Please give me a second chance.*
> *This time come and take the flower from my hand.*
> *Let us say six on Sunday in the park of the States.*

In the dark of the night, Edith and Bennett are walking along the street from the train station to the States. Bennett appears drunk and in need of assistance. "We are almost there," Edith encourages.

"But I dun't wants to go home. The mornin' is still young."

"At least you did not say the night was still young." Edith pulls her weak charge. "Come along, we need to get back to the room before it starts to rain."

With his arm draped over her shoulder, Edith continues to steer Bennett down the street.

Antoinette and Janet watch the display from a corner near the station. Janet grumbles about society, "Dat's what's I mean about not fair. Whats she does for him, is the same as we do to other men but people don't go looking down their noses at her."

"Oh dey look down deir noses at her a plenty. It's jus' da rooms where dey do it we ain't allowed." Antoinette looks wise.

"Don't you wish we had a lot more money?" Janet has a perpetual complaint.

"Yus right 'bouts wun's thin,'" Antoinette concurs, "Wheneve' we ge's a little ahead, Pa comes up with some reason to takes it; so I don't go wishin' any more." "I'll never gives up my dreams." Janet's youth gives her the advantage of escaping reality.

"Den perhaps someday it'll comes true. And yus be able to carry a man home."

It is almost four in the morning and Richards and Morrissey are placing the casino's cash in the safe. Putnam's bored son, Geoffrey, with a deck of cards in his hand, watches. Richards looks at the totally stuffed safe. "Now that was a successful night."

"It all fit?" Morrissey is a happy businessman.

"We could have used the room you gave up." Richards says, reminding Morrissey that much of the space in the safe is being used for no charge.

"I didn't give it up, I helped a neighbor." Morrissey turns his attention to young Putnam. "How is your father coming with the repairs?"

"It will take one more day; however, with it being the Sabbath, no construction can be done around the hotel. We should be out of your way by the time you open on Monday. I understand that the Constitution doesn't even need repairs but Hathorn is going to hire a couple of men to pound away in the cellar so guests think repairs were made."

"Please tell your father that it is no trouble for us. He can use our safe as long as necessary." Morrissey closes the safe door and spins the combination. Richards tests the handle then looks to Putnam to test the handle, which he does. The three walk out into the casino. Morrissey and Richards patrol the casino one last time before the three exit.

A small row boat approaches the shore just outside Amsterdam, New York. The slave family is seated. A teenage white male, Samuel, is rowing the boat and watching the shore line for a signal. A middle-aged man, Robert, wearing a hat to avoid the rain, is waiting on the shore. Robert has a small lantern sitting on the ground. When Samuel sees the glow of the lantern, he pulls the boat into the shore.

"Hurry up," Robert calls out. Samuel pulls slightly harder on the oars. "Hurry, I said, a waiting carriage will draw attention." Samuel pulls up next to a log jutting out into the river. Nate gets out of the front of the boat, pulling it slightly up on the shore to steady it.

Robert begins helping Mattie, who is carrying Eve out of the boat. When Nanny is on land, Robert helps her. Adam gets out, leaving the violin, which is under covers on the floor of the boat. In the background a horse whinnies, causing everyone to turn in the direction of the noise.

Robert points up a small trail. "Hurry, we must get on the wagon before anyone gets suspicious." Nanny and Mattie, who is carrying Eve, start up the trail behind Robert.

Nate is holding Adam's hand. "The violin." Adam is pointing back to the boat.

"Wait sir, wait. We left our violin under the tarp," Nate pleads.

"Not your violin no more." Samuel smiles as he rows away.

"I's sorry pa." There are tears in Adam's eyes. Nate looks helplessly at the boat.

"Can't trust some people; others will risk it all on a stranger." Nate pats his son's head as they climb the trail.

"How dus I know who to trust?" the confused youngster asks.

"Yus figure that out and tell me," Nate admits. Nate and Adam rush up the trail to catch up to the rest.

To stay out of the blowing rain, Smiley is up on the porch near the side of the casino. Morrissey locks the door. Richards tests it and extends his hand for Putnam to test the handle, which he does. It does not move so the three pull towels over their heads and start walking toward Division Street. When they are out of site, Smiley walks down Franklin toward Pauline.

Smiley wipes the rain from his brow as he approaches Pauline. "Still unbearably hot."

"Not as 'ot as it's gunna get," she promises, taking Smiley's arm. "Off's to your place?"

"Can't we go to yur place?" Smiley wonders how he will be lucky enough to sneak her into his boarding house two nights in a row.

"Believe you me, yus don't want dat."

"How good are you at sneaking into a boarding house?"

"Sneaking into bedrooms' my business." It is impossible to tell if Pauline is bragging or ashamed.

Reverend Beecher is in his element addressing a large congregation. Although many dislike the winter in Saratoga, Beecher has an even more severe dread – a small congregation. He believes that he was meant to have a flock constantly the size he has in the season. "It is the sin of greed that plagues us most as a community, as a state, and as a country." He sermonizes.

One in the congregation who has not made it home from the previous evening stands and in a loud drunk voice calls out, "No it ain't Reverend." Those in the audience do not know what to do. The drunk gets louder and more passionate with every word, "The biggest sin is running out of wine. Even Christ knew that - he turned water into wine."

The drunk studies those in the pews, fixating on one older lady. "You know how to do that?" She gasps at the idea. "Nope, didn't think so; that's why you are here all alone." His voice gets softer as if he is becoming philosophical, "You learn to make wine, you will have plenty of company."

Harrison stands and approaches the drunk.

The drunk is not finished. "Last night the establishment where I was frequenting ran out of wine, and the innkeeper didn't know how to change water into wine either." Harrison takes the man by the arm and begins leading him from the church. "Take your hands off me unlessen you know how to change water into wine," the man threatens.

"I do. Come with me."

"You're a saint." The drunk man and the congregation are relieved, even if it is for different reasons. Harrison walks the man out the door.

The service over, those in the receiving line wait to shake Beecher's hand. Cora, her daughters in front of her, is going down the steps just ahead of Cook, Catharine, and George.

Cora shakes Beecher's hand. "A very interesting service. I do not remember one quite like it in Savannah."

"He was filled with the devil alcohol. It is sometimes good when parishioners get to see sin first hand," Beecher reassures her.

"I am sure." Cora has to pull her hand away from Beecher.

She walks away, being replaced by Cook, who speaks while shaking Beecher's hand. "That could have been handled better. The man provided you with an opportunity to talk about the cause of his behavior and its effect on society. Instead you stayed with your prepared remarks."

"I was taken too much by surprise to consider what opportunities were presented."

"Don't you think that we all should be sure enough in our beliefs that we do the right thing without thinking?" Cook walks away.

Catharine attempts to comfort the minister, "My father is a man of strong opinions."

"But he is judgmental." Beecher is still recovering first from the man in church and now from Cook.

"And what is the problem, if the opinions are correct?" She turns and walks down the steps. She is followed by George, who only briefly shakes Beecher's hand.

"Reverend, in this life we are only given a few opportunities to excel." George shows his distaste for Beecher, "It would appear you missed one of yours." George hastens to catch up with Catharine and her father.

Sadie and Sarah are sitting on a bench in the park while Jacob is standing, admiring Sarah. Sadie is holding a long stemmed rose. "You can feel the storm moving in," Jacob says, looking at the dark midday sky.

"I think we have a few hours before it rains," Sarah guesses.

"If you two are going to talk about the weather, will you be so kind as to just move on," Sadie admonishes.

Sarah smiles, stands up, and takes Jacob's arm. "Come dearest Jacob, my sister wants to be alone." Sarah is smiling in delight. A baffled Jacob willingly moves on.

Sadie sits alone on the bench, trying not to look around. Her hands are clasped around the stem of the rose. Walter approaches from behind, reaches over her shoulder and takes the rose from her hand. Surprised, Sadie squeezes the stem and a thorn pricks her thumb. Instinctively Sadie kisses her wounded thumb as she looks a Walter. After a silence, Sadie speaks, "I knew it was you."

"I doubt that."

"Who else would show he cared by criticizing?"

"Listen some time, it happens with most couples," Walter observes.

"Not until they are married."

"May I sit down?"

"No, you must first announce yourself to everyone in the hotel by walking me around the gardens where all can see. Then we can sit together." Sadie rises, takes Walter's elbow as she glances at the family cottage. "Believe me, my mother is watching."

Sarah stops in her walk with Jacob and points politely to her sister. "Did you know?"

"No, but I suspected," Jacob responds.

Edith is looking around the room she shares with Bennett. "Be sure you have everything you need for tonight; we cannot come back today after we leave."

"I don't have too much to take. I can come back tomorrow in the same clothes I have on now." In Bennett's case, no one would notice.

"Unless they get dirty."

"Then you will just have to wash them."

"After tonight, I will never wash another thing except myself again. Of course, I heard that the Stiles' man, Benjamin, can be hired. I might just have him bathe me." They walk out the door and into the hallway.

Edith speaks to a porter who happens to be in the hall. "There should be plenty of time for a walk before the storms move in."

"My mother, who can predict the weather days in advance, says no rain until after midnight," the porter predicts.

"Excellent." A witness established, Edith and Bennett walk out the front door and turn south on Broadway. They walk one short block to Washington Avenue and turn right, walking away from downtown. They cross the railroad tracks and head in the direction of the houses of the working people of Saratoga. After three blocks they turn north, going one block to a stable. They have walked three quarters of a square and are two blocks west of the casino.

In the stable Shorty, Michael, Elmendorf, Nolan, David, Phillips, and Peter are all present when Edith and Bennett enter. "Swanson in position?" Edith asks.

Shorty answers, "He's watching the casino."

Edith steps into one of the stalls. Michael and Elmendorf try to glance over the stall's low edge to watch her changing. "Everyone remember his assignment?" Edith does not seem to care who looks as she reminds everyone, "No names, everyone goes by a number."

Peter is stacking firewood neatly on the front and back of a work wagon leaving a large open area in the middle. There are two draft horses in the stalls. "I'll have the team out back of the casino at 4:00 am iff'n I haven't seen the signal before."

"Don't be a minute late." Bennett tries to show authority and distract the men from Edith.

"I know what I's got to do, I gots to be the Irish charmer. That's as easy for me as waken' up in the afternoon," Nolan brags as they all laugh.

Edith comes out of the stall dressed as a man. Her hair is in a bun. The shirt is padded at the shoulders and waist, hiding any female features.

Swanson is across the street from the casino talking to Pauline and Antoinette. "So how much do you ladies charge?"

Pauline answers, "Depends on what yus looking for."

"I's lookin' for a tumble with the two of you at the same time."

Pauline looks him over then advises, "Yus ain't got dat much money."

"I will have tomorrow," Swanson promises. "How much yus gunna charge me for a double?"

"Yus bring along a five dollar gold piece and we will put a smile on your face that will last until Wednesday. Dat is, iff'n yus survive," Pauline cautions.

"It sure is black out. What's you gunna do iff'n it starts to rain?" Swanson tries to maintain the conversation.

Antoinette speaks for the first time, "Hopefully by then we's found someone that wants us to have a nice dry room to sleep in."

"Or you will go home?" Swanson has an all knowing grin.

"I told yus dry. Our place is many things; dry ain't one of dem," Antoinette assures him.

The church bell rings twelve times, signaling those in the stable. "Okay, it is time," Edith states as it starts to pour. "Perfect. Anyone who is still awake will be closing their windows so the rain doesn't get in. No one is going to hear a thing." With the exception of Peter, who will pick them up, they walk out of the stable one at a time in the direction of the back of the casino. Walking single file, they maintain a separation of two houses.

Swanson watches as one light moves between the back rooms of the upstairs in the back of the casino. He can hear the windows being closed. He looks down the street and watches Pauline and Antoinette rushing for home with their skirts pulled up above their knees. Swanson sees a dark figure walk along the street then duck behind the casino. This continues as one by one the group gathers at the back door. They all pull on simple masks made from the legs of a new pair of pants with eyeholes cut out and the top clipped together.

In a single line they move to the back door. Michael picks the lock and they enter silently. With only the limited light that comes through the windows, Shorty, Michael, Elmendorf, Nolan, Phillips, David, Bennett, and Edith walk as silently as possible through the woodshed and up the back stairs.

There are four rooms off the center hall of the second floor. The group breaks into four prearranged groups of two. Shorty and Edith go to one bedroom door, Michael and Elmendorf to a second door, Bennett and Nolan a third, and David and Phillips are at the final door. One member of each team has a small crowbar in hand. The second, a piece of cloth to be used as a gag.

On a signal from Edith, one member of each pair springs their door with the crowbar. What happens next is simultaneous.

Michael and Elmendorf rush into Jennie's room. Michael grabs Jennie, one of Ringer's twin daughters, and places the gag in her mouth. Elmendorf starts tying her wrists together, then her knees.

Shorty and Edith rush into Jesse's room. Shorty tries to hold Jesse while Edith places the gag over her mouth. Unlike her sister, Jesse struggles violently. She kicks and tries to swing her fist. Ultimately Shorty has to lay on her to hold her down. Shorty, who is enjoying the physical contact, smiles. Edith is eventually able to tie her at the wrists and knees.

David and Phillips rush into Dolly's, the youngest daughter's, room. They have the easiest time as David holds Dolly down and Philip struggles to gag her. They turn her over and tie her wrists together, and like her sisters, they tie her knees together.

Bennett and Nolan have been assigned the Ringers' room. Bennett has a pistol in his hand. At the sound at the door, Ringer jumps from the bed. Coldly Bennett places the gun's barrel to Ringer's forehead. "Not so fast." As Bennett speaks, Nolan puts the gag in Ruth's mouth. "We don't want to do anything stupid now, do we? It would be horrible to make your wife a widow right in front of her eyes." Nolan takes Ruth's wrists and ties each to the metal bed rail. The wrists are tied apart so she cannot untie the knots. He then ties her knees together.

Without any conversation Edith and Shorty pick Jesse up like she is a carpet and carry her out her bedroom door. They carry her across the hall and into her parents' room. Shorty and Edith lay Jesse on the bed beside Ruth. "Look at the gun at your father's head," Shorty insists. When Jesse is quiet, Shorty unties her hands, separates them and ties each wrist to the headboard. Her knees remain tied together.

Edith comes to the door of Jennie's room where she nods her head. Michael and Elmendorf pick Jennie up and carry her out the door. Michael is holding her from under her arms. It appears he is trying to touch her breast. Elmendorf has her legs, which are uncovered to the knee. The two men carry Jennie across the hall like she is a stuffed burlap bag. Michael and Elmendorf lay Jennie face down on her parents' bed. They untie her wrists, then retie each wrist to the footboard of the bed. David and Philip enter carrying little Dolly and place her next to Jennie. They secure her wrists to the footboard. The four women are all tied to the same bed; two facing each way. Their gags keep them from talking while they struggle to communicate with their eyes.

With the women bound, Michael and Elmendorf tie Ringer's wrists behind his back and his knees together. With the family secure, Shorty leaves the group for a planned project. Michael takes up his responsibility, walking to a window in the front where he watches out for any signal from Swanson.

Bennett whispers to Ringer, "Now this can be easy or this can be difficult. We need you to open the safe. If you cooperate, you and your family will be free in no time. If you don't, we will have to start hurting them, starting with the youngest." He tries to extend the threat. "The older two will be treated to a little fun before we hurt them." Bennett squeezes Jesse's breast to show he is serious.

Bennett and David pull Ringer out of the room by his hair. Ringer struggles to stay standing because his knees are tied together. Phillips, Elmendorf, and Nolan remain in the bedroom with the women as Edith exits.

Bennett and David, pulling Ringer, who is struggling to walk with his knees tied together, join Michael, who has been watching out the window. Moments later Edith joins them in the hallway. Shorty is not there. They proceed to the back stairs.

"Who's the fool who tied his knees together? How's he going to get down the stairs?" Bennett says, more than asks. David unties Ringer's legs so the group can proceed to the stairway. The small group walks across the woodshed to the back door of the casino.

"You won't be able to get in the casino, the door is locked from the inside," Ringer attempts to threaten them. When he finishes speaking, the door is opened from the other side by Shorty, holding bolts of dark cloth under one arm.

"Got that one wrong, didn't you?" Bennett grabs the hair on the back of Ringer's head, pushing him through the door. "Let's hope you do better real soon." By agreement, Bennett is the only member of the gang who will speak.

In Morrissey's office, Shorty and Edith hang the two pieces of the dark cloth that Shorty was carrying over the widows. When they are done, David lights a lantern. Bennett leans down very close to Ringer's ear. "Now for the serious part. It is time for you to open the safe."

"I can't; I don't know the combination." Ringer tries a false excuse. Ringer whines in pain when David pulls his hair violently.

"Now do you really expect us to believe that the cashier of the casino doesn't have the combination to the safe?"

"Believe it or not, it's the truth." Bennett nods to David, who then pulls Ringer's hair violently.

To get Bennett's attention, Edith walks over and taps Bennett on the arm - she motions for him to leave the office and come with her into the casino.

Alone in the casino, Edith and Bennett take their masks off. "Pulling his hair until he is bald will not get us anywhere," Edith warns. She thinks for a minute, then suggests, "Let's go upstairs and get the little one."

In the parent's bedroom, Nolan finishes putting a black drape over the window. He takes out a match and lights a kerosene lamp. He keeps the light low enough not to cause someone outside to be alarmed, but bright enough not to bump into furniture. Although three of the gang are watching over the women, Nolan is the only one the women are supposed to hear from. "Now ladies, you need to know that we are just a bunch of fun loving guys who don't want to hurt nobody." Bound and gagged, the women cannot speak; however, the fear is evident in their eyes.

Nolan begins walking around the room looking at the items Ruth brought with her. He goes through the lone dresser and finds a corset. Nolan holds it up, chuckling to himself. "Now this must hurt to wear." He continues to search the room. In a second drawer, he finds a pistol. Nolan takes it out and examines it closely.

Gun in hand, he approaches Ruth. "I'm going to take the gag out of your mouth; if you scream or call out, I will put it back and deeper. Do you understand?" Ruth shakes her head in the affirmative. Roughly, Nolan removes Ruth's gag. "Who does this belong to?" he asks.

"My husband."

"Honesty. Now that is a good concept. Are there any more?"

"No."

Nolan sits in the lone chair pondering what to do next.

Edith and Bennett have put their masks back on before they enter the parents' room.

Bennett sees the gun. "What's that?"

"Belongs to her husband," Nolan answers.

Bennett turns his attention to Ruth. "Your husband needs a little convincing."

Bennett looks at Phillips. "Number 3 (Phillips), give me a hand." Phillips walks over to the bed. Bennett unties Dolly's hands from the bed. He then rolls her over and ties her wrists together behind her back.

Ruth makes a mother's plea, "Not her, take me."

Bennett takes the gag from Nolan's hand and sticks it back in Ruth's mouth. He looks to Phillips, "You carry her." Looking at Elmendorf, "Number 5, you watch out the window in case there is trouble."

Phillips puts Dolly over his shoulder in a fireman's carry. Without further explanation Bennett, Edith, Phillips, and defenseless Dolly leave the room.

Elmendorf follows. His assignment for the next few hours is to replace Michael looking out the front window on the second floor at Swanson, who is hiding under a tree across the street. Michael walks to Morrissey's office.

Eventually Ruth is able to spit the gag part way out. She pleads with Nolan, "What are they doing? Why do they need my baby?" Fearing she may call out, Nolan pushes the gag back into Ruth's mouth.

In the woodshed of the casino, Edith points to an empty cabinet. Phillips realizes what she wants, "I've got it." He ties Dolly's ankles to a rope around her waist so she cannot kick. Gently he places Dolly in the cabinet and closes the door. Edith taps Phillips on the shoulder and he follows Edith and Bennett into the casino.

In the casino and away from any listeners, Edith explains what is next. "We need to make them wonder about the girl." She smiles, "Stay here for a few minutes, then come in the office. Whisper something in my ear and go back to the bedroom. In a little while I will send Bennett up. When I do, bring down one of the twins."

"Smart," Phillips compliments. He exits back through the door to the woodshed. Edith and Bennett move through the door to Morrissey's office.

"Your wife tells us that Morrissey thinks you are a trusted employee. So much so that you have the combination to the safe." Bennett attempts to rationalize with Ringer. "She says to open the safe before one of the girls gets hurt."

"She is wrong, I told her I knew it but I only know the first two numbers. My assistant knows the last two. Morrissey doesn't trust anyone but Richards enough for them to have the entire combination."

"Morrissey is right," Bennett reminds Ringer. "You are a trusted employee to put your family in so much danger." The fright is apparent in Ringer's eyes. Bennett sits and looks through his mask at the scared bookkeeper.

Almost on cue, Phillips opens the door from the casino and walks into Morrissey's office. He approaches Edith and whispers in her ear. "You look better without the mask." No one else could hear his comment. Phillips walks back to the casino.

Edith, mask on, walks away from Phillips to talk to Bennett. Phillips exits through the casino door. Edith whispers to Bennett, "Pretend the little one is dead."

"Shit no!" Bennett swears before turning to Ringer. "Damn little one

212

messed it up." Bennett shakes his head as if truly sorry, "Just remember we did not want to hurt her."

Bennett then turns his attention to his four masked associates (Edith, Michael, David and Shorty.) "Go get one of the twins." On command Edith and Shorty exit the room, leaving Ringer alone with David, Michael, and Bennett.

In the casino Edith, Phillips, and Shorty have removed their masks. Edith reminds Shorty, "You're sure you know what to say?"

"Got it."

Knowing Shorty sees himself as a joker, she adds, "No ad-libbing."

"What?" He does not know the meaning of the word.

"Just say what I told you to - no more," Edith stresses.

In the bedroom Nolan is sitting in the only padded chair, caressing the pistol he found, when Edith, Phillips, and Shorty enter. Shorty goes over and starts untying Jennie and sitting her up. Shorty speaks while he is re-tying Jennie's hands behind her back. "Please be smarter than your sister." Ruth's eyes show fear.

"No one meant to hurt her. She was foolish, but then again, so is your husband," Shorty apprises Ruth.

Shorty looks at Jennie, then at Phillips saying, "You're bigger." Phillips picks up Jennie and starts to carry her over his shoulder in a fireman's carry. He takes the opportunity to place his hand on her buttocks.

Edith holds the door and Phillips carries Jennie out into the hallway, Edith follows. Shorty replaces Phillips in the hostage room. Nolan continues to fondle the gun. Ruth begins to cry; Jesse, the remaining twin, struggles quietly with her ropes.

Phillips enters Morrissey's office with Jennie draped over his shoulder. His hand remains on Jennie's buttocks. Reluctantly Phillips puts Jennie down and starts to leave the room. Edith steps in his way. He realizes he is to wait.

With her knees still bound together, Jennie has trouble standing. Edith stands beside the bound girl trying to help steady her.

Bennett approaches Jennie, putting his hand on her gag. "Now when I take this out, you are going to remain quiet or harm will befall your father. Do you understand?"

Jennie nods her head in the affirmative.

Tentatively, Bennett removes the gag.

Jennie looks to her father, "Where's Dolly?"

"Isn't she with your mother?"

"No, they took her out fifteen minutes ago." Jennie appeals to Bennett, "Where is my little sister?" For the first time, Jennie seriously struggles while Bennett puts the gag back in her mouth. He signals for Phillips to hold her.

"Now Mr. Ringer, are you going to unlock this safe or are you going to be missing another daughter?"

"I told you I only know half the combination. I couldn't help if I wanted to."

"Then you must not want to bad enough." He looks to Phillips, "Get the little princess a chair."

Edith taps Bennett's arm. Realizing that she wants to speak to him, Bennett follows Edith through the door to the casino.

Alone in the casino, Edith and Bennett remove their masks. They are both smiling. Edith leans against the faro table. "Fear works best when it has time to build. Let's let everything cool for a few minutes." She takes out a flask, takes a sip and hands it to Bennett. Bennett takes a bigger sip.

"Nectar of the Gods," he remarks, sitting on the roulette table. "So what are you going to do with your share?"

"First, we have to get the money."

"I'm going to San Francisco. Now that is a place for real men."

"You will be shot within a month," she assesses.

"You fail to see the real me." Bennett puffs his chest. "I am sophisticated, well read, and a bit of a philosopher."

"Who told you that?"

"Several women that I have known over the years."

"Did you trust those ladies?" Edith jokes.

"Never."

"Then why do you trust their opinions of you?"

Three months before, Bennett was sitting on a bench in Pittsburgh, looking worn and tired. Edith, well dressed, walked up to him. Breaking all the codes of Victorian etiquette, she started a conversation with a man to whom she had not be introduced. "Mr. Bennett, I presume."

"Who the hell are you?"

She spun her parasol, "I am about to be your best friend."

"Don't waste your time, I just lost everything in a stock swindle."

"I know."

"Then why are you here?"

"I have a plan that will make both of us wealthier than either of us ever dreamed."

"Wasting your time, I told you, I have nothing left to invest."

"I accept that that is a fact; however, you have what matters to me, your reputation."

Bennett pondered her intentions.

She asked, "How would you like to spend the season at the States in Saratoga Springs?"

"You have not been listening. I couldn't afford a place in a barn."

"But I could."

A wet Pauline and a damp Smiley are sneaking up the stairs of an older house. One of the stairs creak as they climb up. She giggles. Smiley is sure he has pushed lady luck too hard, trying to sneak Pauline into his room a second time.

Nolan asks Jesse and Ruth, "Are your mouths getting dry?" Both ladies nod their heads in the affirmative. "If I take the gags out and give you a sip of water, do you promise not to make any noise?" Ruth and Jesse both nod their heads in the affirmative.

Nolan removes Ruth's gag first. When she remains quiet, he takes out Jesse's. Nolan goes to the wash stand and pours a single glass of water. He gives each a sip. "Can I trust you to stay quiet or do I need to put the gags back?"

"Can I have another sip?" Jesse requests.

Nolan gives both women a second sip.

Ruth quietly asks the mother's question, "Where are my daughters?"

"I honestly don't know."

"They are good girls. Can you please check on them for me?"

"If they are good, they will be okay."

The look Ruth gives Jesse shows she is not sure.

In Smiley's bedroom, he is propped against the headboard of his bed. Pauline's head is resting on his bare chest. She teases, "Two nights in one week, not bad for an old man."

"How long yus been a whore?" Smiley asks, as if he were asking about any other profession.

"I wish I knew. Seems like my whole life."

"Ever want to get out?"

"Every day of my miserable life."

"Why don't yuh?"

"No money, no skills, no prospects, lousy family." She continues to fondle the hair on his chest.

"But surely you make good money."

"Don't matter, Pa takes damn near every cent."

"Your father doesn't care if you are a whore?"

"Hell no. He started me."

"He got you your first client?" Smiley is intrigued.

"No, he was my first client; only he didn't pay for it." Her matter of fact tone shows a sad acceptance.

Smiley goes very quiet.

"Don't go getting all gloomy on me," she directs, "Hell, he an' Ma trained all four of us. I guess Ma used to be pretty good at it."

"Four?" Smiley had been watching her for half the season and only noticed her with two other young women.

"Yeah, I had a sister, Lizzie, went missing a couple years ago." She gently rubs Smiley's chest.

Smiley gets ready to speak when Pauline puts her finger over his lips. "Hush up now."

In the casino, Bennett asks, "Time to go back in?"

"Let's give them a few more minutes." Edith is relaxed. David comes out of Morrissey's office, removes his mask and joins them in the casino.

"What's goin' on?" David asks the natural question.

"We are letting them think," Edith explains.

"I dun't like it. Times a runnin' out." David's anxiety is beginning to show.

"We are fine. Better to use the time wisely than to hurry and lose it all." Edith continues to show control.

In the Ringers' room Nolan continues to tinker with the pistol while Shorty looks out the window. "What should I call you?" Ruth holds back tears for her daughters.

"Number four."

"Could I change places with one of my daughters? I want them safe."

"You changing places ain't gunna change what's already happened."

Jesse speaks for the first time, "What are you going to do with us?"

"Hopefully nothing."

The door opens and Phillips and David enter carrying a tied and gagged Jennie; Phillips' hand is placed directly on her buttocks. Noticing that Ruth and Jesse are not gagged, David is concerned about the change in protocol. "Why'd you take their gags out?"

"They've been quiet. No reason to make this any harder than it has to be."

Shorty attempts to show he is in the line of authority. "Says who?"

"Me." Nolan stands, still holding the pistol. Shorty and Phillips begin tying Jennie to the post with her sister and mother. Nolan walks over to Jennie. "If I take the gag out, do you promise to be quiet like your ma and sister?"

Jennie shakes her head in the affirmative. Nolan adds, "If'n you start making noise, it means I has to gag you an' your sister and mother." Jennie nods her head in the affirmative.

When the gag is removed she turns to her sister, "Where's Dolly?"

"She hasn't come back. Didn't you see her?" Ruth's motherly instincts are being brought to the surface.

"No, she's not with Pa and I didn't see her anywhere in between." Jennie's words concern everyone.

"Oh no!" Ruth begins to cry. Ruth, Jennie, and Jesse all look at Nolan for support.

Shorty gives the order, "Number one (Edith) says to bring down the other twin."

"No, No!" Ruth calls out "What good will that do?"

"Seems your husband needs some more convincing."

Ruth starts to cry as Phillips and Shorty start untying Jesse. "Take me. Please, dear God, take me," Ruth calls.

"This is not a volunteer mission," Shorty barks.

Ruth turns to Jennie, who has been downstairs, "Did they kill your sister? I just know they did…" Phillips puts a gag in Jesse's mouth, then picks her up and carries her over his shoulder like he did Jennie. Again he has one hand firmly on her buttocks; however, this time he is dealing with Jesse, a struggling victim. Shorty, Phillips, and Jesse leave the room headed for the office.

Shorty opens the door to the office and Phillips, carrying Jesse, along with Edith and Bennett, who they met in the casino, walk in.

An exasperated Bennett asks, "Let me put it to you one more time Mr. Ringer. Are you going to open the safe or not?"

"I told you I only know half the combination."

"Your wife tells you to stop lying. She has lost one daughter this evening and doesn't want to lose another."

"I can't."

Bennett removes Jesse's gag saying, "No calling out, understand?"

217

Jesse gives an affirmative nod. "Pa, no one has seen Dolly since they carried her out of the room an hour ago. "If'n you don't help them, I think this is the last time you will ever see me." Ringer looks at his daughter.

In desperation, Ringer offers, "I have an idea what the last numbers might be. I don't know for sure, but I can try."

"Then let's give it a go, shall we." Bennett is confident that things are about to move forward.

Phillips and Bennett pull Ringer to the safe. They don't untie his wrists so he tries to turn the dial with his hands behind his back. After several tries Ringer speaks. "Stupid. You need to untie me."

Bennett mocks anger. "Now why do you feel the need to start calling names? Number 6, untie our guest." Shorty unties Ringer's hands. Ringer quickly goes through the first two numbers of the combination, then slowly does the next two numbers. He tests the door, it does not open. Hands beginning to sweat, Ringer repeats the process, two numbers quickly then two slowly. Again, it does not work.

Ringer tries to relax then repeats the process a third time. The safe doors again remain sealed.

Bennett speaks to Phillips. "Enough, take care of the girl." With a revolting smirk, Phillips moves toward Jesse.

Ringer pleads for time. "I told you I only know the first two numbers; I watched my assistant one time so I think I know the last numbers. What I don't know is how many complete spins in-between numbers." Ringer looks desperately at Jesse and Bennett.

"Five more tries," Bennett concedes.

Ringer repeats the process. On the second attempt the safe handle drops.

As the door is opened, Bennett, Edith, Phillips, Shorty, David, and Michael are all amazed as they look into the jammed cabinet.

Morrissey is holding a drink as he looks out the window of his suite onto the nearly black park below. Susie sits up in bed and realizes her husband is missing. "What's the matter?"

"Nothing, just restless. Must be the rain or maybe just knowing all that is in the safe."

Susie lays back down and pulls the sheet evenly across her body. "You worry too much."

"True enough. This has been a better season than I ever imagined. Where would you like to go to celebrate when it is over?"

"Back to Troy for a week or two to relax. After that, we could go to the City to see some plays."

"That we could."

Concerned about her husband, Susie rises, and joins Morrissey at the window. "Sit down so I can rub your neck, you big moose."

Morrissey sits down and Susie begins to rub the back of his neck. "A week in Troy to be on our own would be good."

"I will write mother and ask her to take Lil' John so we can really celebrate." Susie bends over and kisses Morrissey on the cheek.

In Morrissey's office, Bennett breaks the silence. "It ain't going to unload itself." The men all begin to pull envelopes out of the safe.

Edith taps Bennett's arm and whispers. He turns to the others, "Stop right now."

Those emptying the safe look confused but do as instructed. Edith and Bennett exit into the casino. Those in the office look at each other for guidance. Shorty notices a diamond ring, sapphire ring and several pearl necklaces that have fallen on the floor, one with a big stone. He picks them up. He looks around, notices that no one else is watching and slips them into his pocket.

In the casino Edith speaks, "Here is where we have to maintain discipline. We need to take the girl back upstairs. Make sure Phillips and Nolan double tie the entire family." She thinks of the process. "We can leave Nolan alone with the women. Everyone else, except Elmendorf, comes downstairs; we need him to keep watching the front."

"Did you see that safe? We are going to need plenty of bags." Bennett is amazed. Knowing they have covered the issues, Bennett and Edith return to the office.

Bennett gives instructions. "Number three, take the girl back to her family. Make sure they are tied real tight then come back down. Tell number four that he will be watching the women alone."

Phillips re-gags Jesse then picks her up and places her over his shoulder. This time he does not touch her buttocks as he leaves. Shorty holds the door for them.

Phillips brings Jesse in and places her where she was on the bed. In his hurry, Phillips leaves her wrists tied together behind her back instead of tied to the rail. Phillips reports to Nolan, "Number four, we are in. You would not believe all that is in the safe. It is filled to capacity. She had a great idea to start the fires first."

"Quiet. You talk too much," Nolan responds.

An excited Phillips says, "Number one said you are to watch the women alone. We need everyone else to bag up the prize."

"Okay, get out of here," Nolan says as Phillips leaves. He tries to calm the women. "Ladies, this is going to take a while. You just be quiet and this will end well."

When Phillips returns to the office, Bennett instructs, "Tie him, then tie him again to the chair. We don't need him anymore." Phillips takes some rope and secures Ringer.

Bennett throws five pillow cases onto the floor in front of the safe. "Don't waste space with the envelopes. Number three and six cut them open, dump the contents into these pillow cases. Number seven and eight, you hold the pillow cases open. I'll check each envelope to be sure nothing is left. With a sense of glee the men start tearing and dumping. Two men cut open the envelopes, two hold the pillow cases open. After each envelope is dumped, it is checked by Bennett, who neatly stacks the envelopes on Morrissey's desk.

Standing almost in awe, Edith watches as a king's ransom is piled in inexpensive pillow cases.

Phillips holds up a handful of bonds. "Do we take the bonds?"

"Yes," Bennett says knowing that they can decide what to do with them later.

The men resume the cleaning out of the safe.

Shorty stands in front of the pillow cases filled with bounty. "The pillow cases are full. What do we do now?"

"Now that is a great problem to have," Bennett laughs.

Edith looks around for any type of container, then leaves Morrissey's office. When she enters the Ringers' room she starts opening the drawers to the dresser. In the second drawer she finds and pulls out a crinoline. She puts it under her arm and exits.

As Nolan talks to the women, the sound of Edith opening doors can be heard. "I guess someone needs new clothes."

"The next time he comes in, would you ask where Dolly is?" Ruth worries about her missing daughter.

"Won't do no good."

Ruth begins quietly crying.

In the hallway on the second floor, Edith walks out of Jesse's room. She has three crinolines with her. As she walks, she pulls the strings in the waist of the crinolines tight and knots them, creating makeshift bags. Back in Morrissey' office, Edith throws the crinoline bags to those unloading the safe. Those charged with cleaning out the safe start filling the bags with jewelry and whatever else was put in the envelopes at the hotel.

One of the metal safe-deposit boxes is so heavy that it takes both Phillips and Shorty to pull it out of the safe. It was specially made to be used in commercial safes or stored in a home. To make the issue even greater, the box is equipped with a key lock. "Any ideas on how to open this?" Shorty looks to each person in the room.

Thinking of the bars used to open the bedroom doors, Bennett suggests, "Try one of the crowbars." The men all start looking around. Exasperated, Bennett suggests, "Number 3, they are probably upstairs. Go get one." Phillips heads upstairs.

In Phillips' absence a second strong box is pulled out of the safe by Shorty and David. It is so heavy that it drops to the floor when they pull it off the shelf. They all stare at the safe-deposit box until Shorty begins to snicker. One by one they all start to laugh except Edith.

Hearing the laughter Phillips comes back into the office. "Fell out." Shorty jokes. It takes a couple of minutes for everyone to settle down. Phillips takes the small crow bar and tries several times to force the top of the second box. It does not budge.

Phillips tries to pry open the first box with no luck. "No use. This is too well made." He turns his back to Ringer, takes off the mask and wipes sweat from his brow. He adds, "Damn Troy Safe Company." He puts the mask back on.

"Never mind that for now, we will take it with us," Bennett orders.

"Both of them?" Phillips inquires.

Bennett looks at the two strong boxes. "There is no way we're leaving here without whatever is in them. To want boxes that good means whatever is in them is worth a lot!" Edith taps Bennett and the two go back to the casino.

Back in the privacy of the casino, Bennett and Edith can take off their masks. "It is time to get Peter and the team down here," Edith commands.

"This is where it gets dangerous." Concern is obvious on Bennett's face. "There is no explaining a horse and wagon parked outside."

"No one will give us a chance to explain; if anyone sees the wagon they will sound the alarm."

"Want me to get Peter?" Bennett would like a break.

"The plan called for Phillips to do it. No reason to change now." Bennett and Edith put their masks back on and return to the office.

"Number three, time to get the wagon," Bennett instructs. Phillips stands and looks at his confederates, then starts for the door. Before Phillips can leave, Bennett stops him. "We have too many bags. We need you to carry one with you. Take the littlest one and be careful."

"I'll put it under my shirt, although I doubt anyone will be out in the rain at this hour." Phillips stuffs one of the makeshift crinoline bags under his shirt. It gives him a pot belly and when he walks, the metal jewelry rattles.

"Think you should go on a diet real soon," Shorty jokes.

"I'll be a lot lighter in just a few minutes," Phillips answers. "Going to be a long time before you're funny." Phillips leaves for the stable.

As he leaves the back door of the casino, Phillips removes the mask. He leaves it on the grass behind the casino. It has started to rain more heavily again. Going the two blocks to the stable, Phillips walks as normally as he can. Not having a belt, he has to hold the bag under his shirt.

The horses are harnessed but not hitched to a work wagon. The back and front of the wagon has firewood stacked neatly, although who would be seeking a wagon load of firewood in July would be a difficult question to answer. There is a folded tarp laying over the front stack of wood.

Shaking himself off like a wet dog, Phillips remarks, "It is time to get going."

"How'd it go?"

"As close to as planned as possible," Phillips assures Peter and himself.

Peter has to enquire, "How much did we get?"

"Lots. The jewelry alone is over $300,000." Phillips pulls the bag out from under his shirt, putting it in the wagon. He turns to Peter. "See you in Tom's Tavern in a couple of days."

Phillips starts walking west. Peter begins hitching the horses to the wagon mumbling, "See you in a couple of days. Good luck."

Bennett approaches Elmendorf, who has been watching out the front window. Placing his hand on the watcher's shoulder, Bennett whispers, "It doesn't matter now. Time to help carry everything out." The two walk down the stairs.

It starts to pour even harder as the wagon pulls up to the back door of the casino. Edith holds the back door while David and Elmendorf come through, struggling with one of the personal strong boxes. They lift it up over the side of the wagon and go back inside. Peter holds the old horses steady as they remove their masks and throw them on top of Phillips' mask. David and Elmendorf come out a second time, struggling even more with the other personal strong box. After lifting the boxes onto the wagon, David climbs on and balances the two. Their work done, Elmendorf and David walk south on Franklin Street.

Bennett is nervously watching the door to the woodshed. Edith enters. "They are off. Get ready."

Bennett and Edith each go into Morrissey's office. Bennett is relieved, "Time to finish up." Bennett, Michael, and Shorty pick up bags and walk out the door.

Alone with Ringer, Edith checks over the two remaining pillow cases and the two remaining bags made from the women's crinolines. Satisfied that Ringer is tied sufficiently, Edith goes into the casino, leaving Ringer alone to struggle meaninglessly.

Michael walks in through the woodshed door, followed moments later by Bennett, then Shorty. They are all dripping wet. "Miserable out there," Bennett utters.

"Perfect. Keeps anyone from being out for a walk. Two trips to go." Edith is finally happy.

Michael and Bennett take the two remaining pillow case bags and Shorty takes the first of the crinoline bags, carrying them to the wagon. Edith checks the office one last time then exits, leaving Ringer alone briefly. Ringer struggles uselessly.

Edith, coming from the casino, meets Michael, Bennett, and Shorty in the woodshed. They have loaded the second bags. She instructs, "Bennett, you are done, head for the stable and lay low until the action begins." She turns her attention to Shorty and Michael. "Get the last two bags then head out." She thinks for a minute before focusing on Shorty. "Stick to the plan."

In the Ringer bedroom, Edith walks in and touches Nolan on the arm. She looks over to see if the women are tied. Getting ready to meet with Edith alone, Nolan puts the pistol he has been playing with on the dresser. Edith and Nolan stand in the doorway so they are able to watch the three women. She whispers, "Wait five minutes, gag them, give them the warning, then head out."

"How did we do?"

"Better than even we expected and no one was hurt."

In back of the casino, Michael brings out a bag and puts it on the wagon. He walks to the far side of the wagon, grabs one corner of the tarp and waits. Shorty emerges with the final bag, puts it in the wagon, and takes another corner of the tarp. Michael and Shorty pull the tarp over the wagon and tie it to the back. The wagon looks to anyone who might see it like it is a load of firewood being kept dry by the tarp.

As a sign of congratulations Shorty and Michael pat each other on the back. In the rain, Michael starts walking north following the railroad tracks. Shorty crosses the street; he has one more task to accomplish.

Edith comes out and climbs up on the wagon next to Peter. They pull around the casino and out onto Franklin Street. The sound of the horse's hoofs can be heard as they proceed south. "Take it easy, we don't want to draw attention now," she instructs.

"That was the longest night of my life. Waiting is hell."

"It is the thrill of the chase that keeps us all going," she assures Peter.

Shorty disappears into a group of bushes across the street from the casino. Swanson, soaked to the core, has been standing guard all night. He has huddled under a pine tree seeking whatever shelter was available.

"Went like a dream. I will do any job with that lady," Shorty brags, taking out the two rings and two necklaces that he picked up from the floor. He shares with his friend. "One of each for you. I told you I would take care of you for having this lousy duty." Swanson takes a necklace with the round stone and the bigger of the two rings.

To Swanson, this is like winning the Irish lottery. "Thank you my little friend." He runs his finger over the jewels. "What are you going to do now?"

"I'm headed for Ballston Spa." Shorty is sticking with the plan.

"Going to catch a train?" Swanson asks.

"Yes indeed. One bound for Saratoga. No one will suspect someone coming into the village." As usual, Shorty smiles, "And you?"

"I have a little celebrating to do." Shorty knows his friend well enough that he will have wasted the value of the jewels within two days.

"See you at Tom's on Thursday."

"I should be done celebrating about then." Swanson flips his newly acquired necklace in one hand.

Nolan has just placed the gags back in each woman's mouth. "We have one man guarding Mr. Ringer. He is going to ensure that everyone gets away safely. Don't try anything for half an hour and you will be fine."

Nolan looks at his charges, "Ladies, I am truly sorry to leave you tied up, but the cleaning lady comes in about sunup; she should be able to untie you."

Like his cohorts, Nolan exits via the back door, leaving his mask on the pile by the door. Boldly he walks down Division Street in the direction of the hotels.

Jesse, who is not tied to the bed, but whose legs are tied together, struggles to stand up. She hops around the bed and, with her hands still behind her back, pulls the gag out of her mother's mouth. Jesse puts her own face down near Ruth's tied wrists so that Ruth can take the gag out her mouth. Jesse hops all the way around the bed to get Jennie's gag out while her mother speaks. "You heard him, don't try anything for half an hour."

Jesse removes Jennie's gag. "There is no one out there." Jesse hops around the bed again and grabs the gun.

"Jesse's right, if there was anyone out there he would have been back in here already," Jennie concurs.

"We can't take the chance." Ruth is near panic.

With her hands tied behind her back, Jesse picks up the pistol then hops toward the door.

"What are you doing?" Ruth wonders.

"Sounding the alarm." Jesse exits the room.

"No, don't." Ruth words do not slow her daughter.

Jesse hops across the hall to the back stairs. With her hands tied behind her back, Jesse puts the gun in one hand and tries to grab the handrail with the other. She strains to hop down the stairs. With three stairs to go she falls, dropping the gun, which lands on one of the stairs. She fights to regain her footing. Realizing the difficulty, she sits on the stairs, picks up the gun, then stands.

When she reaches the woodshed, Jesse hops toward the back door. The door has been closed so Jesse grapples with the handle.

Jesse falls for a second time going through the back door. She rolls against the building, regains her footing and hops toward the street. As soon as she is on the street, Jesse fires the pistol and yells, "Murder. Murder."

In the lobby of the States Hotel, the desk clerk and porter are struggling to stay awake when they hear the gun shot. The clerk looks at the porter, "What the hell?"

"Sounded like a gun to me," responds the porter.

"Check it out."

"Why me?!" The porter is panicked.

Jesse's pistol has to be cocked before she fires a second time. She pulls the hammer back and fires a second shot. She hops down the street and fires a third time shouting, "Murder. Sound the alarm."

The desk clerk is losing patience with the porter. "Get out there. You may have to sound the alarm."

Dressed in only a thin soaking wet nightdress, Jesse is in the street yelling for help. Doors and windows from neighboring buildings begin to open.

The wagon, with Peter and Edith, is turning into the yard of a coal and wood company when they hear gun shots. Peter looks to Edith, "What was that?"

"Nothing good."

"What do you want me to do?"

"Pull into the barn just like we planned." The heavy wagon pulls into the sole barn in the small business.

On Franklin Street, Swanson looks over his shoulder. He hustles a little to get further away."

A man exits one of the big the houses across the street from the casino. At the same moment the porter catches up to Jesse in the street and tries to calm her. "It's okay."

"Untie me, you fool," Jesse shouts. Looking over the porter's shoulder, she instructs the man who just exited his house. "Go sound the alarm. There has been a murder and a robbery at Morrissey's." The man looks at Jesse, too stunned to move. "I said, ring the damn alarm or I will shoot you with the one bullet I have left." Others start to come out of the houses.

The man begins running down the street as the porter unties Jesse. When she is free, Jesse, gun in hand, starts running back to the casino.

Jesse puts the gun on the dresser and begins untying Jennie. "We need to find Pa." When Jesse finishes untying Jennie, the two untie their mother and Jesse picks up the gun.

"Did you see anyone?" Ruth asks. The three untied women exit the room dressed only in their nightgowns.

"Not in the building." Jesse, gun in hand, is cautious. "If any of them are left, they know the village is awake, and they are going to be scared." The trio descends the back stairs quietly." Jesse looks around the door from the woodshed. "No one is here."

The three women rush through the woodshed, into the casino, then through the door to Morrissey's office. Jesse looks in. "He's here." Jesse bursts in and rushes to her father, stepping on the opened envelopes laying on the floor. After hugging and kissing his cheek, Jesse begins to untie Ringer. There is the sound of people banging on the front door to the casino.

"Let them in," Jesse orders her sister.

Jennie looks down at herself. "Dressed like this, I must get a wrap." She runs out of the room.

When Ringer's hands are untied, Jesse stands and leaves the room to see who is at the door. Ruth is busy untying her husband's legs.

"Where's Dolly?" The mother is terrified.

Hands free, Ringer helps untie his legs. "I don't know."

The bell on the Village Hall starts ringing. The bell sounds like the notice that someone has died. Ruth runs out of the office yelling, "Dolly, Dolly."

Jesse goes to the front door. "Who is it?"

"The police," Harrison says in a surprisingly calm voice. Jesse opens the door from the inside, allowing Harrison to enter. His pistol is drawn, which adds no authority to his sloppy dress. "Are any of them still here?"

"No, it's just my family. We can't find one of my sisters." Jesse ignores the officer, joining the search for Dolly. Jennie looks under the table cloths of the casino. "Dolly, Dolly, where are you?"

Harrison goes to Morrissey's office as more people start entering the casino. Two help look for Dolly, the rest are just looking around. Harrison comes back into the casino where he finds at least twelve people wandering around. He shouts, "Out. Get the hell out. Now." There is a general hustle for the door.

Jesse pays no attention to Harrison, climbing the main stairs to the private gambling rooms. Her voice can be heard in the casino as she begins opening the doors. "Dolly, Dolly, where are you?"

While the Village Hall bell is ringing in the background Smiley starts putting on his pants. A naked Pauline gets out of bed and looks out the window, "What is it?"

"Don't know, fire or murder, maybe even a robbery."

"One hell of a way to wake up." She does nothing to cover her body.

"Have you seen my watch?" She tries to give him a hug. "I need to get going."

Pauline picks up his watch from the dresser and swings it so he can see. "If you leave, how am I going to get out of here without the landlady hearing?"

"Based on how long they have been ringing that bell, everyone in town will be at whatever it is, even my landlady." Smiley gives Pauline a kiss on the cheek, grabs the watch from her hand, and closes the door quietly behind him.

There is a loud knocking on the door of the tenement. John, the father, calls out "Who is it?"

Swanson is there to live up to his promise. "A guest looking for Miss Antoinette and Miss Pauline."

John has managed to walk to the door. "They're not up."

"Tell Antoinette that I have the money I promised to see both of them."

Antoinette joins her father in the living room. She clarifies, "Pauline's not here. Yus still interested?"

"Yep, but we'll need to talk price. Iff'n I's only gets one."

"Give me a few minutes to gets ready."

There is a load knock on the door to the Morrissey suite. From inside comes a deep voice, "Who is it?"

A very nervous porter responds, "Mr. Morrissey, I have some bad news for you."

Brashly, a naked Morrissey opens the door. The porter automatically looks down at Morrissey, then snaps his neck up where he tries to look around Morrissey to catch a glimpse of Susie in just her thin night gown. "Those bells are for your place. It seems there may have been a robbery." Morrissey grabs his night robe from the chair next to the door and puts it on as he walks into the hall, then toward the stairs.

Morrissey and Marvin arrive in the lobby at the same time, both rushing to get to the front door. "Is it possible?" Marvin asks.

"No, I locked the safe myself; Richards checked it and then the younger Putnam checked it." Morrissey declares as the two rush down the steps to the street. The sun is rising as Morrissey and Marvin rush toward the casino.

Marvin follows Morrissey, who pushes his way through the crowd that has gathered on his casino's porch. It is still only twilight, so the office is lit by three kerosene lanterns. Harrison and two other officers are looking around the office when Morrissey and Marvin enter. They can see that the safe is virtually empty.

"Where's Ringer?" Morrissey bellows.

"Looking for his daughter," Harrison informs those who are listening.

Morrissey leaves his office, looks around the casino and seeing nothing amiss, walks to the open woodshed door. In the dark room are Ruth, Ringer, Jesse, and Jennie. "Ringer?" Morrissey says to a shadow.

"It's Dolly, we can't find her. We have looked everywhere."

Ruth starts crying harder, "They have taken my little Dolly."

Morrissey looks around the room, notices the old cabinet. He walks over to the cabinet and opens the door. "It's okay little one." Morrissey squats down. When he stands he is holding Dolly, who has her arms around his neck.

Aware of all the commotion in the street, Mary is looking out the window, dressed in her nightgown. The bell is still ringing. In the street below she hears a man call out, "It's Morrissey's, they robbed Morrissey's."

She turns, falling back into the lone chair. "Damn, now what am I going to do?"

In the barn of the coal and wood business, Edith is helping Peter unload the bounty from the wagon and stashing it in the barn. "Damn! We needed more time."

On one of the narrow side streets on the west side, Antoinette and Swanson are walking away from the action when they catch sight of Pauline walking toward them. Antoinette whispers to Swanson, "Looks like yus goin' to get the double yus was dreamin' of."

A smiling Swanson cannot help but say, "Damn!"

Author's Imagined Casino

Pursuit!

In the small barn at the coal yard, Edith and Peter place the last pillow case filled with jewelry between two piles of fire wood and begin placing logs over the stolen property. Edith does nothing to hide as she starts changing her clothes, "Take the sideboards off and we'll just pull the strong boxes under the wagon for now. When we get some help, we can hide them."

Peter is alternating between looking out the window and looking at Edith as she continues to change. "Going to be very hot in the village."

"Hot or not, we need to stick with the plan. Take a break until daylight, then take the wheels off the wagon. No one will be suspicious of a wagon without any wheels." Edith continues to change.

Peter talks as he takes the off sideboards and starts to pull the first safe-deposit box, "I won't be able to move these very far."

"You don't have to. The advantage of selecting a coal and wood business - not very busy in the summer."

The first rays of sun are just starting to appear on the horizon, promising a warm day. Elmendorf and David are walking south alongside the tracks when they come to a bridge over a stream flooded by the previous night's rain. "Flooded from all the rain, we should've followed the road," David remarks.

"That would have meant more chances of someone seeing us. Hard to explain why we were out at 4:00 on a rainy night."

"So what do we do now?"

"We ain't going to swim it, we ain't going to go looking for no damn road, so the only thing we can do is go across the bridge,"

231

Elmendorf reasons.

"I hate railroad bridges. No ground to stand on, and you can see through the ties."

Elmendorf pats him on the back in encouragement. "It is not the gaps you have to worry about, it is the water under them."

Knowing there are no good options, the two men start to walk over the long bridge. "Did I tell you I can't swim?" David shows an unexplained bravado. The two men start walking across the bridge. When they are about a third of the way across they hear the sound of an oncoming train that is bound for the station in Saratoga. "This ain't gunna be good." David predicts.

"We can make it across."

In the cabin of the train, the engineer yells to the fireman, "We need to make up some time."

"I'll keep it stoked. We should be on schedule by Saratoga."

"Saratoga, hell, I'll have us on schedule by Geyser Spring." He pushes the throttle forward. The engine picks up speed.

On the bridge, Elmendorf and David are running as fast as they can on the railroad ties. The train is coming at them. "We can make it." Elmendorf looks off the side of the bridge to the water below.

"Damn," is all David can say. With the train bearing down on them, David, then Elmendorf, jump off the opposite sides of the bridge into the water fifteen feet below.

"Did you see that?" The engineer asks the fireman.

"What?"

"Swear I saw someone or something jump off the bridge."

"Nothing you can do about it now. We'll report it when we stop in Saratoga," the fireman rationalizes.

Elmendorf surfaces first. He looks to the other side of the bridge whispering, "David?" With no response, he whispers slightly louder, "David?"

David surfaces and he calls out, "I can't swim."

"Come on, that tree is not so far," encourages Elmendorf.

David struggles to keep his head above water. Appreciating his associate's dilemma, Elmendorf swims in the direction of David's voice. Elmendorf hears David say, while spitting water, "It's no good." David disappears under the water. Elmendorf swims toward the sound of David's voice. When he is near the spot, he dives under the water twice, feeling in the darkness for his friend. With hope gone, Elmendorf swims to the tree. He looks around, sees the outline of a heron standing in the shallows. He swims until his hand touches the bottom, and then he stands and looks one more time for David. Elmendorf's shoulders slump, knowing he is now alone.

To avoid the rain, Nolan is nestled in a clump of trees about twenty feet off the road. He looks around to be sure there is no one there, then lies down on the damp moss.

Michael is outside a small shed near a rural grocery store. Looking around the shed, he is assured there are no dogs. Silently, he slips into the shed and lays down on bags of grain.

Shorty is on a dark rural road singing softly to himself. As he comes upon a stone wall, he hears the growl of a dog. While most might panic or run, Shorty squats down to the dog's level, whispering, "Hey, little buddy, no need to go making all that noise, is there?" Coolly, he scratches the dog's head.

Morrissey's office is crowded. Morrissey, Richards, Ringer, Hathorn, and Marvin are gathered near the safe. Harrison gives instructions to a group of eight men near the door. "Each of you take someone with you to a road leading out of town. It has just rained so you are looking for deep wheel tracks. The wagon is going to be heavy, so there will be wide work wagon wheels." He looks to be sure that each man is listening, "When you find the tracks, one of you stay and stop any traffic from going down the road; send the other man back to get me. We are going to track down these son's a bitches. You don't need to go more than a mile before one of you should find something."

The men start to leave the room, discussing which direction each group will go and which roads each will take, when Harrison has an additional thought. "Jefferson, wait a minute." Jefferson leaves the man he was planning to search with, returning to Harrison. "I want you to go down to the telegraph office and have a message sent to all the police departments in the area. Tell them to be on the lookout for men who are very wet." Jefferson smirks as he leaves the room.

With the deputies having assignments, Harrison walks back to the other four men. "Morrissey, you have any idea who did this?"

"Not yet. May God help the man behind this when I find him." The sound of the first train of the morning can be heard.

Harrison realizes the meaning, saying, "I need to get to the station and stop anyone suspicious from boarding that train. I will be back in a few minutes." He sprints out of the room.

Morrissey turns his attention to Ringer. "We will get to why you opened the safe later. Right now I need you to tell me everything you can about the people. Let's start with how many."

"There had to be at least eight of them, 'cause two went to each of the bedrooms." He tries to frame his answer. "They were well organized and did almost no talking."

Jesse enters the room, still dressed in only her sleeping gown, which has just begun to dry out. "That's not quite true. One of them talked to mother and my sister and me, almost the entire time we were tied up."

"Jesse, that was a very brave thing you did getting the alarm sounded," Morrissey congratulates her. "What did the man talk about?"

"He talked about how we didn't have to worry. I guess he tried to keep us calm." She contemplates where to add a final comment. "He did have an Irish accent, sorry Mr. Morrissey, but he did."

"No need to be sorry." Morrissey fails to see why she would be intimidated by saying he had an accent. "How tall was he?"

"He was average height, about five foot six or seven. With the mask on, there was nothing distinctive about him."

Ringer becomes fatherly, "Jesse, you need to go get some clothes on."

"A little late for that father, half the village saw me in my wet nightgown when I was in the street." As the dutiful daughter, Jesse reluctantly leaves the room.

"There was something that was unusual," Ringer reflects. "One of them never spoke. He seemed to be in charge but he never spoke."

"If he never spoke, how could you tell he was in charge?" Morrissey wonders.

"He was always touching someone and then they would leave the room. When they came back something always changed."

At the train station, Harrison is talking to the conductor. People have been allowed to exit the train but no one is allowed to board. Among those who have gotten off are two reporters, one from Ballston Spa, the other from Albany.

"I checked with all my men, no one has boarded. Can we get out of here?" The conductor has a strict schedule to maintain.

"Go ahead, pull out."

No sooner had Harrison cleared the train, then the engineer approached. "Officer."

"Yes."

234

"I don't know that it means anythin', but I thought I seen a man, maybe even two, jump'n off the bridge over the creek 'tween here an' Ballston. Might've been nuttin'."

Disgruntled passengers start to surround Harrison and the engineer.

"When are we going to be able to leave?" one asks.

"You can't hold us prisoners, I knows my rights," says a second.

A third attempts to threaten. "See if I ever come back to this place if they won't let you leave."

Harrison ignores them all. After scanning the station, he starts back in the direction of the casino, when he is cut off by the reporter from Albany. "Are you the police chief?" Harrison ignores the man. "Can you tell me how many were involved?" Harrison walks by the man as if he was not even there.

Outside the small store north of Saratoga, where Michael is hiding in the shed, three teen-aged boys are on their way to go fishing. "I tell you I seen her," brags the first boy.

"No way." One of his friends is tired of his constant fabricating of stories.

The first boy goes on to explain, "It's Wednesday, you 'member how hot it was. Well I hid on her pa's shed roof and was looking in her window. I watched as she took ever' thing off and puts on her dressing gown."

"Yus makin' this up," accuses his friend.

"Am not."

The third boy sees movement in the shed and reaches his arm out to stop the other two. "You see that?"

"What?" The first boy is looking in the same direction as his friend. "You see a ghost or sump'in?"

"In the shed," the third boy points, "Look see him."

"Yus got good eyes," the second boy says, catching a glimpse of a man's silhouette.

Michael comes running out of the shed and tries to escape through a field of shoulder height cattle corn.

The first boy reasserts his leadership. "Davie, you comes with me. Ernie, yus go gets Colonel French and tell him his hounds got's a good reason to chase today."

A short distance down the road, Colonel French is in his barn dressed in riding gear. The Colonel is saddling his finest stallion. Out of breath from his sprint, Ernie gasps out, "Colonel French, there's some guy tried to rob your store." Ernie points to the cornfield to the north. "He escaped into the field. My brother and Davie Quinn is given' chase."

French tightens the cinch quickly, mounts his horse and calls to his dogs. "Butch, Travis, give chase." He calls to his Russian Wolf hounds as he and the dogs start out at a gallop in the direction Ernie pointed.

The hounds see the direction that French is going and his speed. They sense this is not their normal morning run and immediately increase their pace.

By the time the dogs reach the edge of the cornfield, Michael is already on the other side. He climbs the wood rail fence separating the corn from a field where the hay was recently cleared. Free of the fence, Michael runs in the direction of a clump of trees with thick low brush on the far side.

The dogs run between the rows of corn, while French on horseback breaks off the stalks. The dogs awkwardly climb the rail fence, which French's horse clears with little effort.

Michael looks back at his pursuers and increases his speed. Reaching the tree line, he charges through. What he did not realize was that the brush marked the top of a steep creek bank. Michael trips and slides down the muddy bank into the swollen creek, almost hitting a lone fisherman.

"Now why did you have to go scaring the fish?" Michael fights to get to his feet, then starts walking up the creek. The fisherman slowly stands up, picks up a shotgun that was resting against a tree. "Nows how about gettin' smart and not makin' me waste a shot that was meant for a duck."

Michael looks back at the fisherman, then up the hill where he sees French on his horse. The hounds have come through the brush and are howling on the bank of the creek, leery of getting wet.

"Nice job, Daniel," French congratulates the neighborhood vagrant.

Holding his hands above his head, Michael, knowing he is beat, looks for a place to start walking up the hill in the direction of French.

A couple of miles to the east, Nolan wakes up, stretches, tries to get his bearings, then looks in the direction of a small farm. He is gratified to see a reasonably attractive blonde woman of about thirty carrying a milk bucket headed from the barn in the direction of the house. To avoid being seen, he walks in the woods parallel to the road but away from the small farm. When Nolan reaches a turn in the road, he is well out of sight of the farm. He reverses direction and walks in the road toward the small farm house.

Harrison is back in Morrissey's office after his futile trip to the railroad station. Richards stands at the doorway. Morrissey sits at his desk with Ringer sitting uncomfortably across from him. Harrison announces, "I just heard back from the teams that went north and east. They went two miles and there were no tracks in either directions. I guess that limits the search."

Harrison starts to interview Ringer. "You say there were eight men involved. Can you describe any of them?" At that moment, a deputy enters carrying the eight masks. Harrison examines the masks quickly as Ringer speaks.

"They had those masks on, so I never saw any of their faces."

When Harrison puts the masks down, Morrissey begins examining them. He turns one over, looks inside, and sees a long hair.

"Anything distinctive about their clothes, shape, limp, anything at all?" Harrison is impressing Morrissey, who until now had thought little of the chief.

Pauline, Swanson, and Antoinette are in a room in the same boarding house used by Smiley. "Let's gets da business end of dis arrangement dun befur da action begins." Antoinette is not in this situation for any emotional reason.

Proudly, Swanson takes out the necklace and the ring he got from Shorty and lays them on the dresser. "Ya can take either one, deys both worth a lot more than the five dollars I promised ya." Antoinette looks the jewelry over and selects the necklace. Antoinette looks at Pauline for her approval. Pauline nods her head and the three start taking off their clothes.

Nolan walks around the side of the farm house as the woman dumps clothes into the tub of hot water. "Good morning, miss." The woman is startled and does not reply. "The rain was really heavy last night." The woman picks up a wooden pitchfork and begins stirring the clothes. "Do you have any chores I could do in exchange for a breakfast?"

"My husband is checking the fences. He'll be back in a few minutes. I suggest you keep on walking down the road." She never looks at Nolan.

Nolan picks up a second wooden pitch fork and walks toward the woman. When he reaches the opposite side of the caldron he starts stirring. "This is harder work than men think."

The woman continues stirring the clothes. "This ain't men's work."

"As the youngest of five boys, my ma never taught me the difference between men's and women's work."

The woman stops stirring and studies Nolan's face. "If you keep on with the wash, I'll make you a couple of eggs."

"Sounds fair enough to me." Nolan continues stirring the clothes as the woman walks into the back door of the small house.

Phillips is walking on the road heading west toward Amsterdam when a farmer and wagon come along side of him. "Need a ride, young feller?" The farmer asks.

"Don't mind if I do." Phillips climbs onto the bench seat beside the farmer.

"Headed to Galway myself, where you bound for?"

"Amsterdam."

"That'd be one long walk on a day as hot as this is going to be."

"No denying that, but since I lost my job in Saratoga, can't afford to waste money on a carriage or a train. I heard the mills in Amsterdam are hiring."

"What kind of work you do?" inquired the farmer.

"When I can, I's a handyman, mostly carpentry but I's do most kinds of labor."

"I got's a shed needs some work, can't pay you much but a quarter a day and a place to sleep and plenty to eat."

"I'll take it, but I won't stay more than a week." The two shake hands.

Bennett has changed his clothes in the barn where they started. He discards the clothes he wore in the robbery. Within a block, he does his best to slip unnoticed into the large crowd that has gathered around Morrissey's.

In the coal and firewood company office, Edith has Peter check to be sure no one is coming. Assured the coast in clear, Edith, in a dress suitable for a warm morning, walks out of the office and onto the street. She turns and heads for Congress Spring.

Jesse enters Morrissey's office holding her little sister, Dolly's, hand. "Mr. Morrissey, you need to hear this." Jesse smiles at her sister to give her reassurance, "Go ahead, tell Mr. Morrissey what you told me."

Dolly looks to Jesse for encouragement. "Mr. Morrissey, I know you are not going to believe me but one of them was a woman."

Morrissey's attention is captured, "How do you know little one?" He gives his best Irish smile.

Dolly again looks at her sister for support, "When I was locked in the cabinet, I could hear them talking from time to time. One of the voices was a lady's voice."

Morrissey goes back to the pile of masks, picks one up and pulls out a long hair. "Looks like you were right, little one."

There are at most thirty people at the spring when Edith walks through the gates. Without a crowd, she walks unimpeded up to the dipper boy. She bends over to accept the water from the boy, deliberately showing appreciable cleavage. Sure he will remember her, she asks, "Where is everyone?"

"At Morrissey's, there was a big robbery." The boy does not believe he has actually found someone who does not have some version of the story. "I understand they took millions, but Morrissey already has caught up with two of them."

"Where did you hear all of this?"

"Ever' one's talking 'bout it."

Edith takes a sip of the water, scrunches her face, and starts walking toward the hotel, pouring out the water as she walks past the gates to the park.

On the sidewalk going back to the hotel, Edith passes a group of people going in the opposite direction.

"I heard they have captured three already," says one of the pedestrians.

"One is telling on all the others," a second adds.

"There were surely more than three involved," the first pedestrian speculates.

Becoming increasing wary, Edith picks up her pace as she heads in the direction of the States. She passes the main entrance and turns onto Division Street. As she rounds the corner, it looks like the entire village is in the street looking in the direction of Morrissey's. Edith moves between the groups, which get tighter the closer she gets to the casino. Near Morrissey's, Edith is tapped on the shoulder by Bennett, who says quietly, "There is nothing to see here. Let's go back to the hotel." Edith hesitates, realizing that Bennett is correct and she will get no closer. The two turn and squeeze between groups of people.

Although it is still early in the morning, as soon as they get back to their room Bennett pours each of them a drink. Proud of her ability to scheme, Edith says, "Everything is in the barn, just as we planned. I will go down this evening and Peter and I will start dividing it into containers we can handle."

"I don't trust Peter," Bennett moans.

"I do; that is all you need to know."

"I am suddenly very tired," Bennett pronounces.

Edith offers reassurance, "It was a long night."

In the park of the States, Sarah and Sadie are sitting on one of the benches. Missy stands behind them. "Was Momma's jewelry stolen?" Sadie is concerned.

"It would be hard to imagine it wasn't."

"Then in some small way we are involved in the biggest robbery in the history of the village." Sadie has a misguided sense of delight.

"That is hardly something to be proud of." Sarah attempts to correct her younger sister.

"It is always better to be one of the few who are a part of something than to be one of the many who watch from a distance."

"Sadie, your search for adventure will surely land you in trouble before you are my age."

"I certainly hope so. Just think what it would be like to be that girl who stood in the middle of the street firing the gun sounding the alarm."

"Yes, she can now tell her grandchildren how all the men in Saratoga saw her in her wet nightgown."

Things are quieting down in Morrissey's office. Harrison, Morrissey, Richards, and Deputies Smiley and Jefferson are drinking coffee. Harrison and Morrissey are sitting and the two deputies stand; Richards, pencil in hand, is going through the empty envelopes. "It doesn't make sense. There are no wheel marks on any of the roads leading out of town. Just look how deep the ruts are out back." Harrison is referring to the marks made by the wagon Peter drove.

"That means that what they took is still in the village."

"Not necessarily, they could have divided it up and left," Harrison suggests.

"But they didn't." Morrissey is adamant. "If they were going to divide it up, why have one heavy wagon?"

Richards looks up from his papers. "Seven hundred fifty-three thousand dollars in insured jewelry."

The chief reflects, "Not going to help the reputation of the village at all."

Morrissey thinks out loud. "With that size wheels it had to be a work wagon, not a buggy. It was only minutes after they left when the girl sounded the alarm. They could not have gotten more than eight blocks." Sure he is correct, Morrissey says louder, "What is within eight blocks?"

"Just about the entire village." Harrison responds.

"What is within eight blocks where a work wagon could be hidden?" Morrissey looks at each of the officers.

Harrison looks at his deputies. "Three liveries, couple of grain stores, the ice business, two coal and wood businesses, then there are the alleys and private carriage houses."

"I suggest you send your men to check each of those. You might want to begin by having the men look in each carriage house." Morrissey is sure of his theory. Knowing they are expected to act, Harrison and the two deputies exit the room.

Soaking wet from his morning swim, Elmendorf climbs up the pond's bank and onto the dirt road. He looks back as he hears a wagon coming. The driver of the wagon has a pig tied in the back. The driver, smoking his well-used pipe, stops the wagon when he reaches Elmendorf. "Looks to me like you had one hell of a night. You get so drunk you fell asleep in the rain?"

"Something like that. Don't really remember." Elmendorf does not want to explain.

"You ain't sittin' next to me. Get on the back. We'll get you into Ballston. Yus from there, ain't you?"

Elmendorf gets on the wagon. "Nope. Is that the way I'm goin'? I was on my way to Glens Falls."

"Yus sure 'nough had a good night, hell, couldn't you find the North Star?" The driver laughs at his own joke at someone else's expense.

"Nope, too many clouds; there's no such thing as too much bourbon."

The driver laughs as the wagon starts forward. "Been over a week since I was that drunk. Must be getting old."

Outside Morrissey's, Harrison has called all five of his deputies together. He signals for ten businessmen from the village who are in the crowd to join him. Like a field officer, Harrison starts to give directions. "We need to do an organized search. We are going to start from here and branch out. Search every alley, look in every barn." As soon as he is finished, the men start off in small groups.

In the boarding house, Swanson, finally relieved, is in a deep sleep. Pauline and Antoinette are both getting dressed in their well-worn clothes. Pauline asks, "Where d'ya dink he gots da necklace?"

"I dun wants to know. All I knows is dat is ourn now."

"I's bet it's sometin' to do wid dat alarm we 'eard. Iff'n we goes showin' it 'round, it'll be taken from us or they will tink we dun da robbery," Pauline assumes.

Antoinette looks at Swanson, "Pa's gunna ask us for the money we gots from him."

"How much cash ya's got?" Pauline has a plan.

Antoinette checks her purse. "'Bout a dollar an a half."

"I gots 'bout a dollar. We tells Pa dat's what he paid us."

"Pa won't believe we only gots dat little for the two of us."

Pauline shows her logic. "We tell Pa dat he tried to hold out on us and we robbed him of dat little bit. Pa will be pissed but he'll believe it." Without further discussion, the sisters continue dressing.

There is a gentle, timid knock on Morrissey's door. It is a messenger from the States. "Come in." Morrissey offers.

"Mr. Morrissey sir, I have a message for you."

The messenger hands Morrissey a note. Morrissey looks at Richards, who tips the messenger. Morrissey opens the envelope and pulls out the note. "Who gave you this?"

The messenger is seriously nervous. "The desk clerk at the States; he said a lady gave it to him for a messenger to deliver here."

"Thank you, that is all." The messenger is all too thankful to leave the room.

Morrissey turns to Richards, "Seems someone else knows there was a woman involved and even knows who she is." Morrissey puts the note on the desk. The note reads:

Mr. Morrissey,

I was sorry to hear of your loss. You should be aware that one of those involved was a lady staying at the States.

A Friend

Later that morning Antoinette, Pauline, and Janet are asleep on a single mattress on the floor of their tenement. John slips in the room on his knees and goes through their handbags. Finding only small change, he reaches under the mattress and finds the necklace. John quietly slips out the door.

Minutes later he appears in the tavern next door to the tenement. It is so early that there is only the bartender and one customer in the bar.

"I want a bourbon and I's gunna settle up my tab," John yells to the bartender as he walks in the door.

"You suddenly find a pot of gold?" The bartender counters.

"Nope, one of my daughters is dating a rich man from Baltimore. He gave her this here necklace. She owed me some money and gave it to me in trade."

The bartender examines the necklace, then pours a drink for John. "Where'd you say your daughter got this here necklace?"

"From her fancy pants boyfriend."

"I'll take this to pay off your bill and give you one more drink."

"You meant three more drinks, right."

The bartender examines the necklace closely, "Okay." The bartender turns his attention to the customer. "Cover for me for a few minutes, I gots to use the outhouse." The bartender goes out the back door.

The bartender elbows his way through the crowd in front of the casino. He is dirty and smells, so members of the crowd pull away as he gets closer. The bartender eventually gets to the porch where is confronted by a police officer.

"I needs to see Morrissey."

"What about."

"I've a serious lead in his robbery."

"Really?" The officer is skeptical.

"When Morrissey hears what I gots to tell him, you'll not want to be the officer who 'eld me up even for a minute." The officer looks the bartender over. Reluctantly, he lets him enter the casino.

The bartender looks the casino over on his way through to knock on the open door to the office. At the sound, Richards, Morrissey, and Harrison look up from a map of the village that is lying on Morrissey's desk.

In Morrissey's presence, the bartender gets sheepish. "Mr. Morrissey?"

"Yes."

"I've somethin' dat I thin' you'd like to see." The bartender pulls the necklace out of his shirt explaining. "One of my customer's jus' paid off his bill with dis. Knowin' your situation I thought maybe it came from here." Morrissey takes the necklace. Noting Morrissey's enthusiasm, the bartender gets bolder, "I was hope'n for a reward."

Morrissey examines the neckless carefully. "Where is this customer right now?"

"At my place down on Congress Street."

"What did you say his name was?"

"Don't know his last name, we's jus' call him ol' John. He said his daughter gots it as a gift."

Handing the necklace to Richards, Morrissey says to Harrison and Richards, "Let's go have a little talk with ol' John." Morrissey, Richards, and Harrison rise and leave. The bartender, chest out, follows along. At the door one of the deputies joins the group.

As the group walks swiftly down the street, a portion of the crowd smell excitement and start to follow. By the time they get to the tavern, half the people that were gathered outside of Morrissey's are following.

John has his two free drinks lined up on the bar as Morrissey, Richards, Harrison, and a deputy enter; the bartender follows. In the brief moment the door is open, at least fifty people can be seen who followed Morrissey and the others from the casino.

Morrissey walks over to John. "Ol' John, I think you owe me an explanation."

Without at least three drinks to stabilize him, John is extremely nervous. "I don't even know'd who yus are."

"Where did you come by the necklace you used to settle your account?"

"From my daughters." John may not recognize any one of the men, but he does recognize power.

"And where did she get if from?"

"I dun't hardly know. She's a whore just like her mother. Probably took it in trade."

"Where is your daughter right now?"

John's smile has a sick pride, "Sleeping, she works nights."

Morrissey and Richards each reach under one arm and pick John up from his stool. With little effort they carry him to the door, Morrissey saying, "What do you say we go to your place?"

Janet, Antoinette, and Pauline, all topless to avoid the heat, are still asleep on the floor when Morrissey, Richards, Harrison, and the deputy walk in, carrying ol' John.

"Ladies, I am sorry to disturb your beauty sleep." Morrissey's apology seems insincere.

The three ladies start to wake up. Recognizing Harrison, the girls try to cover up with the lone sheet. They keep pulling the sheet from each other.

Morrissey nods to Harrison to show the necklace, "Where did you get this?"

Antoinette has survived this long because she knows when to fight and when to yield. "We gots it from a gentleman friend."

"Who would that have been?"

"Ever'body calls him Swanson, don't know his real name."

"Did you see any other jewelry?"

"There was a ring with a big ol' stone," Pauline admits.

"Anything else?" Morrissey demands.

"Dat's all we saw." Antoinette wonders what she missed.

"Where is Mister Swanson?" Morrissey demands.

"Mrs. Brown's boarding house."

Morrissey, Richards, and Harrison get ready to leave. The deputy is too engrossed in looking at the girls' breasts to keep track of what is transpiring. Harrison nudges the deputy to get his attention. "Arrest Ol' John. Take him down to the station. Leave the girls, they need to pay his bail." Morrissey, Harrison, and Richards leave for Mrs. Brown's; the deputy continues to look at the scantily clad daughters.

"So it turns out we did do a double for free," Pauline complains.

"Whens he gets out in a day or two I's gunna kill Pa. Mark my words."

The door opens in the rooming house. Richards moves in, followed by Morrissey and Harrison. Richards picks Swanson up like he was a bag of flour and holds him against the wall. "You are the little one that never talked to anyone," Richards notes. Swanson remains held against the wall.

Morrissey holds up the necklace in front of Swanson's eyes. "Where is the rest of it?"

"I dun't know what yus talkin' 'bout."

Morrissey excuses Harrison, who is Swanson's only protection, "If you would be so kind as to go down to the porch, I think it will expedite the situation."

"Dun't go!" Swanson pleads with Harrison.

Swanson goes silent as Richards puts his huge hand over his mouth, continuing to hold the small man to the wall with one hand.

Harrison leaves the room.

Harrison is standing with two deputies who have caught up with him when Morrissey comes out of the boarding house door. He holds the door for Richards, who has Swanson swinging in the air. Swanson's mouth has blood on the edges and his eye shows evidence of having been struck.

Richards throws Swanson to one of the deputy's feet. "This is for you." Then Richards speaks to Harrison, "He wanted to share this with us." Richards shows the ring with the gross sized stone.

Harrison keeps Morrissey up to date on the search for the work wagon. "There is only one work wagon within five blocks of your place. But it can't be the one, the rear wheels are off from it."

"Where would that be?" Morrissey asks.

The deputy who spotted the wagon wants credit. "I spotted it at one of the coal and firewood businesses." From the expression on Morrissey's and Richards' faces, it is obvious they are not willing to write off the wagon just because it has missing wheels.

Harrison is concerned about the information Swanson provided, "What did he say?"

Morrissey answers for Richards, "He did not have much to say. I think he was a pawn in a chess game that was way out of his league." Morrissey speaks quietly to Harrison, "We do know that they did not split up the loot. It is all together some place. He doesn't know where; about that, I can assure you. And yes, he is certain."

Harrison orders his deputy, "Put him in cuffs and take him down to the station."

Morrissey informs Harrison, "You should know that he spent the entire night watching the front of my building. With eight inside there were at least nine people involved. With that many, it will have to break." Morrissey thinks. "One person cannot keep a secret, there is no way nine can."

"Smiley has been on your porch almost every night this summer. Do you think he might have seen something?" Harrison asks Morrissey.

In an alley in Ballston Spa, the wagon with the pig is stopping in back of the butcher's shop. The driver says, "Ever' Sunday I brings a pig to the butcher. You'd thin' he'd do the slaughterin' on some day other than the Sabbath. Wouldn't yah?"

"How far to the train station?" Elmendorf asks.

"'Bout a block. I can drops you after I's drop the pig."

"That'd be right kindly of you," Elmendorf thanks his provider. They both get down from the wagon and start to untie the pig.

Suddenly Grey, the Chief of the Ballston Police, is standing behind Elmendorf. "Who's this you got with you, Slater?" Slater is the driver's name.

"A man whose as big a fool as me; started walking south instead of north." The driver explains.

"Really." The chief is not fooled. Elmendorf looks around for a way to escape. He sees deputies at both ends of the alley. "Now don't go gettin' any fools ideas. No one needs a chase on a hot day like this."

Elmendorf lowers his head, knowing it is over. He turns to the driver, "Thanks for the lift."

"Any time."

"Probably be about five years," Elmendorf declares.

The slave family is huddled in a grove on the edge of an open field. They were awakened by the sounds of hounds howling. Mattie pulls the two children lower into the bush, sheltering them with her body. She tries to quiet them. "Hush now children, we got this far, it's going to be okay."

Nate looks over the bank in an effort to get a better view. He can see that the dogs are on their trail. "They's onto us."

Spread across the open field are five armed men approaching with three dogs. The father, LeRoy, is only thirty-eight, but he has his three oldest boys, Lee, eighteen, Roy, seventeen, and Hammon, fifteen, with him on the hunt; his other four boys and their three sisters are home with their mother. They are joined by LeRoy's brother Ebed, thirty six. All five men are dressed in very old, worn clothes one step above rags. Lee and Hammon, with their two hounds, are flanked out to be sure that they cover the edges of the narrow valley.

Lee, holding back his hound calls out, "Bessy's ontuh sumptin' hot."

LeRoy spits out some tobacco, barely missing his hound. "We's gunna catch us 'nuther one today."

The hounds are yanking on their rope leashes.

Hearing the men's voices and the howling of the hounds, Mattie holds the children close to her. Nanny is gathering the few clothes they have with them into a sack. "The dogs're on tuh us," Nate reports.

Mattie wonders, "Can we run?"

Nate looks around; Lake Champlain is to the east, the mountains are to the west. An escape would be nearly impossible. "Yus run down to dey lake and walk in da water for as far as yus can. I'll run toward the mountains. I'll meet yus in Montreal, if'n not before."

Nanny says bravely. "I can't run anyplace. Da best I's can do is walk and dat gettn harder ever' step. You'll run for the lake and I'll go off toward the mountain. I'll give dem dogs sometin to bray 'bout," "We can't let you do that Ma." Mattie is holding back the tears. "They'll catch you fer sure."

"Dey's gunna catch me anyway, da question is, are dey gunna catch yus?"

The whole family looks at each other. Finally the father picks up the littlest child and starts toward the lake. The older child follows. Mattie hugs the grandmother one last time and runs after the rest of the family.

The men are approaching the little grove when Nanny rises and hustles as best she can toward the mountain. Hammon sees her movement, pointing, "Der she be." Lee, the flanker on the side toward the mountain, stays well to the outside. LeRoy, holding the main dog, rushes in her direction. Hammon, with the dog on the right side, moves toward the old woman. Nanny runs further than she ever imagined she could. When they have her circled, she looks up – she did well.

"Give it up 'ld lady. Yus gone as far as yus goin'," LeRoy orders. Seeing her age, he yells to Ebed, "She ain't alone. She's too 'ld to get dis far on her own."

Having caught up with the group, Ebed agrees, "Yus right. The others must be in da grove or down near the lake."

"Hammon, Lee, deys more, get yus and da hounds back in dat grove and find da trail." Knowing better than to argue with their father, the oldest and youngest boys start for the grove. "Ebed, yus and Roy stay with her." LeRoy follows his two sons toward the grove. The middle boy, Roy, watches as his uncle starts roughly tying up the grandmother.

"What yus lookin' at boy?" Ebed threatens, "I can handle an old woman bys myself. Yus go help yus daddy and yus brothers." Roy knows what his uncle is capable of with those who don't respond quickly, so he hustles off with his hound toward the grove.

Without any discussion, the family knows to cut through the bog in an effort to avoid the dogs. Nate is still holding Eve in his arms, Adam follows in his father's trail, with Mattie last. The parents keep looking over their shoulders, hoping they have escaped.

The sound of the hounds baying gets louder.

Having learned all they could from Swanson, now Morrissey,

Harrison, Richards, and Smiley are seated in four chairs in Morrissey's office, deciding on a course of action. "I swear I never saw anyone hanging around out front," Smiley pleads.

"You know everyone in the village, who would be interested in this big a robbery?"

"No one I know is smart enough to pull it off. Hell, I am watching it be discovered and I don't understand it." Smiley is not exaggerating.

"If they were smart enough to just visit the village and stay somewhere else, where would they stay?" Morrissey asks the group in general.

"Ballston Spa or Glens Falls would be my guesses," Harrison hypothesizes, "they are on the railroad line and big enough for outsiders to blend in, at least to some degree." Harrison asks Smiley, "What about those prostitutes that are always hanging around down the block; think they've seen anything?"

"They ain't from the village and I don't think they is smart enough to know what they saw." Smiley is so dull he does not realize how smart the sisters really are.

"Why don't you go get them and bring them here?" The way Morrissey says it, it is more of an order than a question. "Don't arrest them, let them be our guests."

Smiley and Harrison are all too willing to get out of the office, Harrison, because he wants to blame Morrissey if the case is not solved, and Smiley to see Pauline again.

"Was Ringer in on it?" Morrissey looks at Richards.

"No, he is a good man. And before you start getting too angry at him, ask yourself what you would have done to protect Susie and Lil' John," Richards reminds Morrissey.

Harrison and Smiley walk toward the corner where Antoinette and Pauline are based. "Why you letting Morrissey run this here investigation, yus the chief." Smiley cannot understand political survival.

"Because he hasn't made a mistake yet, and he can do things we cannot." Harrison reflects for a minute. "Besides, Morrissey has more to lose in this than anyone. Iff'n they gets away with it, most of the jewelry was insured, so the people don't lose. The hotel doesn't lose because it didn't happen there. No, Morrissey has the most to lose and if you look at his place you see he is not in the habit if losing."

The women are not on the corner so the officers continue on to the tenement where Antoinette, Pauline, and their family live. Harrison leads Smiley onto the porch.

The chief knocks at the door. John opens the door; he has a swollen eye. "What happened to you?" The chief does not doubt that John has angered someone.

"He fell on my fist." Pauline is unapologetic.

Harrison notices that although the women are barely covered, they are packing their limited possessions. "Going someplace?"

"Yeah. We's done paying for this lousy son of a bitch," Antoinette supports her sister.

"Well, you are going to have to postpone your trip for a little while longer. We need to talk to you down at Morrissey's."

"And if we don't go?" Antoinette takes on the role of the defensive older sister.

"Then we will talk to you at the jail." Janet continues packing, as if she is not involved. "You too," Harrison orders.

Morrissey and Harrison are seated, yet somehow they still dominate the room. Despite having accepted a cup of tea, Pauline and Antoinette are squirming in their chairs. Janet appears oblivious to any peril. The women have dressed hurriedly and have more than normal skin exposed, which pleases a standing Smiley. Richards stands against the wall behind the women. Smiley's eyes are fixated on Pauline's ample chest.

"We never saw anyone jus' hangin' 'round cepting the one yus already got. He calls hisself Swanson." Pauline tells the truth.

"There were those two southern boys but we ain't seen them in two maybe three weeks," Antoinette contributes.

"There was a couple and a single lady I seen mor'n once." Janet speaks for the first time. "Fact is, I seen them most ever day." She has Morrissey's attention. "The couple is one of dem dere nieces and uncles. I seen her helpin' him home more'n once." She looks at Antoinette for backing. "We saw'd them last week; she was kind of carryin' him home."

Antoinette counters her sister while looking at Morrissey, "Can't be dem, I seen him comin' out of your place mor'n once."

"Tell me about the single lady?"

"Not much to tell. She was kind of plain. Not young, not real well dressed, yus know, kind of plain. Maybe like a church lady."

Morrissey realizes that between a man with his niece and a single plain woman they have only eliminated about fifty percent of those in the village. "How old?"

"Ol'." She pauses, coming up with an age. "I'd say 'bout twenty-five."

Morrissey wants the women to feel comfortable, so he suggests, "If you see any of these people again, please do me a favor and tell me right away."

Antoinette understands the meeting is over; her sister looks reluctantly at Richards as he gathers their cups. They cannot remember the last time they were served tea.

Shorty is walking along the sidewalk in Ballston Spa when he notices Elmendorf being brought into the police station by the three officers. The officers are smiling as they brag to those on the street and the local press.

"He got six miles before he were caught," says the first officer.

"Did he really think he was going to escape our grasp? If he wanted to escape, he should have taken off for Glens Falls or Schuylerville," brags the second officer.

"Let it be known that the Ballston Police did their job the only way they know how - to the best of their ability," the chief reminds the two reporters who are present.

Shorty maintains his composure as he climbs the steps to the small safe house. Inside he picks up the infamous suit and walks to the kitchen and starts washing up. Shorty takes the time to shave. While looking in the mirror, he murmurs, "You are such a handsome man, it's time for you to go back to Saratoga and sees what's goin' on."

Morrissey, Richard, and Harrison are having cigars on the porch of the casino. The crowd of onlookers has dwindled to less than fifty. "Still no sign of the wagon?" Morrissey asks Harrison.

"Not one that cannot be explained."

"Where was the one that was broken down?"

"Over at the coal and wood lot on lower Franklin Street."

Walter, pen and pad in hand, approaches the casino. "Mr. Morrissey, everyone in the village has heard what happened. Naturally the rumors fill the air. I was wondering if you would like to make an official statement as to what was taken, how it was taken, where the investigation stands, and if there are any suspects." Walter sounds like an experienced journalist, not a struggling reporter.

"No." Morrissey sounds emphatic.

Walter starts walking toward the newspaper office. When he gets a few steps, Morrissey calls out, "Hey, young man, come back here." Tense to the point of shaking, Walter turns around and walks back and starts taking notes. Morrissey speaks in short clauses giving Walter time to write the quote correctly. "You can tell your readers that we know how many were involved, that we have already arrested one, and that he is talking like a parrot." Morrissey goes silent. Walter, thrilled with having a quote, starts to walk away. "I wasn't finished, tell your readers that the head of the gang was a woman."

Walter is shocked by the news. Not one rumor has mentioned a woman as leading the gang. Walter knows he has broken a story; however, he waits to be sure Morrissey is finished.

"Now, I am done; you may leave," Morrissey instructs. Walter tries to remain calm but after a couple of steps he starts running for the newsroom.

"Why did you tell him so much?" Richards would not have said anything.

"Sometimes it takes a little smoke to find the hot embers." The men return to the casino.

The news room bell rings over and over because Walter ran in so fast through the door. "Morrissey just gave me an exclusive," boasts Walter.

"Why you?" The editor questions Walter's enthusiasm.

"That's not important. What is important is that he told me the head of the gang was a woman!"

"Special edition time." The editor is excited. "Get the press ready. Walter, you start writing. Headline, 'Gang Led by Woman.'"

Susie, the only person who would dare, enters Morrissey's office without knocking. Carrying a wicker picnic basket, she does not close the door. Susie is looking as attractive as ever. A gentleman, Richards rises to help her with the basket. "I was not sure how many were here so I asked Mr. Marvin to order enough for ten." She looks around the room, seeing only Richards, Harrison, and her husband. "I guess we will have a little left over." Susie starts setting up Morrissey's desk like a dining table.

"We will do our very best." Morrissey helps unload the basket. "What have you heard?"

"You have captured somewhere between three and eight men so far. You have not yet found any of the loot and about half the people think you were somehow involved."

"That bad."

"No, that was the good news," Susie assures her husband. "The

252

bad news is that there is a group of citizens who are organizing to have you closed up."

Morrissey takes a half roll and starts putting sliced meat on it. The others join him. "It had to be someone inside. Someone with knowledge of the casino." He thinks about the missing link. "Someone who arranged to have all the jewelry moved here."

Morrissey takes a bite of his lunch then asks Harrison, "What do you know about the fire at the Union?"

"It was set. It was directly under the safe. That's about all." Harrison goes on, "The same was true for the fire at the Constitution."

"How did they know that the jewelry would be moved to here?" Morrissey wonders aloud. No one answers. Morrissey asks Susie, "There was a woman involved, what does that tell you?"

"That all the details were worked out in advance."

A messenger knocks at the open door. "Mr. Morrissey?" Morrissey signals for the messenger to enter. "Mr. Marvin sent me, he wanted you to know the Ballston Police just captured a man that they think was involved."

"Thank you, young man. Why don't you help yourself to some bread and meat?"

"I couldn't."

"Oh yes you can and you will." The messenger is thrilled with Morrissey's generosity. Still, he is hesitant to start to make himself dinner. Seeing how nervous the boy is, Susie helps place food on his plate.

As they begin to finish the meal, Morrissey looks to Harrison. "We need someone to make sure none of them get on the one o'clock train."

"I was just thinking that." Harrison starts to get ready. "We probably need to check every train today." Harrison stands, then starts for the rail station.

"And tomorrow," adds Morrissey.

Richards looks at Morrissey who nods. "I am going to join you," Richards tells Harrison.

Alone, Susie asks, "Do you really believe they are still in the village?"

"Where else could they be?" He thinks, then adds, "Jesse's bravery cut off the amount of time they had to escape."

Richards and Harrison are standing at opposite ends of the train watching the crowd that is getting ready to board. Among those who have arrived are six reporters from across the state, each wanting an exclusive on what has become known as The Great Robbery.

Harrison walks across the deck to Richards. "Waste of time. No one suspicious looking to me."

Richards looks over Harrison's shoulder and notices Shorty wearing the same suit all the men wore. "Maybe." Richards observes Shorty walking in the direction of the hotels and begins to follow.

"Where you going?" Harrison asks.

"Go tell Morrissey I saw an interesting suit," Richards directs. While Harrison scratches his head, Richards starts to follow Shorty. Richards is about a half block behind as Shorty passes the grand hotels and enters Congress Springs.

On Broadway, a group of six newspaper boys pour onto the street outside the newspaper's office. They divide up and begin shouting.

The first boy shouts, "Special! Special! Morrissey says woman involved."

The second boy yells, "One arrested. Woman involved in Great Robbery." Exactly as the editor hoped, people on the street start gathering around the boys, purchasing the special edition.

The sounds of the newspaper boys shouting awakens Edith. She shakes Bennett, "Did you hear that?" She shakes Bennett.

"What?" Bennett is groggy.

Slipping on her sheer robe, Edith walks to the door and looks out. She signals for the hall boy. The hall boy comes to the door and awkwardly looks at Edith. Knowing the value of his job, he struggles to maintain eye contact and not look down. She hands him a dime. "Go get me a copy of that newspaper."

"Which newspaper would you like Miss Bennett?" His eyes slip down to her breasts.

"The one they are shouting about in the street." Edith looking vexed, shuts the door.

Bennett asks a typical inane question, "Are you worried?" Edith just stares at him.

Before Richards gets to Congress Spring, Shorty comes back out of the gates, crosses Broadway and starts walking down Congress Street. Richards follows at what he considers a safe distance. Shorty continues up to the tenement where he finds Pauline, Janet, and Antoinette sitting on the front steps.

Shorty asks all three, "Yus seen my friend?"

"Depends on who yur friend be." Antoinette plays with Shorty.

"Guy who paid with some jewelry."

"He left a long time ago. Police gots him." Pauline is disappointed at the loss of such a sure mark.

Hearing the news, Shorty looks around, spots Richards and starts to run.

"Damn," Richards says to himself knowing that he is going to have to give chase. Richards, who is surprisingly fast for his size, pursues Shorty.

On the porch of the casino, Susie is saying goodbye to Morrissey. "Have a good afternoon."

Morrissey looks down the street where he sees Richards in pursuit of Shorty two blocks away.

"You better get out here." Morrissey says to Harrison, who is inside the casino. Harrison comes out just in time to see Richards disappear over the small hill. Morrissey shakes his head. "I ain't running."

"Me neither." Harrison does start blowing his whistle.

Down the street, Shorty looks over his shoulder and notices Richards gaining on him. In a desperate effort to get away, he ducks into the narrow opening between two small houses. Richards comes to the opening. They are so close that Richards has to turn sideways to fit between the buildings. Shorty comes out the far end of the narrow alley to find himself trapped in a small fenced-in back yard. He looks for any way out and he spots a privy. Without any other choice, Shorty runs to the privy, slipping in before Richards comes out from between the houses.

Coming out of the narrow alley, Richards looks around and sees the privy. Richards walks to the door and knocks.

"Who's there?" Shorty responds in a female voice. "Janet, I told you to leave me alone when I'm in the privy."

"It's your worst nightmare," Richards answers.

Shorty retains the female voice. "Oh no, a man. Don't you try to assault me, my husband is just inside the house."

Richards tries the door, finding it is locked from the inside. Richards moves to the side of the privy and gives the upper portion a push. It begins to tip. "Oh no sir; I am not covered." Shorty is desperate. With that, Richards tips the outhouse on its side.

Shorty's feet protrude from the bottom. Richards grabs Shorty's ankles and pulls him out. Holding Shorty's arms tight to his side,

Richards complains, "You made me work up a sweat."

"Man, where did you learn to run like that?"

Richards holds Shorty's wrists behind his back as they walk back to the alley. When they come out from between the houses, the home owner asks, "Who's going to fix that privy?"

"I'll send over a couple of men in just a minute." The homeowner looks at the size of Richards and decides not to argue.

Harrison, Morrissey, and two deputies greet Shorty and Richards as they come out of the narrow alley. Knowing something is happening, several citizens are standing around. Morrissey greets Shorty, "Ah, my favorite suit."

While the deputies take Shorty into custody, a messenger comes running up to Harrison. "Chief, there was a telegraph from up in Wilton, seems Colonel French caught some of those involved. He is bringing 'em in a buckboard." In the distance the sound of hounds braying can be heard.

A buckboard, pulled by matching chestnut horses, is coming down the center of the street. In the back of the wagon Michael looks uncomfortable. He is standing with his back against a post, his wrists tied at his chest and his arms pulled back and tied to the far side of the post. There is a hound trotting along on each side of the wagon. The entourage is led by Colonel French on his handsome stallion. French has the appearance of a Roman General parading before his victorious troops.

Harrison is un-amused. Morrissey and Harrison have made it to Village Hall, which houses the small jail. Morrissey smiles. "Who's that?"

"One of our local lawyers. It may surprise you to learn he failed the humility exercise."

"Beautiful horse," compliments Morrissey.

"Worth twice what the owner is worth." Seeing Harrison standing on the front steps, French turns his horse toward the chief. "Chief, I captured the perpetrator of last night's crime."

"You may have one, and if so, thank you very much, but there were a lot more than one, who done it."

"That may be, but this is the leader." French is speaking loud enough for all those who have gathered to hear.

"What makes you say that, Mr. French?"

French points to Michael, "Look at his demeanor, the persona he emanates. This is a man who leads, not one who follows. He also has not spoken since we left the farm. It is a smart villain who knows to keep quiet."

"That may be true; however, the leader of the gang who robbed Mr. Morrissey's was a woman."

"Never." French is an arrogant chauvinist. Harrison just smiles and lets the impact settle in.

Catharine is sitting on the swing reading a book; her father is sitting in a rocking chair reading the special edition of the newspaper. "Father, do you think they will capture those who stole from everyone?"

Cook lowers his newspaper and looks at his daughter. "Most assuredly."

"What makes you so sure?"

"A wise thief would not steal from a man such as Morrissey and a foolish thief will get caught."

"But you read the bulletin, it was a woman who was the leader."

"I suspect that story is a rouse designed to make those who committed the crime overly confident."

"I think you are wrong, Father." Cook looks askance at his daughter, who continues, "Father, you must remember, a woman has to be twice as cunning as a man. She has to first plan the actions, then convince a man to carry it out."

"Catharine, you read too much."

Catharine picks up her book. "It always works for me," she says under her breath.

In his dressing robe, Bennett sits in a chair, whiskey glass in hand, reading the newspaper. Edith is behind a dressing screen. "Where do you think you are going?" he bellows.

"I'm going to be sure the money is safe."

"You should stay here. Out there everyone is watching everyone. You will have no excuse for being in the street, let alone going into an old barn."

"Are you coming with me or are you just going to sit here and drink all day?"

Bennett lifts his glass, "I was drinking when we met, I was drinking when you talked me into this, and I will be drinking when you finally leave. It is the drink I am sure of, not you."

"Someone has to take control," Edith says, closing the door.

Bennett raises his glass in a mock salute.

Franklin Street is crowded with pedestrians anxious to see who has been arrested. In the center of the street are deputies walking on either side of a handcuffed Shorty. He struts as if the hero of a parade. "That makes four. The one from Ballston, the one Colonel French brought in, Swanson, and this little guy." Harrison counts on his fingers as he names those found.

"But no woman, no money, and no jewelry," Morrissey reminds the chief. "Any reports from those looking for the wagon?"

"No, and no information on where they might be hiding out," Harrison admits.

Edith walks out the main door at the States, descending the stairs to the nine foot wide sidewalk. She looks both ways before walking up Division Street toward the much smaller crowd in front of Morrissey's.

On Marvin House's porch, Mary is sitting in a wooden rocking chair. She notices Edith going up the street and begins to follow.

Edith, followed in the distance by Mary, approaches the front of the casino where Morrissey is conducting an impromptu press conference. Those of the press and nosey locals are in front of the steps. Under no conditions will anyone be allowed inside. Edith hears Morrissey's news. "Approximately half those involved in the robbery have been apprehended. I expect to have more news at 5:00." Morrissey turns to walk in the door to the casino.

Reporters start calling out. One can be heard above the rest. "Can you tell us how much money and how much in jewels was taken?"

Morrissey turns around, and walks back to the top of steps. His eyes are stern, "Too much. All that was taken will be recovered - that I promise you."

The reporter asks a follow-up question. "Are those involved confessing?"

His response is in a tone that is clear. "They will; believe me, they will." Morrissey spots Walter among the group of reporters. Morrissey points to him and motions him to come onto the porch. Walter elbows his way through the reporters then climbs the steps. Morrissey signals for Walter to follow then takes him into the casino. The remaining reporters are envious.

Having heard enough, Edith leaves in the direction of the coal yard. Mary follows at a safe distance.

Richards and Harrison are in the office as Walter and Morrissey enter. Morrissey walks to his desk and takes a seat. Walter remains standing. "Well, what do you want to ask?"

"Why me?"

Morrissey ignores the question. "Those who have been captured have only provided limited information so far. Richards is about to go visit each of them. Perhaps he can be more persuasive than the police." Walter looks at Richards, not doubting his ability to get answers that those who follow the rules cannot.

Walter asks Morrissey, "Do you really expect to get it all back?'

Again Morrissey ignores the question, "If I give you a story, will you promise not to print it until I give you the go ahead? Then I want it out within an hour." Even without the editor's permission, Walter nods his head.

"Then start writing. The jewels were placed in the safe in envelopes. Those who took the jewels emptied the envelopes to save space. Unfortunately the jewelry is mixed up." Morrissey pauses, giving Walter time to catch up. "Arrangements have been made with Mr. Marvin to use his ballroom to display the gems. Those whose merchandise was temporarily misplaced will be able to make claims. To insure the safety of the gems, five detectives from the New York City police department are on their way to stand guard."

"So you think you will have the jewels back soon?" Walter bravely asks.

"Those who took it will wish that I have it back by evening. That is all for now." Walter starts to leave the room. When he reaches the door Morrissey adds, "I will send a messenger to tell you when it is okay to run the article. Until then not a word."

Reaching the entrance to the coal yard, Edith looks around to be sure no one is following. She opens the door to the office and enters. As the back of Edith's skirt enters the door, Mary cautiously rounds the corner. She stops and looks casually at a vine, giving Edith time to be well inside. Mary walks down the street past the coal yard. As she passes she hears voices from inside.

"They know too much already. We need to get ready to move," Edith warns Peter.

"I can have the wagon back together in an hour."

"No, not yet. The crowd is getting bored and breaking up; the longer we wait, the better. Start getting the wagon back together at 5:00; be ready to leave when the hotels start serving supper at 7:00." Mary turns and walks back in the direction of the hotels.

At the farm near Galway, Phillips is working replacing slab boards on the side of the shed. The old farmer is watching from the fence.

"Gettin' 'bout time for dinner."

"Sounds good - real good." Phillips has not eaten since the day before.

"Well then wash yusself up and meet me and the Mrs. at the table." Phillips finishes nailing the one last board, and then goes to the pump.

Nolan and Gretchen are naked under the sheet. "How you gunna explain this to your husband?

"Whoever told you I was married?"

"You said your husband was in the fields when I arrived."

Gretchen gets up from the bed and starts to dress, her back toward Nolan. Nolan just lays on his back with one hand behind his head. "I don't always tell the truth." She turns and watches Nolan's face.

"Me either."

Two boys of about twelve are carrying their fishing poles. "Yus so lucky, yus parents don't 'xpect you to go to church," says the taller of the boys.

"Ain't luck, my pa's dun got thrown out for some damn reason."

The taller boy looks at the creek bank and then points. "What's dat?" It is hard to make out, but David's body is wedged between tree roots and driftwood. The shorter boy pokes at the object with his fishing pole. The body moves out slightly from the shore.

"Damn, it's a body. Third one I ever seen." David's body rolls over. Mud and weeds cover his face.

The taller boy says, "Yus waits here; I'll go gets help."

The shorter boy wants nothing to do with being alone with a corpse. "I ain't waitin' with no dead body. I'm comin' with you." The two boys start running down the road with the taller boy constantly looking back.

Jacob and George are sitting on a bench in the States Park. "Quite the day," Jacob remarks.

"I think the night was the amazing part."

"I guess you are right, it is not every morning that I am woken up by an attractive young girl dressed in her nightgown shooting a handgun."

"That surprises me. I would have thought you were used to it." George pauses, "Oh that's right, it is the fathers and brothers that are shooting at you."

Jacob ignores the comment. "Will Beach, and you by association, be defending those who have been caught?"

"I think Mr. Beach will avoid the case if at all possible. It is one thing to defend a client, it is another to defend a client whose actions have damaged the reputation of your home."

"So not everyone deserves the best defense possible." Jacob tries to counter the comment about being shot at.

"The best defense, yes. The best lawyer, not necessarily."

"So a lawyer's personal interest can outweigh the rights of a defendant."

"Almost always."

"I wonder how Catharine would accept your answer."

George looks off at Todd standing by the archery range. Jacob stands and starts off toward Sarah, who has just emerged from the family's cottage.

"Going to create a situation to be shot at?"

"No, father's out of town and brother's too young to worry about."

"Yes, but arrows still hurt." George chuckles at his own joke.

Michael and Elmendorf, Shorty, and Swanson are sitting on cots in two cells. The front of the cells are all open so they can see each other. Michael looks at Shorty but speaks to all, "Keep your mouths closed. No one was hurt, so the most we will get is three, maybe five, years. When we get out there will be plenty to live on for the rest of our lives."

"Maybe your life, I like the ladies too much to live for very long on any one heist," Swanson brags.

"Keep your mouth shut or I will shut it for you," threatens Michael.

Swanson and Shorty look at each other, comfortable because they are in a separate cell.

Morrissey, Richards, and Harrison are looking at a map of the village. A messenger is led into the office by one of the deputies. The messenger looks at the deputy as if he is interfering. "Mr. Morrissey, I have a note for you." The messenger hands the envelope to Morrissey. Morrissey picks up an ivory handled letter opener and starts to cut it open. "It was given to me by a lady who is not staying at the hotel. She gave it to me then went out the door. I followed her down the street a block then decided it would be better to get the note to you then to follow her any further."

Morrissey talks while reading the note. "Would you recognize her if you saw her again?"

"Probably not, it would be kind of hard; it was really busy in the lobby and there is not much distinctive about her."

"Thank you, you may leave." Morrissey looks to Richards to tip the boy. Richards gives the boy a nickel. Morrissey says, "More." Richards gives the boy a second nickel.

After the messenger leaves Morrissey turns to Harrison. "Where did you say there was a coal yard?"

"About three blocks south."

"Let's go for a walk," Morrissey suggests to both Harrison and Richards. To Harrison he adds, "Might I suggest you send a couple of mounted deputies ahead to prevent anyone from escaping to the south." As they get ready to leave, he adds, "Tell them not to stop. Just ride by and stop at the next corner." Morrissey throws the note on to his desk and walks out.

Mr. Morrissey,

Might I suggest that you make great haste to visit the coal yard on Franklin Street. I believe you will find most of what you are searching for inside.

You are welcome.
A Friend

Peter is busy placing the rear wheels on the wagon when he hears the sound of horses' hoofs outside. He looks out the window and sees two mounted deputies gallop by. Curious, he walks to the window, looking south in the direction the horses went. There is nothing unfamiliar.

From the north, Harrison is leading a team of deputies toward the front of the coal building. Morrissey and Richards are directly behind the deputies. As they crest the small hill the two mounted deputies are visible on the opposite corner.

Edith is strolling down Division Street. She rounds the corner onto Franklin where she sees a group of men walking in the direction of the coal company. She turns and walks back toward the States. She looks across the street and for the first time notices Mary.

Peter steps away from the window and hustles to the sliding back door. The door is old and its wheels are rusty. He struggles to open the door. Using his legs as levers, the door finally bursts open. Peter steps outside where two more mounted men are waiting with rifles trained on him. He raises his arms.

Smiley looks to Harrison, who nods. Smiley opens the front door; several deputies rush inside, followed by Richards and Morrissey.

The deputies scour the interior of the building, looking for other members of the gang.

Morrissey walks over to a pile of firewood that has been covered by a tarp. He pulls back the tarp and sees the center of the pile has been hollowed out. The open area holds the bags containing what was stolen the night before. Morrissey turns to one of the deputies, "Good! Find that young reporter, Walter. Tell him I said it is time to run the story."

Morrissey returns to examining the bounty. He calls to the deputy who is to find Walter and says, "Stop by the States and tell Mr. Marvin that it looks like we have it all back."

LIFE SKETCHES AT SARATOGA, BY OUR OWN ARTIST—MORNING SCENE AT CONGRESS SPRING.

Frank Leslie's Illustrated Newspaper 27 August 1859
Courtesy of Saratoga Springs Public Library

Returns

A porter opens the door to the States' private dining room for Morrissey and Richards. Inside, over a dozen tables have been set up. Each table is covered with neatly laid out jewelry. There is a burly man guarding each set of four tables. There is also a burly man at the door and one between the two windows. The men all look uncomfortable in suits.

Morrissey looks around and nods his head to the jeweler, David Pratt, who appears to need to talk to him. "Mr. Morrissey, I think we have a problem."

Morrissey stares at him. "What a day!" The clock in the background rings five times.

Earlier that morning, dressed in his night clothes, Bennett packs his trunk. Edith, dressed in clothes to go to the spring, is sitting next to the window in a soft chair. She is biting the knuckle on her right hand. "Wait too long and you will never get out," Bennett admonishes.

"Or try to leave now and be the number one suspect."

"I don't give a damn; I'm too old for anyone to think it were me."

Edith stands. "You're not going anyplace."

"Like hell."

Edith pulls a small derringer out of her pocketbook and holds it directly against Bennett's chest. "You are going to sit back down, have a drink, maybe even five or six. But you are not leaving this room." Bennett holds his hands out and pathetically sits down. Edith walks to the dresser. Placing the derringer on the dresser, Edith pours him a drink of whiskey, and brings the glass and the bottle to a table next to his chair. Edith goes back to the dresser, picks up the derringer, returns it to her pocketbook, and walks to the door. "I'll tell everyone that you have a touch of the ague." Edith opens the door and slips out.

Bennett glowers as he stares at the door, sipping his drink.

The crowd at the springs is the largest of the season, with everyone trying to learn news of the robbery and subsequent arrests. The dowagers are gathered near the walkway to the hotels watching everyone come and go. Edith walks quietly between the groups, trying to reconnoiter.

George and Jacob are at their usual post near one of the pillars. "So will Mr. Beach be using his great skill to represent those who robbed Morrissey's?"

"No, the district attorney has asked him to assist with the prosecution."

"At least he will be involved, which means you will be involved, which means that you will be able to keep me informed." He pauses to catch his breath, "My uncle is relieved that none of those involved were staying at the hotel."

"How does he know, there are still several who are at large."

Jacob seems disgusted. "Looking for the fine points as always. George, you are already sounding like a trial lawyer." Jacob pauses as he looks around. "You must excuse me, I have more important people to talk to." Jacob pats George on the back. Walter has a head start in joining Sarah and Sadie.

Sadie and Sarah are whispering to each other as Walter joins them. "Missy and Josey are so pleased that no one of color has been implicated," Sadie informs Walter.

"As a free man, I would have thought Benjamin would have been more concerned."

"What difference does it make what the servants think? Saratoga is not about the servants," Sarah points out. "It is about the parties, dances, and the attention of the fine beaus; now that this silly robbery has been solved, Saratoga can get back to what is important."

"Walter, how did you get those exclusive stories from Mr. Morrissey?" Sadie asks.

"I guess he is impressed by quality."

"Apparently not modesty or humility."

"Not the qualities apparent in a successful journalist."

Jacob joins the group. "Have you ladies been following the big robbery?"

"It is so exciting." Sarah suddenly becomes interested. "I bet that we have seen the woman who planned the robbery at the springs many mornings. She could be one of the belles at the balls or even one of those awful dowagers."

Jesse and Jennie Ringer walk in. Some in the crowd recognize Jesse and start pointing. Seeing the Ringer girls, Edith tries to remain unnoticed as she quickly leaves.

"Everyone is looking at you." Jennie is proud of her sister.

"It does feel really good."

A teenage boy comments, "She looked better in her wet nightgown."

"How would you know, you never saw her," a friend challenges.

"I sure did. I only live a block away," the first boy contends.

"That doesn't mean you saw her."

"I seen her in wet clothes, yus could see the lines of her legs and they is fine.

"You're such a liar." The second boy has heard the stories of Jesse in her wet gown but will not yield that everyone actually saw her.

"Did you hear those boys?" Jennie is embarrassed for her sister.

"Yes, by tomorrow they will be saying the nightgown was ripped and they saw a whole lot more than the outline of a leg." For a young woman, Jesse is very knowledgeable of men's behavior.

Jennie fears for her sister's reputation. "I don't envy you." Jesse has a satisfied smile.

"I wonder if they ever will capture the woman." The idea of a woman in charge pleases Madam Jumel.

"Why should she be any harder to catch than one of the men?" Van Buren ponders.

"A woman strong enough to lead a group of outlaws is smart enough to avoid capture."

"From what I understand, she was not smart enough to escape with any of her ill gained bounty," he reminds her.

"What matters is that she executed the plan." Madam Jumel has often had to use her wiles to get her way.

"A robbery is not successful without a proper escape," Van Buren contends.

"Mr. President, a woman set up the robbery of one of the largest hotels and the biggest casino in a single night. The failure to escape was the result of the strength of another young woman who went out in her wet night dress and shot a gun from behind her back to sound the alarm."

Madam Jumel sounds like one of those new suffragettes. "This event has all been about women, with men playing the role of pawns." Van Buren stares at her, saying nothing. "Ah, to be a young woman in these modern times. Soon we will invade taverns, play pool, and be allowed in the casino."

Van Buren says what men will say for the next hundred and fifty years, "I am too old for that much change."

LeRoy and his sons Lee and Hammon are standing on the bank of Lake Champlain. The boys are each holding back one of the hounds; their shotguns are at their hips. Nate, waist deep in the water, has Eve in his arms with Adam on his back holding on to his neck. Mattie is in the water above her waist.

LeRoy enjoys having the family trapped. "Now's there's a major drop-off about anoder hundred fifty feet. There ain't no wading der. Yus gunna come out of dat water somewhere might'n well be here as furder up."

Nate and Mattie look at each other, reluctant to give up after having survived so much. "I's sorry Mattie. We's so damn close to freedom." Nate, Eve, and Adam slowly climb up the bank. As Mattie starts to climb up, LeRoy takes her hand and pulls her up. As she reaches the top he grabs her breast.

"Fur a modder of two they's still purdy perky," LeRoy comments, then turns to his oldest son. "Takes a feel fur yus self." Lee goes to touch Mattie's breast but she pushes his hand away.

In vengeance, LeRoy hits Nate in the back of the head with the rifle butt. "Now dunt go gettin' uppity, Missey." He signals for his son to touch her breast. "Yus bounty gunna gives us a chance to have one hell of a party." Mattie makes no further protest as Lee squeezes both her breasts.

Nolan and Gretchen are lying next to each other on her bed. "I'm sure the neighbors have seen you. They are probably talking right now." She ponders her fate under the cloud of rumors. "Whoever's after you will be here by noon."

"There is no one after me," Nolan contends.

"Is that why you look at the road every time a carriage goes by? Or why you split wood in the barn instead of in the yard?"

"I just don't want people talking about you. I care."

"Oh they talk about me plenty. Mostly what they say is about what they wish they was doin'. At least for the last few days they had something real to talk about." She rubs his naked chest. "You'll be leavin' today." She cuddles into her special spot where his shoulder and chest meet.

"Why would I be leaving?"

"Because I want no part of what you're hiding from."

Nolan feels safe, "You don't need to worry."

"I know, because you're leaving." She cuddles deeper into his chest, knowing it is the last time.

Edith enters their bedroom where she finds Bennett passed out in his chair. She walks over, pours into a planter the contents of his glass and the remaining whiskey from the decanter. She looks around and takes the empty decanter to the door. At the door she calls out, "Hall boy."

The hall boy answers his summons, "Yes Ma'am?"

"My uncle would like some more of Mr. Marvin's finest Kentucky Bourbon." The hall boy takes the bottle and walks toward the stairs. Edith is not finished, "Boy." The boy stops. "If no one answers when you return, bring the bottle in and leave it on the stand." The boy heads toward the stairs. Edith looks around the room one final time and exits, knowing that when the boy returns, he will see Bennett passed out.

In the private dining room of the States, in addition to the guards, are Morrissey, Richards, Marvin, and Putnam. There are three couples in the room, each escorted by a clerk. The clerk has the envelope that each couple had placed their jewelry in before the robbery. Each item of jewelry on the tables is numbered. David Pratt, the jeweler, is standing next to one of the tables writing a description of each of the pieces.

"That's it. The envelope says that you deposited three necklaces, two rings, five bracelets and six broaches."

"Do not forget my two sets of cuff links, stick pin, and diamond studs."

The clerk turns over the envelope so that the man can see the numbers next to each item. "Duly noted, they are numbers C215 and C418, S47 and P15."

Pratt whispers to Morrissey, "It would have been so much easier if they had not opened every envelope."

Morrissey speaks to Putnam. "How did Judge Baucus react when he was asked to review any conflicting claims?"

"After the tragedy with his grandson, I believe he was happy to be shown the respect he so strongly deserves."

"We will have the room open to claims today and tomorrow or until everyone who deposited jewelry has come through. Hopefully we can give it back to the owners starting tomorrow night." Young Pratt has supervised the return of the jewelry.

"Nice job everyone," Morrissey calls out, patting Pratt on the back. One couple leaves the room, being immediately replaced by one from the hall.

The slave family is huddled together in a corner of the station in Putnam Junction. Each is tied at their wrists and with their ankles tied close enough to be able to walk but not run. Lee, Roy, Ebed, and Hammon are standing watch. LeRoy enters. "Our agent in Troy said he would go to the station and buy tickets for all of us to go to Saratoga. He's gunna meet us there with the bounty. He'll be taken our little prizes from there."

"How much we gettin'?" Ebed is expecting a long cold winter. He wants to buy his firewood and not have to cut it himself.

"A hundred each for the couple, seventy five for the old lady, fifty for the boy, nuttin' for the girl. Seems she's sickly."

Ebed stares at Mattie, "Dat much for the wench?"

"Seems she's some kind of house maid, and da 'ld lady is a cook." LeRoy explains their worth.

Ebed rubs his crotch. "Gunna be one hell of a night in Saratoga tonight." Ebed pokes Nate one more time with the barrel of his rifle, then grabs Mattie's breast. "Yus headed back to Nord Caroliner, back to dem hot fields."

"Leave her 'lone," LeRoy orders. "We dunt need any damage to da goods."

A couple in their fifties who are awaiting a train walks over to the telegraph office inside the train station.

"I gunna damage nutin', just feel'n the material." Ebed grabs Mattie roughly.

LeRoy places the end of his shotgun at Ebed's head. "I said 'nuff."

In the privacy of Beach's office, George feels safe asking, "You are considered the best defense attorney in the state, why would you even consider helping the prosecutor?"

"You miss the point; I will be putting on a defense. I will be defending Morrissey, Putnam, and the reputation of Saratoga."

"But what if one of those arrested is innocent?" George is showing the optimism of youth.

"From what my sources tell me, the way they are all talking at the jail, they are all guilty," Beach rationalizes. "If not of this, of some other crime."

"I have trouble envisioning you working with a prosecutor."

"I will not be working with him; I will be working in place of him." Beach collects his thoughts, "How are things between you and Miss Cook?"

George blushes. "It is important to believe in the impossible."

"Mr. Batcheller, you are a promising lawyer but a hopeless romantic." Beach throws a rolled up newspaper at his protégée.

In the Ringer family's rooms, Ruth, Dolly, and Jennie are busy packing their trunks. Ringer watches but does not help. Jesse is sitting on the window ledge looking out into the street.

Ringer asks his wife, "But why are you leaving in such a hurry?"

"It is just not safe in Saratoga." Ruth gets more demanding with each word.

"It's perfectly safe now. No one would dare try to rob Mr. Morrissey again."

"Last week you would have told me the same thing, and look what happened. I almost lost my little baby," protests Ruth.

"Dolly is hardly a baby. Look how she was the one who remembered that there was a woman involved."

Ruth turns to Jesse. "You need to start packing."

"I'm not going," Jesse answers calmly.

"You most certainly are. Now start packing." Ruth makes the mother's critical mistake, she tries to argue with a teenager.

Jesse holds her ground. "In Saratoga I am considered brave. I am even a little bit of a celebrity."

"I don't care how much of a celebrity you think you are; you are coming back to Brooklyn where it is safe."

"No, I am not." Jesse does not raise her voice.

Ruth and Jesse both look at Ringer, who tells his wife, "I don't think you should be going, so I am not going to insist that Jesse go." Ruth glares at her husband.

A group of four riders approach the farm where Phillips is working. The four dismount at the water trough so their horses can drink. One rider advances to the farmer. Phillips continues replacing a board on the side of one of the sheds.

"Hi Bill, understand you have a new hired man," one of the deputies reminds the farmer.

"Not really. I do have a new man doin' some carpentry work, but he'll be gone by the end of the week. Why?"

"When did you hire this here new man?" the deputy asks. Hearing the conversation, Phillips lowers the hammer and comes around the barn.

The farmer points. "There he is. Phillips, come on over here."

"Who are you and where did you come from?" The deputy has begun his interrogation.

"Don't matter, yus goin' to 'rest me anyway." Without explanation, the deputy starts putting cuffs and shackles on Phillips.

"Why they arrestin' you?" The farmer asks Phillips.

"Cause when they don't know your history, yus accused of everthin' and when they do know your history, they accuse you of even more." A bound Phillips is helped onto one of the horses. "You are a fair man. When this gets settled, you mind if I drop by and see how things are goin'?"

"You get this straightened out and there be work waiting for you."

"See you in three years."

The group starts riding along the road, with two of the deputies doubled up on one horse.

Morrissey is sitting alone in the office enjoying a cigar. There is a knock on the closed door. "Come in."

The door opens slowly and Jesse enters timidly. "Mr. Morrissey, may I speak with you?"

"Of course, Jesse."

"My ma is planning on going back to Brooklyn soon. I was wondering if I could stay here and work for you."

"I owe you a lot. But you know what kind of business I run. It is not suitable for a young lady such as yourself to work here."

"You's an honest man, Mr. Morrissey. I was thinking I could set up a room in the foyer where men could check their hats, coats, and canes. I would work for tips; it wouldn't cost you anything."

"I'm not sure, a woman, especially a young attractive woman. . . ," Morrissey reflects. "Not a good idea."

"I would even work cleaning up the casino if I have to, but I think I'm cute enough to make money working near the door." Jesse is suddenly immodest.

"I don't think your mother would approve."

"She wouldn't on account of my being a girl. My dad works for you and she doesn't say anything; why shouldn't I be allowed the same privileges?"

"If your mother says it is okay, you can stay on with your father. Why is your mother leaving?"

"Says it's too dangerous here in Saratoga."

Walter is working at one of the standup desks; several other printers are at their desks. They all look up as the bell over the door rings and a telegraph runner enters. The messenger shouts over the sound of the press, "Walter, yous becoming very important. This telegram is for you." Walter walks over to the desk. "The telegraph operator said he guessed it was important."

Walter looks at the messenger, trying to read his eyes as he opens the envelope. "It is not a news story, so I cannot tip you." The runner looks disappointed as he walks out the door.

Walter reads the telegram one more time as he walks to his desk. He puts the telegram on the desk, grabs his jacket and walks to the door.

The telegram reads:

Full family package found. Being returned to Troy on the 2:20 o'clock train.

"Mr. Judson, I will be out on a story for about an hour." Before the editor can respond, Walter is out the door.

There are three groups in the room examining the jewelry. Each is accompanied by a clerk. Mrs. Scarborough, her son Daniel, and her daughter-in-law Julia are perusing the tables under the watchful eye of one of the clerks. The mother lifts one of the necklaces. "That simply cannot be the one."

Julia takes the necklace, "It does seem a little light."

"It is the one, I am certain." Daniel is bored and wants to be at the pool room.

"Impossible! Gold would weigh much more than this."

Hearing the discussion, Pratt joins the group. "Is there a problem?"

"No, everything is fine." Daniel is used to playing mediator between his wife and his mother.

"It most certainly is not," insists Mrs. Scarborough, "This is too light to be the necklace we deposited."

"Mother, it is fine."

Pratt examines the necklace. "There is no other in the room that is similar."

Daniel takes his wife and mother by the arms, "Come along, it is the one; we are taking time from others."

As they walk to the door, Mrs. Scarborough continues her harangue. "Daniel, you are quite mistaken." Daniel continues pushing the two women to the door.

Jacob and Sarah are sitting on one of the benches. "Do you miss your father?"

Sarah taps Jacob's hand. "Only Todd and Mother miss Father. With him gone, I do not have to worry about him limiting our time together. Sadie likes it because she can do those crazy political things that she does."

In the background, Marvin leaves one of the cottages, unnoticed.

"What is she into now, anti-gambling, temperance, women's suffrage?"

"All of those. She did listen to the speech by that Miss Anthony. It filled her head with wild ideas."

"She and Walter make quite the pair."

Sarah changes the subject. "Mr. Jacob Marvin, are you going to ask me to the ball this Saturday or not?"

In a mocking tone, he answers, "Miss Sarah Stiles, would you honor me with your company at the ball on Saturday evening?"

In the background Josey can be seen exiting the cottage Marvin left earlier; she looks both ways.

"Mr. Jacob Marvin, I will consider your offer. A lady must explore all her options; she does not want to commit too soon." Sarah fans herself vigorously as if she has just had a hot flash.

"And what does a young lady get who waits too long?"

"For some, there is no such thing as waiting too long."

Cora exits the same cottage as Marvin and Josey.

Benjamin is working cleaning out one of the stalls in the livery used by the Vanderbilts and other wealthy guests. There are three other men of color present: Jeb Northup, Johnathan, and Elias. Elias is about twenty, the others approximately twice his age. The men are mucking the stalls and brushing down the horses.

"Yes indeed, they wrote that book 'bout my brother." Everyone has heard the story of Jeb's brother, Solomon, as told in Twelve Years a Slave. Those who know Jeb well are tired of him using his brother for fame.

"Dey tells me da book was banned in Charleston and Savannah," Benjamin reminds his coworkers.

"They banned a book? Hell you could buy it in every stationary store in Saratoga. All the soudern people's was reading it!"

"How much of it is true?" Elias makes the mistake of asking.

"Oh, the book is all true," Jeb insists.

Jonathan whispers to Benjamin, "Course Jeb figures none of us can read and when he tells it, he makes the story even worse."

"No need to make it worse," Benjamin assures his fellow workers. "Those field hands work hard for nothing. Elias, how comes Mr. Stevenson brought you up to Saratoga?"

"He doesn't trust no one else to tend to his thoroughbred horses." Elias is proud of his assignment.

"Course he known'd yus'd never try to 'scape to Canada," Jonathan adds.

"They rent my brother out for wages in Charleston. He lives better than some of them immograant workers and dey make better wages." Elias points to his red coat hanging on a peg. "I get's to wear these fine livery."

"I been a slave and now I's free. There ain't no feelin' like the day you wake up a free man," Benjamin clarifies.

"Yes dey is," Elias points out. "The dey yus wake up wid a free woman." They are all laughing when Walter enters, being careful where he steps.

"Benjamin, may I speak with you?" Benjamin shrugs his shoulders to his coworkers, then joins Walter by the door. "I need your help." The two men step outside so they will not be heard. "They found some escaped slaves up near Whitehall. They are going to try to return them south. They are going to be on the 2:20." Benjamin looks questioningly at Walter. "The only thing I can think to do is to have you pose as my slave. We will board the train and get the family off at Mechanicville. I know some people there that will help."

"So's I gots to pose as a slave to help?"

Walter smiles at the irony. "You know me, I will be a kind master."

"What time we get back?"

"We will be on the 4:45."

"I'll ask Mrs. Cora."

"Don't ask anyone. I will talk to Sadie. It will be fine." Walter starts to leave, then gives Benjamin one last instruction. "Meet me at the station at 2:00." Benjamin watches as Walter walks in the direction of the States Hotel.

The Clarks, both in their early thirties, accompanied by a clerk, are looking over the recovered jewelry. The wife, Margaret, is closely examining one of the necklaces. "That is not the one. The one you gave me was longer and had a larger stone."

"I'm sure this is the one my mother owned. I have seen it all my life."

Hearing the discussion, Pratt joins the couple. "Is there a problem?"

"My husband thinks this is one of our pieces, but it is not."

Pratt is suspicious. "Do you see it someplace else in the room?"

"No, we have been through the entire room," Clark explains. "Besides, this is the one my mother gave my wife for an engagement present."

"I am sorry, but it most assuredly is not the one."

"I have the number. We will note it as in the conflict collection." Pratt records the number and starts to place it back on the table to be viewed by others. When he hefts the necklace a final time, his expression shows he thinks something is wrong. He carries the necklace to the window for a closer view.

The faces of the contingent on the piazza have changed over the summer but not the attitude. The crescent of Mmes. White, Brewster, Jackson, and Dallas along with Miss Clark are sitting in what everyone in the hotel knows are 'their' rocking chairs. To mask how much their real purpose is to gossip, each woman has either knitting or a book on her lap.

"Ever since they made the claim that a woman was involved, I have felt accusing eyes fall upon me." Mrs. White reveals her inner concern even if it is imagined.

"What a waste. Clearly you are not nearly clever enough to plan such a robbery and God knows you don't even know eight men," retorts Mrs. Brewster.

Mrs. White starts packing up her knitting, "You are truly a hurtful person."

Mrs. Dallas tries to deflect the conversation, "This is the first time I can remember when a 'niece' is looked upon, by those who judge others, better than being a single woman of high moral standards. I mean, we all know exactly how they make a living."

"It is never better to be a woman of limited morals. The nieces that litter Saratoga are nothing but a bunch of libertines," Mrs. Brewster points out.

Mrs. Dallas' attempt to mollify the situation did not work. Mrs. White finishes picking up. She clutches her knitting, saying over her shoulder, "As are those who make hurtful comments."

Mrs. Brewster ignores her victim. "There probably is not a woman involved. Just some wild story concocted to make everyone distrust the single women."

"Who said the woman was single?" Miss Clark is concerned.

"She would have to be single; a married woman would not have the time." Mrs. Brewster has the last word one more time.

At the entrance to Congress Spring, Edith is sitting on a bench holding up the daily newspaper. Ruth Ringer is sitting on a bench a few feet away. Their backs are toward each other. The women speak in quiet voices. Edith asks, "Why are you leaving?"

"Because I am scared. I never should have let you talk me into this."

"Don't play innocent with me, I'm not father." Edith falls back on a family expression, "You knew how good this could be."

"I'm leaving today on the 2:20 with the girls."

"Where are you going?"

"Back to Brooklyn. Jesse doesn't want to come, but I will make her."

"That should be interesting." Edith folds the newspaper and gets ready to leave. "I will be in touch soon."

"Don't bother. I don't want anything more to do with you or your damn schemes."

In the park at the States, Sadie sits on one of the benches while Walter paces in front of her. "You knew, didn't you?" he speculates.

"You were easy to suspect."

"I'm not asking you to help me."

"But you are putting Benjamin at risk and asking me to be quiet; silence is helping. Admit it, Walter Pratt, you are asking for my help."

"Benjamin is a free man; he will make his own choices."

"Just because Benjamin is free doesn't mean he thinks like a free man. He sees what you ask as an order, not a request."

"It is a whole family." He hesitates. "I must try."

"How can I help?" Sadie has a sincere look.

Bennett looks like a piece of furniture sitting in his chair. Edith ignores him as she finishes getting ready for dinner. "Did you have any breakfast?"

He holds up a half full bottle, "About a pint."

"In your present condition, you better not be planning on going to dinner. Want me to get the hall boy to bring you more water so you can wash up?" Edith is reluctant to help.

"Why do you want me clean?" The sarcasm is clearly present.

"When you are like this, I don't want you at all."

"Sure you do. You need me to tell you how clever you are, how without you, it could never have been done."

Edith checks herself in the mirror, pinching her cheeks to add color. "Do you want me to have one of the waiters bring you dinner?" When

Edith turns she sees Bennett is again asleep in the chair. She walks over and pours the remaining alcohol into the planter as before.

Edith opens the drawer in one of her trunks. Among her undergarments is the derringer, which she takes out. She lifts her skirt and places the small gun in her garter. She picks up the decanter. Looking back one time with disgust, Edith exits the room and calls, "Hall boy." She waves the empty decanter. "We will be needing another." The hall boy takes the empty decanter and walks toward the back stairs. "No need getting the best. Mr. Bennett is not tasting it any more anyway." Edith closes the door and walks down the hall toward the main stairs.

The dining room is full, and for the first time, there is as much conversation about the upcoming ball as the robbery. Several people notice Edith sitting alone. A concerned host, Marvin walks to her. "Miss Edith, where is Mr. Bennett?"

"He is not feeling well. A touch of the ague I suspect. He even complains about his hand being numb."

"I will send the doctor around."

"There is no need, he probably just needs sleep."

"Has he been up late at night?"

"No, he tends to fall asleep in his chair early in the evening and then he is unable to sleep during the night. Of course, going to Morrissey's every night is not helping."

"So you are unable to take advantage of our fine dances. That is a shame."

It is instinctive for Edith to flirt. "It is a shame, I so like to dance. I have such a good sense of rhythm."

Marvin understands her hidden message and walks to the Stiles' table. "Miss Sadie, Miss Sarah, I assume you are both ready for the ball this Saturday?"

Sarah cannot wait to boast, "I will be wearing my blue dress."

"Then I will arrange to have a corsage sent."

Sadie never misses an opportunity to make a comment about her sister's life. "There will be no need for that. I am sure your nephew has made appropriate arrangements." Sarah stares at Sadie.

"If only young Mr. Walter Pratt could afford flowers," Sarah strikes back. Sadie glares.

"I suddenly understand why your father needed to go to Europe; the upcoming war was in his own house." Marvin smiles at Cora and walks away.

"We have details on every newly hired man in the area. Must be a hundred leads to follow up on," Harrison reports.

"A couple of them will be real. The problem is sorting out the real." Morrissey will not be content until all the men are accounted for.

"It's chasing down all the false ones that is driving my deputies crazy."

"The ones who have been captured went north and south. What have you heard from east and west?" Morrissey reminds the chief.

"There are about as many stories in every direction. The reports from north and south are probably because of the railroad."

"Are you watching the train station?"

"Every train in and out."

Three burly men are standing together on the deck of the train station. One has a badge on his lapel. All three are holding short barreled shotguns. There is trepidation in Benjamin's eyes as he stands just behind Sadie. She watches Walter approach from the ticket agent.

"They won't sell us a ticket, the train is sold out."

"What will you do?"

"I have to wire Mechanicville and Troy. My associates will have to do something there." Walter looks back at the ticket agent and sees Ruth with Jenny and Dolly. Each has a ticket in hand. Ringer is watching, dissatisfied.

"How did they get tickets?" Sadie wonders.

"See for yourself." Sadie and Benjamin look over to the edge where Harrison and Richards are standing with several trunks. "It helps to know the right people."

The southbound train screeches to a halt. Several passengers disembark and begin the ritual of looking for their luggage. Reluctantly, Ringer kisses Jenny and Dolly sweetly on the cheeks. He just stares at Ruth. Without further embrace, the three women board the train.

The three burly men with the shotguns board the third class car. Through the widows of the car, they can be seen walking up to the slave family. One of the men takes out some coins and offers them to LeRoy, who counts the money carefully. Then the five mountain men disembark.

As the train starts to pull out, Walter, Sadie, and Benjamin can clearly see the pitiful faces of the slave family. It is Mattie who looks the saddest. Walter touches Sadie on the arm, "My associates will be able to do something."

"What makes you think they will be any more successful than we were?"

Walter looks dejected, like he just failed not only in his mission, but in the eyes of the woman for whom he cares. "Benjamin, sir, please escort Miss Sadie back to the hotel. I have messages to send out."

Walter is surprised when Benjamin extends his hand to shake. "You tried. Dat's more than that Mr. Jacob or even that Mr. Batcheller done."

Walter moves toward the telegraph office, torn between pride and dejection. Sadie leaves for the States with Benjamin a step behind.

On the upper steps on the back of the tenement, Pauline, Antoinette, and Janet are resting in the shade. They hear the whistle of the southbound train as it approaches. It is warm and they have the lifted their skirts above their knees. They make no effort to cover up. Through the train's window, Mattie seems to study them.

Pauline is amazed, "Ain't dat sometin." Antoinette and Janet look at her questioningly. "Someone just went by who done envied our lives." The train continues to pick up speed, carrying people to their fates.

Madam Jumel and the Judge are enjoying tea together in the Judge's parlor. She remarks, "So she still at it?"

"My daughter-in-law will never give up. It is simply not in her nature."

"You cannot blame a mother for defending her child."

"One should always aspire and believe." The Judge continues, "Just not in the impossible."

"Judge, was it not believing in the impossible that made you the man you are today?"

"But there is a difference, I believed in myself, not events."

Madam Jumel takes a moment to ruminate. "It matters not what I believed, or even the truth; rumors and events dictated how others perceived my life."

"I believe that is true for all of us."

"The difference is that, to most, it is families that make the perceptions. In my case, and perhaps yours, Judge, the issue was others' jealousy of our notoriety."

"Notoriety is a much greater burden than people know."

They both raise their tea cups to their lips.

Missy is serving Cora and Sarah as they have afternoon tea in the cottage. Sadie enters slightly winded from the brisk walk on a hot summer afternoon. "Where have you been?" Cora's tone is slightly questioning but more demanding.

"Getting to know a man worth knowing."

The bait is too much for Sarah, "Not another intellectual I hope."

"No, a man of action."

"Oh, so you have given up on Walter?"

"Ladies!" Cora cuts off the comments.

Marvin and Putnam are in the jewelry room as one of the porters opens the door for Morrissey and Richards. Richards moves to one of the other guards standing along the wall. Morrissey looks around and nods his head to the jeweler, who nervously approaches the men. "Mr. Morrissey, I think we have a problem. We have six unclaimed pieces of jewelry, three others with dual claims, and claims that nine pieces are not here." Morrissey stares at the young man; the clock in the background rings five times.

"Has everyone been through the room?"

"Everyone whose name was on any of the envelopes. There were a couple more couples who we did not have on the list but Mr. Putnam said to let in. They are in the dual claims," Pratt explains.

"I suggest we make arrangements to give back the pieces on which there is only one claim." Judge Baucus has assured me that he can hear the dual claims tomorrow."

"How long would it take you to group the single claim pieces on top of their envelopes?"

"About an hour, two at the most." Pratt is jumpy. "Mr. Morrissey, that is not the problem." Pratt goes over to two of the tables where he picks up two of the pieces of jewelry. He moves to the window and urges Morrissey to join him. Pratt hands one of the pieces to Morrissey. He retains the other piece.

"Do you see it?"

Morrissey holds the piece to the light. "What am I supposed to be seeing?"

Pratt holds his piece to the light. "They are both fakes. Good fakes, but both fakes."

Morrissey scrutinizes the piece more closely. "Were they claimed?"

"No, but in each case the man did try to tell his wife that they were hers."

"Who were these men?" Morrissey is as serious as he has been since he arrived in the village.

"A Mr. Theodore Clark of Baltimore. The second was the Scarborough family from Charleston."

Putnam intercedes, "I know Mr. Clark and his family. They are one of the foremost families in the country. His wife is a charming young lady, I believe from New Orleans."

"The Scarboroughs used to stay with me," Marvin adds. "There was some problem with their bill last year and they were not back this season."

"So that is how they came to be my guests." Putnam looks relieved.

Morrissey asks the jeweler, "You are sure both these pieces are fake?" Pratt stares at Morrissey as if to say 'how dare you question my assessment.' Morrissey gets the message. "Then start separating the pieces. About 10:00, I will be back to look at the unclaimed and dual claimed pieces." Morrissey looks at Richards, who has the faintest knowing smile.

Marvin wants inside information. "Any update on those who planned the heist?"

"There are still at least four at large. Harrison is out working one of the hundred leads as we speak."

Morrissey is getting ready to leave as Pratt makes one final comment. "Oh Mr. Morrissey, there was one other person who went through without her name on an envelope."

"Who was she?"

"I don't know. She came in right in front of Mr. Putnam. I nodded to him, he nodded back so I assumed she was okay." Pratt defends his action.

"If you mean when I came about 3:00, I was only nodding hello." Putnam explains his innocent gesture.

Morrissey looks to Richards as if to say pay close attention, "What can you tell me about this lady?"

"She came in just like everyone else and one of the escorts walked her through. She picked up several pieces and put each back. At the end she smiled at me and said 'Good luck.'" He has a sudden realization, "I just realized she picked up the fakes."

"Would you recognize her?"

"Probably not." He tries to focus. "But I would recognize the cameo she was wearing; it was an ivory face set on a blue stone, expensive."

In the Clark suite, he reports the latest news, "I heard they will be giving back some of the jewelry tomorrow evening. Judge Baucus will be hearing from those who have disputes. I am not sure what time we will have to meet with him."

"I cannot imagine what they are going to do since your mother's necklace is still missing." Margaret ponders the options.

"I remain sure it is the one we disagreed about."

"It was not." She insists.

"You are not ready. Do you mind if I go down to the men's parlor and have a cigar?"

"Certainly not."

Clark is relieved to disappear from the room and to be out of the constant bickering. When he closes the door, Margaret pulls up her skirt and takes a bottle from her garter. The bottle is marked laudanum. She takes a small swallow and returns the bottle to her garter. She continues putting on her makeup.

Cook, seated at the head of the table, is joined by George and Catharine. "Apparently it is not going to be a good evening in Troy."

"I heard the same report." George confirms that he has heard the same rumor.

"My agent tells me that there were over three hundred workers from the Burden's Iron Works waiting for the train." Cook tastes a spoonful of the soup. "The engineer would not have stopped except he feared he would kill one of the people on the tracks."

"It always fascinates me that it is the working people who fight so vehemently for the rights of the slaves." George has finished his soup, waiting politely for the next course.

"It is not the rights of the slaves they are fighting for, it is the rights of all." Catharine is comfortable talking politics with her father, the county leader of the new Republican Party.

"Catharine, talk like that will not help you become the first lady," her father corrects her. Catharine and George both look down toward their food. Catharine's foot gently touches George's leg under the table.

At the humble farm east of the village the sun is setting. The windows in Gretchen's bedroom are open, but without a breeze, the room remains hot. Gretchen is alone in the bed wearing a thin nightgown with no sheet over her. Hearing the sound of several horses on the road, Gretchen goes to the window to look out.

Six riders turn into her yard. Four stop in front of the house, the remaining two go to the back. There is loud knocking on the door. Without bothering to put on a robe, Gretchen leaves the bedroom window and starts down stairs. Before she reaches the door she lights an oil lantern. There is a second louder knock. Immodestly, Gretchen opens the door. "Chief Harrison." It is obvious the two know each other.

"Mrs. Thornton, there have been reports that you have had a man staying in the house."

She leans against the door casing, "If you've been talking to some of the neighbors, they would tell you that were true most every night."

"This man is about five feet eight with sandy brown hair, no beard."

"Sounds like Colonel French," she mocks. "He hasn't been by here in several weeks."

"It's hardly Colonel French; the man we are looking for is one of the men who robbed Mr. Morrissey's place in Saratoga."

"I don't know who was talking to you and I don't know any man named Morrissey. A good American lady like me don't take to any Micks."

"Can we look around?"

"You're going to if I let you or not, so I might as well let you; maybe that way nothing will get broken." Gretchen walks out onto the porch. Smiley and Harrison enter the house. The two deputies on their horses stare at the outline of her figure.

Harrison starts into the kitchen. Smiley rushes upstairs to Gretchen's bedroom, where he picks up her worn undergarments and caresses the material.

About five minutes later, Harrison and Smiley come out of the house and start mounting their horses. Harrison says to the deputies who waited outside, "No sign of a man anywhere."

"Just the stacked firewood," Smiley points out. "She would never have that much done in July by herself."

"From what I hear," Harrison talks as the leave her yard, "You can have the good Mrs. Thornton for a full night for far less than a cord of wood." The five ride in the direction of Saratoga.

As they crest a small hill, Nolan, who has been in a grove across the road stands and walks around a tree to watch Gretchen's outline as she reenters the house.

George and Catharine are sitting on the swing at her family porch, enjoying the evening.

"I am proud of you. Your second great case this summer." Catharine is referring to George helping Beach in the prosecution of those involved in the robbery.

"I doubt that there will be much of a trial. I expect they will all confess."

"Have they found the woman or did she get away?"

"I understand that there is still no sign of her. The village is so locked down that unless she was out before the alarm was sounded, I don't know how she could have gotten away." George gently pushes the swing.

"Do you believe there was a woman?"

"Oh there was a woman and she did more for women through actions than Miss Anthony did through her words."

Before Catharine can answer, a group of young people come down the street. "They got a 'nodder one," one of the crowd calls out.

"He's goin' to be at the police station," says a second.

"Where'd they get this one?" a third asks.

"Farm out near Galway," the second one announces.

"None of them was very bright," the first crowd member calls out. The crowd grows as it continues by Cook's house.

"Are you going to see who was caught?" Catharine assumes George will be as curious as the men who just passed and are about his age.

"Why should I leave you to see a common criminal?"

"Mr. Batcheller, comments such as that leave a lady feeling unvalued."

"Then let me say, why would any man leave the grace and beauty you emanate for the company of a poor unfortunate felon?"

Under her breath, she murmurs, "Better, much better."

Two blocks away at the police station, Galway Police Chief Jenson stops the open wagon he has driven into the village. In the back, facing backward, is Phillips, shackled at his ankles and wrist. There are two deputies in the far back of the wagon with rifles across their laps. A group comprised of both members of the community and guests of the hotels continues to gather.

Smiley rushes out the sheriff's door to meet the Galway chief and the horde. "Hey Jenson, I hear you had some good hunting."

"One of our farmers picked him up along the road the night of the robbery. He's got to be one of them."

Harrison comes out the door. "Did he confess?"

"Hasn't said a word since I picked him up."

"Then what made you think he was one of them?"

"Cause he done a lot of braggin' to the other hands before I showed up." Harrison watches as the two deputies in the back of the wagon pull Phillips to his feet and lead him into the jail. Jenson and Harrison remain on the porch. Jenson continues, "Who do I see about getting the reward?"

There is no evidence that Harrison enjoys the company of his contemporary. "That would be Mr. Morrissey. He has the place Mrs. Quinn used to run; I'm certain you remember where that was." Jenson glares at Harrison, then starts to walk toward Morrissey's. "Take this dang fool wagon from in front of the station; we got better things to deal with than your sorry horse's droppings."

Jenson has a scowl as he returns and begins climbing on the wagon. "As always Harrison, it's a pleasure doing yur job for you."

Margaret and Clark are both uncomfortable sitting across from Putnam in his office. Morrissey, whose presence does nothing to alleviate the tension, is sitting in the third chair. Richards is blocking the door. Morrissey starts the conversation. "I believe one of you has something you would like to say to Mr. Putnam."

Clark's voice cracks as he answers, "I have no knowledge of what you are talking about."

Morrissey says nothing he just looks at Margaret. She remains silent. Morrissey puts an empty bottle of laudanum on Putnam's desk. "Which of you has been sleepy lately?" Clark instinctively looks at Margaret. Margaret looks down. "I assumed as much. Laudanum is the ladies' solution to unhappiness."

Margaret continues to look down as she speaks, "I only use it when I am truly sad or when it is my time." To reassure her, Clark moves behind her and touches her shoulders.

"Why would you be sad? You have everything: a grand house, maids, and a carriage to take you places." His voice is barely above a whisper.

"But I don't have a child, do I?" Margaret begins crying.

Clark looks at Putnam, "Does this explain the necklace?" Putnam shakes his head. "Can you prepare our bill; we will be checking out in the morning. Please accept my sincere apology for any insinuations I, or my family, may have made."

Morrissey rises and offers Clark his hand. "We all have our issues to deal with."

"Are you sure you do not wish to stay and take advantage of our curative springs?" Putnam attempts reassurance.

Clark takes Margaret in his arms and leads her to the door. "I think not."

Before they reach the door, Morrissey asks, "Mrs. Clark, might I ask where you got the replacement necklace?"

"There is a lady in the village who makes all the arrangements." She is holding back tears.

"Who is this lady?" Morrissey's voice is firm but caring.

Margaret weeps harder, "I only met her twice. One of the ladies in the park pointed her out."

Putnam is curious, "Is she a guest in the hotel?"

"No. I have seen her many times on the porch of the States." Richards opens the door for the Clarks to leave.

Morrissey tries to comfort. "Good luck, Mr. Clark. Be well, Mrs. Clark"

Richards and Morrissey take off their hats as they enter, handing them to Jesse. Jesse has set up a table with a rack behind on which to hang men's hats, coats, and umbrellas. It is a warm night so there are hats and coats checked. On the table is a pile of cards. Morrissey picks up one of the cards. "What's this?"

"Just an idea I had to make a little extra money. Is it okay?" Morrissey looks at the card. It is an action picture of Jesse dressed as she was when she sounded the alarm with the gun showing from beside her hip. Although the picture was clearly shot indoors, the photograph is of a wet Jesse. Across the top it says 'Sounding the Alarm.' "I sell them for a dollar. The photographer gets fifty cents and I get the other fifty cents."

Morrissey smiles for the first time in two days. "Nice little enterprise. How does your mother feel about the picture?"

"She will probably never see one."

"You hope." Morrissey hands back the card and walks into the gaming room.

In her suite Susie is sitting in her dressing gown reading a book. There is a knock on the door. Susie moves to the door. "Who's there?"

"Message for Mrs. Morrissey," the messenger says. Susie opens the door anxiously. The messenger hands her a note. As Susie takes the note, he examines her robed body closely. "I was not expecting any messages this evening, so I don't have any money for a tip." The messenger continues to stare. "Do you know who I am?" The messenger nods his head. "Then my tip for you is this: never look at the wife of a man such as my husband the way you have been looking at me." The messenger hustles from the door.

Susie looks at the message.

"Please tell your husband to be in the hotel's park tomorrow afternoon at 5:00. I have information of interest for him."

The handwriting is that of a woman.

LeRoy, Ebed, Lee, Roy, and Hammon are standing outside the tenement door in the glow of the gas lantern. They have all (including the youngest) been drinking since they got their reward. "Well boy, today we gets you taken care of." They knock.

John, smelling money, opens the door. "What can I do for yus gentlemen dis fine evenin'?" Ebed doesn't answer, he just pushes past John, followed by the rest of the family.

The men look over Antoinette, Pauline, and Janet, who are all dressed in corsets, bloomers, and stockings. LeRoy grabs his youngest son. "Well Hammon, tonight's yus lucky night. We's gunna gives yus the young-un." Hammon looks appreciatively at Janet.

Janet looks Hammon over more than he looks her over. "Dat'll cost yus ten dollars."

"Ten dollars, are you crazy? Dats more than the three of you are worth fur da whole night. Da boy won't last ten minutes," LeRoy complains.

Pauline is joining in the fun. "And it's another ten dollars for me."

"And it be another ten for me." Antoinette raises the ante.

LeRoy takes out his wallet. He hands John the thirty dollars. Antoinette and Pauline walk over to John. Pauline knees her father in the crotch and takes the money from his hand. Afraid of Pauline, LeRoy and Ebed take Antoinette's hand. "Let's go little lady. I aims to get my money's worth and yus gonna gets a littl' brotherly loven." LeRoy attempts being funny. The three go into the lone bedroom. Lee and Roy look longingly at Janet but eventually take Pauline's hand. She just smiles and leads them into the kitchen.

Hammon cannot stop looking at Janet as she starts removing her corset. "You want me to leave da stockings on or not?"

Hammon just stares.

In the morning, Gretchen is working on the fence near the road. A worn out buckboard carrying a women slightly older than Gretchen and a ten year old boy comes down the road toward her. "Well if it isn't Doris Peck. I've been meaning to thank you, had five men go through my bedroom last night." The woman and boy remain silent as they pass, staring ahead. "That would be a couple less than your daughter." The wagon keeps going in silence. "How old's your Ellie now, fifteen, sixteen? You a grandma yet?" The wagon continues down the road.

A smiling Nolan listens behind a tree as the wagon pulls away.

Janet, Antoinette, and Pauline are on the back steps recovering from the night before. Janet is almost starry eyed like she enjoyed the previous evening. Antoinette is rubbing her arms and legs. "So you really think that slave lady was envious of us? We was paid for same as her."

Pauline sees the issue differently, "Yes but despite it all, we could have said no."

"But we didn't," Antoinette reminds her sister.

"But we could a'." Pauline holds to her conviction.

The grounds surrounding the springs are beyond full. Between the robbery and the riots in Troy, those gathered cannot get enough news, even if most of it is unimpeded by truth.

"It must have been hell on earth in Troy with thousands of people in the streets screaming and waving clubs." Mrs. Brewster is on her pulpit.

"It said in the Troy newspaper that they got the family off the train and onto some boat that dropped them in Waterford, wherever that is." Mrs. Jackson is unusually concerned.

"They will never be seen again. I understand that the agents trying to take them back to North Carolina were tarred and feathered. Aren't you from North Carolina?" Mrs. Dallas inquires of Mrs. Brewster, who ignores the question.

"The newspapers all told how the mob was totally out of control. Father shall most certainly call me home to Hartford." Miss Clark has mastered the art of putting a whine in her voice.

Mrs. Brewster can never miss a chance to get in a taunt. "Yes, and to get to Hartford would mean you would have to go through Troy."

In her simple way Miss Clark asks, "Why do you always have to demean what I say?"

"Because most of what you say is such foolishness." Mrs. Brewster smiles.

"I believe that simple is better than having the manners of a fool." Mrs. Jackson stares down Mrs. Brewster.

Glaring at Mrs. Jackson, Mrs. Brewster declares, "You go too far."

"And you offer so little," Mrs. Jackson pushes.

Miss Clark, who has been reading a newspaper, asks Mrs. Brewster, "What is the name of your plantation?"

"Why Twin Oaks, thank you for asking."

"Very interesting," says Miss Clark. "The newspaper interviewed the family, who said they were from Twin Oaks."

"That must be another Twin Oaks." Mrs. Brewster is adamant.

"Yes it must. It says that they ran away because the women were constantly abused and their husbands flogged." Miss Clark reads the quote from the newspaper.

"Yes it must be a different Twin Oaks." Mrs. Jackson smiles; nothing like that would ever happen on Mrs. Brewster's Twin Oaks.

Across the springs, Van Buren is talking with Madam Jumel. Watching the dowagers has forced the fine lady to smile. "The issue of runaway slaves who have gotten this far having to be returned is causing a deep divide among the guests."

"At the time they passed the Fugitive Slave Act, it seemed like a fair trade, no more slave states and runaways get returned. With Dred Scott allowing slaves to be taken anywhere, they should have ended the Fugitive Slave Act." Van Buren takes the high road, missing the personal level that Madam Jumel is so pleased to watch.

"If you were still President, how would you handle the situation?"

"Since I have no answer, I shall never again be President."

George, with Catharine on his arm, is walking past the former President and Madam Jumel, who for a second time leaves George feeling awkward. "Mr. Batcheller, I am not sure you remember me, but you allowed me to rekindle my friendship with Judge Baucus."

George stammers his answer, "I remember you well. Madam Jumel, may I present Miss Catharine Cook." Both women extend their gloved hands. Catharine curtsies slightly.

It is totally natural for Madam Jumel to introduce George and Catharine. "I assume you both know the honorable Martin Van Buren."

"I am most pleased to meet you Mr. President." George offers his hand.

"You are the young man who worked with Mr. Beach on the Frank Baucus case?" Van Buren knowing of him embarrasses George.

"Yes, that was I."

"Then I would like an opportunity to talk with you. Are you free at 4:00?"

"I will be." George is elated.

"Let us meet at the men's parlor of the States?"

"Ideal."

Madam Jumel looks to George and Catharine, "Might I make another suggestion, why don't the two of you call at my house at that time for tea?"

Catharine takes control of the social aspects of the relationship. "It would be our pleasure; thank you for your kind offer." Catharine and George continue talking to Van Buren and Madam Jumel.

Jacob and Sarah have watched the scene develop. "There will be no talking to them now," Jacob assures Sarah.

"Was that said out of jealousy?"

"But of course, as the future operator of the States, I am supposed to be the one invited to everything."

In the Morrissey's suite, Susie is combing her long hair in front of the mirror and Morrissey is tying his tie. "Are you going to bother with the note that came last evening?" Susie is interested in her husband's business affairs.

"Yes."

"You know it is from a woman."

"Yes. A well informed woman. She knows to meet me in a public place."

Susie looks at his reflection in the mirror. "Do you want me to accompany you?"

"No, but it would not hurt for you to be watching out the window at say, 5:00." Morrissey walks behind her and gently touches her shoulder; she reaches up and pats his hand.

At dinner Marvin joins Morrissey as Susie stands up, getting ready to leave. "I understand that the jewelry was all returned."

"Yes, the ball on Saturday will not be disrupted for lack of appropriate accessories."

"What lessons have you learned?" Marvin inquires.

"That in small towns, everyone knows everyone and more importantly, knows when someone new arrives." Morrissey pauses, "And what have you learned?"

Marvin is caught off guard. "One of my fundamental assumptions was reinforced. Everything matters; the Union Hall and Constitution fires were to get the jewelry moved to one safe; the most impregnable safe in the village was robbed."

Morrissey interrupts, "and so far, with the exception of a probable drowning near the railroad tracks, no one has been hurt."

Edith enters her suite, finding Bennett sitting in a chair. His glass is empty. "So you are up," she asks rhetorically.

"And I will be leaving on the morning train." Bennett shows unusual strength.

"You will be leaving, that is for sure," she says under her breath.

Late in the afternoon, Morrissey is sitting on one of the chairs in the park, feeding the pigeons a piece of bread. Mary walks up to him. "Do you like birds?"

"Roasted."

Mary smiles, "Would you like to know the name of the woman

behind your misfortune? Or are you more interested in who makes the counterfeit jewelry?"

"Please be seated," Morrissey offers. "I will stand." As Morrissey stands, Mary sits on the bench.

There is an afternoon shower, so Gretchen walks off the porch, holding a towel over her head. She walks directly toward the small grove where Nolan has been hiding. She calls into the trees, "You been sittin' out here for two days now. You might as well come in till the storm passes." Nolan rises and runs to the porch of the house. She follows at a trot. Graciously, he holds the door for Gretchen to enter.

Gretchen throws Nolan the towel she used to cover her hair and grabs a fresh one for herself. "How long were you planning to stay out there?"

"Don't know. Had no place else to go anyway."

"So, were you involved in some big robbery?" Gretchen takes off her simple dress.

"Don't matter none, my life started the day I showed up here."

"Mine started over the same day." She takes Nolan's hand and leads him to the stairs.

Bennett, wearing nothing but a robe, is sitting in the chair he has been in all day. It doesn't look like he has moved except to raise his glass to his lips. Edith, dressed for an evening concert, comes in the door. "So, you are still up."

"Where you been?"

"At the concert."

"Until this hour of the night?"

Edith ignores his question, pours a washbasin full of water, and begins disrobing. "Why don't you get out of that chair and get into bed?"

"Because I like watching you wash."

Edith, dress off, begins removing her corset. "After all this time, you still like looking?"

"It seems as if all I get to do any more is look."

Edith washes her upper body. "Why don't you get into bed and we will see just how much you want to do more than just look."

Bennett struggles to get up from the chair then struggles again to sit on the side of the bed.

Edith pulls up one leg of her bloomers and pushes down her stockings. "Is this what you still like to watch?" She repeats the process, lowering the other stocking.

"You can be such a woman, but never a lady."

Edith looks in the mirror. "We both know that is not a complaint."

Bennett settles into a seated position with his back against the top of the bed.

Edith removes her chemise and uses a cloth to wash her upper body. "I want to be nice and clean for you." Edith looks at the various perfumes on the dresser. She selects one and sprays it on. Edith removes her bloomers and washes her lower body with a cloth. "Why don't you settle on down and we will see how much you missed me."

Bennett slides down on to his back. Edith comes over and straddles him at his waist. She takes his left hand and puts it palm down under her right knee.

"What are you doing?" he asks.

"Those colorful girls, whose father found the necklace, were talking about how this position puts the woman in control. They say the men appreciate a woman showing what she likes." She pulls his right hand and puts it palm down under her left knee. "Now who is in control?"

Still drunk, Bennett smiles, "You are."

Edith reaches up, takes the second pillow and places it over Bennett's face. At first he does not react, assuming it is part of the game. Bennett begins to struggle and tries to pull his hands out. Edith divides her weight between confining his hands and holding the pillow in place.

Bennett begins to thrash about. Slowly his struggle ends.

Edith fluffs the second pillow and puts it at the top of the bed. Everything in place, she starts screaming, "Oh God, get a doctor. Get a doctor."

She gets out of bed, grabs her robe and rushes to the door. Struggling to put the robe on, she opens the door and calls to the hall boy. She makes sure the boy sees her nearly naked. "Quick, summon doctors, my... my uncle is sick, I think he had a heart attack." The hall boy runs off.

The desk clerk and two porters are talking at the front desk as two men carry Bennett's body down the stairs on a stretcher. "That's the way I want to go," the desk clerk jokes.

"Not me, I want to be on top so she has to climb out from under."

"I will never be able to look at that Miss Edith the same again," the clerk says with admiration.

"Me either." The porter is lustful.

"Well, I guess we will have an open room soon."

United States Hotel

The Grand Ball

Morrissey is standing and Mary is sitting in the park. Susie watches them from the window above. "How did you come by your information?" he inquires.

"Have you ever heard of Lady Bluestockings?"

Morrissey is confused by the question. "The gossip writer for the Gazette?"

"Do I look as dreadful as I am portrayed?"

"But how did you come by your information in this case?"

"By being invisible."

Morrissey looks questioningly at her.

"I literally live out of a trunk," she explains. "I am in all the best places when they are in season: the fall in New York, the cold of winter in the Capital, the spring in Charleston. Last year I was in Cleveland for the South Shore Bank robbery. I was in New York City for the great jewelry scandal." Mary takes a drink from her spring water. "I listened to the theories and rumors. The difference is that I thought, but what if it was a woman? From there on, it was just a matter of looking for the logical choice. You do know, Mr. Morrissey, that there is nothing more dangerous than a logical woman."

"Perhaps a cunning one," Morrissey adds.

"You have made such an assessment already?"

"No, I learned from experience; I married a logical, cunning woman."

"I ask that you not name the people until my next article on Saturday."

"Fair enough." Morrissey thinks for a moment. "Your article will be on the day of the ball."

"Yes, and the Gazette will be sending over an extra thousand newspapers just for Saratoga."

The Day before the Grand Ball

To avoid the crowd at the springs, Jacob and George are having coffee in the States dining room.

"I assume Catharine said yes to your invitation to the ball?"

"Yes, she did."

"If memory serves, this is the first time she will have attended the ball on a date."

"I do wonder how her father will handle going alone."

"Mr. Cook is quite the catch. I am sure he will find some widow who wants his money."

"Jacob, not everyone is like you. There are many women who would enjoy his company and are not after his fortune."

"But unless they are like cream, and rise to the top, they will be lost in the crowd. He will never find such a partner because he will be drowning in the milk of those who are after his money."

"There is another way, women will try to get him to take their sisters, cousins, and mothers."

"I notice you did not say nieces."

Jacob spits out his coffee as they both laugh.

Michael, Swanson, Shorty, Phillips, Peter, and Elmendorf are being loaded into a police wagon bound for the county jail. The men's wrists and ankles are shackled, making it difficult for them to walk. "Not a word," Michael reminds his cohorts.

"My one chance at fame and notoriety. If you think I am going to miss it, you are the fool. I will have all the young ladies in Ballston lining up to see me at the trial," Shorty brags.

"That sounds good to me. Do you think we will be allowed out on bail?" Swanson asks, certain that he could do lots of entertaining before the trial.

Elmendorf shakes his head while looking at Michael. "Where did she find these guys?"

Michael's voice is barely a whisper, "You just said she!" He then calls out, "Not another word."

Swanson nudges Shorty. "You know'd we is goin' tuh be famous."

The men are loaded into the enclosed wagon. When they are inside, Shorty and Swanson start kicking each other and laughing. Michael lifts his feet up, over Shorty and Swanson's legs. He slams his heals down on their shins. They both call out in pain.

"I told you to be quiet."

Mary Vanderbilt chairs the final meeting before the grand ball. She has made an agenda, which she is checking off. This meeting is traditionally contentious but with all that has occurred this summer, the members are behaving. Mary reads the agenda. "Appetizers and punch will be available starting at 8:00. The dance will start at 9:00. There will be a ten minute break each hour on the hour with ice cream, cake, and punch served at midnight."

"Are we going to insist that all the children leave by midnight? They absolutely should not be up later than that." Nothing infuriates Mrs. Corning as much as children eating with their fingers at a buffet.

Mrs. Astor is not her supporter. "As much as I do not believe that children should even be allowed to attend the ball, it is the parents' right to say when bedtime should be."

Mrs. Osgood offers a compromise. "Perhaps we could put a note in the program that children are encouraged to be in bed by midnight."

To avoid a rift, Mrs. Davidson changes the topic. "The band has made its list of dances. It would still be possible to add a sentence to that effect to the dance cards." The women all nod in agreement.

"Mr. Marvin has agreed to donate fifty dozen roses. On Saturday, men can buy individual roses for a nickel in the park and if they can get a lady to agree, in advance, to save them a dance, they will give the lady a rose," reports Mrs. Devereux.

Ever the caregiver, Mrs. Corning wonders, "Will not several young ladies arrange for their own flowers to avoid being embarrassed by not being asked?"

"I am quite sure that will happen, but the money goes to the relief fund," reconciles Mrs. Devereux. Again they all nod in agreement.

"How many are we expecting this year?" Mrs. Davidson, as the youngest, wonders about the future of great balls.

Mary has an estimate. "At least a thousand. Mr. Marvin has told me he will have food enough for two thousand."

"Can we make arrangements for the train to not blow its annoying whistle during the ball?" Even the fine details attract the attention of Mrs. Astor. The women look at each other, not knowing if that is even an option.

"I will ask Mr. Marvin if it is a possibility." Cora accepts the responsibility.

Mrs. Astor looks directly at Cora. "What will we do if anyone is inappropriately dressed?"

Mrs. Corning does not want to be involved with trivial issues. "Like with the children, it is up to each family to be dressed as they believe is appropriate. Beyond that, Mr. Marvin will be the judge."

Mrs. Astor has one more detail. "Whatever are we going to do about all the servants and villagers that will be standing at every door to watch the dance?"

"Entertain them by dancing every dance," declares Cora.

Judge Baucus has once again joined Madam Jumel for tea. "I have not asked a lady for her company since my wife died, but I was wondering if you would go to the ball with me."

"Judge, I would consider it an honor. You do know we can only dance two dances together, least others think we are engaged." They both laugh. "How is Amanda doing in her quest?"

"I fear it will keep her occupied for at least two years." He pauses, escaping a deeper thought. "At least we will not have to worry about her being at the ball; she is in Auburn."

"Will Clara attend?"

"I do not know. If she should want to go, would you mind if she rides with us?"

"Such a silly question. I doubt she would want to go with two old fogies, but I would enjoy the company of a young person who is in the prime of life."

Still in their nightgowns, Pauline and Antoinette are making their own plans for the night of the ball. "The ball was our busiest night of the season last year," Pauline reminds her sister.

"All the men get so excited dancing with all those high fluten' ladies that don't do nothing. They comes to us to gets some relief."

"There was also the group that came to us before the dance to get relief so's the ladies at the dance didn't think they was bumping into them." They both laugh.

"All I knows for sure is I was sore for two days." Antoinette rubs between her legs.

John knocks on the door jam. "Can I's come in?"

In unison Pauline and Antoinette respond, "No!"

Richards and Morrissey check the machines, tables, and cards in the closed casino. Morrissey recaps the investigation. "Assuming the man who drowned near Ballston Spa was one of them, I think we have three who are unaccounted for. Two men and the woman."

"That is, if there was a woman."

"Oh, there was a woman and I know who she is."

"Why aren't we doing something?"

"It will all be clear on Saturday." The two men go out on the porch where they light up a cigar. Morrissey looks calmer than he has since the robbery. "I have decided to close the night of the ball."

"I understand you want to take Susie, but I can cover the casino in your absence."

"The only men that will be here are those who have no one to take to the ball. They will have little money and more than likely drink too much."

"Good point. I can take an evening to myself."

"Don't make any plans, you already have a date." Richards looks at him confused. "What should we do about Miss Jesse Ringer?"

"I suppose we could buy her a ticket to the ball. She did help with the robbery."

"Yes, she did. I will have Susie take her shopping for a gown. She can join Susie and myself."

"I thought you wanted me to take her."

"No, I told you, you already have a date." As the two men continue to smoke, Nolan and Gretchen go by in a wagon headed west.

Gretchen and Nolan have their limited possessions in two trunks on the back of the wagon. "So how long have you wanted to ditch it all and go west?" Nolan asks.

"Ever since I can remember. Had to get rid of a couple of men before I could get started."

"Why not south or east?"

"South is a bunch of snotty people or people too poor to afford dirt. East is a bunch of people who are too religious. They all think they are the only ones who know how you should live your life. North is just too cold."

"Why didn't you want to sell the farm; the money could have given you a fresh start."

"The county's going to take it for taxes next month." Nolan gives her hand a reassuring squeeze, giving her the comfort to add, "There's things in my past I don't want to share."

"That don't make you special. Everyone I know can say the same." Nolan encourages the horse on. "How far west do you think we should go?"

"I hear the road ends at an ocean. I sure would like to see that."

Amidst a room full of fabric and flounce, Cora and Sadie are mending the hems on their dresses. "Which gown will you be wearing?" Cora asks.

"I am not sure I will be going. No one has asked me. Sarah will be going with Jacob and I don't want to go with my mother."

"What about young Walter?"

"I doubt if he has the money to afford a ticket. Five dollars is a high fee for one night."

"It is the jewel in the crown of the season. Start planning what you will wear and we will see what happens."

For a station as popular as Saratoga, the ticket agent's office is small and cluttered. Marvin has come on a mission that may prove impossible. "Palio, how good to see you. How has your season been going?"

"When I took over as freight agent, I never expected so many problems. No one is ever happy and all the trunks look alike."

Marvin ignores Palio's complaints. "Saturday is the ball. Is there any way that you could arrange for the trains not to blow their whistles?"

"The railroad's policy is to blow the whistle at all street crossings. The only way to avoid a whistle is if there is a man on horseback preceding the train to warn people of it's coming."

"If I supplied such a man, could you make the arrangements with the engineers?"

"In the village the trains would have to move at the pace of a person walking."

"That is only for a mile. Surely the conductor could make up the time."

"There are three trains during the time of the ball. It would probably cost you ten dollars per train."

"You set up the trains, I will find someone to ride my stallion." Marvin leaves the office; passing through the open door he sees Walter. "Well hello, Walter. Getting another inside story?"

"Could be." Marvin walks back in the direction of the hotel. Walter says again, even softer, "Could be."

Walter and Missy are in the alley behind the Stiles cottage. What neither realizes is that Benjamin is listening through the kitchen window and Sadie is listening through the open window on the second floor. Walter speaks in a whisper. "I know how to do it. The thing you need to do is tell everyone who wants to join us, they will only have twenty minutes to be ready."

"Why not more? It will take me that long to pack."

"You are going to a new life. You need to leave the old one behind. The only thing you really need are the clothes on your back. How many do you think will be coming?"

"I know of five, maybe six."

"Will Josey join you?"

"I's hinted but she don't sound interested."

Edith is in the furniture store picking out a casket for Bennett. Like all salesmen of the time, it is high pressure. "He was a simple man with few friends. That is why I want the funeral here in Saratoga."

"We have many options, from a simple pine casket to a fine mahogany, fabric lined, padded model with silver handles." The salesman lists the options.

"Where he is going, we need something that burns quickly. He will go out in pine."

"Do you want it cloth lined and padded?"

"A cloth lining would be sufficient; he did not like padding in the end."

"When would you like the funeral?"

"As soon as I can make arrangements with a minister. Perhaps this afternoon."

"So soon?"

"Like I said, he did not have many friends and those he did have are tied up at the moment." The police wagon is rolling by.

Saturday: the Grand Ball

The dowagers, except Mrs. Jackson, are holding court at the springs. Mary is standing alone near the road at a spot where she can see all that transpires. As expected, Mrs. Brewster is directing the conversation. "Tomorrow we will be the only ones here."

"Many will just be going to bed when some come to the springs." Mrs. White wrings her hands.

"I do hope I get to dance several times. I suppose we will all have some idea this afternoon when we see who gives us a rose."

Mrs. Jackson comes into the park carrying several copies of the Gazette. She hands them out to her friends. "It seems Lady Bluestockings has been here all season. She has written an entire page on Saratoga. It is entitled 'The Springs Bubble Up.'"

"I am sure there has been enough trivial information for her to print. Is it her usual fiddle faddle about who wore what and who danced with whom?" Mrs. Brewster's critique is right in character.

"No, she has changed her style. She has become a detective. She claims to know who has been selling fake jewelry and who was behind the robbery of the casino." Mrs. Jackson is happy to be the purveyor of this news.

Mrs. Brewster looks very concerned.

Mrs. Jackson continues, "She even claims to know the lady who owned the slave family; you know, the one where the wife was raped regularly and the husband was severely beaten. That family that escaped a second time during the riot in Troy. Well, it seems that the lady who owned them has been staying in the village the entire season."

"Oh my, my; she has been amongst us all this time?" Mrs. Dallas hopes to be mentioned in Lady Bluestockings' column.

"On my, my, such an evil person staying right here? We might have seen her every day. Just imagine if we talked to her or she took a meal at our table." Mrs. White is so innocent she seems to melt under stress.

Chief Harrison and two deputies pull up in a wagon. One deputy stands with the horse, while the second and the chief walk into the crowd.

Everyone in the park is watching as Harrison walks up to Mrs. Brewster. "I am sure you know why we are here."

"I certainly do not," she responds.

"We have a warrant for your arrest."

"On what charge?"

"Jewelry fraud."

"Surely you have the wrong person. I am the owner of a fine plantation in North Carolina."

"And a ready supply of fakes stones - we have searched your room." Harrison is proud of his arrest. He is up for election in the fall and between this arrest and solving the casino robbery, he is assured reelection.

Mrs. Brewster heads toward the wagon.

"Not so fast." Mrs. Brewster stops. Harrison takes shackles out of his belt and binds her wrists together.

The crowd begins to applaud as she is taken away. She turns and calls out, "Someone send for Mr. Batcheller."

The crowd applauds even louder.

Serendipity strikes as George and Catharine walk into the springs. Hearing the crowd roar, George gets sarcastic. "Must be the water is getting better, people are applauding."

Catharine points to Harrison. "I warned you that disparaging remarks about the springs is treasonous talk in Saratoga. See, the chief is here to arrest you."

Bishop Sleight looks Reverend Beecher directly in the eye, "There seems to more than a little concern about your humility and your relationships with those in your congregation."

"I am sorry Bishop, I have no idea to what you are referring."

"Over the course of the summer, three other ministers attended your services. The first two because they were here for health reasons. The third was at my request." The bishop does not stop staring. "In each case they noted a degree of discomfort among the women in the congregation, especially when the women were in close proximity to you."

"Discomfort?" is the best Beecher can respond.

"Please don't ask for me to be more specific. Accept your new assignment with grace and dignity."

"New assignment? I have had a full service every Sabbath this summer."

"And you will have a full congregation beginning next week. You are being assigned to the Auburn prison, where we have a great many souls in need of salvation."

"But who will see to the needs of this church?"

"That is not your issue. Your issue is to be on the 6:20 train."

Pauline and Antoinette have taken over their finances. They rented the second apartment on the floor where they have stayed all summer. The second apartment is for business, with mattresses on the floor of each room. Pauline is overjoyed by the new arrangements. "This is much better. Having them come to us means we don't have to stand in the rain, hot sun, or just plain stand!"

"Having Bob sitting outside the door guarantees our safety."

There is a knock on the door. "Already?" Pauline is pretending to not be ready.

"Going to be one busy day."

"And a busy night. Wouldn't it be nice to actually go to the ball?" Pauline's eyes drift off.

"There you go dreaming again. Yus don't knowd how to dance."

"Oh I knowd how to dance just fine. Why yus thin' so many men come back for more?" They both laugh.

The unattached women have taken up stations around the park of the States Hotel. They have their dance cards ready so they can sign up a dance with any young man who gives them a flower. A proud Sadie has six flowers already. Sarah has only five. "So we finally know who is the most popular," Sadie tells her sister.

"It is not about the number of flowers, it is about the number of dances."

"Then I win again. Six flowers five dances."

Sarah reminds her sister, "I have three from Jacob and one from Mr. Marvin and one from Mr. Banks."

"Mr. Marvin doesn't count; he will be dancing with every woman there. Mr. Banks is an immoral man who will grab you too tight and look down the top of your dress."

Sarah counters, "And the boys who gave you flowers will be grabbing you too tight and looking down the top of your dress."

"Yes, but the difference is, I want them to."

"Sadie Stiles, you are really becoming a tart."

"You must be proud to have taught me so well."

Miss Clark looks dejected, having only received a flower from Marvin.

Cora is not sitting, but walks across the park on an errand. Marvin, roses in hand, cuts her off. "Miss Cora, how many roses would you allow me to give to you."

"You, of anyone, knows that a rose means a dance."

"My question remains unanswered."

"The polite answer is one, the bold answer is two, and the correct answer is many." She looks down, suddenly experiencing a flash of shyness. Marvin hands her three flowers. They make out their dance cards, selecting three slower dances spread across the evening.

Susie Morrissey has been watching the scene from her window. Seeking to be part of the action, she joins the others in the park.

"Miss Susie, would you accept a flower?" A smiling Marvin asks.

"I would have been offended had you not offered one." Marvin smiles and they check their dance cards.

Walter comes into the park with five flowers. He starts by giving one to Miss Clark, then catches Cora. "Mrs. Stiles, I would consider it an honor if you would allow me the privilege of one dance this evening."

"Very well spoken. I should enjoy that." They compare dance cards, then he walks to Sarah.

"Miss Sarah, may I have the pleasure of one dance this evening?"

"But of course, Walter. You are the first man who has asked who may make one of the others jealous." Sarah looks around for Jacob.

"I doubt that he would be jealous of me but thank you for the compliment." They match cards and he goes to Sadie.

"I have two flowers left. I know it is bold; however, I would consider it an unmitigated honor if you would accept both." Walter has grown this summer.

"I would have considered it an unmitigated insult if you had not offered. In truth, I was expecting a third."

"Wait a moment." Walter rushes back to the porch where they are selling the flowers and buys another. After giving Sadie the third flower, they compare cards. "I will be busy from nine-thirty until ten-thirty," Walter confesses.

"Something I should know about?"

"You would be better off not knowing."

"So I must ask one of the young men who asked me for a dance during that time to reschedule." She looks him in the eye. "You will not be alone."

Walter smiles at her courage.

Morrissey comes out the back door looking for Susie. Seeing her, he remembers the meaning of the flowers. He buys a dozen. He gives all but three to her.

Susie mocks jealousy. "And who are those for?"

"One is for Miss Jesse, the other two for Richards' date."

Susie looks at her husband dumbfounded. "Richards has a date?"

Morrissey signals for a messenger and hands him the two flowers and a note.

Edith is standing at the head of a freshly dug grave in Greenridge Cemetery. An old minister, who appears to have been drinking for some time, holds a Bible. Bennett's simple coffin has already been lowered down. There are two men leaning on shovels and smoking, waiting to fill the grave.

"Would you like say a few words?" the minister mumbles.

"No."

He is surprised, "Are you sure?"

Edith walks to the waiting black carriage.

In their parlor, Cook is writing a letter while Catharine reads a book. "Would you like me to walk you to the park so you might receive flowers?"

"Thank you dear Father, it is not about a bunch of flowers, it is about a bouquet."

At that moment there is a knock on the door. The butler opens the door, finding a messenger with a dozen roses.

Missy helps Sadie and Sarah dress for the ball. Sarah has the fancier of the two dresses. Sadie's is lower cut in the front. Sarah's is white on white. Sadie's is forest green. "I only have three dances open all evening," Sarah reminds her sister.

"My card is as full as I want."

"I certainly hope you are wearing a collar or scarf with that dress."

"I am not. The first day we were here Mr. Marvin said that he wanted this to be the Grand Ball that the children would be telling their children about. I plan to help that plan along."

"You should watch out for your reputation. Father would not have let you wear it."

"Father is not here; however, I assure you he would have appreciated it on any other young woman."

Josey is helping Cora put on an elegant burgundy dress that emphasizes her tiny waist. It is as low cut as Sadie's. She looks in the mirror, knowing that she will draw the attention of the men and the vile of the women. She is satisfied.

One of the maids is helping Catharine put on her dress. She is in white with a lace bodice and white over skirt.

"Is it really okay to watch from the back porch?" the maid asks.

"Of course. I would be insulted if you did not want to watch me dance."

There is a knock on the door. The maid opens it and finds Cook standing in the doorway. The maid steps to the side. Cook speaks as he enters. "Catharine, it has been too long since this cameo was worn at a ball. Would you honor your mother by wearing it this evening?'

Her eyes water as he fastens the gold chain behind her neck. "You will be grander than the ball."

For the first time this season, Mary looks sophisticated. Her modest dress is royal blue with a high collar. Nervous to be on her first date in over a year, Mary has difficulty selecting her jewelry, which is real.

In the living room of his suite, Morrissey is straightening Richards' tie. They are both in their evening black frock coats. Susie and Jesse emerge from the bedroom. Susie is overpowering. She has sprinkled white dust in her hair to make it reflect any light. Her dress is as low cut as Cora's or Sadie's. In contrast, Jesse has on a new red dress, also cut deep in the front. They join the two men.

"Doesn't she look beautiful?" Susie says of her protégée. Unable to find the correct words, Morrissey and Richards nod assurances.

"Do you think anyone will recognize me with clothes on?" Jesse jokes, relieving the tension.

"John, Jesse has a great idea for your casinos in Troy and Brooklyn. She will hire a series of girls who will work the door taking hats and canes; however, they will also sell cigars and tobacco and it will not cost you a cent."

"Interesting, very interesting."

Susie takes Richards' arm. "Well my big friend, I expect you to behave as well as you look."

The four walk out the door with Morrissey and Jesse walking behind.

Mary is standing in the center of the lobby on the arm of Morrissey's best looking dealer. Susie steers Richards to her. "Richards, this is Mary Barden. Mary, I must apologize, I have known Richards for years but do not know his first name." She looks at Richards to introduce himself.

Richards bends slightly at the waist, "Miss Mary, it would be a great honor if you would accompany me this evening."

Susie smiles at Mary. "That is the most words I have ever heard him say in a day."

As they walk to the ballroom, Susie points out. "John, you are with three women, each of whom saved your season." He smiles knowingly.

Susie whispers to Morrissey, "What is his name?"

"I don't know. I heard someone call him Hollis once, but the man could not talk for days after."

At 9:00, those on the planning committee, Marvin, and other dignitaries, walk out of the hotel to a specially constructed dance floor in the park. Marvin, as host, is last in line. When he reaches the dance floor, the band starts to play. There is merriment and a few minutes between each dance so that dancers who have agreed to share a particular dance have time to find each other.

As soon as the procession ends, the waiters start replacing the snack trays. Women have already begun visiting the ladies' parlor, ostensibly to freshen up, but really to avoid explaining why they were not asked to dance.

Walter and Sadie finish their first dance together. He advises, "It is

9:30; I must take my leave."

"I told you earlier, you are not doing this alone."

"If you wish, join me on the piazza."

Walter walks out onto the piazza where men are gathered in small groups having cigars. Sadie joins him and they walk down the steps and out onto Broadway. Arm in arm, they walk north a few hundred feet to Division Street, turn west and walk in the direction of the railroad station.

When they reach the end of the States hotel they turn south, away from the station, and proceed along the back of the cottages. At the furthest end of the hotel they turn one more time into the alley behind the best cottages. There they find Missy, two other slaves, and Benjamin. Those gathered each have a simple bag holding what they consider most valuable.

"It is time to move." Walter is prepared.

"Not yet, there are others." Missy holds.

"How many?"

"Many," Missy assures him.

Walter paces; he knows that they only have a few minutes to spare. In desperation he makes a decision, "Sadie, it is dangerous to wait. You take those who are gathered past the train station. Turn right on Walden Street. The tracks start a left turn at that point. Go about a block. Be sure you are on the right side, that way you will be obscured from both the front and the back of the train. It will be going slow." Sadie has been listening intently.

He uses his hands to illustrate what will happen, "As the cars go by you will see an open door on the second baggage car. There is a man inside who will help get the people aboard."

Sadie takes charge. "So no one suspects, you will act as my slaves. This is the last time you will ever have to act like one." Sadie takes Missy and the two other slaves and begins walking.

Missy holds Benjamin's hand, "Don't you dare be late."

"Don't you worry, we will have the rest of our lives together." Missy and Sadie head to the meeting point.

When Sadie's group gets about a block away, two other slaves join Benjamin and Walter. Minutes later, two more slaves join the second group.

Walter is getting concerned about the time. "Benjamin, I will take these people to the meeting point. You wait here and bring any who come later. You must cross the tracks ahead of the train; if the train gets by you, you will not get to the pickup point in time." Walter makes sure

Benjamin knows the plan, "Do you know the way?"

"I know the way."

Walter speaks to the escaping slaves. "Stand tall, don't act like you are doing anything wrong. Act like I am your master and people will not be suspicious." Walter starts out with the four slaves. Walter's group walks up Clinton Street to Walden where his group turns. From the crest in the small hill Walter looks back. He thinks he can make out Benjamin with others following.

Sadie, Walter, and seven slaves are gathered next to a livery at the turn in the tracks. "Because they are not using a whistle, the train can go no faster than a walk. When I give the signal, you are to run up next to the car I show you and jump in. There is a man in there to help you."

In the distance they can see a horse and rider in front of the train. The rider is getting ready to start out. Suddenly Benjamin and ten more slaves cross the street. Walter signals them to hide next to the barn.

Walter whispers to Sadie, "Seventeen. More than I ever suspected we could help."

"Eighteen," Benjamin whispers. Walter counts again then looks at Benjamin. "I may be free, but I don't have my freedom in this here country."

Walter looks to Missy. "I's gunna take my chances on Canada," Benjamin pronounces.

Missy takes his arm. "We's gunna takes our chances." Affirmed, Benjamin smiles.

The rider is coming along ahead of the train. Being careful that the horse does not stumble on the rails or ties, he passes those gathered at a slow walk without noticing. He and the engine are just out of site when Walter runs out and the others follow. The door to the baggage car opens. A man reaches down and lends a hand to the first woman. One by one he pulls the escaping slaves inside. When half are inside he says aloud, "My God, how many are there? We only expected seven."

"Just keep pulling." Walter says.

By the time they are up to fifteen, they are already full to the door. Walter pushes Missy, "Missy get on."

"Not without Benjamin."

Benjamin lifts her so the man in the car can pull her up. "Just get on, I'll make it." In desperation the man inside throws two trunks out to make room. Benjamin is the last to jump on. He only makes it because he is strong enough to hold onto the pole outside the baggage car door. He and the man who was in the car try to move the people around so they can all fit. People are climbing onto the trunks to pick up space. As the train finishes the turn, Walter watches as three of the slaves' bags are thrown from the train. The train door shuts.

Walter turns to Sadie. In her excitement, she kisses him on the lips. "That was the bravest thing I ever did," she boasts.

"We need to get those bags before someone gets suspicious." Walter picks up the three bags, then pushes them down the newly installed storm sewer. Walter pulls the two trunks that were thrown off and puts them next to the barn.

Sadie takes Walter's arm as they walk toward Broadway. A block from the hotel they have caught their breath and look like any other couple out for a romantic stroll.

Six hours later, at the first train station in Canada, the train slowly comes to a stop. On the station deck are twenty people. The family that escaped from North Carolina, then were recaptured, are among those present. The baggage car opens and a minister, among others, is waiting to help those in the baggage car get down.

"Welcome to Canada. Welcome to freedom," greets the minister.

One by one the escaping slaves get off. They stretch, bend, and rush to the water closets.

Benjamin bends down and kisses the ground. "Missy, would you do me the honor of being my wife?"

Missy takes his hand and leads him to the minister. "Reverend, would yus say the words that will make us man and wife?"

The dowagers are drinking the water, hoping their curative powers will allow them to recover from their second scandal of the season. Mrs. White defends her previous behavior. "I suspected from the beginning. She always had money."

"Of course you did." Mrs. Jackson rolls her eyes.

Mrs. Dallas is amazed at the deception, "To be both the manufacturer of fake jewelry and the owner of the escaping slaves. However did she fool us all?"

Mrs. Jackson has the unique ability to capture life. "By casting aspersions on others, we never looked at her faults. If women could vote or hold office, she would have made an excellent politician. By the way, has anyone seen Miss Place?"

Sitting alone on her trunk, Miss Clark occasionally uses her handkerchief to remove a tear from her eye. She looks out onto the park.

Harrison sees her and walks over. His badge shows so she knows he is safe. "Leaving so soon? There are still two weeks in the season."

"With the ball over, there is nothing to look forward to."

"There is always something to look forward to and there is always next season."

"I fear my time is running out."

"I used to feel that way, then along comes Mr. Morrissey and changes my life completely."

"I wish I could say the same." She cannot look at the chief. She turns and faces the door.

Cora rushes in, sees three other southern families and hurries to them. "My Missy and Benjamin are missing."

"Do not speak too loud," says one of the men. He looks around. "There are several slaves missing. It seems they ran off during the ball."

"Have you sounded the alarm?" Cora is too excited to keep her voice down.

The man tries to soothe her. "In Saratoga, it would just bring them support. I fear we will have to see if they are picked up." Angry, Cora leaves for her cottage.

Getting back to her cottage, Cora takes the stairs to her daughters' room two at a time. She bursts in and finds Sadie and Sarah still in bed. Cora shakes Sadie, "Were you involved?"

Sadie tries to rub the sleep from her eyes. "In what?"

"You know what."

"No I don't."

"Missy and Benjamin are missing. So are many other slaves."

Sadie straightens her pillow. "All I can say is that Missy was in a family way. The father would not own up to his responsibilities." She pounds the pillow, "Benjamin has stepped up and is planning to marry her."

"Your father will be livid."

"Father will be glad the problem is solved."

Cora slams the door on her way out.

Sarah turns on her side. "And they think I am the wild one!" She turns and pulls the blanket over herself.

Jacob finds Walter near the newspaper office. "You were involved, weren't you?" Walter just stares. "Had to be you or George. No one else could help close to twenty slaves escape at the same time." Walter continues to stare. Jacob grabs his hand, "Good job my man. Good job." Jacob shakes Walter's hand and then walks away.

"I am tired, sore, and rich. I must have done thirty last night." Pauline is rubbing between her legs.

"Thirty-four to be exact," Antoinette informs her.

John walks in without knocking.

"What are you doing here?" Antoinette demands.

"Making myself coffee."

"That is an excellent idea. Make yourself a large cup, take it down on the porch, and never come back to this floor again," Antoinette informs her father.

John looks to Pauline. "Where's I supposed to go?"

Antoinette answers for her sister, "Ma can go with you or not, that is up to her."

"Yus can't throw me's out, I raised yus. Yus gots to take care of me in my o'd age."

"That is not all you did to me. Make your coffee and leave before I throw you down the stairs." John looks to Pauline. Pauline just takes a sip of her coffee. John mumbles on his way down the stairs.

Empowered, Antoinette asks, "You seen Janet?"

"I was wondering when you would find her missing." Pauline takes another sip of her coffee. "She run off with the young mountain boy."

"Good for her."

George, Cook, Beach, Van Buren, and four other businessmen are having a sherry in Beach's office. Cook looks at George, "Mr. Batcheller, we would like you to stand as the Republican candidate for the Assembly."

George shakes his head. "I am only 21, and new to Saratoga."

"True, true, but you believe in ending slavery, the rights of women, protecting the environment, and taking care of those who cannot take care of themselves. That is the Republican code. You are the man," Cook states. The other men all nod in the affirmative.

"I doubt if I could win, no one knows me."

"Oh they know you." Cook smiles. "True success is when more people know you than you know them."

George takes a sip of his sherry. It is a different trail than he planned, but if successful, it will prove to be a shortcut.

Richards and Mary are taking a romantic walk, arm in arm, in Greenridge Cemetery. There are many other couples also taking walks. "Strange place to walk," Richards says.

"Not if you want privacy." She waits for a comment; when none is forthcoming, she continues, "I doubt if any of the couples we see are married … to each other. This is where one goes not to be seen."

"Interesting."

"My dear Richards, we are going to have to work on your communication skills." He touches her hand. "That's a start." She smiles.

Susie, still in her nightgown, is having breakfast in bed. Morrissey is dressed and ready to go out. "You looked ravishing last evening. You were the most beautiful woman at the ball. We shall have to build a grand home in Troy where you can entertain everyone of importance."

"You give Troy more credit than I think it deserves. I think we shall be shunned in Troy."

"Why?"

"To you, life is a gamble. The snobs of Troy will never accept us or your profession. They will come to your club but they will not invite us to their homes."

"You are so wise, why did you marry me?"

"Because dear John, underneath that rough exterior you have a heart, and you love me."

Gretchen and Nolan are sitting on one of the benches in the Amsterdam Train Station. They have sold the horse and wagon and have used the money for tickets. "So what do you think St. Louis will be like?" Gretchen asks.

"Dirty, dusty, corrupt, full of crime."

"I thought you said you had never been there."

"Haven't been. But it's a city and all cities are pretty much alike."

"So why are we going there?"

"Just a matter of time till it gets too warm for us here. Besides, we ain't got money enough to get to Denver." Nolan looks at her. "Are you married?"

"I don't think so," she answers.

At the Saratoga Train Station, Edith is standing by her bag waiting to board the south bound train. She tries to hide as Morrissey approaches. "Miss Edith, it was a terrible thing that your benefactor passed so suddenly."

"Do I know you?" Edith pretends to be a lady who would not talk to a stranger in a train station.

"Oh you know me. Let me put it this way. When the season is over

313

and I return to Brooklyn, you will not be there. In fact you will not be any place east of the Mississippi." Edith just stares. "You may be a woman but you are not a lady and if I ever, ever see you again, mine will be the last face you ever see."

The train stops and Edith boards. Morrissey hands her her travel bag and tips his hat. He says, as if in oversight, "Tell your sister I will deal with her when I get back."

Two Weeks Later

Jacob and Sarah are sitting next to each other on one of the benches in the park. "Can I visit you this winter?" Jacob has waited until the last day to ask.

"Send my father a letter, but I am sure he will say yes."

"I have always been a bit of a rascal. That is probably because I never before felt the way I feel about you."

"Mr. Marvin, never, never forget that." She studies his eyes as she asks, "You do know I saw you looking in my window in July." Jacob blushes. Sarah continues, "I left the curtains open on purpose." She watches his face for signs of his feelings.

There is a long uncomfortable pause. "Will you write my father to see if you can visit?"

"Does your window have curtains?" They both laugh.

Across the park, Sadie and Walter are sharing a bench. Her speech is well rehearsed. "Walter, you are a far more interesting man than that Mr. Batcheller, wealthier in spirit than Jacob is in money, and braver than any man I have ever known."

"Then you will be back next summer?"

"No, Walter, I will not. Father and mother will never let me cross the Mason Dixon line again." Walter looks sad. "Cheer up. With your help, I became a woman this summer and for that I thank you." She kisses him on the lips, in the middle of the park, in daylight, a move beyond bold.

Cora and Marvin are at one end of the piazza, well away from the thinning crowd. He remarks, "Reality is painful."

Looking, Cora confesses, "You know I wanted to be alone with you."

"And I you. Another time, another place, another life."

"We both have burdens to bear, a secret liaison is not one of them."

"Will you be back next season?"

"No, I resisted once, I shall not challenge myself a second time."

Frank Leslie's Illustrated Newspaper
Courtesy Saratoga Springs Public Library